#1 *NEW YORK TIMES*

#1 *USA TODAY*

#1 *WALL STREET JOURNAL*

#1 *WASHINGTON POST*

#1 *SEATTLE TIMES*

#1 *HOUSTON CHRONICLE*

#1 INDIEBOUND

#1 *PUBLISHERS WEEKLY*

THE MASSIVE #1 BESTSELLER

P9-DMO-188

RUN, ROSE,
RUN

RUN, ROSE, RUN

DOLLY PARTON

and

JAMES PATTERSON

GRAND
CENTRAL

New York Boston

Copyright © 2022 by James Patterson and Dolly Parton
All song lyrics copyright © 2021 Song-A-Billy Music. All rights administered by Sony Music Publishing (US) LLC, 424 Church Street, Suite 1200, Nashville, TN 37219. All rights reserved. Used by permission.

Grand Central Publishing
Hachette Book Group
1290 Avenue of the Americas, New York, NY 10104

Originally published in hardcover and ebook by Little, Brown & Company in March 2022
First trade paperback edition: April 2023

Grand Central Publishing is a division of Hachette Book Group, Inc. The Grand Central Publishing name and logo is a trademark of Hachette Book Group, Inc.

The publisher is not responsible for websites (or their content) that are not owned by the publisher.

The Hachette Speakers Bureau provides a wide range of authors for speaking events. To find out more, go to www.hachettespeakersbureau.com or email HachetteSpeakers@hbgusa.com.

Grand Central Publishing books may be purchased in bulk for business, educational, or promotional use. For information, please contact your local bookseller or the Hachette Book Group Special Markets Department at special.markets@hbgusa.com.

Library of Congress Control Number: 2021936295

ISBNs: 9781538723968 (trade paperback), 9781538756270 (Walmart trade paperback), 9780759554375 (ebook)

Printed in the United States of America

LSC-C

Printing 1, 2023

RUN, ROSE,
RUN

PROLOGUE

The Louis Seize–style mirror in the bedroom of suite 409 at the Aquitaine Hotel reflected for little more than an instant a slim, fine-featured woman: wide blue eyes, clenched fists, dark hair streaming behind her as she ran.

Then AnnieLee Keyes vanished from the glass, as her bare feet took her racing into the suite's living room. She dodged the edge of the giltwood settee, flinging its throw pillow over her shoulder. A lamp fell with a crash behind her. She leaped over the coffee table, with its neat stack of *Las Vegas* magazines and tray of complimentary Debauve & Gallais truffles, her name written in chocolate ganache flecked with edible gold. She hadn't even tasted a single one.

Her foot caught the bouquet of Juliet roses and the vase tipped over, scattering pink blooms all over the carpet.

The balcony was up ahead of her, its doors open to the morning sun. In another instant, she'd reached it, and the hot air hit her in the face like a fist. She jumped onto the chaise longue and threw her right leg over the railing, struggling to push herself the rest of the way up.

Then, balanced on the thin rail between the hotel and the sky, she hesitated. Her heart beat so quickly she could hardly breathe. Every nerve ending sparked with adrenaline.

I can't, she thought. *I can't do it.*

But she had to. Her fingers clutched the rail for another split second before she willed them loose. Her lips moved in an instant of desperate prayer. Then she launched herself into the air. The sun flared, but her vision darkened and became a tunnel. She could see only below her—upturned faces, mouths open in screams she couldn't hear over her own.

Time slowed. She spread out her arms as if she were flying.

And weren't flying and falling the same?

Maybe, she thought, *except for the landing.*

Each millisecond stretched to an hour, these measures of time all she had left in this world. Life had been so damn hard, and she'd clawed her way up only to fling herself back down. She didn't want to die, but she was going to.

AnnieLee twisted in the air, trying to protect herself from what was coming. Trying to aim for the one thing that might save her.

ELEVEN
MONTHS EARLIER

CHAPTER

1

AnnieLee had been standing on the side of the road for an hour, thumbing a ride, when the rain started falling in earnest.

Wouldn't you know it? she thought as she tugged a gas station poncho out of her backpack. *It just figures.*

She pulled the poncho over her jacket and yanked the hood over her damp hair. The wind picked up, and fat raindrops began to beat a rhythm on the cheap plastic. But she kept that hopeful smile plastered on her face, and she tapped her foot on the gravel shoulder as a bit of a new song came into her head.

Is it easy? she sang to herself.

No it ain't
Can I fix it?
No I cain't

She'd been writing songs since she could talk and making melodies even before that. AnnieLee Keyes couldn't hear the call of a wood thrush, the *plink plink plink* of a leaky faucet, or the rumbling rhythm of a freight train without turning it into a tune.

Crazy girl finds music in everything—that's what her mother had said, right up until the day she died. And the song coming to AnnieLee now gave her something to think about besides the cars whizzing by, their warm, dry occupants not even slowing down to give her a second glance.

Not that she could blame them; she wouldn't stop for herself, either. Not in this weather, and her probably looking no better than a drowned possum.

When she saw the white station wagon approaching, going at least twenty miles under the speed limit, she crossed her fingers that it would be some nice old grandpa pulling over to offer her a lift. She'd turned down two rides back when she thought she'd have her choice of them, the first from a chain-smoking lady with two snarling Rottweilers in the back seat, the second from a kid who'd looked higher than Mount Everest.

Now she could kick herself for being so picky. Either driver would have at least gotten her a few miles up the road, smelling like one kind of smoke or another.

The white wagon was fifty yards away, then twenty-five, and as it came at her she gave a friendly, graceful wave, as if she was some kind of celebrity on the shoulder of the Crosby Freeway and not some half-desperate nobody with all her worldly belongings in a backpack.

The old Buick crawled toward her in the slow lane, and AnnieLee's waving grew nearly frantic. But she could have stood on her head and shot rainbows out of her Ropers and it wouldn't have mattered. The car passed by and grew gradually smaller in the distance. She stomped her foot like a kid, splattering herself with mud.

Is it easy? she sang again.

No it ain't
Can I fix it?
No I cain't
But I sure ain't gonna take it lyin' down

It was catchy, all right, and AnnieLee wished for the twentieth time that she had her beloved guitar. But it wouldn't have fit in her pack, for one thing, and for another, it was already hanging on the wall at Jeb's Pawn.

If she had one wish—besides to get the hell out of Texas—it was that whoever bought Maybelle would take good care of her.

The distant lights of downtown Houston seemed to blur as AnnieLee blinked raindrops from her eyes. If she thought about her life back there for more than an instant, she'd probably stop wishing for a ride and just start running.

By now the rain was falling harder than she'd seen it in years. As if God had drawn up all the water in Buffalo Bayou just so He could pour it back down on her head.

She was shivering, her stomach ached with hunger, and suddenly she felt so lost and furious she could cry. She had nothing and nobody; she was broke and alone and night was coming on.

But there was that melody again; it was almost as if she could hear it inside the rain. *All right,* she thought, *I don't have* nothing. *I have music.*

And so she didn't cry. She sang instead.

Will I make it?
Maybe so

Closing her eyes, she could imagine herself on a stage some-where, singing for a rapt audience.

Will I give up?

Oh no

She could feel the invisible crowd holding its breath.

I'll be fightin' til I'm six feet underground

Her eyes were squeezed shut and her face was tilted to the sky as the song swelled inside her. Then a horn blared, and AnnieLee Keyes nearly jumped out of her boots.

She was hoisting both her middle fingers high at the tractor trailer when she saw its brake lights flare.

CHAPTER

2

W as there ever a more beautiful color in the whole wide world? AnnieLee could write a damn ode to the dazzling red of those brake lights.

As she ran toward the truck, the cab's passenger door swung open. She wiped the rain from her eyes and looked at her rescuer. He was a gray-haired, soft-bellied man in his fifties, smiling down at her from six feet up. He tipped his baseball cap at her like a country gentleman.

"Come on in before you drown," he called.

A gust of wind blew the rain sideways, and without another second's hesitation, AnnieLee grabbed onto the door handle and hauled herself into the passenger seat, flinging water everywhere.

"Thank you," she said breathlessly. "I thought I was going to have to spend the night out there."

"That would've been rough," the man said. "It's a good thing I came along. Lot of people don't like to stop. Where you headed?"

"East," she said as she pulled off her streaming poncho and then shrugged out of her heavy backpack. Her shoulders were killing her. Come to think of it, so were her feet.

"My name's Eddie," the man said. He thrust out a hand for her to shake.

"I'm...Ann," she said, taking it.

He held her fingers for a moment before releasing them. "It's real nice to meet you, Ann." Then he put the truck into gear, looked over his shoulder, and pulled onto the highway.

He was quiet for a while, which was more than fine with AnnieLee, but then over the road noise she heard Eddie clear his throat. "You're dripping all over my seat," he said.

"Sorry."

"Here, you can at least dry your face," he said, tossing a red bandanna onto her lap. "Don't worry, it's clean," he said when she hesitated. "My wife irons two dozen for me every time I head out on a run."

Reassured by news of this wife, AnnieLee pressed the soft bandanna to her cheeks. It smelled like Downy. Once she'd wiped her face and neck, she wasn't sure if she should give it back to him, so she just wadded it up in her hand.

"You hitchhike a lot?" Eddie asked.

AnnieLee shrugged because she didn't see how it was any of his business.

"Look, I been driving longer than you been alive, I bet, and I've seen some things. *Bad* things. You don't know who you can trust."

Then she saw his big hand coming toward her, and she flinched.

Eddie laughed. "Relax. I'm just turning up the heat." He twisted a knob, and hot air blasted in her face. "I'm one of the good guys," he said. "Husband, dad, all that white-picket-fence business. Shoot, I even got a dang *poodle*. That was my wife's idea, though. I wanted a blue heeler."

"How old are your kids?" AnnieLee asked.

"Fourteen and twelve," he said. "Boys. One plays football, the other plays chess. Go figure." He held out a battered thermos. "Got coffee if you want it. Just be careful, because it's probably still hot as hellfire."

AnnieLee thanked him, but she was too tired for coffee. Too tired to talk. She hadn't even asked Eddie where he was going, but she hardly cared. She was in a warm, dry cab, putting her past behind her at seventy miles per hour. She wadded her poncho into a pillow and leaned her head against the window. Maybe everything was going to be okay.

She must have fallen asleep then, because when she opened her eyes she saw a sign for Lafayette, Louisiana. The truck's headlights shone through slashing rain. A Kenny Chesney song was on the radio. And Eddie's hand was on her thigh.

She stared down at his big knuckles as her mind came out of its dream fog. Then she looked over at him. "I think you better take your hand off me," she said.

"I was wondering how long you were going to sleep," Eddie said. "I was getting lonely."

She tried to push his hand away, but he squeezed tighter.

"Relax," he said. His fingers dug into her thigh. "Why don't you move closer, Ann? We can have a little fun."

AnnieLee gritted her teeth. "If you don't take your hand off me, you're going to be sorry."

"Oh, girl, you are just precious," he said. "You just relax and let me do what I like." His hand slid farther up her thigh. "We're all alone in here."

AnnieLee's heart pounded in her chest, but she kept her voice low. "You don't want to do this."

"Sure I do."

"I'm warning you," she said.

Eddie practically giggled at her. "What are you going to do, girl, scream?"

"No," she said. She reached into the pocket of her jacket and pulled out the gun. Then she pointed it at his chest. "I'm going to do *this*."

Eddie's hand shot off her leg so fast she would've laughed if she weren't so outraged.

But he got over his surprise quickly, and his eyes grew narrow and mean. "Hundred bucks says you can't even fire that thing," he said. "You better put that big gun away before you get hurt."

"*Me* get hurt?" AnnieLee said. "The barrel's not pointing at me, jackass. Now you apologize for touching me."

But Eddie was angry now. "You skinny little tramp, I wouldn't touch you with a tent pole! You're probably just another truck stop hoo—"

She pulled the trigger, and sound exploded in the cabin— first the shot, and then the scream of that dumb trucker.

The truck swerved, and somewhere behind them a horn blared. "What the hell're you doing, you crazy hobo bitch?"

"Pull over," she said.

"I'm not pull—"

She lifted the pistol again. "Pull over. I'm not kidding," she said.

Cursing, Eddie braked and pulled over onto the shoulder. When the truck came to a stop, AnnieLee said, "Now get out. Leave the keys in and the engine running."

He was sputtering and pleading, trying to reason with

her now, but she couldn't be bothered to listen to a word he said.

"Get out," she said. "Now."

She shook the gun at him and he opened the door. The way the rain was coming down, he was soaked before he hit the ground.

"You crazy, stupid, trashy—"

AnnieLee lifted the gun so it was pointing right at his mouth, so he shut it. "Looks like there's a rest stop a couple miles ahead," she said. "You can have yourself a nice walk and a cold shower at the same time. Pervert."

She slammed the door, but she could feel him beating on the side of the cab as she tried to figure out how to put the truck into gear. She fired another shot, out the window, and that made him quit until she found the clutch and the gas.

Then AnnieLee grabbed hold of the gearshift. Her stepdad might've been the world's biggest asshole, but he'd taught her to drive stick. She knew how to double-clutch and how to listen to the revs. And maybe songs weren't the only thing she had a natural talent for, because it didn't take her long at all to lurch that giant rig off the shoulder and pull out onto the highway, leaving Eddie screaming behind her.

I'm driving, she thought giddily. *I'm driving!*

She yanked on the horn and shot deeper into the darkness. And then she started singing.

Driven to insanity, driven to the edge
Driven to the point of almost no return

She beat out a rhythm on the steering wheel.

Driven, driven to be smarter
Driven to work harder
Driven to be better every day

That last line made her laugh out loud. Sure, she'd be better tomorrow—because tomorrow the sun would come out again, and tomorrow she had absolutely *no plans* to carjack an eighteen-wheeler.

CHAPTER

3

Ruthanna couldn't get the damn lick out of her head. A descending roll in C major, twangy as a rubber band, it was crying out for lyrics, a bass line, a song to live inside. She tapped her long nails on her desk as she scrolled through her emails.

"Later," she said, to herself or to the lick, she wasn't entirely sure. "We'll give you some attention when the boys show up to play."

It was nine o'clock in the morning, and already she'd fielded six pleading requests for Ruthanna Ryder, one of country music's grandest queens, to grace some big industry event or another with her royal presence.

She couldn't understand it, but people just failed to get the message: she'd *retired* that crown. Ruthanna didn't want to put on high heels, false eyelashes, and a sparkling Southern smile anymore. She wasn't going to stand up on some hot, bright stage in a dress so tight it made her ribs ache. She had no desire to pour her heart out into a melody that'd bring tears to a thousand pairs of eyes, hers included. No, sir, she'd put in her time, and now she was done. She was still writing songs—she couldn't stop that if she tried—but if the world thought it was going to ever hear them, it had another think coming. Her music was only for herself now.

She looked up from the screen as Maya, her assistant, walked into the room with a crumpled paper bag in one hand and a stack of mail in the other.

"The sun sure is bright on those gold records today," Maya said.

Ruthanna sighed at her. "Come on, Maya. You're the *one person* I'm supposed to be able to count on not to harass me about my quote, unquote, career. Jack must've called with another 'once-in-a-lifetime opportunity.'"

Maya just laughed, which was her way of saying, *You bet your white ass he did.*

Jack was Ruthanna's manager—ahem, *former* manager. "All right, what does he want from me today?"

"He wouldn't tell me yet. But he said that it's not what *he* wants. He's thinking about what *you* really want."

Ruthanna gave a delicate snort. "*I* really want to be left alone. Why he thinks he knows something different is beyond me." She picked up her ringing phone, silenced it, and then threw it onto the overstuffed couch across the room.

Maya watched this minor tantrum serenely. "He says the world's still hungry for your voice. For your songs."

"Well, a little hunger never hurt anyone." She gave her assistant a sly grin. "Not that you'd know much about hunger."

Maya put a hand on her ample hip. "And *you* got room to talk," she said.

Ruthanna laughed. "Touché. But whose fault is it for hiring Louie from the ribs place to be my personal chef? You could've picked someone who knew his way around a salad."

"Coulda, woulda, shoulda," Maya said. She put a stack of

letters in Ruthanna's inbox and held out the paper bag. "It's from Jack."

"What is that, muffins? I told Jack I was off carbs this month," Ruthanna said.

Not that Jack believed anything she told him lately. The last time they'd talked she'd said that she was going to start gardening, and he'd laughed so hard he dropped the phone into his pool. When he called her back on his landline he was still wheezing with delight. "I can't see you out there pruning roses any more than I can see you stripping off your clothes and riding down Lower Broadway on a silver steed like Lady Godiva of Nashville," he'd said.

Her retort—that it was past the season for pruning roses anyway—had failed to convince him.

"No, ma'am," Maya said, "these are *definitely* not muffins."

"You looked?"

"He told me to. He said if I saw them, I'd be sure you opened them. Otherwise he was afraid you might chuck the bag in a bin somewhere, and that'd be…well, a lot of sparkle to throw away."

"Sparkle, huh?" Ruthanna said, her interest piqued.

Maya shook her head at her, like, *You just don't know how lucky you are.* But since lovely Maya had a husband who bought her flowers every Friday and just about kissed the ground she walked on, she was considerably fortunate herself. Ruthanna, divorced seven years now, only got presents from people who wanted something from her.

She took the bag. Unrolling the top, she looked inside, and there, lying at the bottom of the bag—not even in a velvet box—was a pair of diamond chandelier earrings, each one as long as her index finger, false nail included. "Holy sugar," Ruthanna said.

"I know. I already googled them," Maya said. "Price available upon request."

Ruthanna held them up so that they caught the light brilliantly and flung rainbows onto her desk. She owned plenty of diamonds, but these were spectacular. "They look like earrings you'd buy a trophy wife," she said.

"Correction," said Maya. "They look like earrings you'd buy a woman who made you millions as she clawed her way to the top of her industry and into the hearts of a vast majority of the world's population."

The office line rang, and Ruthanna put the earrings back into the bag without trying them on. She gestured to Maya to answer it.

"Ryder residence," Maya said, and then put on her listening face. After a while she nodded. "Yes, Jack, I'll pass that information along."

"He couldn't keep his little secret after all, could he?" Ruthanna asked when her assistant hung up.

"He says they want to give you some big giant honor at the Country Music Awards—but you'd actually have to go," Maya said. "And he'd like me to tell you that you really shouldn't pass up such a perfect opportunity to wear those earrings."

Ruthanna laughed. Jack really was something else. "That man can buy me diamonds until hell turns into a honky-tonk," she said. "I'm out of the business."

CHAPTER

4

E than Blake's aging F-150 coughed and belched as he pulled through the wrought-iron gates of Ruthanna's sprawling compound in Belle Meade. It was a good thing the security cameras didn't record audio, because the Ford sounded downright embarrassing. It needed a new exhaust system plus half a dozen other repairs. But until he had more than a few grand in his bank account, vehicular maintenance was on the back burner.

Ethan pulled up under the shade of a massive oak and looked at his watch. When he saw that it was 11:02, he jumped out of the cab so fast he was halfway to the door before he realized he'd forgotten his guitar. By the time he was on the stoop outside the kitchen door, it was four minutes after the hour, and he was sweating through his white T-shirt.

He gave the knob a tug, but it was locked. Then, as the seconds ticked by, he started banging on the glass. There was no response. He fired a volley of curses into the ivy creeping up the sides of the Greek Revival mansion that Ruthanna jokingly called the Castle, and then he went around to the front and began stabbing madly at the doorbell. Ruthanna was going to kill him.

Maya finally opened the door. "May I help you?" she asked. She looked him up and down like he was a stranger trying to sell her a set of encyclopedias.

"Maya," Ethan said, exasperated. "I'm here to record."

"Mm-hmm," she said. But she didn't step aside to let him in.

"I'm late," he said. "I know, I'm sorry. I couldn't get Gladys started."

Maya's dark eyes widened. "I sure don't want to hear about that!" she exclaimed.

Ethan blushed right down to his neck. "Gladys is my *truck*."

Maya laughed at her joke, and then her face grew serious again. "Well, you know where you're going, and I guess you'd better get yourself there quick. You-know-who's waiting."

He ducked his head in thanks, nerves jangling, and hurried through the marble-floored foyer, passing the magnificent living room on his left. Ruthanna probably called it the parlor or the salon or something fancy like that, because it looked like one of those roped-off period rooms in a museum. There were leaded-glass windows; massive, glittering chandeliers; and walls hand-painted with tumbling English roses. It was ten times bigger than his entire apartment.

He'd never gotten a tour of the mansion, since all Ruthanna cared about was that he knew where the basement recording studio was, but the house had to be nine thousand square feet at least. He'd even gotten lost in the halls once. But now he took a deep breath—he could just *feel* Ruthanna waiting on him, simmering with impatience—and then he practically ran down the basement stairs.

Though it seemed as though the majority of music these days was recorded and mixed using little but a MacBook and Pro

Tools, Ruthanna was old-school. She had an old tube mixing board she'd saved from some legendary Nashville studio or another, and she liked all her musicians playing together rather than overdubbing for days. She said she loved the raw, natural way the songs came out sounding when people actually played their parts at the same time.

Opening the door to the live room, Ethan saw most of the band already assembled: Melissa, with her fiddle tucked under her arm; Elrodd, perched behind the drums; and Donna, tinkering around on the upright bass.

"Hey," Ethan said. He didn't see Stan, though, which meant—thank God—that he wasn't the last one to arrive. Relieved, Ethan was just setting down his instrument when the lead guitarist came out of the isolation booth with his Stratocaster in his hand.

Stan gave Ethan a look that said, *Uh-oh, bro.*

Ruthanna's voice came at Ethan over the intercom. "I know you're the new one in the room, but I did think you'd know enough not to keep your fellow musicians waiting. Didn't they teach you about punctuality in the army, Captain Blake?"

He turned toward her; she was in the control room with the engineer, on the other side of a gleaming pane of glass. "I'm sorry, Ruthanna. I couldn't—"

She cut him off with a flip of her hand. "Absolutely not interested in your excuses," she said. "You think you're so special that you can roll in whenever you want to? Sure, you're real cute, you've got a nice voice, and on a good day you could be Vince Gill's pale imitation, but Nashville is lousy with guitar players with tight jeans and a tight butt *who can show up on time.*"

Stan gave a low whistle under his breath. He was clearly glad not to be on the receiving end of the dress-down. And though Ethan's cheeks burned, he kept his mouth shut for once. He didn't want to lose this job. He *couldn't* lose this job. His part-time gig bartending at a karaoke dive wouldn't even cover the rent, let alone get Gladys running the way she should.

"I'll never—" he began.

"Damn right 'never,'" Ruthanna said. "Now take your guitar out and get tuning."

As he did what he was told, he glanced over at Donna. "Are my jeans too tight?" he whispered.

But she just laughed at him.

After he'd tuned, he warmed up by playing the song Ruthanna had written yesterday, a smart-ass send-up of certain music industry types called "Snakes in the Grass." He picked the bass line with his thumb and the melody with his other fingers, Chet Atkins–style, until he realized that Ruthanna had left the control room and was standing right next to him.

"Mr. Blake, let me remind you that we *have* a bassist," she said. "So don't think you need to do her job."

He turned to meet her fierce eyes. Ruthanna was twice his age but still beautiful. She had a smile that could light up a whole concert hall and a tongue sharper than a serpent's tooth. He just about worshipped the ground she walked on, and he couldn't believe how lucky he was to get to play music with her. But he also couldn't understand why she wouldn't release any of her new songs.

"I'm sorry, ma'am," he said.

She landed a light smack on his shoulder. "The word you're looking for," she said, "is *boss*."

Then she turned on her heel and walked over to the microphone.

"All right, then," she said. "Let's play some damn music."

CHAPTER

5

U nderneath a buzzing neon sign that read CAT'S PAW SA-
LOON, AnnieLee smoothed her hair and took a deep
breath.

"You can do this," she whispered. "This is what you came
here for."

It wasn't much of a pep talk, but AnnieLee figured she
shouldn't stand around on a city sidewalk muttering to herself like a crazy person, so short and sweet would have to
do. She took another deep breath, yanked the door open, and
strode inside.

The bar was cool and softly lit by Christmas lights draped in
multicolored strands along the ceiling and walls. On a stage at
the back of the room stood a man in a big black cowboy hat,
playing a battered guitar and singing a Willie Nelson tune in a
low, mournful voice. To her right was a long wooden bar, and to
her left, a woman in a DON'T MESS WITH TEXAS shirt was racking
balls on a red-felted pool table. AnnieLee scanned the crowd,
such as it was, and decided everyone looked reasonably friendly.
The air smelled like beer and French fries.

In other words, it was a perfect dive bar, and it would do just fine for her Nashville debut. AnnieLee walked over to the bar and climbed up onto a stool, ignoring the admiring eyes that followed her progress.

The bartender, a middle-aged man with a handlebar mustache, slid a cardboard coaster toward her. "What can I do for ya, miss?" he asked.

AnnieLee swallowed down her fear and smiled her klieg light smile at him. "You can put me up on that stage after that guy's done," she said.

The bartender gave a snort and swiped the coaster back. He bent down behind the bar, reappearing with a knife in one hand and a giant lemon in the other. AnnieLee watched as he started cutting the lemon and pitching the slices into the garnish station, next to a tray of crimson-dyed maraschino cherries. He didn't look at her again or say another word.

Is that it? she wondered. *Is he going to ignore me now?*

She tapped her fingers on the bar as she glanced over at the singer, now playing the opening chords to a Garth Brooks number. No one in the room seemed to be paying much attention to him. AnnieLee wondered if he felt bad about being background music, or if being up there with a guitar and a microphone was reward enough. Because if he wasn't enjoying himself sufficiently, she'd trade places with him in a heartbeat.

AnnieLee gave her hair a nervous flip. She knew she could shine on that stage—she just needed the chance. And Mr. Mustache here had to be the guy who'd give it to her, because her feet hurt too much to walk any more today.

She turned back to the bartender, who was now hacking away at a bunch of limes. She cleared her throat, but he still didn't look up.

Her courage wavered. She had the songs, but she hadn't prepared the sales pitch.

Listen, she said to herself, *you didn't carjack your way to Nashville to watch someone cut up a damn fruit salad, so you better open your big ol' mouth and start talking.*

"I'm sure you get people coming in here wanting to sing all the time," she said to the bartender. "But I think I've got something that you'd really like to see."

"Your titties?" The voice was a low, lewd growl, and it came from right behind her.

AnnieLee whirled around, heart pounding and hands curled into fists. An old man with gin-blossom cheeks took a wary step backward, even as he kept leering at her.

When she realized she didn't know him, she unclenched her fingers. "Pig," she said.

"Just a peek?" he asked, his voice pleading.

But the bartender had overheard him. "Oh, damn it, Ray, that's it," he yelled, snapping his towel at the old man. "You're eighty-sixed. Go home."

Ray blinked drunkenly. "But Billy—"

"Don't make me repeat myself, you old creep," the bartender said.

Suddenly chagrined, Ray looked over at AnnieLee. "I beg your pardon," he said, bowing, and then he lurched away toward the door.

"I'm really sorry about that," Billy said as he watched the old man leave. He filled a glass of water and set it in front of AnnieLee.

She was rattled, but she did her best not to show it. Vulnerability was never a good look. "I was ready to defend myself," she said.

"I noticed." He briskly wiped down the bar top. "What are you drinking? I'll put it on Ray's tab. He owes you now."

"I'm okay, thanks." AnnieLee paused, steeling her nerves, and then the words came out so fast there was hardly a breath between them. "Look, I can't tell you how I got to Nashville without incriminating myself—which is too bad, because it's a really good story—but I can tell you *why* I'm here. I'm going to make it as a singer or else I'm going to die trying. My name is AnnieLee Keyes, I turned twenty-five years old last week, and I'm asking you to give me a chance to sing up there on that stage. Will you be the one to give me my first big break? I really hope so. And then when I'm famous, I'll tell everyone that I owe it all to Billy the bartender at the Cat's Paw Saloon."

He gave another snort, but this one was gentler. "Like I need *more* desperate wannabes coming into my bar." He narrowed his eyes at her. "Though you don't look desperate, if I'm being perfectly honest."

"That's because I look *ambitious*." She leaned forward like she was about to tell him a secret. "And I also look like I did my makeup in a Popeyes bathroom." She held out a slender arm. "Seriously," she said. "I really did. On this here wrist is nothing but pure eau de fried chicken."

The bartender stared at her for a moment and then burst out laughing. "You're funny. Country music's a tough business. Maybe you should consider a career in comedy."

She said, "Yeah, that's on my bucket list, right after climbing Mount Kilimanjaro and becoming a contortionist in Cirque du Soleil. But I need to get this dream accomplished first because it's in the number one spot. So do you want to keep chatting me up or do you want to hear what I've got?"

"Can you sing?" he asked.

"Like my name was Melody," she said.

Billy didn't say anything for a moment. He got a bottle of whiskey down from the shelf and poured some into a shot glass. But instead of giving it to a customer, he knocked it back himself.

She watched him, her heart fluttering in her chest. She couldn't fake confidence like this much longer, but she couldn't let this chance slip away, either.

"Okay, listen," she said, more serious now. "I was kidding just then. I don't care about mountains or circuses. I only care about this."

Billy dropped his shot glass into a sink of bubbly water. "Do you have any idea how many people come up to me every week, just like you're doing?" he asked.

"Probably about a million," AnnieLee acknowledged. "But I'm one *in* a million—not one *of* a million. That's a big difference there."

Billy pursed his lips thoughtfully. "Well," he said, "I did just kick out my filler act."

"Ray?" AnnieLee gasped.

"That man can out-Cash Johnny when he's sober."

AnnieLee sat up straighter. "I guess this is my lucky night," she said.

"I guess it is," Billy agreed.

AnnieLee bit her lip. "Just one thing," she said. "Do you happen to have a guitar I could borrow?"

CHAPTER

6

If AnnieLee had been jittery trying to talk her way into singing, it was nothing compared to how she felt as she stood at the back of the bar, waiting for her turn to go up onstage. Nerves made her chest hurt so bad she almost wondered if she was having a heart attack.

Deep breaths, girl, she told herself. *This ain't the firing squad.*

She touched the edge of a picture of Emmylou Harris that was hanging on the wall and then brushed a speck of cigarette ash off the frame of Ruthanna Ryder's photo, wishing that somehow the spirits of these great country women would give her strength.

She scanned the room, trying to breathe long and slow. There were only a few dozen people in the bar, most of whom probably wouldn't even look up from their beers when she started playing. So why did she feel so damn nervous? Her hands were sweaty, and her cheeks felt as hot as frying pans.

Maybe she was so jumpy because this was the only first chance she'd ever get. Or maybe it was because she was scared and alone and she needed some kind of proof that this all wasn't some giant mistake.

The singer with the ten-gallon hat and the battered Martin came striding off the stage to the sound of half-hearted applause. He passed close by AnnieLee on his way to the bar.

"Good luck, kid," he said gruffly, and then it was her turn to walk up those three impossible steps.

She made it onto the stage without tripping—and without turning tail and running, which she did for one instant consider doing. Her legs were trembling, and her heart had shot so far up into her neck she wasn't sure she could speak. She sank onto the folding chair. Keeping her head down, she moved the lower microphone so it was positioned right in front of the sound hole of the guitar and then adjusted the vocal mic so it was close to her lips. When she looked up, ready to face her audience, she realized she could barely see anything or anyone with that stage light in her face.

Well, she thought, *that's probably good, all things considered.*

She cleared her throat. "Good evening," she managed, and the microphone squealed. Startled, she jumped back before collecting herself and trying again. "Sorry," she said. "I'm kinda new at this. But I guess I'll at least sound better than *that.*"

A low chuckle floated up from the front row. Encouraged, AnnieLee gave the guitar's strings a light flick of her fingers. "I want to thank you for sitting here with me tonight," she said as she twisted the tuning peg on her high E. "Living in Nashville, you've probably seen more live music than I've seen hot dinners."

She began to strum a chord progression she figured they'd recognize—"Crazy"—and she could see Billy behind the bar, nodding his head in approval.

The safest thing to do was to play a cover—she knew that. Something old and beloved, or else a song the middle-agers in the room would've sung in high school. "Strawberry Wine," maybe, or "Friends in Low Places."

But as she got ready to channel Patsy Cline, AnnieLee hesitated. This was her stage right now—this was her chance. Why sing someone else's words when she could sing her own?

She stopped on the C7 and let the notes hang in the air. "You know what? I think I'm going to play a song you've never heard before," she said. "A song so new I've never sung it for anyone else." She strummed G, then E minor, then a D. "No one's going to mistake me for Maybelle Carter on this thing, but I can play the chords all right. And that's what I hear you need—just three chords and the truth?"

Someone in the back gave a whoop, but whether it was because of what she'd said or because a billiard ball had just gone spinning into a pocket, she couldn't tell.

"Anyway, I guess I should stop talking and start singing, huh?" She smiled nervously as she gave the body of the guitar a jaunty little slap. She knew how to do this. She was ready. She just had to relax.

The fingers on her left hand found their positions. Tapping her foot on the worn floor, she began to pick out the intro. She fumbled once, stopped, began again. And then, when her fingers felt steady, she started to sing.

Is it easy?
No it ain't

Her voice wavered and fear tightened her throat. *Dear God, don't let me blow it,* she thought.

Can I fix it?
No I cain't

She sounded so tentative, and nerves gave her voice a thin, quivering vibrato.

But I sure ain't gonna take it lyin' down.

Somewhere in the room, a beer bottle fell to the floor and smashed.

Will I make it?
Maybe so

Closing her eyes against the hot light, AnnieLee imagined she was far away and long ago from the Cat's Paw Saloon, when she was a kid who'd sing to her teddy bear with a hairbrush microphone. Back then, she'd imagined a huge, awed crowd hanging on her every note. Now she pictured the opposite: one lone teddy bear, half drunk on Miller Lite, not even bothering to listen.

The thought made her feel ten times better, and when it came time for the chorus, her voice came out stronger. It growled, then hollered, then implored.

Gotta woman up and take it like a man

She could feel the crowd's new attention. Her fingers flew over the strings, and by verse number two she was belting out the song at the top of her lungs. She sang for joy, and she sang as if her life depended on it.

Because, she knew, it did.

CHAPTER

7

Y ou sure weren't lying when you told me you could sing," Billy said as he poured a round of shots for a rowdy table in the back.

AnnieLee took a sip of her club soda and then pressed the cool glass to her burning cheeks. Her heart still hadn't stopped pounding, and the sound of the audience cheering and clapping echoed in her ears.

"I don't lie," she said, brushing her damp bangs away from her forehead. Sure, she might break a law or two, or fail to answer certain pointed questions, but she always told the truth unless she absolutely couldn't. Her stepdad had been a cheat and a liar, and she never wanted to be anything like him.

"So maybe you'll let me come back sometime?" she asked Billy.

He waited a beat, and then he gave a single nod. "I reckon maybe I will," he said.

"Well, I'd be honored," AnnieLee said. She'd played just four of her own songs and then, figuring she shouldn't wear out her new Nashville welcome, she'd tucked that old bar guitar under her arm and headed offstage. That was when the Cat's Paw regulars started stomping their feet on the floor, and Billy began waving madly at her from over by the beer taps, shouting, "Stay up there, girl! Go on!"

For a moment she'd stood there, frozen in the bright light, truly doubting this moment was real. She'd imagined a night like this for so long that suddenly she was afraid she'd conjured it up, straight out of her wild and grandiose imagination. Maybe she was dreaming as she slept on a park bench somewhere. Or maybe she'd flipped that big, dumb semi into a ditch, and the Cat's Paw Saloon was just a hospital bed hallucination no realer than a young girl's secret, most heartfelt wish.

"Is it easy?" someone shouted. "No it ain't!"

Those six simple words had broken the spell and brought AnnieLee back to herself. She'd sat down on the rickety stage chair again. And then, with sweat beading on her upper lip and trickling down her neck, she'd had to confess that she couldn't play any more originals.

"I've been traveling a bit lately," she said, "and so I'm kinda rusty on my back catalog." She laughed. "But I could play you an oldie but a goodie—something I didn't write."

She'd just started to strum the chords to the old hymn "I'll Fly Away" when someone in the back said, "Play *your* songs again!"

And so, not knowing what else to do, she had—one right after the other. And everyone seemed to like them even better the second time around. Some people even sang along with the choruses.

Now, perched comfortably on a barstool, AnnieLee wasn't sure if she was glad her set was over or if she wanted to run back onstage and do it all over again.

Billy held out a menu to her, but she waved it away. She couldn't very well admit that she didn't have enough money to pay for dinner. She wanted to be remembered for her performance, not her poverty. Besides, she had granola bars and gorp in her backpack, so she wasn't going to starve.

Not yet, anyway.

"Suit yourself," Billy said amiably.

"They make a good burger here, you know," came a new voice. "Of course, it's cat meat."

AnnieLee swiveled around on her stool and saw a man in a denim shirt and faded blue jeans smiling at her. He was dark-haired and coal-eyed and as long-legged as a young Johnny Cash, and her heart gave a little skip in her chest. He had just about the nicest face she'd ever seen.

"I'm kidding. I hope that's obvious." He held out his hand. "I'm Ethan Blake," he said. "I'm a big fan."

She drew in a slow and deliberate breath. She'd die a thousand deaths before she'd let him see that he'd flustered her. "Are you, now?" she asked.

His smile got wider, and a dimple appeared in each lightly stubbled cheek. "Yes," he said. "I'm really a fan, and my name is really Ethan." He gestured to the empty seat next to her. "Do you mind if I join you?"

She gazed down into her drink; the ice cubes had all but melted. "Suit yourself," she said.

"Can I buy you a beer?" he asked. "Or a glass of wine, or a carton of milk?"

She bit back a smile as she stirred the club soda with her straw. "No, thank you."

"You were really something, though," he said. "You wrote those songs?"

That made her look over at him again, and this time there was fire in her eyes. "Of course I did. Does that surprise you, Ethan Blake? Do you think I look too young to write them? Too meek? Too female?"

He held up a hand. "No, no, not at all. Sorry. I'm just trying to make conversation."

AnnieLee scooted her stool a few inches away from him. The last thing she needed was a man hitting on her; it didn't matter one bit how handsome he was. "Well, I don't generally talk to strangers," she said.

"Okay, I get it," he said, and he sounded good-natured as opposed to defensive. "That's totally fair. But Nashville's a small town, and maybe someday we'll be friends."

"I doubt it," she said.

He put a twenty down on the bar and called, "See if you can buy her a drink for me, will you, Billy? She did good up there."

Then he walked away. AnnieLee watched him go, prepared to look the other direction if he turned back around. But he didn't. He just picked up that same old bar guitar and started heading toward the stage.

Her stomach gave a terrible lurch. *Keyes, you utter fool,* she thought. *You were rude to the next act.*

CHAPTER

8

AnnieLee grabbed her coat and ducked out of the bar before Ethan Blake started to play. If he was bad, she didn't want to hear him. And if he was good—well, she didn't want to know. No sense kicking herself all night for being snotty to the next Luke Combs. She'd been kicked enough already.

Outside the air was cool and the street empty and quiet. Lower Broadway, Nashville's honky-tonk hotbed, was just a few blocks to the southeast. But from where she stood, AnnieLee could hear nothing but the electric hum of a streetlight and the whir of a police siren far in the distance.

After glancing around to make sure that she was alone on the block, AnnieLee hunched up her shoulders and started walking. The early spring breeze was chilly and her shirt was still damp with sweat. She walked quickly, alertly, occasionally stopping to look behind her, wary as a rabbit in a wide-open field.

But no one was following her. She slipped along the streets, beneath flowering crab apples whose blossoms seemed to glow in the darkness. She turned one corner, then another, heading for the water.

Along the Cumberland River, which snaked its way around and through Nashville, lay a narrow strip of a park that AnnieLee had called home for two nights now. She'd slept in better places, that was for sure. But she'd also slept in worse.

She crossed Gay Street and climbed over a low stone wall, and in another few steps she was standing beneath trees just coming into their leaves. Though it'd been eighty degrees the day she'd left Houston, spring was late this year in Tennessee. She could hear the river sliding along its banks and the sound of traffic on the bridge.

Ducking down between two giant hydrangeas, AnnieLee pulled her backpack from its hiding place. She took out her tarp and lay it on a smooth patch of ground beneath an elm tree, humming softly, almost tunelessly, to herself. Then she unrolled the lightweight down sleeping bag she'd gotten— along with a knockoff Swiss Army knife, forty dollars in cash, and a lewd proposition—in exchange for Maybelle at Jeb's Pawn.

A folded sweater served as her pillow. Light from a neon Coca-Cola sign on the other side of Gay Street flickered through the tangle of branches.

Sleeping outside reminded AnnieLee of summer nights when she was a kid, when she'd lie in the back of her mom's pickup truck as it sat parked in the driveway. Mary Grace had been alive and happy then, and sometimes she'd join her daughter under the stars, singing her to sleep with old folk lullabies like "500 Miles" and "Star of the County Down."

It had felt like a wonderful adventure to slip into dreams with her mother beside her and the whole sky of stars hanging right there above them. But bedding down outside like this now? It was nothing but a cold and lonely necessity.

A gust of wind blew last winter's dead leaves and a torn scrap of notebook paper toward AnnieLee's face. As she brushed them away, she saw words scribbled in black marker on the paper: *...ave never felt like this before, and it...* The rest was ripped away.

She wondered if the note had ever gotten to the person it was meant for, or if it was just wadded up and pitched into the bushes.

Lines written but never read
Like a song only played inside your head, she sang softly.

Then she stopped to readjust her makeshift pillow. If she had a nickel for every scrap of a tune she'd ever written, she'd be curled under six-hundred-thread-count sheets in a fancy hotel instead of stuffed inside a polyester pawnshop sleeping bag underneath a damn elm.

She closed her eyes and thought back to earlier that evening, when she'd stepped onstage for the first time and sung her scared little heart out. Maybe there was a song in that experience. Certainly there was a story in how she'd got there, and what she was running from. And as she drifted off to sleep, she thought of Ethan Blake and the warmth of his dark eyes.

Eventually AnnieLee began to dream, and inside that dream, she spoke out loud. The words were nonsense at first, and then came a name. "Rose," AnnieLee muttered as she curled tighter inside her sleeping bag. "Rose!" Her arms flew up as if to ward off a blow. "Oh, Rose, be careful!"

CHAPTER
9

E than Blake got to Ruthanna's so early on Tuesday he had to wait twenty minutes in his truck before it was time to let himself into the kitchen. "Morning," he said as Ruthanna's cat, Biscuit, twirled itself around his legs. He reached down to pet its soft gray head.

"It sure is," Ruthanna said. She was tucked into her favorite spot in the entire enormous house, against the cushions in the bay window, and the sunlight was falling on her red-gold hair. "You want coffee?"

"Thanks, I'm good," he said. He'd made a stop at Bongo Java on the way, plus Maya, who was over by the stove, made coffee so strong he could practically feel it stripping the enamel from his teeth. He set his guitar case on the Florentine tiles and took an apple from the enormous fruit bowl on the kitchen island. "So I saw an amazing new singer last night," he said.

Ruthanna gave Maya the side-eye, and Maya giggled into her fist. Ethan braced himself for the ribbing he could tell was coming.

"So, Blake," Ruthanna said, "what was so amazing—her face or her boobs?"

"How do you know the singer was a girl?" Ethan asked, his mouth full of apple.

"Because I'm not dumb," Ruthanna said.

"Fine," he said. "But give me a little credit, why don't you? It was her *voice*."

"Mm-hmm," Maya said, pouring herself a mug of her killer brew.

"Sang like an angel, did she?" Ruthanna asked.

"If you don't mind a cliché like that," Ethan said, "then yeah, she did." He still felt moved by the blunt power of AnnieLee's lyrics and the soaring ache of her voice. "She sang like an angel who's been cast out of heaven, yearning to fly back up to where she belongs."

Ruthanna stared at him. "That's some highfalutin poetics for nine a.m. Also, to be perfectly honest, she sounds depressing."

Ethan rolled his eyes, and Ruthanna laughed at him. "She *was* hot, though, wasn't she?"

"That's not the point," he said.

"Of course it is," Ruthanna said. "What'd that old bird Tennyson say? 'In the spring a young man's fancy lightly turns to thoughts of love.'"

"*Now* who's got the poetics?" Maya asked. "Also, I think that poem ends sort of tragically."

"Seriously, Ruthanna, I'd think you'd care," Ethan protested. "She's good, and she was playing at the Cat's Paw. That's *your* bar, if you recall, and in my mind, that gives you dibs."

Ruthanna got up from her window seat and slid across the kitchen in her gold velvet slippers. "I don't know what you're talking about dibs for. She's not mine because she sang in my bar, you big oaf. I've got no interest in wannabe country singers, anyway," she said. "I don't care if they sing like angels or pick like Doc Watson. I don't care if that girl was born with a Dobro in her hand and a harmonica in her mouth." Ruthanna was on a roll now, and her sentences became lines of a song she was making up as she went. *"I don't care if she's pretty as a daisy or if she can belt out the high notes in 'Crazy,'"* she sang.

Maya came in with her low, rich alto. *"Ruthanna's retired and she deserves to be lazy…"*

Ethan started laughing—he couldn't help it. "Are you two about done?" he said.

They turned toward him, grinning. "Probably," said Ruthanna. "I can't think of anything else that rhymes with *lazy*."

"Jay-Z?" Maya offered.

"Look," Ethan said. "I'm not telling you this for my own good. I'm just here to say that I think you'd really like this girl." He patted Ruthanna on the shoulder. "She's a lot like you," he said. "Beautiful, talented…and mean as tobacco spit."

Ruthanna looked at him in surprise, and he froze. Had he crossed a line? Ruthanna had a legendary temper, and few people could get away with talking to her like that. What on earth made him think he was one of them?

"I'm sorr—" he began, and then she threw a kitchen towel at him, hitting him squarely in the chest.

"For your information, I take all of those things as a compliment," she said.

He let out a sigh of relief. "That's good," he said. "Because I meant them that way."

"I still don't care about your singer, though," she said. Then her face brightened and she held up a finger. "Wait—I've got it: *Martin Scorsese!*"

"I thought you said you were done," Ethan moaned, as Ruthanna laughed all the way down to the recording room.

AnnieLee woke at dawn to the sound of voices. She was frigid and sore from sleeping on the ground, but she held herself perfectly still, not even breathing as she strained to listen. How close were they?

And more importantly, were they coming *closer*?

She could hear a man and a woman, the latter saying something about an "EDP" she'd talked down off a bridge the day before: "...couldn't convince him I wasn't the ghost of his dead aunt," she said. "Dude was whiter than a bedsheet and he's got a Black aunt? I doubt it. But being confused about who I was had to be the least of his problems, poor thing."

They were definitely getting closer, and AnnieLee didn't have to know what an EDP was to know that they weren't just a nice couple out for a morning stroll. They were cops. She could hear the swagger in the male cop's voice as he talked about tracking down a man suspected of holding up a Circle K.

AnnieLee quickly slithered out of her sleeping bag and tried to stuff it into her pack as she ducked into the bushes to hide. She was about to get down on her hands and knees to crawl deeper into the greenery when the man said, "Hold up there."

AnnieLee cursed under her breath as she slowly turned around, straightening the backpack on her shoulders. Maybe they'd think *she* was out for a sunrise walk?

"Good morning, officers," she said, trying to keep the tremor from her voice.

In the branches above her, a crow coughed out three loud, hoarse squawks. AnnieLee glanced up at the shiny black bird, bobbing near the treetop, and then looked back at the cops, who'd failed to wish her a good morning in return.

"Did you know that crows are songbirds?" she asked. "That always seems kinda funny to me, because they have such terrible voices." She shrugged in a way that she hoped seemed both innocent and charming. Maybe she could pass as a slightly eccentric urban birder? "A thrush, on the other hand," she said, "sounds like some kind of magical flu—"

"You spend the night here?" the man interrupted. He stood with his legs spread wide and his thumbs tucked into his belt.

"Welllll…" AnnieLee said. Wasn't it obvious?

"Sleeping in the park is illegal," he said.

The woman took a step closer to her. She had a cup of steaming coffee, and it smelled so good and warm that it nearly brought tears to AnnieLee's eyes. "There's a shelter on Lafayette Street," she said gently. "The Rescue Mission—are you familiar with it?"

"Um, okay, sure," AnnieLee said, taking a corresponding step backward. She saw the other cop scanning the ground, probably looking for needles or bottles of cheap liquor.

"I don't do drugs," she blurted, and then flushed. "I'm not from here," she added. But that was probably obvious, too.

"Are you okay?" the woman asked. "Do you need help?"

"Yes," AnnieLee said. "No. I mean, I'm just fine. I'll be moving along, I guess, if that's okay with you." She took another small step away from them.

The cops looked at each other—they clearly didn't consider her a threat to herself or others—and when they turned back to her, she gave them a little wave. She'd take their silence as permission to get the hell out of there. "Thanks, and, um, have fun patrolling," she said, and then she hurried away, holding her breath until she was safely out of sight. They didn't call after her.

It's your lucky day, kid, she said to herself. And then she tried very hard to believe it.

CHAPTER
11

AnnieLee walked south through the park for a quarter mile before she came to a long, sloping lawn. To her left was the slow-moving river, and on the far side of it, Nissan Stadium. To her right, up the hill, was a row of brick buildings, including one that said GEORGE JONES COUNTRY in big white letters. She headed up the lawn toward the city's edge, singing to herself Jones's "These Days (I Barely Get By)," a bleak song if there ever was one.

In a little café on Commerce Street, she spent three precious dollars on the largest coffee on offer, adding a big splash of cream and four packets of sugar. She didn't actually like her coffee that way, but she needed all the free calories she could get.

Then she brushed her teeth in the café bathroom and tried to comb out her hair with her fingers. As she did so, she turned her face this way and that, gazing into the mirror appraisingly. Her mother used to tell her that she looked like a young Jacqueline Bisset, though AnnieLee barely knew who that actress was.

What she looked like now, she thought, was *hungry*.

"Well, there are worse things to be," she reminded her reflection. "And you've been a few of them."

She spent the rest of the morning wandering the streets and gazing into shop windows, feeling awkward and conspicuous with her big lumpy backpack. Though live music began at 10 a.m. all along Lower Broadway, she knew she'd never be able to talk her way onto one of those big stages. The people who played on them were seasoned professionals.

In the afternoon, she returned to the park to stash her belongings. A crow—the same one or not, she certainly couldn't tell—was the only witness as she placed her pack in the hollow, covered it with leaves and branches, and then trudged back into town.

She'd decided to try her luck at a little spot on the corner of Church Street called the Dew Drop Inn, but when she asked the bartender if it might be possible for her to sing there, the woman didn't even speak—she just started laughing. She laughed until a tear shone in the corner of her eye, and AnnieLee wondered if she'd been drinking more of the booze than she'd been serving.

"Every day," the woman finally said, wiping her face with the back of her hand. "Every livelong day there's a new face asking me if they can perform in my bar. Is there a farmer growing a whole field of you somewhere? Some bumper crop of wannabes?"

AnnieLee bristled. "You can just say no. You don't have to call names."

"Sorry," the woman said, though she didn't sound it. She pointed vaguely east. "You can try over at Patsy's."

AnnieLee moved toward the door. She didn't know where Patsy's was, but she certainly wasn't going to ask.

"Just take those leaves out of your hair before you walk in," the woman called after her.

Flushing, AnnieLee pulled a tiny twig from the park that'd gotten caught in her dark waves. "Thanks," she said tartly, and dropped it on the sidewalk outside the Dew Drop.

After only a few wrong turns, she found Patsy's and began to make her inquiry, but before she'd finished, the bartender interrupted and told her to put her CD on the bar.

"My what?"

He didn't answer; he'd moved away to help an actual customer.

A lady in cat-eye glasses and bright-pink lipstick leaned over and poked AnnieLee in the forearm. "Your demo, hon," she said.

"My what?" AnnieLee said again. She knew she wasn't what anyone would call worldly, but she was starting to feel like there was a whole heck of a lot she didn't know about the way things worked in Nashville.

"Most people who want to play here leave a CD they've made—you know, with them playing their music?" The woman pointed to a tall stack of CDs leaning on a counter behind the bar.

"Does anyone actually listen to them?" AnnieLee asked. They looked dustier than the picture frames at the Cat's Paw.

"Who knows? But it's like a calling card, sweetheart. You oughta get one."

"Okay, thanks," AnnieLee said. She'd add it to the list of things she needed, right behind a hot meal, a bed, a shower, and a guitar. "Can you recommend another spot for me to try?" she asked. "Someplace small—a bit out-of-the-way, maybe?"

The woman scribbled a few names on a bar napkin and then pushed it toward AnnieLee.

"Here you go," she said. "You're real pretty and you've got a nice figure, so you might have a little luck."

Is that what matters around here? AnnieLee thought.

"Then again," the woman went on, "you might not." She pulled a long, gold-filtered cigarette from a pack and put it between her lips without lighting it. "And if it seems like all those folks are trying to stop you from getting anywhere, hon, that's because they are. They're the gatekeepers, whether they deserve to be or not, and they don't want anyone but the best and brightest coming through."

"Separating the wheat from the chaff," AnnieLee said. The Gospel according to Matthew had been her mother's favorite.

"Mm-hmm. If you want to make it in this town," the woman went on, "being talented is just one little tiny part of the battle. Fearlessness is mandatory. And shamelessness sure as hell don't hurt."

AnnieLee nodded. "You've been really helpful," she said. "I hope I get to sing for you someday."

"Oh, I bet you will, sweetie. I see hunger in your eyes."

"Yeah, literal and figurative," AnnieLee said. "Thanks again."

Outside, she closed her eyes and leaned against the sun-warmed brick building. She told herself that she wasn't discouraged. She knew she was going to have to knock on a lot of doors, and it was only to be expected that some of them would get slammed in her face.

After another moment's rest, she righted herself and started walking toward the next watering hole. She thought of her stepdad, lurching from dive bar to dive bar, trying to remember which place hadn't eighty-sixed him.

Just like him, she needed a bar desperately. Not for a drink, though: for a chance.

B ut it wasn't desperation that took AnnieLee back to the Cat's Paw Saloon two nights later. It was loneliness.

Not that she cared to admit it to herself.

She slid into the cool, dim bar well after sundown. Dirty ol' Ray was nowhere to be seen. The stage was empty; Carrie Underwood sang softly on the radio. AnnieLee was relieved to see Billy polishing glasses behind the bar. She hopped onto a stool near the soda gun and waited for him to notice her.

When he did, he looked as though he was actually glad to see her. "The songbird returns," he said.

"I thought you were going to say, 'Look what the cat dragged in,'" AnnieLee said. She didn't think she had any leaves in her hair tonight, but it'd been a long time since she'd seen the inside of a shower stall.

He laughed. "I don't keep my job by being rude to guests of my establishment."

What if the guests aren't paying customers? she wondered but didn't say.

He poured her a club soda without asking her if she wanted

one, which she did. If only he'd toss a free hamburger her way! Between rationing her food, walking around all day, and shivering to keep warm all night, she was losing weight. Pretty soon she'd be skinnier than a guitar string.

"You get yourself an instrument yet?" Billy asked.

AnnieLee shook her head in mock gloom. "My fairy godmother quit."

"Sorry to hear that."

"Me, too. Now I have to *buy* a guitar instead of getting handed an enchanted gourd. Can you believe it?" AnnieLee slapped the bar for comedic emphasis. Noticing her fingernails were dirty, she quickly put her hands back under the counter. "But that takes money that I don't have." She looked at Billy hopefully. "Do you happen to need any housekeeping help around here or anything?"

"Sorry," he said. "We're fully staffed on that front."

She considered mentioning the dusty picture frames and the slightly grimy sheen to the tile in the women's bathroom. Certainly no one could ever accuse the Cat's Paw cleaners of trying too hard. But then she grinned—suddenly, brilliantly. "Great. No problem. So how about you ask me to sing again, and you pay me a little bit of money this time?"

Billy stood there and stared at AnnieLee as if he couldn't figure out where a person like her could come from. And she half wondered the same thing. She'd always been *shy*. But that lady with the cat-eye glasses had said that success took fearlessness and shamelessness both. Sure, she might've been a fading barfly, but she'd sounded as though she knew what she was talking about.

Billy pulled a pint of Miller Lite and walked it over to a table near the stage. When he came back, he said, "You can't just keep coming in here and hoping I have a slot for you."

She ran her fingers through her tousled hair. She *knew* that. But so far Billy's was about the friendliest face she'd seen.

"Fair enough," she said. "But since I'm here now…"

He sighed. "No one's up there, so what the hell? You might as well be."

"Can I use…" she began, glancing over his shoulder at the orphan guitar.

"Guess you'd better," he said gruffly.

She was halfway across the stage before she turned around. "Thank you," she called.

And then she sat down in the rickety chair and began to play, without any preamble and without any amplification. As the songs unspooled their beauty into the quiet, half-empty room, the pool game halted. Someone ordered a whiskey in the barest whisper. The only sound, besides the raw, aching sweetness of AnnieLee's voice, was the whir of the old ceiling fan.

When she was done playing, AnnieLee came floating off the stage, happier than she'd been in days. The euphoria lasted all the way up until she saw Ethan Blake having a beer at the other end of the bar.

Her cheeks went hot with shame. She knew she should apologize for being rude to him, especially since he was a fellow musician. But it was impossible to show the tiniest glimmer of vulnerability. If she did, her whole brazen facade would shatter.

And so she simply pretended she hadn't seen him. She sank onto her seat, still breathing a little heavy from her vocal exertions. Billy came over and placed two twenty-dollar bills on the scuffed wooden bar.

"Really?" she said, forgetting about Ethan instantly.

"You were dynamite, kid."

Though she was nearly speechless with gratitude, she knew

she had to keep playing the proper part. "When I'm back on my feet you won't be able to get me with such bargain-basement prices," she said.

Billy snorted. "Ethan," he called. "You've played here a hundred times. When did I start paying you?"

"*Are* you paying me?" Ethan called back. "It's so little I guess I hadn't really noticed."

Billy snapped his bar towel in Ethan's direction and turned around, grumbling something about the world being full of ingrates. From opposite ends of the bar, Ethan and AnnieLee laughed together, and the next thing she knew he was standing beside her, and his handsome face was like a light that was too bright to look at.

"You were great—again," he said. "Your voice sounds even better when it's not coming through Billy's crappy amp."

"Thank you," she said. She kept her tone cool but perfectly polite.

"I won't offer to buy you a drink this time," he said. "But I've got these French fries…"

He shoved a steaming basket toward her. AnnieLee's mouth watered and her stomach clenched when she smelled the oil and salt. She glanced up and saw him smiling at her.

But she couldn't let herself. She shoved her hands with their dirty fingernails deep into her pockets. "I have to go," she said.

Then she scooped up her money and stalked toward the door, stubborn and hungry, full of nothing but stupid pride.

CHAPTER
13

E eny, meeny, miny, moe," Ruthanna whispered as she stood barefoot in her mammoth closet, flipping through a rack of glittering gowns. Was she in an emerald-green mood, or a scarlet one? Did she want short or long? Fitted, flowing—or perhaps both?

Maya had carefully painted Ruthanna's nails a rich red, and Ruthanna herself had bronzed, highlighted, and tinted every inch of her still-lovely face; now came the vexing task of picking out her dress for the annual Book Garden gala and fundraiser.

Though Ruthanna didn't miss the army of makeup artists and hairdressers who'd fussed over her for decades, she did slightly mourn the loss of her personal stylist, who'd often seemed to know what Ruthanna felt like wearing before she knew it herself. But retired stars shouldn't require stylists, Ruthanna felt, or the Secret Service level of security detail she'd once employed. She was trying to keep things simple these days.

And so, in the spirit of that simplicity—and because the proverbial clock was loudly ticking—she decided to pluck a gown from its hanger and call the job done.

"Voilà," she said. "Haven't seen you for a while."

The dress her fingers had selected at random was a snow-white sheath with intricate swirls of sparkling crystals, tiny pearls, and silver beads that cascaded like a shimmering, wintry waterfall from neckline to hem.

The dress was perfect, she realized: glamorous but not over-the-top, and body-hugging enough to help her stick to that infuriating low-carb diet she'd committed to for a month.

Carefully she stepped into the dress, feeling its cool satin slide up her skin and settle onto her narrow shoulders. With all the beading, it must have weighed seven pounds at least. Next she slipped her feet into tiny high-heeled shoes, and finally she put on Jack's gorgeous, outrageous earrings. She gave herself a quick final glance in the mirror—she now sparkled as if she was made of ice—and then she hurried downstairs to wait for her car and driver.

Her phone buzzed with a text from Ethan as she stepped onto her porch. Her feet hurt already.

Gotta come 2 Cat's Paw 2night she's here

Ruthanna rolled her eyes and hit Delete. She was busy to-night. Hell, as far as Ethan's girl singer was concerned, she was busy until the end of *time.*

The white limo pulled up, and bald, big-shouldered Lucas got out to open the door for her. He'd been her driver for nearly three decades, and he doubled as her bodyguard when the need arose.

She was silent as they drove, preparing herself for the only kind of public appearance she made anymore. Though she might have wished herself still at home, curled up in silk pajamas with a glass of wine and a good novel, she believed in giving back, in showing up for good causes. The Book Garden was created to put books in the hands of needy kids, and that was a mission she took very seriously.

Thirty minutes later, Ruthanna was mentally running through her speech one last time as she minced her way to her table near the front of the ballroom. She hadn't picked her most comfortable pair of shoes, that was for sure.

Jack Holm was already sitting down and halfway through his second old-fashioned. He looked up at Ruthanna and smiled.

"I didn't think you'd come," she said as she sank into the chair across from him. "You hate these things."

"I couldn't pass up a chance to see you," her former manager said. "Though this coat and tie is choking me."

She immediately recognized the line as one from Waylon's "Luckenbach, Texas."

"You look great," she said, which was true. Jack had aged in the last couple of years, but he was still handsome. Distinguished-looking, too, with his bespoke suit and hand-tooled boots, his head of silver hair, and his hideously expensive Patek Philippe. And, she couldn't help but note, with his newly bare ring finger.

Sometimes she teased him about how far he'd come from where he'd been when they first met. In 1979 he wore a dented Stetson and played slide guitar with a socket from Sears on his pinkie while singing backup in the Tootsie's house band. But he'd quit performing after only a few years, and he'd never looked back. He preferred a desk to the stage, a phone to a mic.

He took a sip of his drink. "What's black and white and red all over?"

"Any number of things," Ruthanna said, "as I recall." Her phone buzzed with another text from Ethan.

> You gotta see her
> really

Her fingers were poised to write him back: *Quit it.*

"Ahem," Jack said.

So she hit Delete and looked up at him again. "I hate guessing—you know that. Just tell me the punch line."

"A bunch of Nashville bigwigs in too-tight tuxes," he said. "Doing their best to breathe. Is it hot in here or what? I'm sweating like a sinner in church. Those earrings look dynamite, by the way. I assume my thank-you card's in the mail."

She laughed. "Oh, definitely."

"I know you're lying, but it doesn't matter," Jack said. "I don't need your gratitude. I need your attendance at the Country Music Awards. Don't say no! Just…think about it."

A waiter appeared at her shoulder and before either he or Ruthanna could say anything, Jack said, "Bubbles, if you please. The lady would like bubbles. Preferably a grand cru."

As he spoke, Ruthanna noticed that he had missed a spot shaving, and there was a tiny patch of salt-and-pepper beard— mostly salt—near the edge of his jaw. She touched her own cheek wistfully. Whatever time was doing to good old Jack, it was also doing to her. But at least she had dyes and paints to cover it up.

Quit deleting my texts flashed on her screen.

Ruthanna almost laughed aloud. How'd Ethan even know? She tucked her phone into her clutch.

The other table guests arrived right after her champagne, people from Jack's office plus his well-coiffed niece and nephew. Ruthanna hadn't wanted to invite anyone, so she smiled and nodded and picked at her dinner, a salad scattered with flower blossoms and a fillet of salmon balanced on a mound of buttery potatoes that she wasn't supposed to eat.

She took the stage during the dessert course and gritted her teeth through the laudatory introduction, which went on at great length about her achievements: eight Grammys, a National Medal of Arts, "one of the most successful musicians in the history of humankind," blah blah blah blah. Then she made her way to the podium, feeling her heart fluttering quickly in her chest.

She'd been in the spotlight so many times that she shouldn't have been nervous. But it was different to speak than it was to sing; she felt like a bird forced to walk when its job was to fly.

But, she reminded herself, retirement had been *her* idea.

She gave her speech quickly, from memory, barely glancing at her notes. It was short, sweet, and simple.

"If time is money, my friends," she said in conclusion, "just think of all I've saved you by not rambling on and on. So be generous tonight, please, and help us give books to kids who need them. Who crave them. And whose lives will be forever changed by them. Because books, my friends, are true magic bound between two covers. Thank you."

The audience clapped wildly, and at every table she could see checkbooks pulled from purses and pockets. She was about to make a joke about the number of zeros she wanted to see people writing when a deep-throated yell came from the back of the room—a loud, insistent shout that sent a spike of fear up her spine.

She looked to the wings where Lucas stood waiting, and she wondered if she needed to call him out for protection.

And then she realized what the voice was saying. It wasn't a threat. It was a plea.

"Sing! Sing! Sing!"

Within seconds, the entire room was chanting with him, stomping their feet and clapping.

Ruthanna stood there, stunned. Back when she used to perform, her audience would clap for a quarter of an hour to get her to come back out and sing one four-minute encore. And she'd loved it, she really had, even when she was exhausted, body and soul, from performing night after night to thousands of adoring strangers.

But now she straightened her shoulders and motioned to Lucas, who came onstage to offer her his arm and lead her away.

It wasn't so much for them to ask her for a song.

At the same time, though, it was far more than she could give.

CHAPTER

14

S afely ensconced in the back seat of the limo, Ruthanna kicked off her masochistic heels and breathed a sigh of relief. She'd failed to say goodbye to Jack—or anyone else, for that matter—so she pulled her phone from her Swarovski clutch to text him that she was sorry for dashing off. Then she checked her notifications and saw four new texts, two missed calls, and a voicemail, all from Ethan Blake. Wincing a little, she pressed Play.

"I know you hate it when I beg. So you leave me no choice: I'm going to have to *pray*," he said. The sound on the call was terrible, full of bar noise and cell static. "Oh, Ruthanna," Ethan went on, "Saint of Southern Sopranos, will you take pity upon this poor wretch and get your divine, sublime self to your hole-in-the-wall drinking establishment, such that you may hear the dulcet tones of one AnnieLee Keyes? Please, oh rare, remarkable Ruthanna, hear me in my time of need—"

She clicked off, smiling in spite of herself. His prayer would've sounded a lot more convincing if he hadn't been choking back laughter the whole way through.

Ethan was funny, though, and Ruthanna had quickly developed a soft spot for him, partly because he thought he was so tough. One of these days she was going to tell him that a bullet wound and a Purple Heart didn't make him hard as nails. They made him just like everyone else. Sometimes you could see the scars and sometimes you couldn't. But everybody had them.

Her phone vibrated again, and she nearly threw it out the window. He wasn't ever going to leave her alone, was he? She could be undressed and lying on her Beautyrest Black, listening to the meditation app Maya had downloaded for her, and he'd still be pinging her about that girl, no doubt some fresh-faced, wide-eyed little idiot with a decent voice and the ability to string three chords together.

Of course she'd be beautiful. But as far as Ruthanna was concerned, all young people were beautiful. They just had all that *collagen*.

You should see her, he'd texted.

> Not kidding
> Voice like a celestial being
> Bar sink's overflowing

She sighed and tucked her phone back into her bag. Billy could obviously handle the plumbing issue, if there even was one. She wouldn't put it past Ethan to use any weapon in his persuasive arsenal, including outright invention.

She was tired, but the champagne she'd drunk still fizzed pleasantly in her head. How awful would going to the bar really be? Billy made a mean martini, and she could treat herself to one.

She leaned forward. "Actually, Lucas, take me to the Cat's Paw, please."

"You got it, Ms. Ryder," he said. After so many years, he still insisted on calling her that.

When Billy saw Ruthanna come in, his eyes went wide, and his mouth fell open like a trapdoor. She held her finger to her lips and quickly slid over to a small empty table that was almost hidden behind the bar. She didn't want to make a scene if she could help it.

The smell of the Cat's Paw—the funk of old beer, fryer grease, and Bar Keepers Friend—worked like a time machine, and for an instant Ruthanna was her younger self again, cocky and scared at the same time, aching to take Nashville by storm. The Cat's Paw was the first place she'd ever sung. Five years later, when she hit number one with the gut-punching "Don't Lay the Blame on My Pillow," she'd bought the place in celebration. She'd kept it exactly the same.

But she couldn't even remember the last time she'd been here. Like her other properties, the Cat's Paw seemed to run itself—which meant, in fact, that she had responsible people taking care of it for her. Ruthanna simply signed the checks and deposited whatever meager profits there were. Though she well knew the value of a dollar, money was far from her primary concern. She had more than she could ever spend.

Billy hurried over to her table, still looking like he thought he might be hallucinating. "Are you gonna sing?" he whispered. "You look like it."

She kicked her shoes off for the second time that night, thinking she just might leave them there under the table for good. "They asked me that at the last place. The answer is a most emphatic no." She paused. "Is the bar sink working okay?"

"Huh?" Billy said. Then, "Um, yeah. Far as I know."

"I figured."

"Can I get you anything?" he asked.

"Tanqueray martini," she said. "You can glance at the vermouth if you need to, but don't bother touching it. Lemon twist. *Please*."

"You got it," he said, and practically sprinted away.

The bar was crowded, but the stage was empty and ready for its next act. Maybe it'd be Ethan's angel, or maybe it'd be some other hopeful—it really didn't matter to Ruthanna. She wasn't here for the music; she was here, however reluctantly, for Ethan Blake.

She couldn't see him from where she sat, which was just as well. He'd sniff her out eventually, but she wasn't ready to admit he'd won this round.

Not yet.

CHAPTER
15

As Ruthanna waited for her drink, a middle-aged cowboy climbed onstage, tipped his hat, and proceeded to entertain the crowd with a solid Keith Urban imitation. By the time her martini arrived, with its bright slice of lemon floating in ice-cold gin, he'd been replaced by redheaded twins on guitar and mandolin. They played a couple of old-timey numbers that sounded almost but not quite familiar, like the phantom B side to one of the famous Bristol Sessions records.

It was obviously open-mic night at the Cat's Paw, which meant that everyone and her in-laws had come out to get their six minutes in the spotlight. And if Ruthanna had known this in advance, she'd have thought twice about showing up.

"Boo!" said a voice right near her ear.

Ruthanna socked Ethan in the arm without even looking. "Blake, don't scare a lady," she said. "Sit down and have a drink." She gave him a sidelong glance. "Where's your crush? Don't tell me she's immune to your charms."

He started to jokingly protest, but suddenly his face got serious. "Shh," he said. "She's on."

Ruthanna turned and saw a small, slender young woman standing alone in the center of the stage. Her head was bowed, and the lights shone on her dark, tousled hair. Her posture was tense, wary, as if one loud noise would make her bolt like a rabbit.

Oh, Lordy, Ruthanna thought. *This is going to be painful.*

But then the young woman straightened up, and the hair fell away from her face, and Ruthanna saw that she was beautiful, with big eyes and high cheekbones and a rose-bud mouth. She looked as perfect and innocent as one of those Madame Alexander dolls Ruthanna's mother had collected.

Ruthanna started laughing deep in her throat. "Good Lord, Blake, that girl's so gorgeous she could sing like a barn cat in heat and folks'll be calling her the next Maria Callas," she said.

"Shh," Ethan said. "Just you wait."

"Don't *shh* me, soldier boy," Ruthanna warned. Half a dozen choice insults were right on the tip of her tongue, but another glance at Ethan told her that they'd be wasted. Ethan Blake had neither eyes nor ears for anyone but that dark-haired woman on the stage.

"It's nice to be back here," she was saying. "I'm AnnieLee Keyes, and I'm kinda new in town." She tapped on the beat-up instrument she held in her lap. "This here is the Cat's Paw, um, community guitar. It's got old strings and slippery pegs, so it doesn't always like to stay in tune. But the two of us'll do our best for you tonight."

People chuckled, and quite a few of them clapped enthusiastically. Either they knew her already, Ruthanna thought, or she was charming them real quick.

As AnnieLee began to strum her intro, Ruthanna could hear how dull the strings sounded, and she quickly decided to get a better instrument sent to the bar tomorrow. She was wondering whether she should get a Martin or a Gibson— or maybe a Taylor?—when the girl opened her mouth and started singing. And Ruthanna sat up and started paying attention.

Dark night, bright future
Like the phoenix from the ashes, I shall rise again

The girl's voice was a honey-colored soprano, clear and luminous. Ruthanna forgot about her tired, aching feet—and even her excellent drink—as she listened, mesmerized. Where did this girl come from? AnnieLee Keyes looked barely older than a teenager, but she sang as though she'd lived for ninety-nine years and seen tragedy in each one of them.

And yet that voice of hers wasn't sad. It was strong, and it was *wise*.

In any other instance, Ruthanna would've expected Ethan to nudge her in the ribs and whisper *I told you so*. But she didn't have to look at him again to know that he was entranced. The whole room was under AnnieLee's spell.

When she started a new song with a quicker tempo, her voice became a roar rather than a trill. Ruthanna tapped her bare foot on the sticky bar floor. Ethan was right. She *did* sing like an angel—and like a devil, too. Underneath that sweet, doll-faced exterior, there was something fierce and furious about AnnieLee Keyes. Some dark pain powered those pipes; Ruthanna was sure of it.

It wasn't just the girl's voice, either; it was the stories her songs told. Words and melody alike pulled the listener in, so that everyone in the room, no matter who they were, felt exactly what AnnieLee Keyes was feeling.

Ruthanna took a deep breath and beckoned to Billy for another martini. She'd seen more than a lifetime's worth of brilliant, accomplished professional musicians, but this girl was a natural.

It took one to know one.

CHAPTER
16

When AnnieLee finished her set and went to the bar for her celebratory club soda, Billy waved her off. "Not here," he said, and his voice sounded almost strangled.

Her stomach lurched—had she done something wrong?

Well, you insulted the guitar he was nice enough to let you use, for one thing, she thought.

Then a thousand other possible slights began tumbling through her mind. Maybe she hadn't thanked him enthusiastically enough from the stage for letting her sing, or she'd failed to say how honored she was to share the stage with all the other songwriters. And had her pitch been off in that last number? That high E string kept going flat, and she *had* flubbed the bridge a little...

She felt herself shrinking down into something small and uncertain. "What'd I do?"

"You can have your drink at the back table," he said. "Somebody wants to meet you."

AnnieLee straightened up instantly. "Oh!" she said. "They do, do they? Well, for your information, I'm not going to just go sit down with some random stranger just 'cause he wants me to. Shoot, Billy, I thought I was in trouble."

"It's not 'some random stranger,'" said Billy. "It's Ruthanna Ryder."

AnnieLee blinked at him. Surely she hadn't heard him right. There was truly no way—it was like saying Patsy Cline had floated down from heaven on a pair of gilded wings so she could buy AnnieLee a drink. "Come on," she said. "Can I have my club soda, please? My throat hurts. I don't even need the lime slice if it's too much trouble."

Billy's eyes flicked toward the back of the bar. *"Ruthanna Ryder,"* he said again, still sounding a little choked. "She's here, AnnieLee, and she wants to meet you."

AnnieLee still scoffed at him. "Didn't your mother teach you not to lie?"

But then Billy walked out from behind the bar, and he came right over and put his big, calloused hand on AnnieLee's elbow. "The Cat's Paw is her place," he said. "Now why don't you put your pretty smile on and come meet her?"

"Oh, my God," AnnieLee said as he gave her arm a little tug. "You're not kidding."

She slipped off her stool, and Billy began to steer her through the crowd. "She's a hell of a lot ornerier than your average fairy godmother, but that woman can work all kinds of miracles."

AnnieLee still couldn't believe what he was telling her. "Is this really happening? What am I going to say? Am I really about to meet the queen of country music?"

"Now, honey, that's what they call Loretta Lynn. But get all that gee-whiz crap out of you now," Billy said through clenched teeth. "Ruthanna doesn't suffer fools."

Billy gave her a gentle shove and then they broke through a knot of people to find themselves standing in front of a small battered table, in the very back corner of the bar, where the biggest star in Nashville was sitting, clicking her nails on the rim of a martini glass.

Perfumed and painted, with smoky eyes and candy-red lips and her spectacular hair coiffed in studiously messy curls, Ruthanna Ryder was so dazzling that AnnieLee gasped.

As Ruthanna extended a slender arm, gesturing for AnnieLee to sit, her beaded dress reflected the colored lights dripping down from the ceiling. "Damned if I don't look like a disco ball in here," she said, almost to herself. Then she looked up at AnnieLee. "Have a seat."

Tongue-tied, AnnieLee did as she was told. Only then did she notice Ethan Blake sitting in the shadows to Ruthanna's left. *Wait,* she thought, *they* know *each other?*

"Ruthanna," Ethan said to the glittering queen beside him, "I'd like you to meet AnnieLee Keyes. AnnieLee, this is Ruthanna Ryder."

At first AnnieLee could only nod, but a moment later, a torrent of words came rushing out of her mouth before she could stop them. "I pinched myself already, but I still think I might be dreaming. It is such an honor to meet you, Ms. Ryder. I've looked up to you since I was old enough to know anything." She felt her cheeks growing hot, but she kept on going. "We had a poster of you in the kitchen, right next to the Sacred Heart of Jesus, and I thought you were one of the saints! I figured you *had* to be, to sing like that. I even prayed to you. I was about seven years old when my mom finally had to tell me that while your talents were divine, you weren't actually *holy.*"

Ruthanna laughed. "I am far from holy, AnnieLee." Her speaking voice was rich, and lower than AnnieLee had thought it would be.

"See?" Ethan said, nudging Ruthanna's sparkling arm. "I'm not the only one who prays to you."

"What'd you pray for back then, AnnieLee?" Ruthanna asked.

"To sing," AnnieLee said without hesitation. There had been other prayers, too, more desperate ones, but she didn't need to bring them up now.

Ruthanna folded her beautifully manicured hands on the table. Her expression was serious. "You're a very talented girl," she said. "I've been in this business for over forty years, and I've seen more singers than I've seen Sundays. But honestly, you stand out, AnnieLee Keyes. You've really got something special."

AnnieLee's heart swelled with relief and gratitude. "Thank you," she whispered. "That means the world to me."

"I don't do this very often," Ruthanna said, "but I'm going to help you out."

By now AnnieLee was nearly trembling with anticipation. Forget joking about a fairy godmother: one of the greatest musicians in the whole world was going to take her under her wing! This was an honest-to-God miracle. AnnieLee almost laughed out loud to think how her childhood prayers had paid off, even though they'd been sent in the wrong direction.

She could already imagine the story she'd tell about this night. *I was only in Nashville about two weeks before I met Ruthanna Ryder, and she's the reason I'm playing here at the Ryman Auditorium today.*

AnnieLee's life had been so hard. Was it crazy to think that this one thing might be easy? She could feel the huge, wild smile spreading across her face.

But Ruthanna didn't smile back. She pointed one perfect, blood-red nail at AnnieLee's heart. "Here's my advice for you, AnnieLee Keyes," she said. "Get the hell out of Nashville while you still can."

AnnieLee swallowed. "Pardon me?" she gasped.

"It's a hard, rough business," said Ruthanna. "A tiny thing like you? You'll get chewed up and spit out like a hunk of gristle. Sure, you might taste success, but you're more likely to end up broke and alone. Do something sensible with your life, AnnieLee. Get a job. Find a man and marry him." She looked over at Ethan Blake. "Take this guy, for example. He'd make someone a real nice husband."

Elation turned to dismay, just like that. AnnieLee had to remind herself to breathe. Next, though, she had to remind herself who she was.

Can I fix it?
No I cain't
But I sure ain't gonna take it lyin' down

Steeling herself, she spoke slowly and calmly to her idol. "I admire you more than anyone else on this whole green earth," AnnieLee said, "but with all due respect, Ms. Ryder, you can go screw yourself."

CHAPTER
17

Too agitated to stand still but too infuriated to leave, AnnieLee was pacing back and forth in the alley behind the Cat's Paw when the door swung open to reveal Ethan and Ruthanna, backlit by the bar's colored lights.

AnnieLee pulled up short and put her hands on her hips. "Are you here to give me more advice I won't take?"

Ruthanna threw her head back and laughed. "You were right about her, Blake—she's a little firecracker!"

This made AnnieLee even madder. She hated being called small, no matter that it was accurate. "You ain't so big yourself, you know," she said. "I bet I could take you in a fight."

Ruthanna, falling into paroxysms of laughter, held on to Ethan's shoulder for balance, while he looked back and forth between the two of them as if he didn't have the faintest idea what to do or say.

Pretty soon the confounded expression on his face made AnnieLee start laughing, too. How ridiculous was this? She'd thrown a hissy fit in an alleyway and then challenged a country music *goddess* to a street fight. What on earth was she thinking?

"Oh, sugar, that would be the funniest thing," Ruthanna gasped. "Us going at each other like cats. You'd pop all the beads off my fancy dress!"

Ethan, however, had decided that he was not nearly so amused. His eyes met AnnieLee's. *Are you* crazy? *Apologize,* he mouthed.

AnnieLee ignored him. She couldn't apologize because she wasn't sorry. When a girl didn't have anyone to stand up for her, that girl had to stand up for her own damn self. She didn't expect that hunky Ruthanna groupie to understand.

"Your shoes look like they could kill a person, Ruthanna," AnnieLee said, giggling.

Ruthanna kicked out a leg to show off a pointy-toed stiletto. "They're killing *me*," she said. Then she brushed a red-gold curl away from her cheek and said, "I like you. And that's not something I say very often."

"No, it is not," Ethan muttered.

"I know you're new in town," Ruthanna went on. "Where are you staying, AnnieLee Keyes?"

AnnieLee looked down at her hands. She didn't want to lie. "Well, *around*," she said.

"Around," Ruthanna repeated.

Ethan's brows knitted together. "That sounds kinda questionable," he said.

AnnieLee thought of her dirt bed and her cop alarm clock. "It is."

Ruthanna and Ethan shared a meaningful glance before Ruthanna turned back to AnnieLee with an almost maternal smile. "You're welcome to stay with me for a little while," she said.

AnnieLee didn't say anything right away because she was too shocked. How in the span of a few minutes had she gone from threatening Ruthanna to being invited to her house? When she looked over at Ethan, she was surprised to see him nodding, as if he thought this all made perfect sense.

"I stayed there once," he said. "Woke up feeling like the king of England."

Ruthanna stepped into the alley. "Come on," she said to AnnieLee, her voice gentle now. "Don't be too proud. The car's waiting."

AnnieLee hesitated for only a moment. The prospect of an actual bed to sleep in was just impossible to resist. And so with one last wide-eyed look at Ethan, she followed Ruthanna along the cobblestones and into an idling white limo.

CHAPTER
18

AnnieLee sat tensely on the soft leather seat as the car glided along the dark streets. Ruthanna, who was gazing out the window with a thoughtful expression on her face, didn't seem to be in the mood to make conversation.

It still made AnnieLee nervous to look at her, and so she stared at the back of the driver's big bald head. Every once in a while, she caught his eyes in the mirror. But his expression was unreadable.

After half an hour, they turned into a driveway almost hidden beneath towering trees. An enormous pair of wrought-iron gates swung open, and replicas of old gaslights flickered on as they passed. The driver proceeded a full quarter mile before coming to a stop under a porte cochere to the right side of the house.

Although *house* was hardly the right word for it.

Would you call it a manor? A country estate? AnnieLee wondered. Neither did the place justice. Hell, it looked big enough to be the state capitol building.

"You live here?" she asked incredulously—and by mistake. She'd promised herself she wouldn't act like a poor dope who'd hardly ever seen a two-story house or had a meal fancier than the all-you-can-eat pancake breakfast at Denny's. What had that guy Shakespeare said? *The truth will out.*

Ruthanna laughed. "It's a bit much, I know. I was younger and dumber when I bought it, and I got upsold. Here, we'll go in the side."

Feeling more self-conscious than ever about her faded jeans and old Gap T-shirt, AnnieLee followed her into a warm yellow kitchen, where Ruthanna kicked off her shoes and immediately shrank at least four inches. AnnieLee bent down to tug off her beat-up Ropers. Her big toes stuck out of the holes in her socks.

"Now it's time to get out of this preposterous dress," Ruthanna said. "And I bet you'd like to take a shower."

AnnieLee nodded mutely, suddenly worried that she smelled like sweat and dive bars. But she refrained from sniffing her pits as they walked up a wide, curving staircase and then down a long hall lit by a series of glittering chandeliers.

"Voilà!" Ruthanna said, pushing open one of the many heavy wooden doors. "The Lilac Room."

At Ruthanna's urging, AnnieLee stepped into the largest bedroom she'd ever seen. Besides the king-sized four-poster bed with its matching mahogany end tables, there was a sitting area, with a silk brocade couch and two matching armchairs, and a work area, with a beautiful old-fashioned rolltop desk. The walls were painted a soothing shade of the palest purple.

"The en suite's through that door," Ruthanna said.

The what? AnnieLee thought.

Ruthanna gave AnnieLee's shoulder a pat. "I'll leave you to it."

"I really don't know how to thank you—" AnnieLee began.

Ruthanna cut her off. "Hush," she said. "It's nothing."

The en suite turned out to be a bathroom with a heated

marble floor and a soaking tub so big AnnieLee could've swum laps in it. She turned on the shower and peeled off her dusty, sweat-stained clothes. When the water was as hot as it could go, she stepped into the stall and stood beneath the downpour until her skin turned bright pink and billows of steam filled the room. It was the most wonderful thing she'd felt in…well, she didn't really want to count the days. The number was just too high.

Half an hour later, smelling like jasmine and orange blossoms, AnnieLee tiptoed downstairs in an oversized fluffy white bathrobe and found Ruthanna at the kitchen table with a steaming mug of tea.

"You look like you feel better," Ruthanna said. "You also sort of look like a polar bear in that thing."

AnnieLee smiled shyly and sat down across from her. "I'm clean, but my clothes are pretty dirty."

Ruthanna just gazed at her for a moment, and AnnieLee wondered if she'd somehow said the wrong thing, even though it was the obvious truth.

Then Ruthanna got up and walked over to the counter, where she squeezed a thin stream of golden honey into her tea. "I think I might have some things that would fit you," she said.

When she looked up again, her eyes were steady on Annie-Lee's. "Where are you from, AnnieLee? Where's *home*?"

AnnieLee had been dreading this question, since it wasn't one she could answer the way she wanted to. True honesty just wasn't possible. She pulled the collar of her robe tighter around her neck. "It's complicated," she said.

"Life's complicated," Ruthanna said, coming back to the table. "And seeing as how I let you into my home, I don't think it's too much for you to answer a question. Do you?"

AnnieLee twisted a napkin in her lap.

"Well, then?" Ruthanna was persistent.

"I don't really have family," AnnieLee said.

"We all come from somewhere," Ruthanna said gently.

Nervously, AnnieLee straightened the napkin back out. When she spoke, she kept her lips so close together that her words were barely audible. "My parents were survivalists in the backwoods of Tennessee."

There. She'd done it.

God, forgive me, she thought. *I never knew lying could be so easy.*

"It doesn't sound like you were too fond of them," Ruthanna said. "Well, parents can be tough. My own mother was— if you'll excuse the phrase—an incorrigible, dyed-in-the-wool, redheaded bitch on wheels."

"My mom died when I was ten," AnnieLee said. That much was true.

"I'm so sorry," Ruthanna said. "What happened?"

But AnnieLee just looked down at her lap. She wasn't ready to talk about her mother's slow and grisly death from cancer— not tonight, and maybe not ever.

"All right," Ruthanna said. "I won't press you further. You go on to bed. I have to finish drinking this tea. It's nettle. Maya, my assistant, says it's good for me."

"I really appreciate you letting me—" AnnieLee began.

Ruthanna held up a hand. "Say nothing more," she said. "I've got more space than I know what to do with. It's nice to have another body around." She took a sip of her tea and made a sour face. "Needs more honey. I swear it tastes like boiled weeds. Anyway, when you go upstairs, open the last door on your left, and you'll see a bedroom that's all white." She stopped abruptly, and she closed her beautiful green eyes. But after another second, she opened them. She gave herself a little shake, as if she were shrugging something off. "In the closet are all kinds of clothes that will fit you. You can take whatever you need."

"Oh, Ms. Ryder, I can't take your clothes on top of everything else," AnnieLee said.

Ruthanna almost seemed to flinch, and her fingers tightened around her mug. "No one's worn them in a long time," she said quietly. "So you just go on ahead and take whatever you like."

Ruthanna woke to sunbeams filtering softly through sheer French linen curtains. Her window was open, and she could hear the low hum of bees in the apple blossoms outside. She lay in bed for another minute, thinking about the girl down the hall. Dark-haired AnnieLee Keyes was like a half-broke horse: bold and skittish at the same time.

Ruthanna wasn't sorry for telling her to go home—or somewhere else, if home wouldn't do. The music business was different than it used to be, and Ruthanna Ryder herself wouldn't want to be finding her way through it these days.

She sat up slowly and stretched, working out the kinks in her neck as she walked into the bathroom. After a quick, cold shower—another one of Maya's ideas for improving her health, which was perfectly good already, thank you very much—she put on a cream-colored linen jumpsuit that her former stylist had sent her for her birthday in May. Ruthanna had fudged her age for so many years she barely knew what number she'd turned, and she certainly didn't care to think too hard on it.

She pulled her hair into a loose ponytail and then headed downstairs through the big, silent house. It hadn't always been so quiet in these rooms, but a lot had changed over the years. *Some things for the better,* she thought, *and quite a few for the worse.*

"But time marches on," Ruthanna said out loud, a truism for sure and the name of a Tracy Lawrence song, too. She hummed the melody as she fixed herself a pot of coffee, making a lot of noise as she did so to let that nervy girl upstairs know that she was awake and it was okay to come down.

Then Ruthanna got the wild idea to make pancakes. AnnieLee needed to put some meat on her bones, and Ruthanna figured she could live vicariously by watching AnnieLee put away a stack of flapjacks. Meanwhile, she could sip her coffee and wait for whatever nasty spirulina smoothie Maya would show up with and then badger her into drinking.

Ruthanna kept humming as she worked, remembering how much she liked having someone to care for. She didn't want the girl moving in permanently, of course, but it would be nice to keep her around for a little while at least. Maybe they could do a bit of gardening together. The roses were just beginning to bloom, and the lilies would be coming up soon. She had thousands of them, from every corner of the world.

When she'd finished making the pancakes, she stuck them in the oven to keep them warm, and then she sat down to read the paper. Her assistant would be arriving any minute, and she looked forward to introducing the two women. AnnieLee certainly wouldn't challenge Maya to a fight, would she? That *would be something to see,* Ruthanna thought.

It was nearing 9 a.m. when she finally decided to go upstairs and wake her guest. She knocked lightly, and when there was no answer, she slowly pushed the door open.

The bed was made, and the room was empty. A scrawled note lay on top of one of the throw pillows.

Dear Ms. Ryder,

Thank you so much for everything. I want you to know that I took a pair of sweatpants and two shirts from that closet. And…well, I also borrowed the guitar that was in there. The case was real dusty. I know you didn't offer me that, but something told me you wouldn't have refused me if I'd asked. I promise to take good care of it, and I'll return it just as soon as I can.

All my gratitude and admiration, and then some,
Firecracker

"Well, I'll be damned," Ruthanna whispered. She felt a rush of so many feelings at once that she couldn't have put words to any of them. Then she crumpled the note in her hand.

CHAPTER
20

Ruthanna was standing in the rose garden when Maya got out of her Lexus bearing two bright-green smoothies.

"You're looking thoughtful this morning," Maya said, handing her one of the cups.

"I guess I am," Ruthanna said. "Thanks for—whatever this is."

"Spinach-celery-kale-pear. You'll like it."

Ruthanna gave the drink a dubious sniff. "I let that girl Ethan discovered stay here last night, but she vanished sometime before six a.m. Why do you suppose she did that?"

"I don't know," Maya said. "Did anything else vanish with her?"

"She took a guitar. But she left a note about it."

Maya clucked her tongue. "This is very unlike you."

Ruthanna acknowledged that it was. But something about that girl had touched a nerve.

"Should I go count the silver?" Maya asked, half joking.

"That won't be necessary," Ruthanna said. "AnnieLee wouldn't do something like that. But if she did, would I really even care? I mean, when was the last time we used that stuff?"

"Oh, I remember," Maya said. "It was—" But then she snapped

her mouth shut and turned quickly on her heel, walking up the steps to the house.

Ruthanna felt a jolt of pain as she remembered, too. A gorgeous June Sunday, a celebratory brunch for her daughter—

But she wasn't going to think about that now.

She turned and followed Maya into the kitchen and watched as her assistant brewed another pot of coffee.

"You gonna have some?" Maya asked. "I'm making this so strong it'll lift weights."

"Sure," Ruthanna said, pushing her mug over. "There's pancakes in the oven if you want some."

"Do I ever," Maya said. "I don't know how a person's supposed to just have juice for breakfast."

Ruthanna took an exploratory sip of her smoothie. "It's not bad, though." She folded herself into the window seat. "I really like that AnnieLee. I wanted to help her, but I don't think I told her what she wanted to hear."

Maya peered at her over her glasses. "What'd you say?"

"I told her to get out of Nashville as fast as her tiny little feet could carry her."

Maya snorted. "In other words, you crushed her dreams."

"If you want to be negative about it, go ahead," Ruthanna said. "But I was trying to save her, actually."

Maya sat down at the table with a plate of pancakes dripping with syrup and melted butter. "You think she took your advice?"

"Not hardly," Ruthanna said. "I think she's as stubborn as—"

"As you are?" Maya interrupted.

Ruthanna grinned. "Basically." She took the cordless phone down from the wall and held it out to Maya. "Can you call Jody at BMH?" she asked. "If the girl's going to stick around, I guess the least we can do is let some people know she's here."

"Can I eat while I'm doing it?"

"Obviously."

Maya took the phone and dialed as she chewed. She had the number memorized, but Ruthanna knew Maya still had her old Rolodex if she needed it. A shared penchant for doing things the old-fashioned way was just one of the reasons they worked so well together.

Maya put the phone on speaker as soon as Jody picked up.

"Please, dear God, tell me Ruthanna's got a new song," Jody said in lieu of "Hello."

"She's got about a hundred," Maya said. "But you know her feelings on the matter."

"Unfortunately, I do," Jody said. "Let me say that all of us at BMH Music look forward to the day she changes her brilliant and infuriating mind."

"She does have something for you, though," Maya said. "A new singer."

Ruthanna could practically hear Jody's eyes roll. "I don't go out anymore. I can send one of my underlings—as a favor to Ruthanna, of course. She around?"

Ruthanna waved her hands. *Noooooo, I am not here.*

"Not at the moment," Maya said smoothly. "All right, so you're going to sit home and binge-watch British baking shows while you let some kid discover her? Sign her to a publishing deal and take all the credit?"

Jody gave another theatrical sigh. "What's her name?"

Maya looked over at Ruthanna, and Ruthanna quickly wrote the name on a piece of paper and held it up.

"AnnieLee Keyes," Maya read.

"Yeah, I don't love that," said Jody.

"Why?"

"AnnieLee? Keyes? It sounds like she should be stick-thin and toothless, playing spoons on some Appalachian porch with a bunch of flea-bitten hounds steaming around her bare feet."

"Hell, tell us what you really think," Maya said.

"Okay, it's not that bad," Jody said. "But it's not good, either."

"Well, change it, then. That's what they did with Ruthanna Ryder."

"I wasn't responsible for that, as you know, but whoever was had a fine idea. Pollyanna Poole? That's a name for a baby doll— you know, the kind that opens its eyes and pees in its diaper."

Ruthanna couldn't keep her mouth shut any longer. "You're pretty opinionated today, Jody Decker," she said. "But if I was singing those songs, you know people would've listened, even if my name was Toot-a-lee McDoo-Doo."

Maya giggled while Jody somewhat awkwardly cleared her throat. "I didn't know you were on the line, Ruthanna," she said. "Is this girl we're talking about a friend of yours?"

"I barely know her, to tell you the truth. But I've seen her, and she's something else."

There was a pause. "Is she pretty?"

Ruthanna wasn't at all surprised by the question—everybody liked a good-looking package to promote—but it still bothered her. She sat back and crossed her arms.

"You'll have to go see her to find out," she said.

CHAPTER

21

AnnieLee strode into a bar called the Lucky Horseshoe a few minutes before four o'clock happy hour. She was clean, well rested, and only moderately starving, a state of being far better than usual these days. The guitar bumping against her thigh gave her an extra boost of confidence. She'd written another song on the eight-mile walk back to the city proper, and she was excited to see how it played. She had an instrument now; she only needed a stage.

As her eyes adjusted to the bar's dimness, she looked around for someone to appeal to. A neon Budweiser sign flickered; a couple watched a golf game on the big TV; four fan-tailed, multicolored fish swam lazily in a small tank near the lowest row of liquor bottles.

She was about to try her luck elsewhere when a tall, ruddy-cheeked woman came out of the back, a bar towel slung over her tanned, tattooed shoulder. She wore her long blond hair in two fat braids, but her brows were thin and painted almost black. She slid in behind the bar, washed her hands, and then began polishing pint glasses. She didn't look up at AnnieLee.

"Hi there," AnnieLee chirped.

The woman's eyes shifted from her glass to AnnieLee, and then down to the guitar she was carrying. "Hello," she said warily.

"I was wondering if you'd like to hear some live music tonight," AnnieLee said. "Performed by me and my new guitar." She patted the case protectively. When the woman didn't say anything, AnnieLee added, "I've played at the Cat's Paw a lot. They love me there."

The woman lifted one of her overplucked eyebrows. "Do they, now?" she said.

"I'd say so," AnnieLee said. She wondered if she should mention Ruthanna Ryder—how they were practically friends now, even though AnnieLee had snuck out of her house just after the sun came up. But she was pretty sure the woman wouldn't believe her, for one thing. And for another, she didn't think Ruthanna would appreciate being name-checked like that. She'd told AnnieLee to go find a real job, after all, not traipse around Nashville looking for a place to perform and using her name as grease for the wheels.

"So why aren't you singing at the Cat's Paw tonight?" the woman asked. She wasn't unfriendly, but she looked like she could snap AnnieLee in half.

"I'm branching out," AnnieLee said. "Trying new things." She glanced around her. "I thought this looked like a good place to play. I, um, like your fish."

The woman looked over at the tank and her expression softened. "They're pretty, aren't they? Like a painting that moves." Then she turned back to AnnieLee. "We have live music Friday and Saturday nights. The rest of the time, we use that." She gestured toward a giant, old-fashioned jukebox.

AnnieLee walked over to it and peered through the smudged glass. Hank Williams. George Jones. Kitty Wells. "How come the newest song you got in here is at least twenty years older than I am?"

"The jukebox only plays 45s," the woman said proudly. "It's an antique."

AnnieLee scanned farther down the list. It was nothing but classics: "I Walk the Line," "Crazy," "Coal Miner's Daughter," and "I'm So Lonesome I Could Cry." "Friends in Low Places" was as close to contemporary country as it got.

Then AnnieLee turned back to the bartender. "I can play all of those songs," she said.

"Congratulations." The woman had opened a magazine and was flipping through it.

"What I mean is," AnnieLee said, "*I* could be your jukebox."

The woman flipped another page, squinting at it as though she needed glasses. "I love Rebel Wilson," she said thoughtfully. "I wish she'd record a country album." She looked up at AnnieLee. "What?"

AnnieLee talked quickly so the woman wouldn't go back to her *People*. "It'd be really fun," she said. "If someone wants to play any of the songs on the jukebox, they can just ask me to play it instead. They won't even have to put a quarter in!"

The woman gave AnnieLee a quick up-down. "I'm sure the guys would want to stick more than a quarter in you," she said.

AnnieLee shuddered but decided to ignore this. "Everyone will get a big kick out of it—I know they will," she said.

A small, needling voice in the back of her head reminded her that she did not in fact know every single one of the songs. But she'd grown up listening to all of them, and singing most of them, and she hoped she'd be able to fake the rest well enough. Three chords and the truth, right? Or six, maybe seven—plus some decent fingerpicking?

She could see the bartender thinking it over. "Tuesdays are a little slow," she said, more to herself than to AnnieLee. "And it's not like I'd die if I went a day without hearing 'Folsom Prison Blues' straight from the Man in Black's mouth."

"You don't have to pay me," AnnieLee said. "I'll sing for my supper."

The bartender snapped her magazine shut and stood up straight. "Supper?" she said, tossing her thick braids behind her back. "I've got the best chili dogs south of the Mason-Dixon, girl, so let's not get ahead of ourselves."

CHAPTER 22

F ollowing the bartender's curt instructions, AnnieLee perched herself on a stool by the jukebox and waited for someone to walk over and request a country classic.

And waited.

And then she waited some more. Soon an hour had gone by—sixty lonesome, tedious minutes during which she sat there unnoticed, cradling Ruthanna's beautiful rosewood guitar on her lap and tapping her feet on the cement floor.

Maybe no one saw her because it was two-dollar Tecate Tuesday until 6 p.m., and they were too busy knocking back cans of Mexican lager to notice a dark-haired girl hunkered in the corner. And maybe it'd be too loud to hear her play anyway. But AnnieLee had no intention of calling it quits. She told herself that she was just doing what she had to do for her art. For her love of music.

Anyway, there were far worse ways to spend a Tuesday night; this she knew from experience.

She shifted around on the uncomfortable stool and sighed. Then she hummed the beginnings of a new melody. Later she killed a few minutes thinking of words that rhymed with bored: *chord, sword, horde, snored*...

As she watched the bar clock tick its way toward six and her stomach began to grumble, AnnieLee realized that her reason for sticking it out at the Lucky Horseshoe had shifted. It was no longer about dedication or pride; it was about *dinner*. She wanted one of those chili dogs, damn it, and she wasn't going to leave until she'd earned it.

Ingrid, the bartender, had told her to sit tight and wait for someone to come up to her, but hunger finally wore AnnieLee's patience too thin. When a man in a Charlie Daniels T-shirt passed by on his way to the bathroom, she leaned out and called, "What's that you said, mister? You asked me if I could play 'The Devil Went Down to Georgia'?" It was the only Charlie Daniels song she could think of.

The man turned toward her in confusion. "Huh? I didn't—"

"Well, I can't play it, actually," she interrupted, giving him her brightest, most irresistible smile, "because I don't have a fiddle player. But you look like a man of great taste and discernment, so what if I played you a little Willie Nelson instead? Say, 'Yesterday's Wine'? I know George and Merle went to number one with their version, but I've always loved Mr. Nelson's take on the tune."

Still looking somewhat baffled, the man told her that he wouldn't mind hearing the song at all, especially not from a pretty little thing like her. And AnnieLee swallowed her objection to being referred to as such, and thereby tricked her way into her first live performance at the Lucky Horseshoe.

When she'd finished the song and the sound of the final E chord had faded into the background noise, she thought the Charlie Daniels fan would move along on his personal errand. But he stayed there, peering at her curiously, as if she were some kind of rare bird.

"I never heard it sung like that before," he said. "Can you do 'On the Road Again'?"

"I sure can," she said.

"Spider," he called over his shoulder, "come check this girl out."

"Woman," AnnieLee said under her breath.

Then an extremely large man in an extremely large cowboy hat—Spider, AnnieLee could only assume—strode over to hear her version of Willie's ode to being on tour, and pretty soon a whole cluster of people had gathered around her stool. Spider wanted her to sing "Two Doors Down" next, and she'd barely gotten the last line out before everyone started calling out more requests from the jukebox lineup. A very young couple with their arms around each other's waist asked if she could play their wedding song.

"Our first dance was to 'I Cross My Heart,'" said the woman, who hardly looked old enough to be in a bar, let alone in a marriage.

AnnieLee clipped a capo onto her guitar's first fret. "George Strait, right?" she asked.

"Damn straight!" the woman said, and then she blushed and giggled as if she couldn't believe she'd said the word *damn.*

AnnieLee closed her eyes and thought back to being a kid, listening to KCMN— *"That's* Country Music Now *at 95.5 on your FM dial, cowboys"*—on the truck radio, clutching her banged-up, twenty-dollar guitar in sweaty hands as she tried to figure out where her fingers were supposed to go. She could remember the tune, but…

"Can you help me a little with the lyrics?" she asked.

And just like that, AnnieLee's performance turned into a

sing-along. The young woman put her arm around Spider, who was three times her size, as he joined the chorus with his deep baritone. And then more people started drifting over and adding their own voices. AnnieLee played Patsy Cline next, and then Tammy Wynette. A tip jar appeared at her feet, and within half an hour it was full to the rim with small bills and loose change.

When AnnieLee had played at least half of the songs in the jukebox, the man in the Charlie Daniels shirt stepped forward to ask her if she had any songs of her own she could play.

Her fingers were aching and her throat was sore, but she wanted him—and everyone else, for that matter—to hear the words that she herself had written. She'd prove she wasn't just a human jukebox. "I've got loads," she said. "You really want me to play one?"

"Damn straight!" the young woman shouted again.

"Hell yes!" said her baby-faced husband.

The crowd fell silent as soon as AnnieLee played the first little lick of her song. Her voice was tired, but it still had power, and she felt her spirits lifting even higher as she played song after song of her own.

Finally she had to put the guitar aside and stand up. Her legs were cramped and her fingertips felt blistered and raw.

"I'm sorry," she said to everyone. "I think I might be done for the night."

They began to boo loudly but playfully, and then Ingrid the bartender appeared and wagged her finger at all of them like a tattooed Viking den mother. "Give her a break, you guys," she said. "A girl's gotta eat."

She set up AnnieLee at a little table in a corner and brought her a chili dog and a huge pile of cheese fries. The food smelled so good AnnieLee very nearly cried. "I could eat this three times over," she said.

"You must got a hollow leg," Ingrid said.

AnnieLee put a warm, greasy fry in her mouth. "I've got a lot of hollow." She saw a waitress walking by with a basket of tater tots. "Could I have some of those, too, please? And a Coke? I'm sorry, I'm just—" But she couldn't speak anymore, because she had to get the food in her mouth. And though she tried to eat politely, it was impossible. For one thing, she was starving, and for another, consuming a chili dog was an inherently messy operation.

Ingrid came back a few minutes later with more food and said, "Here you go, Takeru."

AnnieLee looked up. "Who?"

"Takeru Kobayashi," Ingrid said. "You know, the Japanese eating champion."

"Oh, sure, of course," AnnieLee said, nodding as if she'd heard of him, which she hadn't. She took a grateful sip of her Coke. "This tastes funny." Then she flushed. "Sorry, I don't mean to be rude—"

"It tastes funny, dummy, because there's Jack Daniel's in there," Ingrid said, giving AnnieLee's shoulder a quick pat. "It's good for the voice box." She grinned. "*And* the mood."

The whiskey burned AnnieLee's throat a little, but she got used to it quickly enough. Soon, a pleasant, warm feeling began to spread throughout her body. Her calloused fingertips stopped hurting so much, and she felt a new but fierce affection for every single person in the Lucky Horseshoe.

By the time AnnieLee got to the bottom of the glass, her worries seemed as far away as clouds on a distant blue horizon. She was finally safe, right here in Music City, and she knew without a doubt that pretty soon, she was going to make all of her dreams come true.

CHAPTER
23

AnnieLee was still giddy from her performance as she left the Lucky Horseshoe almost eight hours after she'd arrived. She'd given Ruthanna's guitar to Ingrid for safekeeping, and she'd then bid a fond and only slightly tipsy farewell to all her new friends, promising that she'd come back to sing for them again as soon as she could.

She'd refused a ride home from Spider, and then from the nice kids who'd requested George Strait. AnnieLee figured that a quiet walk would help her wind down, and anyway, she didn't want anyone finding out that "home" was a pawnshop sleeping bag on a bare patch of ground underneath a tree in Cumberland Park.

After tucking her money a little deeper into her back pocket, AnnieLee began to walk northeast toward the river. She had only about a mile to go, the night was clear and warm, and she was feeling very pleased with herself. She'd arrived in Nashville hungry and poor, with nothing more than what she could carry on her back. And every single day, things were looking up.

Of course, when you started at the very bottom, up was pretty much the only way to go.

As she passed under a streetlamp, AnnieLee gave a little skip and spun around the pole like Gene Kelly in *Singin' in the Rain*. Maybe it was the unexpected money, or the song she was writing in her head—or maybe it was just the Jack and Coke—but AnnieLee found herself letting her guard down a little. She didn't look around continually as she walked toward the river. She didn't pause at every corner to check her surroundings, holding her breath and listening like a doe. She let herself be carried along by a thrilling and unfamiliar happiness. Humming her new melody, she even bent down to sniff a cluster of purple dwarf irises in a café's window box. They smelled like Easter candy.

And then suddenly, some ancient, animal part of AnnieLee that she'd tried to ignore, just this once, rose up and grabbed her by the throat. *Hunter,* it said. *Danger.*

She froze, still bent over, every sense alert and every nerve electric and prickling. She heard the tiny hiss of her exhale, the buzz of a distant motorcycle, and the leaves on a potted magnolia rustling against one another.

And then there it was—a different, human kind of noise. A metallic jangle of keys. The scrape of a boot along a sidewalk. How such a simple sound could be sinister, AnnieLee didn't know, but she'd already started running when a man came charging toward her in the dark.

She felt fingers snatching at her arm, and instinctively she kicked backward. Her foot connected with something hard. A knee, maybe, because she heard a crack and then a curse of pain.

She didn't turn around. She flung herself forward.

Fast but relaxed—that was what her middle-school track coach used to say. *Running's about stamina as much as it is about speed.*

But this wasn't a track race; this was the flight of an animal pursued. A hunted doe did not run with grace. It ran desperately so that it would not die.

AnnieLee leaned into her pace as her feet swallowed ground. She didn't look back to see if she was being followed because it would slow her down and because she knew that she was. Her breath exploded out of her mouth, hard and fast. She focused on moving her arms, because if she could move them faster, then her legs would have no choice but to follow.

Adrenaline fueled her, but still her lungs screamed. Her boots slid on the pavement and her legs nearly went out from under her as she took a corner at top speed, but she grabbed onto a windowsill and caught herself, pushing away with all her might, barely breaking stride.

Up ahead, she saw an opening between the buildings. If she could only make it in before her pursuer rounded the corner—

She pitched herself into the dark, narrow passageway, passing overflowing trash cans lined up against the brick wall. She leaped over pallets that spilled into the path. And then she looked up to see a dead end, not fifty yards ahead.

She couldn't go on and she couldn't turn back. So she ducked down, crawling on hands and knees across the gritty cobblestones until she could shimmy into a tiny space between two greasy, stinking dumpsters.

She couldn't hear anything over the pounding of her heart and the roaring in her ears. Her throat was raw, and her chest heaved as she mentally implored whoever it was who'd followed her, *Keep going, keep going, keep going.*

She kept as still as she could, even while her legs began to shake and cramp. When her breathing finally slowed, the sweet, rotting smell of the trash became almost unbearable.

She listened, hearing nothing but silence. No silhouette appeared at the end of the alley. No one pushed aside the trash bins and saw her there, crouched in the alley like cornered prey.

AnnieLee stood up slowly on aching limbs. The world seemed to spin all around her, and she gasped. Reaching out and pressing her palm against the rough brick, she bent over. She coughed and wretched. Her stomach gave an enormous, terrible lurch, and then she vomited up her entire dinner.

"Shit," she said when she could finally speak again. She wiped her mouth on her shirt. "What a waste of those chili dogs."

Then she turned and started walking back toward the park. She cast wary glances in all directions as she hurried down quiet streets. But no one followed her.

That man just wanted to rob you, she told herself as she climbed over the wall and vanished into the park. *That's all.*

But that old, subconscious part of her knew this wasn't true. Whoever it was hadn't wanted her money. He had wanted her.

24

For the next five nights, AnnieLee woke at every twig snap, and often she lay awake until dawn pinkened the sky. Only when the crows began their earsplitting morning chorus would she rise, pack her gear, stow it in its hiding place, and make her exhausted way into town.

She'd pick up her guitar from its storage spot at the Lucky Horseshoe, which started serving its famous Bloody Marys at 8 a.m. If AnnieLee was lucky, Ingrid would be working the opening shift and would give her a free coffee. Then she'd walk down to Lower Broadway to busk on a corner not already staked out by other street musicians. After a few hours of singing to passersby, many of whom hardly seemed to notice her, she'd go looking for a dive bar to play in. Most nights she got lucky enough to earn either a meal or a bit of money, and sometimes she hit the jackpot and got both.

By the sixth night, AnnieLee had made enough that she'd decided to splurge on a cheap motel in East Nashville. Her room was so pink she felt like she'd checked into an oversized Pepto-Bismol bottle, and the lime-green chenille bedspread belonged to 1974 at the latest. But the floors seemed clean, and the air didn't smell of mildew or cigarettes, and anyway, AnnieLee was too grateful for running water and a mattress to complain about questionable color schemes.

The other upside of being inside was that now when she woke at 2 a.m., heart pounding, from a nightmare about being chased, she could lie in a soft bed and watch the motel sign flicker on and off, and listen to the ice machine going *kachunk kachunk kachunk* on the sidewalk outside her window.

Things were really looking up.

On a sunny Thursday morning, AnnieLee decided it was time to play tourist and visit Music Row, which was the heart of Nashville's music business. She wanted to see the Quonset hut that legendary record producer Owen Bradley had built as a studio back in 1954, and RCA Studio B, where so many country stars had recorded so many chart-topping hits.

But as soon as she got to the quiet parallel streets a mile and a half west of the river, she realized that Music Row wasn't the industry's heart so much as its *brains*. Here were the music publishers, recording studios, and organizations that made the city sing. Here were businessmen with brief-cases and powerful-looking women with expensive haircuts and soft, manicured hands that couldn't hold a barre chord if they tried.

AnnieLee couldn't exactly put her finger on why she felt disappointed. It wasn't as if she'd expected to see Reba McEntire walking out of the Starstruck Entertainment build-ing. She hadn't thought she'd be discovered by a BMI exec just because she strolled by on the sidewalk with a guitar in her hand.

Maybe it was because she suddenly understood that even though she might play her heart out every night in bars across the entire city, she was still a little nobody, and these imposing doors would be closed to her for a long time.

Can I fix it? she sang softly.

No I cain't

She threw her head back and stared up at the glass pyramid at the top of the ASCAP building. "Not yet, anyway," she yelled. "But just you wait!"

As far as she could tell, not a soul heard her.

Then, to cheer herself up, AnnieLee turned around and headed back toward the café she liked, the one with the antique furniture and the basket of cheaper, day-old pastries.

A bell on the door jingled as she walked in, and AnnieLee's mouth was already watering. She'd eaten cold beans from a can for breakfast, so she felt as though she deserved an orange-cranberry scone, dusted with sparkling sugar and slathered in butter.

She pointed to the one she wanted. "May I have that big guy right there, please?" she asked.

The girl behind the counter grabbed it with a pair of tongs and set it on a pretty vintage china plate. "Hey," she said, peering at AnnieLee. "Haven't I seen you somewhere?"

AnnieLee flushed. "Well, *here*," she said. "I mean, I've come in once or twice."

It was four times, actually, and she'd drunk endless free coffee refills and washed goodly portions of her body in the restroom. But she definitely didn't want to be remembered for these things.

"No, I mean *out*," the girl said. She cocked her head. "Do you sing—like, around?"

AnnieLee's cheeks began to tingle with pleasure. Was it possible she'd actually been recognized? "Sure, I've played here and there," she allowed as she reached for her pastry.

The girl pointed her tongs at AnnieLee. "I saw you in Printers Alley—that's it. You were great! I loved your song, the one about the girl who imagines that she's a phoenix?"

"You're too nice," AnnieLee said, flustered.

The girl smiled. "The scone's on me. Coffee, too. I hope I get to see you play again."

AnnieLee thanked her warmly and then took her coffee and pastry to a cozy window table, where she sank into an antique armchair, feeling very gratified and just a smidge famous.

25

The Cat's Paw already had a decent crowd when AnnieLee waltzed in wearing a new-old pair of Frye booties she'd gotten at a thrift shop sale. They made her three full inches taller, and she loved them, even if they pinched her toes as her Ropers never had.

She made her way to the bar, where Billy was mixing up a pitcher of margaritas.

"Well, hello, little songbird," he said. "You ready for your set?"

She'd talked him into giving her the 7:30 slot, and she'd brought three new tunes to debut.

"Of course I am. But don't call me *little*—sheesh," AnnieLee said as she hoisted the guitar case onto the only empty stool. "I'm five foot five tonight."

"I beg your average-height pardon," he said. "And wait—am I seeing things, or did you get yourself an actual instrument since I saw you last?"

"Fairy godmother came through after all," AnnieLee said.

"Well, I hope she brings you a pair of jeans next."

AnnieLee looked down in consternation at her ragged

Levi's. "Dang, Billy," she said. "I bought boots. I can't buy the whole world. Anyway, I thought torn-up was the fashion these days."

"I sure wouldn't know," he said.

"Of course you wouldn't. I mean, didn't the handlebar mustache go out with Wyatt Earp?"

"It's called an *imperial* mustache, for your information," Billy said, "and it's European in origin."

AnnieLee laughed. "Well, I guess a hillbilly like me wouldn't know the difference. Europe, you say? Is that anywhere near the Texas Panhandle?"

"And for a minute I thought I was glad to see you," he grumbled.

"Oh, don't pretend like you didn't miss me," she said.

Billy just rolled his eyes at her and disappeared into the kitchen. AnnieLee looked down along the bar. Most of the seats were filled with regulars whose faces she recognized but whose names she didn't know. But down at the far end, with an untouched beer in front of him, sat Ethan Blake and his knife blade cheekbones. She couldn't see his eyes under the brim of his baseball cap, but they were probably smoldering enough to start a fire.

She gave him a small wave, as if she were neither surprised nor especially pleased to see him when in fact she was both. Would he fall for it? Ethan opened his mouth to say something, but then Billy shot out of the back with a basket of fries he practically threw onto the bar in front of AnnieLee.

"I missed your voice—I can admit that," Billy said. "Your attitude? Maybe not as much." He glanced over at Ethan, too. "Blake, though, he missed everything about you," he added.

"I don't know why you're putting words in my mouth, Billy," Ethan said.

"Because you're too chickenshit to put them in there yourself."

"Oh, yeah? Is mind reading a talent of yours?" Ethan asked. But he made no effort to deny that it was true.

"Every bartender on earth has an honorary PhD in human psychology, son. No mind reading necessary."

AnnieLee was staring down at her fries, pretending she wasn't hearing any of this. It was better not to get into a conversation she wasn't sure how to get out of.

But there was a small part of her, somewhere *very* deep down, that thrilled at this exchange. There wasn't room for a man like Ethan in her life, not the way she was living it. But finding out that he might have a soft spot for her? Well, it made her feel nice. Cozy. As if the knowledge was a sweater she could put around her shoulders when she was cold.

"Are you gonna answer the man?" Billy asked.

AnnieLee looked up. "What?"

"He asked you if you really ran away from Ruthanna Ryder's."

"Oh." AnnieLee picked up a fry and gazed at it contemplatively. She felt it was important to seem nonchalant. "I think a better word is *strolled*."

Ethan gave a short, sharp laugh as he came over to stand beside her. Even in her heels, AnnieLee barely came up to his shoulder.

"Wow," he said. "You really might be nuts."

AnnieLee didn't bother to dispute this, since she'd concluded the same thing. "I didn't want to overstay my welcome."

"I heard Ruthanna made you pancakes you didn't stick around to eat."

AnnieLee stood up straighter. "For real?" She grimaced. She never would've dreamed of such a thing. *Regular* people hadn't taken care of AnnieLee—why would she ever expect someone that famous and fabulous to do so?

She felt awful. But guilt meant vulnerability, and she had a policy against weakness of any sort. So she said, "Doesn't she pay someone to do that for her?"

The rich, familiar voice came from behind her. "I most emphatically do *not*."

CHAPTER

26

AnnieLee froze in dread.

Then, her shoulders hunched up as if she was expecting a blow, she turned around. Ruthanna Ryder was standing a foot away from her in a gold lamé blouse, high wedge sandals, and skintight jeans, her long red-gold hair cascading down her back. In that dim bar, she almost seemed to glow from within.

Now *that* was what you called imperial, AnnieLee thought, awed.

"I can see I've startled you," Ruthanna said, "by the way your jaw's hanging open like a dying trout's. Don't worry, though, AnnieLee. My skin's grown real thick over the years, and you'll have to work a lot harder to offend me."

AnnieLee shut her mouth and swallowed. "Hello, Ms. Ryder."

"I don't know why I have to keep coming downtown to see you, though," Ruthanna said.

Fearlessness, AnnieLee reminded herself. *Don't give yourself away.*

Her posture straightened. "Well, it *is* a good idea to come to your own bar," she said, trying to sound jaunty and playful. "You can keep an eye on your employees. Make sure they're treating the talent right." She gave Billy a sly look.

"Oh, git, you pint-sized smart-ass," he said.

"I told you not to call me small," AnnieLee warned.

"Clearly you two get along just fine," Ruthanna said. "Anyway, AnnieLee, I knew you were playing tonight, and I came down here to have a listen—and a word with you."

AnnieLee could hardly believe that one of the most successful musicians in the history of the business had troubled herself to come to see her for a second time. But pride and stubbornness made her thrust up her chin. "I'm honored, ma'am, and I hope you'll forgive me for saying that you know how I feel about your 'get out of Nashville' advice," she said.

Ruthanna leaned against the bar. "When someone doesn't appreciate my advice the first time, I'm not dumb enough to give it again. I don't waste my breath like that, not when there's songs to be sung. Or French fries to be eaten." She reached over and plucked a handful from AnnieLee's basket.

"I heard you weren't supposed to have those," Ethan said.

"I'm not. What are you going to do about it?"

Ethan threw up his hands in a gesture of surrender. "Absolutely nothing."

Ruthanna turned back to AnnieLee. "Listen," she said. "Everybody needs an ally. And the more powerful that ally is, the better."

AnnieLee took a deep breath, waiting for what Ruthanna would say next. Was it possible that she meant to help AnnieLee for real now? Or was this some kind of trick—a new, back-handed way to run her out of Dodge? Flustered, she tried to meet her idol's cool, green-eyed gaze and failed.

"I didn't get where I am alone, AnnieLee," Ruthanna said. "A lot of people helped me along the way. Some of them did it because they loved me, and some did it because they knew they'd make money from me. I'm not saying that I couldn't've done it without them, but it would've taken a whole lot longer. So *you*, little firecracker, you can keep on begging and sweating, just like you're doing, and I'm sure you'll make it somewhere. It might be just the second stage at Tootsie's, though. Or it could be top billing at the Cat's Paw. The CMAs might never be anything more than a wish you make on a falling star. Or on another damn birthday cake, one that's got so many candles on it you could use it to roast marshmallows. So what I'm saying—"

"The CMAs?" AnnieLee sputtered, interrupting Ruthanna's speech. "I might as well wish to sprout a horn and turn into a unicorn."

Ruthanna cocked her head and laughed. "Well, all right, if that's what you think. But I'm sure you could use a break from the dive bar hustle."

"Billy wouldn't know what to do without me, though," Annie-Lee said, loud enough for the bartender to hear as he walked by. He grunted and swiped some fries out of her basket.

"I'm not saying you can't keep playing here," Ruthanna said. "Or anywhere else that'll have you, if that's what you want to do."

"AnnieLee's starting to get a reputation, you know," Ethan told her. "I heard her called the Princess of Printers Alley the other day."

"That's impossible!" AnnieLee exclaimed. Printers Alley, which was once home to a thriving publishing industry, was now one of Nashville's most exciting entertainment districts. "I only played there twice."

"Once is all it takes sometimes," Ruthanna said.

"If you're really good," Ethan added.

"I think you are, AnnieLee," Ruthanna said. "Which is why we need to get you into a recording studio."

AnnieLee nearly choked on the fry she was eating. "Seriously?"

"Ruthanna's got one in her basement," Ethan said. "It's incredible. You should see the mixing board. It's fifteen feet long."

Ruthanna gave him a playful elbow jab to the ribs. "Just like a man, to be concerned with how *long* something is."

AnnieLee started laughing, which kept her from blurting out that she barely knew what a mixing board did. Then she asked, "Do you really think I should record some of my songs?"

"I do," Ruthanna said. "I want to hear what you sound like in a decent mic, backed up by real musicians."

AnnieLee's heart was in her throat. She felt equal parts thrilled, grateful, and terrified.

"Yeah—five or six great recordings and she can self-release an EP on streaming," Ethan said. "Is that what you're thinking, Ruthanna?"

Ruthanna took a few more of AnnieLee's fries. "One step at a time, cowboy."

"But I've never sung with anyone else before," AnnieLee said. "It's always only been me and my guitar."

"Well, once upon a time you'd never sung on a Nashville stage before, either," Ruthanna countered.

"And you'd never met a charming, handsome man by the name of Ethan Blake. So really, there's a fine first time for everything."

AnnieLee considered throwing him an elbow, too, but decided not to.

"So, what do you say?" Ruthanna asked. "Are you ready to try something new?"

AnnieLee bowed her head and gazed down at her thrift

store boots, remembering the lyrics she'd written on the way to Nashville.

Reaching out to take what life has given
One thing you can say for me is…
I'm driven

Then she lifted her head, and her eyes met Ruthanna's. "Yeah," she said. "I believe I am."

CHAPTER
27

The day had dawned soft and tropical, and Ruthanna was reclining on a chaise longue beside the placid, glass-tiled pool, playing with a few lines of lyrics. A song about a girl, falling in love. *Hmm, that was nice,* she thought. And there would have to be a boy, of course—preferably a handsome one. Together...

With love in their eyes
'Neath the wide open sky...

But then her phone buzzed, hornet-like, from deep inside her big straw tote. She fished it out.

"Hello, Jack," Ruthanna said. He was the only person whose calls she rarely screened.

"How are my earrings, love?" Jack asked.

"*My* earrings," she corrected him. "The damn things sparkle so much I can signal aliens."

"I'm glad you like them," he said, and she could hear the amusement in his voice. "So now tell me about this girl I hear you found."

She wasn't surprised he'd already heard about AnnieLee. "Ethan Blake found her."

"Never mind, say no more," Jack said. "I'm sure he wasn't listening with his *ears*, if you know what I mean."

Ruthanna laughed. "He probably wasn't, but she's great. Her voice is even prettier than she is."

"I'd like to meet her. Let's get a lunch on the books."

Just then AnnieLee popped out of the house in a borrowed bathing suit, and Ruthanna watched as she dipped a toe into the cold water and yanked it back with a surprised yelp.

"I know patience isn't one of your strong suits, Jack, but she needs time to figure things out," Ruthanna said. "Because I swear, she couldn't get any wetter behind the ears if I threw her in my pool. She'd never seen a pop filter or a loop pedal before two days ago. And God's honest truth, she'd never even heard her own voice played back to her! She says she's been writing and singing songs for as long as she can remember, but as far as I can tell, her audience must've been a bunch of trees and some squirrels."

"She sounds delightful," Jack said. "I guess you better promise to let me know when she's learned her way around a recording session. And in the meantime, when do I get to see you?"

Ruthanna ran her hand through her hair and didn't answer right away. Though she didn't perform anymore, she still had plenty of business dealings, and Jack was her most trusted counsel. But something about the tone of his voice made her wonder if he was asking for a different reason.

"Jack," she said. But then she stopped there.

"You're busy pruning roses—I get it," he said quickly. "I'll call you in a few days."

When he hung up, she put the phone up to her chin thoughtfully. Whatever did he want? In all the years they'd known each other, had they ever spent an afternoon together and *not* talked business?

Maybe not, she thought. But they hadn't both been single, either.

AnnieLee walked over, now wrapped in a robe and eating a slice of brioche she'd grabbed from the kitchen. "You get me a record deal yet?" she teased as she sat down on the chair opposite Ruthanna.

"Hardly." Ruthanna eyed the bread, which was dripping with honey butter. "Darling, you're still just…rising."

"What?"

"You need more time. Like dough. If someone puts you in the oven too early, you're not going to come out right."

AnnieLee pushed the rest of the bread into her mouth and chewed, gazing out at the pool and the beautiful gardens surrounding it. "You're just thinking about carbs."

"That may be true," Ruthanna allowed, "but regardless, the analogy works. You're too raw. Now let me see that new song you're working on."

AnnieLee handed her a scrap of paper and Ruthanna squinted to make out the scrawl. She'd left her readers inside, but she didn't like to admit that she needed them.

They knew in their hearts
They could not live apart
So they started making their plans

Ruthanna looked up from the page. "So wait—did the guy propose to her? Or did he just trip and fall? Is she going to say yes?"

"I don't know yet. I just started it. It might be tragic."

"'Blue bonnet breeze' is nice. But you've got to nail down your story, AnnieLee. That's what a good country song is: a story about real things and real people and real emotions, set to a really good tune."

AnnieLee licked her fingertips to get the last of the honey off. "Is 'real' the same as 'true'?" she asked. "Because all my true stories are bummers."

"No, they're not the same thing." Ruthanna twisted one of the many rings on her fingers. "But a made-up song should still contain real emotion. And the point is, AnnieLee, you need to keep developing your own sound and tone and vision. Your own unique *voice.*"

"I don't sing like anyone else and you know it," AnnieLee said defensively.

"But if a label gets their hands on you now, you will," Ruthanna said. How could she possibly explain the kind of armor it took to stay true to yourself? "They'll mold you into whatever they think the market wants and turn you into someone you don't want to be. And you'll be so seduced by their promises that you'll let them. You wouldn't know a good deal if it bit you on your scrawny butt. You'd sell that song you were working on earlier this morning for five hundred dollars."

"That's a lot of money," AnnieLee said.

"It is not!" Ruthanna sat up and pointed her finger at AnnieLee. "You listen to me, missy: don't make any deals without me."

AnnieLee's eyes were the same color as the pool, but they were hardly placid. Instead, they were bright and wary. "I'm not making any deals yet, don't worry," AnnieLee said. "But this promoter's been calling."

"Who? What's his name?"

"Mikey Shumer."

Ruthanna gripped the arm of her chair. "How'd he get your number?"

"Billy gave it to him, I guess."

"You stay a million miles away from that man," she said.

AnnieLee appeared startled by her tone. "You know him?"

"I wish I didn't. He's dirty, AnnieLee. You can't trust Mikey Shumer any farther than you can drop-kick him."

AnnieLee frowned. "But I can trust *you*," she said slowly.

"Yes."

"So what's in it for you? There's got to be something, right?"

Ruthanna sighed. "Honestly, I don't even know," she said. "Maybe I'm just trying to be nice."

AnnieLee lay back on her chaise longue and crossed her arms. "Nobody does anything just to be nice."

"Is that really what you think?" Ruthanna asked.

"It's what I know," AnnieLee said quietly.

"You must've had a rough life."

"I'm doing all right. I've got a place to stay now and everything."

"Dream big," Ruthanna said dryly.

"I do," AnnieLee said, suddenly earnest. "But I try to be real pleased by the little things along the way."

Ruthanna smiled at the prickly, lovely girl. "That's about the smartest thing I've heard you say yet." She reached into her straw tote and handed AnnieLee a bottle of sunscreen. She could see the girl's nose getting pink. "Look at me," she said. "I've got everything. I don't need anything at all, but if I *did* need something, I certainly wouldn't try to take it from you." She sighed. "I don't know why I'm being so nice. Maybe it's that you make me stop and remember someone."

AnnieLee turned to Ruthanna. "Who?"

But Ruthanna had closed her eyes. "Hon," she said quietly, "I don't think I want to talk about it right now."

CHAPTER
28

E than high-fived the regulars perched on barstools as he made his way toward the Cat's Paw stage, his acoustic guitar slung across his broad back. He'd made the instrument himself from East Indian rosewood and western red cedar. It was beautiful, the product of six months' worth of sweat and concentration.

If he was honest with himself, the guitar didn't sound a whole lot better than a good factory-made Blueridge from China. But he didn't care. He knew every inch and every joint of the instrument, every hex head bolt and fret wire, and it felt solid and right in his hands.

He'd recently begun making a second guitar. It would be smaller, with a mahogany face, curly maple back and sides, and mother-of-pearl inlay around the sound hole. When he worked on it late at night, he tried not to think about the blue-eyed girl he hoped would someday play it.

He checked his tuning in the shadowed corner near the pictures of Ruthanna and other Nashville greats, and then he hurried onto the stage, tipping his Tar Heels baseball cap to the crowd as he dropped onto the folding chair. He wasn't the bantering type; half the time he'd start playing without even introducing himself. That, Ruthanna had told him, was a bad sign. A man who couldn't remember to tell the audience his own name was a man who did not sufficiently hunger for fame and fortune.

But who said he had to want them in the first place? There were plenty of other things to hope for—like a bit of money so he could get a new exhaust system for his truck, for example. Or the ability to keep writing songs. Or a night without troubled dreams.

Of course, there was no guarantee that even such modest hopes would be realized. Fate granted some people their wildest, greatest wishes while leaving the simplest pleas of others unanswered.

But damned if he wasn't philosophical tonight! If he wasn't careful, he'd end up singing "Whiskey Lullaby" and weeping onto his one-of-a-kind guitar. The Cat's Paw regulars would never let him hear the end of *that*.

He did manage to introduce himself, giving the room a wry half smile as he explained how he'd taken the night off from KJ'ing over at the Rusty Spur. "So head on over there one of these days," he told the crowd, "grab a mic, and give me the chance to clap after *you* sing."

He warmed up the crowd with some Dwight Yoakam and Merle Haggard. Ethan wrote his own songs, but he didn't always like to play them onstage—which, as Ruthanna had pointed out, was another big hurdle on the road to fame and fortune.

"More like a sinkhole," Maya had said.

Ethan was fifteen minutes into his set, strumming a sloweddown version of "Achy Breaky Heart," when Billy placed a beer at his feet. Ethan finished the song and sipped gratefully, and then raised the glass in a toast to the entire room. The air conditioner was battling the heat of a hundred bodies, and the stage lights made everything hotter. "Thank you, kind stranger," he said to the crowd. "I was getting thirsty up here."

As he set down his drink, he shielded his eyes from the glare, trying to get a sense of who'd bought him the beer. That was when he spotted AnnieLee Keyes standing way in the back.

She'd actually come out to hear him play. And he was pretty sure she'd coaxed Billy into delivering the brew.

When Ethan straightened back up, he'd forgotten what he'd planned to sing next. He could feel her eyes on him now, and the hand on the neck of his guitar grew sweaty. Had he played "Good Hearted Woman" yet? What about "Smoky Mountain Rain"?

He strummed the opening chords to "Good Hearted Woman," but he stopped before he got to the first verse. Adrenaline pulsed in his fingertips. He couldn't understand why she made him feel this way, and he didn't particularly enjoy it, either.

But if there was a silver lining to his present discomfort, it was this: his nerves couldn't get worse. So why worry about playing covers?

"Screw it," he said to the room. "I've got a few of my own songs to sing for you tonight."

When he was done playing, the crowd clapped like crazy, and over the sound of their applause came a piercing wolf whistle. Ethan didn't have to look to know who it was coming from. He waved to the room in thanks, turned off the mic, placed his guitar in its case, and then headed straight for AnnieLee Keyes.

But by the time Ethan got to the front of the bar, she was gone.

CHAPTER
29

AnnieLee was already halfway down the street by the time Ethan Blake stepped off the stage. She hadn't even meant to run, but her legs had carried her like he was someone to be afraid of.

It was ridiculous—Ethan had never been anything but a gentleman to her. He was a great guitar player, too, and he had a rich tenor voice that could hit the high lonesome notes with ease. She felt bad she hadn't stuck around to tell him so.

You'll let him know the next time you see him, she told herself as she unlocked the door to her motel room. *And you'll apologize for being such a jumpy little freak.*

She tossed her sweatshirt onto the ugly chenille bedspread and went into the bathroom to turn on the shower. The water came out in a tepid, rust-colored trickle. She undressed the rest of the way and stepped into the shower, unwrapping a thin rectangle of motel soap and lathering it up into lemon-scented bubbles.

"You spent too much time in low-down places," she sang. *"You up and forgot all your social graces."*

Then she laughed at herself because the rhyme ripped off Garth Brooks's thirty-year-old hit. And anyway, wouldn't Ethan Blake forgive her for her imperfect manners when her songs were playing from every car radio and earbud in the free world?

Oh, she thought, squeezing her eyes shut, *if only. If only.*

AnnieLee was working out better lyrics and shampooing her hair when the first blow came.

A fist she didn't even see collided with her chest with a wet thud. The shock was greater than the pain at first. Her knees buckled and she ducked down into the tub, hiding behind the shower curtain. She couldn't see her attacker, but she knew he couldn't see her, either, so she slid-scrambled to the other end of the tub and rocketed out.

She felt someone grab at her as she ran, but she was slippery with soap and he couldn't hold on. In another four steps she'd made it into the bedroom. She meant to grab her sweatshirt and run outside half naked—

But she couldn't because there was someone else waiting for her.

He'd been sitting on the bed, but he stood up as she came running into the room, long hair streaming, soap in her eyes. She let out a shriek as the man behind her grabbed her hair to hold her head back, and the one who'd been waiting stepped forward and punched her in the stomach.

She wanted to scream but she couldn't get enough air into her lungs. She twisted sideways, then doubled over. The man let go of her hair, and she fell on all fours, gasping.

She stayed down, covering her head with her arms and trying to make herself as small as possible as the men rained blows down on her shivering body. Every strike made a flash of light flare behind her eyes, and her ears started ringing.

She tried inching toward the bed because she could see her backpack peeking out from underneath the dust ruffle, and she knew the gun was in one of its pockets. She was reaching out for the strap when a boot to her ribs knocked her back toward the bathroom.

"What the hell do you think you're doing?" a voice growled.

For a moment, she didn't move. The pain was almost overwhelming. But then she dug her fingernails into the carpet and popped her hips up like she was taking off from the starting block, and she exploded toward the door. She was halfway to it when one of the men grabbed her around the waist, and she could feel his teeth as he bit her on the back like an animal. She cried out as the other man shouted, "Shut up! Shut the hell up!"

"It's your own fault for running," hissed the one who'd bit her, who still had her around the waist. "You know how this works."

She did indeed know, and she went limp. There was nothing more she could do. Realizing he'd broken her, the man let her go, and she fell to the floor, her cheek pressed against the carpet. The other man walked over so his boots were an inch from her face.

"Please don't hurt me anymore," she whispered.

"*Hurt* you?" The first man laughed. "This is just a friendly how-do-you-do," he said. "If we really wanted to hurt you, you wouldn't still be talking."

"There's a price for breaking the rules," the other man said.

"No." AnnieLee raised her head, and he cuffed it back down. She could taste blood in her mouth. "I'll get you," she said through clenched teeth. "Someday I will, so help me God."

The boot pulled back, and she squeezed her eyes shut. Pain, excruciating pain, flashed on the side of her head as his foot made contact. Then—blackness.

CHAPTER

30

AnnieLee knocked on Ruthanna's side door and then leaned against the railing in exhaustion. Every inch of her body ached, and the bruises she couldn't see hurt worse than the bruises she could. Sometimes the deep ones took days to come to the surface.

The door opened. "Dear God," Ruthanna gasped when she saw her. "What happened?"

AnnieLee quickly ducked past her into the kitchen, and then limped through the hall and into the closest of Ruthanna's sitting rooms. She sank onto the velvet couch without being invited, arranging her limbs carefully to keep pressure off the sorest spots. Her head hurt, and sounds seemed muffled, as if she'd wrapped towels around her head.

"I'm sorry," she said to Ruthanna, who'd followed her in, looking aghast. "I just really had to sit down."

"Maya," Ruthanna called without taking her eyes from AnnieLee's face. "Can you get ice packs and Advil? And bring some water?"

AnnieLee heard a sound of assent from somewhere deep inside the huge house.

"What happened?" Ruthanna asked again.

AnnieLee looked down at her lap. "Strangers," she said. That much was true, at least—she hadn't known their names.

Ruthanna sank down on the cushion beside her. "What do you mean?"

AnnieLee shivered, and Ruthanna pulled a blanket off the back of the couch and gently draped it over her shoulders. "Maybe we should go to the hospital."

"No, I'll be okay." AnnieLee tugged the blanket tighter around her neck. "I've had worse." She took a deep breath, which made her ribs ache. "I got mugged," she said. "Jumped by a bunch of kids."

"Kids?" Ruthanna said, frowning.

"Yeah, big ones. Three of them."

"Did you call the police?"

"No, they ran," AnnieLee said, "and I couldn't have said who they were or what they looked like. It was my own fault. I should've just given them my money instead of mouthing off the way I did."

Now that the story had come to her, she could see the scene playing out just as she described it. How she'd walked down an empty street with her pockets bulging with tips, whistling as if she didn't have a care in the world. How in the darkest stretch of the sidewalk, the first kid had jumped out in front of her and said in a low, cruel voice, *Gimme all your money.* How she'd gone to turn around and run, but suddenly there were two other kids behind her, and they'd caught her by the arms and held her. *Gimme all your money.*

"Oh, you poor thing," Ruthanna said.

AnnieLee said, "I was dumb and stubborn. I didn't think they'd jump me." She squeezed her eyes shut and quickly apologized— to God, to Ruthanna, to the universe—for lying again.

Ruthanna got up and began pacing in circles around the couch. "This has something to do with Mikey Shumer. I know it."

AnnieLee watched her go, marveling at how quickly she could walk in high heels, and who wore high heels at 9 a.m. anyway? Ruthanna's toes were probably as black-and-blue as AnnieLee's arms.

"No offense, Ms. Ryder," AnnieLee said, "but that doesn't make a whole lot of sense. Why would he want to beat me up if he says he wants to help me build my career?"

"I don't claim to know how criminals think," Ruthanna snapped. Stopping by the fireplace, she wrapped her fingers around the end of a poker as if she might use it to strike against the very idea of Mikey Shumer. Then she turned and stared at AnnieLee. "Have you heard from him lately?"

AnnieLee thought a moment before answering. "He left a message this morning." She hadn't returned any of his calls, but that hadn't stopped him from making them, sometimes multiple times a day.

Ruthanna started pacing again, this time with the poker in her hand. "Maybe he thought he could scare you. Show you what could happen to girls who try to go it alone," she said.

As ridiculous as it was, AnnieLee wished she could believe Ruthanna's theory. It would be better to have a new enemy, wouldn't it, instead of an old one? The demons of the past were the hardest to slay.

Maybe that could be a line for a song, she thought, and then pressed her thumbs into her aching temples.

Maya came into the room with water, Advil, Tylenol, aspirin, and an armful of hot and cold packs. "I didn't know what you wanted, so I brought everything I could carry," she said. "I'm so sorry you got hurt." She turned to Ruthanna. "And hon, you better put that thing down before someone *else* gets hurt. Like you, when you trip in your heels and impale yourself."

Ruthanna scoffed. "I've been wearing heels since I was twelve years old. I don't trip." But she put the poker back where it belonged.

AnnieLee couldn't help smiling at their fond bickering. "Thank you, Maya," she said. "You know what else I could really use? Coffee. I hear you make it pretty strong."

"So strong it'll beat you in arm wrestling," Maya said. "You sit tight. I'll be right back."

A moment later she returned with a steaming mug of ink-black coffee, which she set on a marble-topped end table. "How about some breakfast, too?"

AnnieLee's stomach twisted at the mention of food. She was starving. She only hoped it wouldn't hurt too much to chew. "That sounds great," she said.

"Why don't you sit, Maya?" Ruthanna said. "Help her with whatever the hell these things are." She held up a box that said CryoMagic InstaCold. "What happened to using a good old bag of frozen peas?"

Maya took the box as Ruthanna clicked into the kitchen on her five-inch heels. "Ruthanna likes to do everything the old-fashioned way, in case you hadn't noticed," she said. She broke open one of the cold packs, shook it, and then handed it to AnnieLee, who tucked it against her hip.

"Better already," AnnieLee said, and she meant it. She swallowed four Advil, and then she reached out and took the coffee, cradling the hot mug between her palms.

She felt cared for—a feeling so unfamiliar that it brought the sting of tears to her eyes.

She'd barely begun to build up her life. What if it all came crashing down?

CHAPTER

31

I've got to be at work in an hour," Ethan said as Ruthanna ushered him into the kitchen on an unseasonably muggy afternoon. "So please don't tell me you called me here to get another possum out of the pool house."

Ruthanna gave a delicate snort. "I have a job that's better suited to your talents than possum wrangling," she said. "As I recall, that poor creature was no more scared of you than you were of it."

"That's not how I remember it."

"Then we will just have to agree to disagree," Ruthanna said. "In any case, I think you won't mind this assignment." She gave him a sly look. "In fact, I think you might like it a lot. Now sit down and shut your trap."

He did as he was told, of course. It still gave her a tiny thrill to order around someone twice her size.

"I want you to look after that dark-haired little firecracker you found," she said.

Ethan reached into the fruit bowl for an orange. "What for?"

he asked, tossing it up and catching it, again and again. "She's got *you* looking after her."

Ruthanna paused. She knew AnnieLee wouldn't want her telling Ethan what had happened, but there was no way around it. "She got mugged the other night."

Ethan dropped the orange, and it rolled under the table. "When? Where?"

Ruthanna told him all that she knew while Ethan listened with a dark expression on his face.

"I don't want anything else bad happening to her," Ruthanna finished. "And I know you don't, either." She nudged him with her elbow. "You're the protective type, I can see it from a thousand miles away. You love taking off your jacket on a chilly night so you can give it to your girl."

"I don't have a girl," Ethan said.

"Once upon a time you did."

"You know how that ended, Ruthanna."

She resisted the urge to put her hand over his. "And there's been nobody since?" She found it hard to imagine he'd been alone so long. But then again, so had she. She wouldn't have imagined that, either.

Ethan said, "Nobody."

"You can't stay solitary and wounded forever," she said gently.

"Says who?"

Ruthanna opened a cabinet and pulled out two cut crystal glasses. "You know what? You're about as ornery as AnnieLee Keyes is."

"And as you are," Ethan pointed out.

"Yes," Ruthanna said, pouring them each a nice, smoky Scotch. "We're a regular ol' bunch of barnyard mules, I guess. Ice?"

"I have to go to work, remember?"

"It'll make your job easier. You'll feel ever so much more kindly toward those bridesmaids belting out 'Girls Just Want to Have Fun.'"

He caved, as she'd known he would. "Sure, ice."

She looked pointedly at his biceps as she set the drink in front of him. "I bet you've got a mean right hook."

"I could hold my own in a fight, supposing I got into one." He gave the Scotch an appreciative sniff. "What makes you think AnnieLee needs protection? I mean, she had an unlucky walk home, but..."

"I don't know," Ruthanna said. "Maybe I'm crazy. I'm just not sure that mugging was random."

"Well, you are crazy," Ethan said. "But that might not have any bearing on the matter at hand."

"Very funny, cowboy. I could be wrong, and I hope I am. But does it even matter? A girl doesn't have to be in mortal danger to be worth protecting, does she?" She pulled out her phone and clicked on a video Maya had shown her. Someone had taken it during one of AnnieLee's performances at the Cat's Paw and posted it online. "Here," she said, giving Ethan the phone.

She looked over his shoulder as he watched. The camera was shaky and the sound was terrible, but even in a tiny iPhone video, AnnieLee's talent was outsized. Her mix of power and vulnerability commanded the stage; Ruthanna could practically sense the crowd holding its breath so as not to miss a single sweet note.

"Take the wheel and just believe," AnnieLee sang, *"that you can change your life..."*

When it was over, Ethan handed back the phone. "So you really think she's got what it takes," he said.

"I know she does. But *she* has to know she does, or it doesn't mean a thing. Sustaining that kind of belief in yourself—that's the hard part."

"Tell me about it," he said.

"That's why AnnieLee needs us," Ruthanna said. "So tell me, Ethan Blake. Are you in?"

He didn't hesitate. "I'm in," he said.

CHAPTER

32

AnnieLee closed her eyes, breathing in the rich scent of good, fertile soil. It was still early, but she'd been working for two hours already, tucking lettuce and cucumber starts into neat rows and hilling up soil around the potato plants. This was on top of the week she'd already spent clearing out the space for the garden itself.

It was part of the deal she'd worked out with Ruthanna: in exchange for the singer's musical guidance, AnnieLee would plant a big four-square kitchen garden in what had been just another patch of emerald-green lawn. It'd been years since she'd tilled a vegetable bed, but she hadn't forgotten how.

Just like riding a bike, she thought. *Or playing a G chord.*

Of course, Ruthanna had protested vehemently at first. For one thing, she could pay a professional to do it a thousand times over; for another, she "didn't need some scrawny hillbilly digging a giant hole in the yard." But AnnieLee had insisted. She wanted to feel as though she was taking care of her debts, even if she could never truly repay Ruthanna for taking her under her wing, not if she died trying.

Anyway, she liked the work. It distracted her from life—unlike songwriting, which demanded that she face everything head-on, no matter how painful it was. And though it was the writing that'd gotten her through the worst times, every once in a while she needed to take a tiny break from it.

AnnieLee shoved the spade into the dirt and wiped her sweaty face. Any minute now, she hoped, Ruthanna would swan outside in designer sunglasses and an enormous sun hat and regale AnnieLee with tales of her rise to fame.

AnnieLee couldn't get enough of the stories. She'd learned how it took two full years for a kid named Pollyanna Poole to get a label to listen to her songs—and how the first thing they'd told her to do was change the name her beloved mama had given her. Six months later, the newly christened Ruthanna Ryder got a publishing deal with AMG Music, wrote "Big Dreams and Faded Jeans," and watched another singer take it to number one on the charts and keep it there for sixteen solid weeks. "Didn't know whether to jump for joy or cry for jealousy," Ruthanna had mused.

Yesterday, as AnnieLee sowed beet seeds, Ruthanna had told her about how hard it was to be on tour. "The day starts at four thirty a.m. so you can hit the morning radio shows to promote your concert," Ruthanna had said, sipping on Maya's rocket fuel coffee. "And it doesn't end until you've played your heart out onstage and then signed your last autograph outside the venue. You stumble onto the tour bus somewhere on the wrong side of midnight and fall into your bed, and by the time the sun comes up you're in a different town. And then *you do it all over again.* Because the only thing harder than getting to the top, kiddo, is staying there."

It sounded impossibly glamorous to AnnieLee, even if Ruthanna tried to convince her otherwise. She talked about working around the clock and barely having time to eat, about sweating blood trying to make enough money to pay the band, the production staff, the promoters, the organizers, and the concert spaces, "not to mention forking out a regular four figures on your spangly outfits."

"It's not a normal way to live," Ruthanna had said.

Tell me more, was all AnnieLee could think.

She was lying in the sunshine, taking a five-minute break, when Ruthanna threw open the back door and said, "Tomato-gate."

AnnieLee sat up and looked over at the Early Girls she'd planted and staked the other day, wondering if Ruthanna thought she needed to put a fence around them. Because that would be...well, weird.

"Do you know why *salad* is significant to country music?" Ruthanna said, coming outside and folding herself onto a cushioned bench at the garden's edge.

"Um, because salads are good for you, and country music is, too?" AnnieLee guessed, slipping her work gloves back on.

Ruthanna said, "Yeah, I'd laugh if the truth weren't so damn maddening."

Then she told AnnieLee about what a powerful radio consultant had said about women in country music. Male musicians, he'd argued, were the truly important artists—the "lettuce" in the playlist salad. Female singers should just be sprinkled into airplay now and again as garnish.

"'The tomatoes of our salad are the females,'" Ruthanna said. "That was his *exact* quote. And that's why they call it Tomato-gate."

"I hope you called him up and gave him the what for," AnnieLee said, angrily weeding now. It wasn't as if she couldn't believe a man would think that—men had all kinds of dumb and crazy ideas—but to say it out loud seemed like another thing entirely.

"Program directors have been telling their DJs not to play two women back to back for as long as there's been radio," Ruthanna said. "Labels didn't think women could headline on the road or even make hit records. As far as they were concerned, we could sing our pretty little hearts out and just be happy opening for George Jones."

AnnieLee yanked out a dandelion and threw it over her shoulder. "But that's BS," she said. "I mean, look at you. You're a *superstar.*"

"But I had to work ten times as hard to get half the attention."

AnnieLee was letting that fact sink in when she heard the rumble of a car coming up the driveway. She turned to see Ethan Blake pulling up in his battered truck, and her heart gave a tiny little hop. Did *he* know about all this? she wondered. Did it make him mad, too?

"And all the while," Ruthanna went on, "a good-looking guy with a big hat, tight jeans, and a *thimbleful* of talent could get a record deal."

AnnieLee watched Ethan swing his long legs out of the cab. He was wearing broken-in Levi's, a faded chambray shirt, and lace-up work boots, and his hair was still wet from a shower. "Ethan's got more than a thimbleful, though," she said. "I've seen him play."

"I wouldn't give him the time of day if he didn't," Ruthanna said. "He's one of the good ones—as a musician and a man." Then she nudged AnnieLee with a perfectly polished toe. "You two getting along better now that I've asked him to look out for you?"

AnnieLee felt her cheeks get warm. "We get along fine," she said.

She hadn't wanted a bodyguard, or whatever he was calling himself. An escort? *That* was a laugh.

But as much as she hated to admit it, she liked being around Ethan Blake. And she felt better knowing that he was looking out for her. After she played a showcase, he'd drive her home. Then he'd follow her into her hideous pink motel room so he could check in the bathroom and under the bed. "No bogeymen, no alligators," he'd say, because she'd told him that when she was little, she was afraid that an alligator lived under her bed.

She didn't talk about what she was afraid of now, but it certainly wasn't alligators.

When he'd assured them both that the room was empty and AnnieLee was safe, he'd remind her to lock and bolt the door behind him. He'd tip his cap to her and say good night. But then he'd linger a little while in the doorway, as if he wanted to stay.

Goodbyes got awkward when it seemed like neither party wanted to say them.

Ruthanna's expression was smug as she watched AnnieLee work. "I thought you two might take a liking to each other," she said, "being young and cute and all that. But you don't have to tell me anything."

Don't worry. I won't, thought AnnieLee.

Then Ruthanna looked up from beneath her giant hat and called out to Ethan. "Go see if there's an extra shovel in the shed, why don't you? These beans won't plant themselves."

AnnieLee quickly wiped at her face with the hem of her T-shirt. She must look a mess—sweaty and dirt-smudged.

Ruthanna laughed. "You look gorgeous," she said, as if reading AnnieLee's thoughts. "You could put on a potato sack and go roll around in a hog pit and you'd still be the prettiest thing for miles."

AnnieLee flushed as she coaxed a squash start from its container. As she gently placed it in its row, she marveled at the turns her life had recently taken. She'd come to Nashville with nothing but desire and a backpack, and here she was, planting an icon's garden as a handsome guitar player walked over to help her do it. For most of her life, she hadn't felt lucky at all. But maybe, finally, she was.

CHAPTER
33

"The important thing is not to be nervous," Ethan said, patting the stickered side of his guitar case. "We're all friends here."

That was easy for *him* to say, AnnieLee thought as she followed him down the steps to Ruthanna's basement recording studio. He'd been playing with her band for six months, whereas she'd never even met them before. And though she'd spent the last few nights singing and playing in the studio—"No pressure: we're just messing around," Ruthanna had assured her—today was the day she was supposed to teach the other musicians one of her songs, and AnnieLee felt as though she'd been having a low-grade panic attack ever since the sun shone its first light into her motel room window.

Ethan led her along the hallway lined with gold records and then stopped in front of the heavy metal door. "Ready?" he said, grinning at her with those damn dimples of his. "No alligators in here, either. I promise."

"No, I'm not ready," she said, in a sudden fit of honesty, but he opened the door anyway, ushering her into the large, carpeted room full of microphones, instruments, and Ruthanna's studio band.

"This is Elrodd, Donna, Melissa, and Stan," Ethan said, pointing to each one in turn. "Guys, this is AnnieLee."

AnnieLee managed to get out a "Pleased to meet you" as some of the best session players in Nashville greeted her with a mix of personal warmth and professional skepticism. They'd played on more hit records than AnnieLee could count, and not just Ruthanna's. They were virtuoso musicians, and country music history in the flesh.

Elrodd, sitting behind a drum kit, was a wiry sixty-something with a smoker's laugh. Donna's black hair hung so far down it brushed the top of her bass. Melissa was long-limbed and graceful, a ballerina who'd traded her pointe shoes for a fiddle. Round, white-bearded Stan was her opposite: a mall Santa in a Stetson. He gave his Stratocaster a big, amped-up strum and laughed when AnnieLee jumped back in surprise.

Ruthanna's voice came over the speakers. "All right, AnnieLee Keyes," she said. "I've got my producer, Janet, here in the control room with me, and my genius engineer, Warren, on the mixing board. Are we ready to make some music?"

AnnieLee tried her hardest to say yes. But instead she bolted into the hallway and pressed herself against the wall, her eyes shut tight. There she forced herself to take ten deep breaths. *This is what you want,* she told herself. *You can do this. It's going to be fine.*

After another minute, her heartbeat slowed, and she went back in and picked up her guitar. "I'm sorry, everyone," she said. "My feet have a mind of their own sometimes."

"Don't worry about it," Donna said in a voice that was surprisingly kind. "We've all been nervy before."

Stan nodded in agreement; maybe he felt a little bad for scaring her. "What do you got for us today, Ms. Keyes?"

AnnieLee knew that session players usually worked off a demo in order to record a track. But Ruthanna had wanted her to play her song for them live and unaccompanied. That way, Ruthanna said, everyone could build up the song together.

"It'll still be your song," Ruthanna had said. "But it can change and grow once other people start playing on it."

AnnieLee placed her fingers on her guitar's fretboard. "Okay, I start with this little lick right here," she said, demonstrating. "And then the song's got this really basic one, four, five structure." She played the chords as she spoke, feeling more self-conscious than she'd ever felt in her whole entire life.

"You don't need to explain it, hon," Donna said. "Just play, and we can take it from there."

"Okay. Sure, ma'am. You bet," AnnieLee said earnestly, and Ethan shot her a look, like *When did you get so polite?*

She gave him a sheepish smile and began to sing.

Driven to insanity, driven to the edge
Driven to the point of almost no return

Her voice was shaky at first, but she grew more confident as she played, and by the time she got to the second verse she'd hit her groove.

When the song was over, the other musicians started talking immediately. They had ideas about the bass line and the way the fiddle should curl around the opening notes. They offered tweaks to the bridge, and Elrodd suggested slowing the tempo after the second chorus. Ethan wondered if there should be a key change as the tension rose. AnnieLee listened to their ideas in awe and gratitude. They weren't trying to take her song away from her—they were focused on making it as good as it could possibly be.

After they'd agreed on the basics, everyone practiced their own parts for a while. Then they ran through it, with Ethan on lead guitar, Stan on pedal steel, and AnnieLee playing rhythm. She leaned into the pop filter on her mic and closed her eyes as she sang.

"That's sounding just killer," Ruthanna said from the control room. "Raw and driving. I think it needs more bass, though. Elrodd, I'm loving that kick drum."

On the next run-through, Melissa added a soaring fiddle line. Later, Ethan worked out a fantastic guitar solo. AnnieLee couldn't believe how rich the song sounded now. After three hours and multiple versions, AnnieLee's voice had grown hoarse and Ruthanna declared it was time to stop.

AnnieLee turned to Ethan. "For good?" she whispered. "Are we done?"

Ethan stared at her. "Stop *for good*?" he repeated. "Try 'for lunch.'"

When he saw her confused expression, he laughed. "Blazing-hot singles don't come quick, girl," he said. Then he slung his arm over her shoulders, a gesture so casual and intimate that it made her knees weak. "But you're doing great," he said. "I promise."

AnnieLee wanted desperately to believe him.

Ruthanna came in, eyes sparkling. "We'll get your vocals in an isolation booth later, but don't even *think* we're going to use Auto-Tune," she said. "It's better to let the audience hear you reaching for that note. Passion's more important than perfection." She rubbed her hands together. "Oh, this is exciting!"

"What's for lunch?" Elrodd asked, taking a swig from a water bottle that just might've had whiskey in it.

AnnieLee flashed him a nearly ecstatic grin. "We're having a *big* ol' tomato salad," she said.

The Ford's engine belched as Ethan downshifted, coming to a stop across the street from Nashville's biggest radio station. WATC, "All That Country on 99.5," was housed in a big brick building on Music Row, a stone's throw away from the bronze Owen Bradley statue and its steady parade of picture-taking tourists.

AnnieLee gripped the lever of the manual window, nervously rolling it down. "We're early," she said.

"Well, you're the one who made me pick you up at eight a.m.," Ethan reminded her. "Did you think it was going to take us an hour to get here?"

"Not exactly," she admitted. But as her mother always said, *Don't ever be late. It's like proclaiming that your time is more important than someone else's.*

Anyway, sitting in Ethan's Ford was better than pacing the perimeter of her Pepto-Bismol room, which she'd been doing since 5 a.m. And that was because last week, Ruthanna had made a call and worked her magic, and now AnnieLee was moments away from walking into Nashville's number one country station and pitching the single she'd recorded in Ruthanna's studio to the program director.

She pulled down the visor mirror and looked at herself for the fiftieth time that morning. She was wearing a low-cut black thrift store blouse, cropped jeans, and her new-old Fryes. A single pearl on a delicate gold chain floated in the hollow of her collarbone. "I bought this after my first album came out," Ruthanna had said when she gave it to AnnieLee. "I like to think it's good luck."

"Does my hair look okay?" AnnieLee asked, turning to Ethan.

"Terrible," he said. He reached out and playfully flicked a long, dark wave over her shoulder. "But now it's perfect."

She grew suddenly serious. "What if they don't like my song? What if they don't want to play it?"

"They're going to love it. They're going to love you." He tapped out a swinging little beat on the steering wheel. "There's no way I could do what you're trying to do, AnnieLee. But I've got faith in you."

This didn't make any sense to her, because she'd seen him sing and play at the Cat's Paw, and it seemed as though he could do anything. "What do you mean?"

"I couldn't say to myself, 'I'm going to be a star, and I'll do whatever it takes to make it happen.'"

Is that what he thought she said to herself every morning? Not hardly—she was still worried about *survival*. But Ethan was right that she wanted more—much more. And if she had to sell herself to a radio bigwig to help her build her career and her reputation, she'd do it just as well as she could.

"Ruthanna says you're one of the best musicians she knows," AnnieLee said. "Although she made me promise not to tell you that."

"Well, I'll keep the secret," Ethan said, smiling. But then

his smile faded. "Maybe I'm jaded, but it seems like too many people around here just want to be famous. They don't even care if they're talented or not—they just want the attention, and as much of it as they can possibly get."

"But what does that have to do with you?" AnnieLee asked. "You're *great*. How come you don't want everyone else to understand that?"

Ethan's eyes smoldered at her. "You really want to know?"

"I do," she said. She wanted to know all kinds of things about him—she couldn't help it.

"When I got out of the army, I was in a rough spot," Ethan said. "I'd...well, I'd had some problems, I'll leave it at that. I didn't know what I was going to do with myself. But I did one thing every single day. I'd wake up, grab my guitar, and put on a country record. Johnny Cash, Merle Haggard, Chet Atkins, Lester Flatt. Merle Travis, for the Travis picking style. The Carter Family, for Maybelle's Carter scratch. I taught myself to play that way—by listening." He stared out the windshield, quiet for a moment. Then he turned back to AnnieLee. "I studied the greats more than a preacher studies the Bible," he said. "I played the gospel of country music."

"And you got really good," AnnieLee said. "So—again—why don't you want to try to really make it?"

"'Making it' has different meanings for different people, AnnieLee," Ethan said. "Honestly, I like being a studio musician. I want to write songs, and every once in a while, I want to perform them. I get to do that now, so isn't that 'making it'? I don't know, but I'm happy with the way things are."

"But you don't always seem that happy," AnnieLee blurted. Then she flushed. What had made her say such a thing? They'd known each other for only a matter of weeks. But she saw a kind of sorrow in him—she was sure of it: some guarded, secret hurt lurking beneath his good humor and good looks.

And why shouldn't she recognize it? She was hiding something, too.

Ethan cleared his throat and placed his palm on the gearshift. "I think it's time you went inside, AnnieLee," he said. "You want me to come with?"

"Shoot," she whispered. For a moment she'd managed to forget where they were and what she was supposed to be doing. But she came back to herself, and she straightened her shoulders.

Fearlessness. Shamelessness, if necessary.

"No, thanks," she said. "You stay here." She slid out of the cab and slammed the door. Then she poked her head through the open window. "But just so you know, when I get famous, you can be part of my entourage," she said. "As long as you agree to walk a few steps behind me at all times."

He rolled his eyes. "You're infuriating."

"Thank you. Now wish me luck."

"You don't need it," Ethan said. "But good luck, anyway."

I nside WATC, the air-conditioning had been turned to an antarctic setting and there was no one at the front desk. AnnieLee twiddled her thumbs in the frigid reception area for only a few seconds before taking a deep breath, pushing through a pair of glass doors, and waltzing down the hallway as if it were her own. She was determined to make her case. She was also ready to get this meeting over with. As Ethan had reminded her, it was one thing to play a song, and an entirely different thing to try to market it. Though AnnieLee was proud of her single and wanted to share it with the world, she really just wanted to run back to her crappy motel room—or the café downtown, or anywhere she could be alone—and write more songs.

A moment later, she'd walked straight into the actual broadcast room. It was dimly lit, with concert posters on all the walls and a huge audio console. A man in headphones was leaning toward a microphone, speaking into it in a rich, drawling bass.

"…and that's how you do a blue yodel, y'all, practically a century after Jimmie Rodgers first recorded his versions. There's been many an imitator, but no one can compare to the Singing Brakeman. And that concludes today's lesson in country music history. Now we return to our regularly scheduled programming, with a hot new song from Maren Morris."

AnnieLee watched as the man poked a series of mysterious buttons and then turned to her with a furious look, one that softened so quickly she almost didn't catch it. "Did you *not* see the on-air light?" he asked.

She shrank back, mortified. "No."

"Well, it's a good thing my mama told me to always be kind to strangers," he said. He was middle-aged and dressed head to toe in denim, with a silver belt buckle the size of a tea saucer.

"I'm here to see Aaron Price," AnnieLee said. "You're not—"

"No, I'm not," he interrupted, "and you must live under a rock somewhere, or else you'd damn well know who I am. I'm the talent; Aaron's the suit. His office is two doors up on your left."

Well, I was *living under a tree,* AnnieLee thought. But she could hardly say that, or admit that she didn't even own a radio she could listen to. So she thanked him, apologized, and skedaddled.

When she got to the right door—she knocked this time—a deep voice said, "Yep," which she took to mean, "Come in."

Aaron Price was a big man, with a full head of silver hair and a goatee. He rose to his feet as AnnieLee entered, coming over to hold out a red, meaty hand for her to shake. AnnieLee felt her cheeks get hot, the way they often did when she was nervous.

"Hello, sir," she said. "Thanks for letting me come in today."

"So you're the sweet-voiced young thing everybody's been talking about," he said. His teeth looked tobacco-stained, and he was still holding on to her hand.

AnnieLee smoothly removed her fingers from his grip. "Maybe

I am," she said lightly. "Though I'm not a thing so much as a person."

He rumbled out a laugh. "Just a figure of speech, doll."

She opened her mouth to tell him that she wasn't a doll, either, but he was already talking, telling her about how many people tuned in to WATC every day, and how the station had been key in launching the careers of countless singers over the years.

"Of course," he said, "most of these guys and gals had full promotion campaigns and major labels backing them up. That certainly helps a song get good airtime." He sat down on a large black leather couch and patted the cushion beside him. "You're just trying to put your tune out independently, aren't you? That's…well, maybe I'd call it *quaint.*" He gave a deep-throated chuckle. "Anyway, have a seat."

AnnieLee perched delicately on the edge of the couch. She didn't really know what a promotion campaign would look like, though she suspected that Mikey Shumer did. She still hadn't called him back because Ruthanna had told her to stay away from him—but was AnnieLee dumb to have come here alone? Would Mikey Shumer have swaggered into WATC and made this pitch for her? Surely he wouldn't flush with fear sweat the way she did.

"But let me get to the point," Aaron Price said. "The thing is, you can be God's gift to the radio waves and it's still rare that you get something for nothing."

"Pardon?" AnnieLee said.

"When I was coming up in the business," said Aaron Price, "label promoters came rolling in with piles of cash, AnnieLee. And they'd make sure you knew that there were girls and white powder to be had, too—or maybe a nice trip somewhere, if your tastes were more wholesome. All you had to do was spin their record *when* and *how often* they wanted you to." He laughed again. "Those were some crazy times."

"It isn't like that now, though," AnnieLee said. She didn't phrase it as a question, but it was one.

"No, no, that's all illegal now. And heck, you don't have a label yet anyway. But there are always ways to buy spins." He held up a hand. "Don't get me wrong—if you walk in here with a briefcase full of bills, I'll be the first man to show you the door. But artists still need help getting their songs on the air. And the people who help them do it don't mind…expressions of gratitude, let's call it."

"Like what kind of expressions?" AnnieLee asked, feeling a slight flare of alarm.

Aaron Price slid closer to her on the couch. "Maybe we should go to dinner tonight and talk about it," he said. "You're a smart girl—I can tell. You know it pays to have powerful friends, don't you?"

AnnieLee lifted her chin and looked him straight in the eye. Maybe she shouldn't have been shocked, considering he'd just been talking about bribery. But she was definitely offended. He was hitting on her in the slyest, lowest sort of way; he was making it out to be a business transaction.

"What do you say? I'll have my assistant book us a table at Etch."

She stood up and walked to the other side of his office, just in case he'd been thinking about putting a hand on her knee. "I think you should just listen to my song," she said. "And then *you'll* be the one expressing gratitude, because it'll be the best thing your dang station has played in months." She gazed at him defiantly, and he stared back at her in surprise.

God, I hope he likes my song, she thought, *or I'm going to look like an even bigger fool than he does right now.*

Then Aaron Price blinked. "Huh," he said, almost to himself. "Huh." It seemed as if he was about to say more, but instead he went over to his computer and clicked on the WAV file Maya had sent him earlier.

The song's opening chords blasted into the room, followed by AnnieLee's fierce, plaintive voice.

Driven to insanity, driven to the edge
Driven to the point of almost no return…

AnnieLee watched as Aaron Price started drumming out the rhythm on his desk. She paced in the corner, bopping her head to the beat. She was mad, and the song seemed like a perfect accompaniment to her feelings. She remembered pointing the gun in the trucker's face, and then shooting a hole in his window and stealing his semi. It wasn't a bad memory at all, now that she'd gotten away with it.

Maybe she should've told Aaron Price that story, so he'd know who he was dealing with. She made her fingers into the shape of a gun. *Pow,* she thought, and imagined shooting the fern on his desk to smithereens.

Take the wheel and just believe
That you can change your life

"Damn," Aaron Price said when the song ended.

"Well?" said AnnieLee, eyes blazing. "Are you going to play it or what?"

Aaron Price smiled at her in a totally new way. He didn't look sleazy—he looked thrilled. "Hell yes, I'm going to play it," he said. "Just about every hour for the next week."

AnnieLee gave a little squeal of excitement. It sure wouldn't be appropriate to throw her arms around his neck in thanks, but she almost wanted to. She wasn't at all mad anymore.

Aaron Price opened the door to usher her out. "All right, then, I'm guessing this won't be the last time I hear from you, AnnieLee Keyes."

"It sure won't be," she said, and then she floated down the hall, grinning from ear to ear. When she got outside, she burst into a sprint. And she ran whooping and hollering all the way to the shady bench where Ethan Blake sat waiting for her.

CHAPTER

36

Walking into the motel lobby to pay her rent for the week, AnnieLee had to skirt an enormous cellophane-wrapped gift basket half blocking the door. At the front desk, Rhonda, the no-nonsense motel manager, was nearly invisible behind a Technicolor bouquet of gladiolas.

"Whoa, Greg must've done something really bad this time," AnnieLee said. AnnieLee had never met Rhonda's boyfriend, but to hear the stories, Greg seemed less like a love interest and more like an eternal thorn in Rhonda's side.

Rhonda gave a quick snort of a laugh. "Fool drove the riding mower into the duck pond last night," she said. *"Again."* She flicked a bit of the bouquet's decorative greenery out of her way. "But he only sends me flowers when I catch him hitting on other girls. For that tractor stupidity, he just apologized real nice and gave me a foot rub."

"So you've got a secret admirer, then," AnnieLee said as she poured herself a big cup of the motel's coffee. It was terrible, but it was free. "Spill the beans!"

"All this is for you, girl," Rhonda said.

"What? Really?" Bending down to peer through the cellophane, AnnieLee saw boxes of Belgian chocolates, champagne, pears wrapped in gold foil, dried Spanish cherries, tea biscuits, and glass jars of candied nuts, all nestled in creamy tissue paper and tied up with a silk bow. "This looks seriously expensive," she said.

"No shit. Who's it from?" Rhonda asked. "Who's *your* admirer?"

Ruthanna was the only person AnnieLee knew who could spring for a present like this. "Just a friend, I'm sure," AnnieLee said. She plucked the card from the bow at the top of the basket, expecting to see the singer's name and a message of congratulations for getting "Driven" on the WATC playlist.

So she felt a jolt of unpleasant surprise upon seeing that the gift basket was from Mikey Shumer. So were the gladiolas, and a smaller package she hadn't even seen right away. It contained a pair of classic Ray-Ban Aviators.

AnnieLee put on the sunglasses to disguise her unease. Mikey Shumer was sending her a very clear message: he knew where she was and how to get to her, and he wasn't going to give up.

"Those look hot on you," Rhonda said.

"Could I use the phone?" AnnieLee asked. If she didn't call him right now, she'd lose her nerve.

Rhonda looked pointedly at the basket. AnnieLee sliced open the cellophane with her room key, reached in to grab a sleeve of extremely delicious-looking ginger cookies, and held them out to Rhonda.

"*Now* can I use it?" AnnieLee asked.

Rhonda smiled and lifted the phone onto the counter where AnnieLee could reach it. Then she opened the cookies. "Dial nine to get out," she said, breaking off a piece of a cookie and popping it in her mouth. "Do you know how much that champagne is worth?"

"Of course not," AnnieLee said. She'd never tasted real champagne in her life, let alone tried to buy herself any.

"Five *hundred* dollars. I googled it."

"So can I give you the bottle instead of the rent money?"

Rhonda snorted again. "Not when Two-Buck Chuck'll get me just as drunk on a Saturday night."

"Well, it was worth a try," AnnieLee said, sliding an envelope of cash toward the motel manager. She wasn't stone broke, not anymore, but handing over a solid three figures still wasn't what she'd call enjoyable.

Someday, though, she was going to have enough money to blow her nose on twenties if she wanted to.

I'm on my way, I start today
I'm gonna be all right

AnnieLee held the handset to her cheek and tapped her fingers on the counter as the phone rang. *Sound tough*, she reminded herself.

"Shumer," said a brusque voice.

"Mr. Shumer, this is AnnieLee Keyes."

Immediately the voice warmed. "Please, call me Mikey, AnnieLee. It's great to hear from you."

"What's with the loot in the lobby?"

"A small token of my esteem," he said smoothly. "And, apparently, the only way to get you to return my calls. I want to meet with you, AnnieLee. I've seen you play—you're incredible—and I happen to think I could be extremely beneficial to your career."

AnnieLee was surprised by how earnest he sounded. "You came to one of my shows? Why didn't you introduce yourself?"

After a beat, he said, "I saw a video, actually, taken by one of my people."

"Oh. I don't know if that really counts," she said.

Mikey Shumer laughed. "Well, it's obvious that a cell phone video doesn't do you justice. That's why I want to meet you in the flesh, just as soon as you're willing. I'd like to talk about what I can do for you."

AnnieLee gazed out the streaked lobby window. The sun was already beating down on the asphalt, and the air shimmered in the heat. She could hear the shouts of kids splashing in the pool—kids who were visiting the country music capital with their parents, and for whom sleeping in this cruddy motel was a wonderful adventure.

Aside from her night at Ruthanna's, this cruddy motel was the nicest place AnnieLee had stayed in years.

She curled a strand of hair around her finger as she considered Mikey's request. Ruthanna wanted her to take things slow—AnnieLee knew that. Ruthanna said she should build a strong local fan base and a big catalog of songs. "Go out too soon, and you risk being a one-hit wonder," she'd said. "You've got to be a little bit patient."

But this morning, with a big cup of cheap, industrial coffee running through her veins and an expensive pair of sunglasses turning the world a new, warmer color, AnnieLee didn't feel patient.

"Where are you?" she asked Mikey Shumer. "I'll call a cab."

"Please, don't do that," he said. "I'll send a car."

CHAPTER
37

⁀

"Y ou're even prettier than I thought you'd be," Mikey
Shumer said, looking at AnnieLee appraisingly. "The
photo editors are going to love you."

Then AnnieLee stood very still as Mikey Shumer walked
around her, scrutinizing her as carefully as a truck he was thinking about buying. This wasn't how she'd imagined their meeting
would begin. But then again, everything about this morning—
from Mikey's extravagant gifts, to the Jaguar he'd sent to pick
her up, to the sleek steel-and-glass conference room in which
she now found herself—had surprised her.

"Is that actually important?" she asked. She didn't know what
photo editors had to do with country music.

"When they're putting together glossy spreads to accompany
all those glowing AnnieLee Keyes profiles, you'll make their job
incredibly easy," Mikey said, brushing what might have been a
speck of lint from her shoulder. "Unlike a certain diva I know,
who looks like an alley cat until she's been in hair and makeup
for three hours, and then she *still* needs a week's worth of Photo-
shop." He came back around to the front and gave a satisfied

nod. "Hair: great. Face: great. Height: well, nothing to be done about that but teach you how to walk in heels. Have a seat."

AnnieLee sank into one of the sleek ergonomic chairs surrounding the gleaming conference table, gazing at Mikey Shumer as frankly and appraisingly as he had at her. He was clean-shaven, with blond hair swept back from his wide forehead. He had broad shoulders and well-tanned skin, and his eyes were a bright, sharp green. He was so slick she could smell it—the kind of guy who could sell mud to a hog. But Mikey Shumer hardly looked like the monster Ruthanna had said he was.

"If I'd known I was coming in for an inspection, I'd've worn my clean pair of jeans," AnnieLee said.

"I hope you're not offended. Everyone in the business *thinks* these things," Mikey Shumer said. "I believe in saying them out loud. It makes everything simpler." He held out his hands, palms up, as if he were offering her something invisible. "If you think labels don't care at least as much about what you look like as about what you sound like, well, then you've got a lot to learn. So it's extremely lucky for you that you have other…*assets* besides your lovely voice."

Two people—a stern-looking woman and a man with a baby's face and a pro wrestler's build—came into the room. Once Mikey sat down, they silently took their places at the table on either side of him. Mikey introduced Meredith and Hitch, calling them his "A team," and then he crooked his finger, and a pretty assistant appeared to ask if anyone wanted a cappuccino.

AnnieLee asked for a double. She also wanted one of the fancy doughnuts on the platter in the center of the table, but she didn't want to get powdered sugar all down the front of her shirt.

"Don't be shy," Mikey said, pushing the platter toward her.

"I didn't come here for breakfast, Mr. Shumer," she said.

"Well, you've got a giant basket of food back at your motel anyway, don't you?" He grinned. "So let's talk business. Your single's on the radio. People are calling in, saying they love it— they're trying to figure out who this AnnieLee Keyes chanteuse is. Have you checked your streaming numbers?"

AnnieLee looked at him blankly. Ruthanna had told her that she needed to focus on the music, and so that's what she'd done.

"Well, Meredith here did. She can go over all the figures if you want her to. They're pretty solid for a non-album single with absolutely zero promotion, paid or otherwise, but you've got a long way to go." He leaned back as the assistant placed their coffees in front of them. "You're not even on social media, are you, AnnieLee?"

"I've been writing songs, not tweets, Mr. Shumer. I've finished seven real good ones, just in the last couple weeks."

"Seven, huh? Good for you," he said. "That'll keep you onstage for about thirty minutes. What'll you do for the rest of the time? Magic tricks? You gonna pull a bunny out of a Stetson?"

AnnieLee laughed, but she knew that Mikey was challenging her. Maybe he was even doubting her abilities. "I'll write more songs," she said. "No problem. I've been rhyming since I could talk, and I've been singing longer than that. I can write a verse faster than you can eat one of those doughnuts."

Mikey Shumer reached slowly and deliberately for a doughnut. "On your mark," he said. "Get set. *Go.*"

AnnieLee grabbed her guitar out of its case and strummed a quick C, then F, G, back to C. Basic. Familiar. Then she began to sing, looking Mikey Shumer right in the eyes as she did.

You walk into the room like a big man, do ya
Never seen you before, but I can see right through ya

You tell me you can help me go high and go far
While you're sittin' in a chair that's worth more than my car

Then she took her hands from the strings and grinned. "I'm just kidding," she said. "I don't even own a car."

Mikey Shumer stared at her. He'd taken two bites of the doughnut.

AnnieLee felt her palms begin to tingle. Had she gone too far? Had she offended him? She couldn't tell what he was thinking at all. "These chairs are really comfortable, though," she added, just to break the silence.

Mikey Shumer began to laugh. After a moment, the others began to laugh, too.

"You've got fire, girl," Mikey said. "I like it."

"Damn straight I do," AnnieLee said. "Because I ain't got nothing else."

"I've got fire, too," Mikey said. His voice grew softer, confidential. "That's why we'll make such a good team. Your friend, Ruthanna, she's been out of the game for too long. She doesn't need the hustle. She's gone soft. Me, though, I *live* the hustle."

"She doesn't seem to like you much," AnnieLee said.

"That's true. I can't understand why, though. I'm an extremely charming person, once you get to know me." Mikey Shumer set the half-eaten doughnut on the table, and the assistant appeared out of nowhere to take it away. "Tell me, AnnieLee, how much longer does Ruthanna think you ought to keep grinding it out in honky-tonks?"

AnnieLee plucked lightly at her guitar strings. "She wants me to get experience. You know: easy come, easy go, put your time in—that kind of thing?" Even as she said it, she wondered if Ruthanna was right. Why do something slow if you have the chance to do it fast?

"Maybe she doesn't have your best interests at heart," Mikey said lightly.

AnnieLee frowned. "If she doesn't, why's she doing everything she's doing? You think *I* know how to get a song on Spotify?"

"I'm sure you're familiar with the phrase 'Keep your friends close and your enemies closer.'" Mikey smiled at her with teeth that must've cost ten grand in bleach and crowns.

"I don't believe it," AnnieLee said. "There's no way."

Mikey shrugged. "I'm only suggesting...different interpretations? Anyway, we can discuss Nashville's favorite daughter later. Let's hear you play a song—one that's a little less spontaneous, how about?"

"Okay," AnnieLee said, relieved. This, finally, was ground she felt comfortable on. Her fingers curved around the fretboard again. After thinking for a moment, she strummed the opening to "Dark Night, Bright Future." She closed her eyes as she sang so she didn't have to look at Mikey's shrewd, avid face.

Like the phoenix from the ashes, I shall rise again

The song was yearning and insistent, and her voice flew around the glass-walled conference room, as bright and spectacular as a mythical bird.

Got so much ahead of me
The past is gonna set me free
Learn from it and just believe
That I can touch the sky

When the song was over, Mikey and his A team—and the assistant, too, who'd reappeared to listen—clapped so hard that the noise hurt AnnieLee's ears. Mikey Shumer was giving her a one-man standing ovation.

Her cheeks felt hot, and she could feel a trickle of sweat running down between her breasts. "Thank you," she said. "I can play another one if you want."

"You don't even need to. AnnieLee Keyes, you're the real deal," Mikey Shumer said. "I'll bet anything on it. If you sign with me, I can get you a four-continent tour. Sixty dates. Paris, Barcelona, Tokyo—all the places you've ever dreamed of going. It won't be tomorrow, but it'll happen. I can *make* it happen for you."

AnnieLee looked down at her guitar. What would it mean if she agreed to work with Mikey Shumer? He was smart and confident, he knew a thousand things she didn't, and he wasn't afraid to think big.

He's dirty, AnnieLee, Ruthanna had said. But it wasn't as if she'd given her any proof.

For a moment, AnnieLee allowed herself to imagine an easier path to the top. "I guess—" she began.

"We have a deal, don't we?" Mikey Shumer interrupted. But it wasn't a question. He was so convinced of his charms and his power.

It was that presumption that gave AnnieLee pause. "I guess," she said again, "I guess I'd better consider your offer a little bit longer."

Mikey Shumer was a man used to getting his way, and AnnieLee could see how he tried not to let his disappointment show. But his expression had darkened, and she watched as he reached into his pocket, his eyes never leaving her face. He began to pull something out of it, and for a crazy, stupid instant, AnnieLee thought he was pulling out a weapon.

But it was a brand-new iPhone in a glittering black case.

"This is for you," Mikey Shumer said.

AnnieLee's eyes widened. "Oh, no, I've got a prepaid," she said. "It's nothing special, but it does what I need it to do. I mean, it recorded about fifty messages from you, didn't it?" She laughed nervously.

Mikey waved this information away. "I took the liberty of putting my number in the contacts. You call me, anytime, day or night." He wasn't smiling anymore. "You made it out of the gate, AnnieLee, but if you're not careful, you're going to stumble at the first curve. Don't screw yourself." He put the phone down on the table. "And don't screw me, either."

Ruthanna plucked an antique milk glass vase from its kitchen shelf, filling it with water and then with the flowers she'd just cut from her garden: bursting dahlias, heavy-headed roses, feathery pink beeblossoms. On four-inch heels, she carried her bouquet to the narrow farm table that had been in her family for five generations, and which she'd already set with linen napkins, Spode china, and vintage silver she'd bought on one of her tours through France.

She looked around the lovely room with satisfaction. The salad was ready, Alice Waters's cheese and pasta gratin was browning in the oven, and a bottle of rosé sat chilling in a silver ice bucket. Everything was perfect, and perfectly calm.

But it didn't matter. Ruthanna Ryder felt like screaming.

When she thought about getting through the next hour, she wanted to pour herself three fingers' worth of Scotch, neat. She wanted to crawl into bed. She wanted to call Jack.

Too late, she wished she'd asked him to join her tonight. He knew the story she had to tell, and, if need be, he could take over its telling. She reached for her phone, saying, "Siri, call—" But then she stopped. Jack was a busy man. Though he'd drop every-thing and come running, she didn't want to ask it of him.

AnnieLee walked in at three minutes after six. She wore her hair in a messy bun, and there was a touch of pink gloss on her full lips. "I'm so sorry I'm late," she said, her voice harried as she kicked off her boots at the door.

Ethan, no doubt, had shared with her Ruthanna's feelings about punctuality. "Two more minutes and I might've locked the door," Ruthanna said.

"I was writing, and I lost track of time. I feel terrible." Then AnnieLee straightened up and noticed the beautiful table, and her expression turned to delight. "Wow, it's gorgeous—a romantic dinner for just us two?"

"I like a civilized meal," Ruthanna said a little stiffly; it was the truth but hardly the whole of it. She'd made everything perfect because the alternative was to lie on the floor, sobbing. She poured a glass of wine and held it out to AnnieLee. Then she poured herself twice as much and took a delicate sip. It was ice-cold, its color a hazy sunset pink, and it tasted of strawberries.

"Cheers," said AnnieLee.

"It's a Willamette Valley rosé."

"I'm not going to pretend I know what that means," AnnieLee admitted.

"You will, I hope, learn about the finer things in life someday," Ruthanna said dryly.

AnnieLee giggled. "Just don't ruin me for vending machine Cokes and cold beans from a can, okay?"

"That's the most depressing dinner I've ever heard of."

"No, the most depressing dinner is the one without any food at all," AnnieLee said, "and believe me, I've had my share of those."

"Well, you won't starve tonight," Ruthanna said. She quickly dressed the salad with a simple homemade shallot vinaigrette, and then she turned around with the wooden spoon in her hand, which she pointed at AnnieLee. "Do you want to tell me where you were yesterday?"

AnnieLee looked startled. "I don't mind, but why?"

"Because I want to know if I've been wasting my time with you."

AnnieLee flinched. "I met with Mikey Shumer."

"I know," said Ruthanna.

"Then why'd you ask?" AnnieLee cried.

"I wanted to see what you'd say."

"Well, I wouldn't lie about that," AnnieLee said.

Ruthanna bent down and pulled the gratin from the oven. It smelled cheesy and buttery and rich as she set the pan on the table in front of AnnieLee. "I thought I told you to stay a million miles away from him." She handed her a serving spoon. "Go on. Help yourself."

AnnieLee meekly piled her plate high with food while Ruthanna sipped her wine.

"Well?" Ruthanna eventually asked.

"I guess I didn't see what harm a single conversation could do," AnnieLee said.

"It could do plenty with the likes of him," Ruthanna said. "Mikey stuck a gun into a man's mouth last year—he told him that if he didn't play his artist's song, he'd be back to pull the trigger."

AnnieLee's eyes went wide.

"There are plenty of stories like that about Mikey Shumer," Ruthanna said. "But I have my own story, and that's the one I think you need to hear."

She took a deep breath. The sun was shining into the kitchen, slanting and golden, in what Ruthanna always thought of as the angel light of evening. This was when memories of her daughter came to her most frequently. Often she tried to push them away, but other times she let them flow over her like water. She never could tell which hurt more.

"Do you remember when I told you that you made me think of someone?" Ruthanna asked.

AnnieLee nodded, her mouth full of food.

"Well, that person was my daughter."

AnnieLee went pale. "Was?" she whispered.

"She would've been twenty-seven this year. Her name was Sophia." Ruthanna drew in another breath. It was hard to know where to start the story. Hard, too, to acknowledge that not all the blame belonged where she wanted to put it, which was at the feet of Mikey Shumer.

"Sophia was a banjo player," Ruthanna finally said. "She was very good, and she could've been great. But hard work didn't come to her naturally, not the way it came to me. Maybe because she was born having everything."

Ruthanna took another sip of wine; she hadn't touched the dinner she'd worked so hard to make. Whatever. It was glorified mac 'n' cheese, and she wasn't supposed to eat it anyway.

"She had everything, that is," she went on, "except for a normal childhood. Imagine having flashbulbs snapping in your little face when you went out with your daddy for ice cream. Or unscrupulous reporters asking you for dirt on your famous mom. The world cared *so much* about me—Sophia couldn't escape that. And she also couldn't escape realizing that the world didn't care as much about her. What a cruel lesson that was, and I didn't even know that she was learning it."

"I'm sorry," AnnieLee said, sounding so young and small herself.

Ruthanna told AnnieLee about how Sophia had rebelled in high school, partying too hard and sneaking out at night while Ruthanna was on tour. After a stint in rehab, she graduated a year late, but with a good GPA. She was supposed to go to college. She wanted to be a music teacher.

"But then she met Trace Jones," Ruthanna said, and the name tasted bitter in her mouth.

"I know him!" AnnieLee exclaimed. "I mean, I know who he is."

"Of course you do. He's been on the charts for a decade. He's nothing but a hat act, if you ask me, but people buy his records. Anyway, Sophia and Trace were in love. She wanted to go on tour with him—a tour Mikey Shumer had booked and was managing. I didn't want her to go, because she still seemed too fragile to me. She argued that it was time she went out on her own. I pointed out that she wasn't going out on her own, that she was following someone else. She wasn't even going to be playing, because Trace already had a banjo player in his band. We fought. And Sophia left."

Ruthanna unfolded her napkin and then folded it back up again. AnnieLee had stopped eating her dinner.

"Somewhere on the tour, she started drinking again. And a little while after that, Mikey decided that it wasn't good for Trace Jones's image to have a girlfriend. Mikey told him that if he was serious about his career, he needed to break up with Sophia."

Ruthanna poured more wine into her glass.

"So he did. I'm not saying it wasn't hard for him. All I know is that he did it. And that night, in her hotel room, before she was supposed to fly home to me, Sophia drank all the bottles in the minibar and took some pills she'd gotten from a roadie. I don't know if she was trying to die. Maybe she was just trying to drown her sorrows. Trying to get to the place where she didn't feel the pain. But she went to sleep, and she never woke up."

Ruthanna had been looking out the window as she spoke, and she could feel the tears trickling down her face. When she looked at AnnieLee, she saw that the girl was crying, too.

"I'm so sorry," AnnieLee said. "I can't even imagine."

Ruthanna put her hand on top of AnnieLee's. "I know your life hasn't been easy, and I bet you've felt loss, too." She pulled her hand away and her voice grew firm. "That's why I don't want you talking to Mikey. There's a darkness in him, and a coldness. A man who would do anything to win is not the kind of man you want on your side."

She got up and walked over to the sink to get herself some water. "'I have been in sorrow's kitchen and licked out all the pots,'" she said softly.

"Is that a line from a song?" AnnieLee asked.

"It's from a book—*Dust Tracks on a Road*, by Zora Neale Hurston."

"Sorrow's kitchen," AnnieLee repeated. "I might've visited there once or twice."

Then they were silent, and the sun passed down into the garden, illuminating every flower in one last bit of angelic light.

Ruthanna gripped the edge of the sink to steady herself. "Good night, Sophia," she whispered.

CHAPTER
39

AnnieLee half woke to the sound of an urgent whisper. A figure, dressed all in white, stood by the side of her bed. *Sophia,* she thought, still in sleep's clutches. The ghost reached toward her, even as she rolled away from it, and then it yanked the blankets back.

"Ahem," the ghost said, and AnnieLee woke up enough to realize that it was Ruthanna standing there, her red-gold hair shining like a halo around her head. She was telling AnnieLee that it was time to get up.

Last night, after they'd talked and cried and drunk a bottle and a half of rosé, they'd agreed that it made little sense for AnnieLee to wend her way back to her motel, not when there were six empty beds in Ruthanna's beautiful house.

"It's almost eight a.m.," Ruthanna said, saying "eight" as if it were as scandalous as "noon." Then she bent over and picked a piece of paper off the carpet, peered at it, and began to read out loud as AnnieLee tried to burrow back under the covers. Her head felt like someone was hitting it with a hammer.

I was standing up just as tall as I was able
Already begging for a seat at the table
Feeling like a shadow, pressed against the wall
All those years he didn't see me at all
I was invisible, invisible
Like shade at midnight, a ghost in the sunlight
Invisible

Ruthanna looked at AnnieLee. "What's this?"

"A song I started last night," AnnieLee said groggily, sitting up and blinking as the world came into focus.

"We went to bed at two!"

"I like to write late," AnnieLee said. She ran her fingers through her tangled hair. "Though it makes getting up at eight unpleasant."

"So does drinking too much wine." Ruthanna shook the paper at her. "You got any more lines?"

AnnieLee cleared her throat and sang the next two, which she hadn't written down yet. Her voice was still jagged, and she yawned midway through.

But then I grew up pretty and I grew up wild
Didn't look no more like a hungry child

She looked up at Ruthanna. "I got stuck on the next bit," she said, "the part where the girl's old enough to realize that being noticed by a man can be worse than being ignored by him." She paused. "So, yeah, it's kind of a tragic song, too."

The sadness of Sophia's story had moved AnnieLee, and in the middle of the night, she'd allowed fragments of her own story to come back to her. But they were memories so unspeakable that the only way to survive was to deny them—at least in daylight, when such things seemed a little easier.

"It's good so far," Ruthanna said. "Maybe we can work this up."

AnnieLee threw off her covers and plucked the paper from Ruthanna's fingers. "I think I need to burn it," she said.

Ruthanna sniffed. "You're a baffling little thing," she said, heading for the door. "Anyway, meet me downstairs in half an hour. We're going down to the studio to see what else you've got."

"Don't call me *little*," AnnieLee called after her.

And you're *the baffling one*, she almost added. Last night Ruthanna had revealed an unimaginable grief, and now here she was, ready to work.

AnnieLee stumbled into the bathroom and turned on the shower, as hot as it would go. She guessed she was a little like that, too.

After a quick breakfast of scrambled eggs and an English muffin, AnnieLee descended to the studio, where the band was already gathered. Everyone was full of congratulations for AnnieLee; they'd all heard her song on WATC.

"Maybe just a little too often," Stan admitted. "No offense. But that thing's an earworm."

"That's a good thing, though, isn't it?" AnnieLee laughed, but then she grew serious. "I couldn't have done any of it without you," she said. She glanced over at Ethan, who was tuning his guitar. Their eyes met and held until AnnieLee flushed and looked away. "Thank you for playing with me, you guys," AnnieLee said, suddenly too moved to look at any of them. "I can't tell you how grateful and honored I am. And I'm so happy to be here working with you again."

Ruthanna's voice came through the control room speakers. "Can we get started now? Or do we need to hold hands and have a dang gratitude circle? Maybe light a candle and write some thank-you notes?"

AnnieLee flushed again, but she wasn't quite done yet. "I'm grateful to you, too, Ruthanna," she called, and she thought she heard Ruthanna give a kind of harrumph of acknowledgment. "Okay," AnnieLee said. "*Now* I'm ready to work."

"So you better give us the tune, then," Ethan said. "What are we learning today?"

Elrodd offered up a drumroll and Donna tossed off a goofy little walking bass line—they were all eager to get started. But AnnieLee didn't answer because she didn't actually know. Instead, she brought out a canvas tote bag and turned it upside down. Sheets of notebook paper, bar coasters, napkins, and Post-its went fluttering down to the floor, all of them covered with AnnieLee's neat, tiny handwriting.

"What the hell is that?" Ruthanna demanded.

"Songs," AnnieLee said simply. "Y'all want to help me pick some out?"

This was *not* how things were done, Ruthanna informed them as she came barreling out of the control room. This was disorganized and indecisive, not to mention downright *messy,* and in case AnnieLee hadn't noticed, there wasn't a speck of dust in the whole 9,312 square feet of Ruthanna's house, and if AnnieLee didn't clean up those papers right quick she'd find out she wasn't too grown-up to have her skinny little fanny tanned.

AnnieLee let Ruthanna's tirade wash over her. She wanted the musicians to find lines that spoke to them. She'd usually jotted down the chords along with the lyrics, so even a glance at a scrap of paper could give them a sense of what the song might become.

Donna squinted at the margins of a bar coaster. "I like the look of this one," she said, and so AnnieLee played it for her while everyone listened carefully, critically.

Elrodd wanted something with a driving drumbeat, almost like a train, he said, and Ethan admitted he wouldn't mind something with a spot for a hot-shit guitar solo. By midmorning, after much discussion and many friendly arguments, they'd settled on five new songs to record.

After that they met every day, early, and they worked until dinner; sometimes they'd work again afterward. "Woman Up (and Take It Like a Man)" took them three days to get right; "Dark Night, Bright Future" took less than eight hours.

"Does that mean it keeps getting easier?" AnnieLee said to Ethan as they walked through Ruthanna's garden on one of their breaks.

"No," Ethan said, "it just means we were lucky that time."

After a couple of weeks, they had six songs ready to be mastered, which was enough for an EP. And that final night, after ten hours in the studio, Ruthanna, Ethan, and AnnieLee celebrated with take-out pizza by the pool. AnnieLee was barefoot, swinging her legs in the chilly water, while Ethan lounged on the deck with a beer.

Ruthanna, though, paced back and forth along the deep end. She was talking to Jack, her former manager, and AnnieLee could hear the laughter in her voice. She'd never met him, but Ethan said he was salt of the earth. "Played a killer slide, too, before he decided to become a suit."

AnnieLee lay back so that she was staring up at the evening sky as swifts darted above her. The next thing she knew, her vision was blocked by Ruthanna's perfectly made-up face.

"I was telling Jack about your love song. You know, the one with the blue bonnets?"

AnnieLee sat up. "But I haven't done anything more with it."

"Well, I was thinking it'd work with a few lines I've got. And maybe it could have a kind of trilling, lilting melody…"

AnnieLee's eyes went wide. "Like, you and me could write a song together?"

"Yes, genius," Ruthanna said, "that's what I meant. We can't sing it together, though, obviously, or at least not in public. I'm retired."

AnnieLee was speechless—astonished at the idea of actually writing a song with her hero. It was thrilling. Or maybe the word she wanted was *terrifying.*

"For being retired, you sure spend a lot of time working," Ethan said mildly.

Ruthanna turned on her heel and started pacing again. "What else am I supposed to do with my time?"

"Hunt wabbits," he said. "I can see six of them over there near your lilies."

"They've gotten into my vegetable garden," AnnieLee added. Not that she cared one lick about the lettuce or the tomatoes. She was going to write a song with Ruthanna Ryder!

Ruthanna gazed thoughtfully at the little creatures. "When she was little, Sophia used to call this the Bunny Hour," she said.

AnnieLee got up and went to stand beside her. "It's nice to hear you talk about her," she said.

"It's been a long time," Ruthanna said. "I'm out of practice."

"You'll get better," AnnieLee said.

Ruthanna flashed a wicked grin. "Like Ethan did on the solo—but Lord, what torture along the way."

Ethan genially raised his bottle of beer to them. "It's okay to use me as the brunt of your jokes," he said.

"Wouldn't matter if it weren't," Ruthanna said.

And AnnieLee laughed, feeling tired in body and soul, and happier than she'd ever thought was possible.

CHAPTER

40

B illy gave AnnieLee and Ethan a look of genuine surprise when they walked into the Cat's Paw on Saturday night. They'd been so busy in the recording studio that it'd been a couple of weeks since they'd sidled up to the bar or climbed onto the stage. But since Ethan was scheduled to play that night, AnnieLee assumed Billy was just surprised to see them coming in *together.*

Billy was topping off a pint of Budweiser for Ethan when he turned around and said, "Well, I'll be damned."

"What?" AnnieLee said, plucking a cherry from the garnish station and popping it into her mouth.

Billy snapped his bar towel at her in annoyance. "Normally I'd eighty-six you for that—but listen!" He bent down and turned up the volume on the stereo, and AnnieLee heard the sound of Ethan's wailing guitar, and then her own sweet, fierce voice doing melodic somersaults over it. "Your single's playing right now on WATC," Billy said, looking as proud as if he'd written "Driven" himself.

AnnieLee grabbed the lip of the bar. "Oh, wow," she whispered. "Honestly, Billy, that's the first time I've heard it."

"You mean besides the five thousand times Ruthanna made us sing it, and then the ten thousand times we listened while Warren mixed it," Ethan corrected her.

She shot a light punch at his well-muscled biceps. "I meant on the radio, dummy." It was amazing—and so *strange*—to hear her own voice coming through the speakers. She couldn't imagine ever getting used to it.

"Nice work, kid," Billy said to her. "Reckon that's about the fastest I ever saw someone go from begging for a set to getting herself on the radio."

AnnieLee tossed her hair back. "I told you so when I walked into this place, didn't I?"

"I guess you did," he said. "The vast majority of *Homo sapiens* are full of BS, though, so forgive me for assuming you belonged in their ranks."

AnnieLee laughed. "I don't know what I'm full of."

"Piss and vinegar," Ethan said, scooting his stool closer to hers and slinging his arm ever so casually over her shoulders.

She thrilled to the warmth and weight of it, though she didn't know what he meant by the gesture. Friendship? Flirtation? All she knew was that he'd showed up at her motel half an hour earlier and demanded that she come watch his set. "And you're not allowed to just stand in the wayback and bug out the second I'm done," he'd clarified. She hadn't even pretended that she didn't want to go. She'd loosed her hair from its braid, swiped on a hint of red lipstick, and jumped into his truck.

"You be nice," she said to Ethan now. "I had big plans I had to cancel for this." She waggled her fingers at him. "I was going to paint my nails something fabulous: Cosmic Glitter was the name of it."

Ethan laughed, a low, thrilling rumble in his chest, and his arm tightened around her.

She was thinking about slipping her own arm around his waist—in a similarly casual way, of course, easy to laugh off if she needed to—when Billy said, "Well, Blake, you better get yourself ready. The mic's looking lonely up there."

Ethan released AnnieLee and swung off his stool. The bar was still quiet, especially for a Saturday night, but he'd asked to play early: his KJ shift at the Rusty Spur started at nine. As he grabbed his guitar case, he looked back at AnnieLee as if he wanted to say something. But then he frowned almost imperceptibly and walked toward the stage.

She watched as he took his place and adjusted the leather strap over his shoulder, the spotlight shining on his dark hair, his long, tanned fingers tenderly holding the neck of the guitar.

"Evening, everybody," he said, and there was a smattering of claps from the room. He began to fingerpick the intro to a song AnnieLee didn't recognize.

"What's your name?" she shouted.

Ethan laughed and leaned into the mic. "I always forget that part. I'm Ethan Blake, and I'm looking forward to playing a few songs for you guys tonight."

He started the song over again, and AnnieLee closed her eyes to listen. He sang about a person asking to be trusted and fearing that he wouldn't be. The song was slow and sad and gorgeous.

No matter what's gone on before,
Don't hold it in a moment more

She whistled and clapped when he finished, and he shot her a grateful look.

"Now for a bit of the Boss," he said, and he played a coun-trified version of "I'm on Fire" that made a trio of tipsy college girls scream in delight.

There were no bells and whistles at the Cat's Paw, no possibility of showmanship beyond the skill of a person's hands and throat. Ethan's warm voice filled the room, sometimes vaulting into an old-fashioned cowboy falsetto before tumbling back down to a richer and darker range. As AnnieLee sat there, entranced, she felt like he was singing only to her.

And maybe he was. Because every time she opened her eyes, she met his from across the room.

He was halfway through a Gram Parsons cover—"$1000 Wedding"—when AnnieLee found herself pushing through the growing crowd to get outside. In the narrow alley, she could still hear Ethan singing, but only faintly. She leaned against the wall, a fingernail of a moon hanging in the sliver of black sky above her. She hoped he hadn't noticed that she'd bolted. How could she explain it? *I ached when I saw you up there, Ethan, because your voice showed me a picture of a life I never thought I could have. A summer evening, you and me on a porch, watching the sun go down. You're playing and I'm singing, and we're barefoot, and the porch is all ours because the house is ours, and oh, my God, I have to get air.*

Her reaction was ridiculous, if not downright insane, for so many reasons. For one thing, she barely even knew Ethan Blake—not really. Which was partly her fault, for pushing him away all the time, but who was keeping track? And for another thing, that vision, as sweet as it was, didn't fit at all with her restless, relentless ambition. She'd meant the words to "Driven," after all.

Driven to keep on and on
To achieve the things I want

She kicked at a can lying in the alley and heard an echoing noise a few yards away. Squinting into the dark, she could see nothing but shadows. She stayed very still, holding her breath as she listened.

Nothing but silence all around, and from inside, the reassuring sound of Ethan Blake's voice.

After another moment, she let herself relax. Her shoulders dropped, and she began to tap her foot against the cobblestones. Ethan had moved on to "Mammas Don't Let Your Babies Grow Up to Be Cowboys," which he had sung as a slow, almost mournful waltz. AnnieLee began to sway a little, *one-two-three, one-two-three,* as she turned to go back inside.

As her fingers closed around the doorknob, something hit her between the shoulder blades. Whatever it was crashed to the ground, shattering. She looked down and saw the glittering pieces of a whiskey bottle at her feet at the same time she realized that the bar door had locked behind her.

Her heart gave a painful hitch in her chest as she whirled around, shouting, "Hey—what the hell?"

Even in the darkness she recognized them: the men from her motel room. There was now one on either side of her.

"Gutter trash," the smaller of them said. "That's all you are."

"Then why do you keep *coming* for me?" The question felt ripped from her throat. She'd tried so hard to run from her past, but it just kept following her. Cornering her. Demanding that she face it.

"You broke the rules." The bigger man lunged toward her, and she wasn't quick enough. He caught her shoulders and shoved her to the ground. Her head slammed against the cobblestones. AnnieLee felt more rage than pain as she rolled to her side, flinging her leg out and connecting her boot to his kneecap. He stumbled, cursing, and then she saw the flash of a knife. She heard herself screaming.

"Ethan! Ethan!"

Instead of straightening himself back up, the injured man fell down on top of her. She gasped as air was forced from her lungs. The man's big hands became vises around her as he turned her over, so she was lying on her stomach and her cheek was grinding into the ground. He let his full weight press down on her back. The second man came over and knelt down by her face.

"Rose isn't really getting the message," he said, and he flicked open a Zippo lighter. "I don't know what's wrong with her." The flame bloomed to life, and she could feel its heat as he pushed it toward her. Grabbing a lock of her hair in his fist, he lit it. The ends curled and crackled, making a horrible stench before burning out.

"Flesh doesn't smell as bad, but it hurts a lot worse," he hissed.

AnnieLee was bucking her hips up and down beneath the big man, but she couldn't get him off her. She didn't have enough air to scream.

Then there was a crash as the bar door flew open and a shape came hurtling out. Ethan Blake knocked the big man off her, and she saw the glint of metal in his hand. *A gun.*

The men were up and already running away, melting into the shadows. Ethan fired after them, over their heads—once, twice. And then he was bending down over her, and lifting her up, and asking her if she was okay. She didn't know how to answer that, so instead of speaking she put her arms around him.

She let him pull her close and hold her there, shaking against his warm chest. Crying tears of shock and relief. Safe, if only for now.

CHAPTER
41

S o she wouldn't tell you anything?" Ruthanna asked.

Ethan followed Ruthanna through her garden, his head foggy from lack of sleep. "No, ma'am. Nothing."

AnnieLee hadn't even let him bring her to Ruthanna's last night the way he'd wanted to. She'd insisted on being driven back to her terrible motel, to a room that made Ethan's humble apartment look like Windsor Castle, but she wouldn't let him come inside. So he'd waited outside her door until he heard the locks click into place, and then he'd sat in his truck like a sentry until the sun peeked over the horizon.

It was strange to feel so fiercely protective of her, especially when he knew she didn't want him to be.

"Does she think she can't trust us?" Ruthanna asked.

"I'm not sure that's the problem," Ethan said. But he couldn't articulate *what* he thought the problem was. There was something unreasonable, almost pathological, about AnnieLee's refusal to answer any of his questions. She'd always seemed tough yet innocent. But was he misjudging her? She was certainly one of the most tight-lipped females he'd ever encountered.

"Those men last night—" Ruthanna began.

"They weren't from around here."

Ruthanna plucked a big pink flower from its stem and tucked it behind her ear. In the soft morning light, she looked as young and fresh-faced as a girl. "How do you know?"

Ethan shrugged. He couldn't pretend he knew every tough in town, but he knew a lot of them. It came with the territory of late nights and liquor—and, no doubt, the Rusty Spur's tendency to hire ex-cons and bad boys as bartenders and bouncers. "Instinct," he said.

"So is our girl just in the wrong place at the wrong time? A lot? Or is there more to the story?"

Ethan took out his utility knife and began opening and closing it as they walked, an old, nervous habit. His friend Antoine had given it to him for his birthday when they were stationed together in Afghanistan, wrapping the gift in toilet paper and tying it with a spare shoelace. Two weeks later, Antoine was dead, killed by an IED in a dusty Kandahar street. Now the blade flashed and gleamed in the sunlight—a beautiful, lethal thing.

"Ahem," Ruthanna said.

Ethan startled. It'd been a while since memories of his service had come on strong like that. "What? Sorry, Ruthanna."

"I said, let's get her out of town."

He waited for her to explain what she meant.

She began to cut tall stems of hollyhocks for a bouquet, and she handed them to him as she walked. "I'm going to set up a meeting with ACD," she said.

"Really?" Ethan said. ACD was a huge record label. It wasn't based in Nashville, either, but nine hundred miles away in New York City. "I thought you said she should put out her EP, get good streaming numbers, and then look for a label."

"Well, that was your idea, actually, and it was a pretty good one. But I want her to have more support right off the bat. I thought about calling Jody at BMH here in Nashville again, but she never sent the scout she promised. So I've reached out to the big guns, and they've agreed to a meeting with AnnieLee." She poked Ethan in the side with a red-nailed finger. "And you're going to New York with her, Blake—as chaperone."

"Says who?" he blurted, regretting the words even as they came out of his mouth.

"Says me," Ruthanna said, severing the head off a fading rose with a slash of her clippers. "Your boss. You got a problem with that?"

"I just…don't think…" But then he stopped. What were his objections, honestly? Of course he'd go anywhere AnnieLee went. So what was the problem? He dug a toe into the soft grass. Was he worried that AnnieLee Keyes would go all the way to New York City with her big voice and her borrowed guitar and fail to win them over?

Or that she'd succeed?

And then she might leave you behind. The voice was so small he could almost pretend he didn't hear it.

Ethan knew he didn't understand the business, not the way Ruthanna did; he was only on its fringes. But he'd seen the way it could grind people up and spit them back out. AnnieLee seemed truly driven. But so had his friend Jake, who'd signed with Warner Music, put out an album that no one bought, and suffered such a crisis of confidence he nearly drank himself into an early grave.

Willie Nelson himself once lay down in the middle of Lower Broadway, considering the possibility that a car might roll over him. It was a tough business.

But Ruthanna seemed to have no worries about AnnieLee's prospects.

"If she won't tell us what's going on," Ruthanna said, "then fine. I don't have to know." She glanced down at her long, dangerous-looking nails. "I'll deal with the professional side only. I was always extra good at that part."

Ethan thought he heard a sudden note of sorrow in her voice, and he reached out and touched her shoulder. He could guess what Ruthanna was thinking: how she'd lost a daughter and then a husband, and now she was rattling around in a huge mansion alone, writing and recording songs that she didn't want anyone but a handful of studio musicians to hear.

Some people said you should never meet your idols: you'd only see their feet of clay. But Ruthanna, as ornery as she could be, had never shown herself to be anything other than magnificent.

"You're good at everything," Ethan said gently. "You're a shining light."

She looked up at him with glittering eyes. "And you're a good man," she said.

He smiled, and then he sang a line of her song, the very first Ruthanna Ryder tune he ever knew.

They say a good man is hard to find
Damn straight they're right—but I don't mind

He'd heard it when he was just a kid, and its honky-tonk swing, its mix of yearning and audacity, had lifted his spirits every time he heard it. His mother had loved it, too, and she'd always turned up the volume and sung along. Ethan hadn't had the faintest notion of learning to play the guitar back then, but he understood the lines about chasing a dream. And he'd known, deep down, what it felt like to want something more than what you had.

He still knew that feeling.

"Oh, Lord, that's an old one," Ruthanna said quietly.

"It's a good one," he said.

Ruthanna laughed. "Oh, sure," she said. "I did all right by it, I guess." She patted him on his big strong shoulder. "Anyway, you better go home and pack your bags. You two leave tomorrow."

CHAPTER
42

The ACD offices were in a towering high-rise a few blocks north of Times Square. AnnieLee's boots echoed through the vast marble lobby, and she felt wide-eyed and mouse tiny as she made her way to the big security desk.

After printing a sticker with her name and the word VISITOR in big black letters, the desk attendant pointed AnnieLee toward the turnstiles, which she pushed through with far more confidence than she felt.

On the fifty-third floor, she was directed to wait in a reception area, where a tinkling Zen fountain did nothing to calm her nerves. Her meeting was supposed to be at ten, but by ten thirty no one had come to fetch her.

Whoever these New Yorkers were, AnnieLee thought, they clearly felt that their time was more important than hers.

Nervousness turned to annoyance the longer she sat, and by the time an assistant appeared to escort her to the conference room, AnnieLee wasn't sure if she wanted to play her guitar or knock someone upside the head with it.

Then, quick as whiplash, she was back to being anxious

again as she stood before a roomful of executives, PR people, and marketing managers from one of the world's biggest record labels. A large, bald man with Kix Brooks facial hair and a top-brass attitude smiled at her, but not with his eyes.

"AnnieLee Keyes," he said. "Tony Graham. I've heard a lot about you." He glanced over her shoulder. "Where's your team?"

My team? AnnieLee thought. Ruthanna was in Nashville, Ethan was two blocks away at an Au Bon Pain, and who else was there? She stood up as tall as she could, and she still didn't even come up to Tony Graham's armpit.

"I'm my own team," she said.

Tony Graham glanced back at his underlings. "Interesting," he said.

"Is it?" AnnieLee asked, a hint of challenge in her voice. "I wrote the songs alone. It's how I first performed them. I figure it's how I can sell them, too." Then she flashed him one of her own smiles, eyes and all, and set the guitar on top of that big table as if she owned it.

No doughnuts in the middle this time, she noted, as the coffee she'd drunk roiled in her stomach.

Tony gestured for her to take a seat as he introduced her to every polished and formidable person in the room. AnnieLee felt like a yokel in her old jeans and her new, emerald-green blouse. She thought she'd splurged at the Gap—sixty bucks for a single shirt!—but these people obviously spent that much on a single pair of socks.

Her hand slipped into her pocket and she thumbed the guitar pick Ethan had given her.

"I know it doesn't look like much," he'd said to her, "but it's a lucky pick."

She'd asked him how he knew, and he'd said it was because good things happened when he used it.

"Like what?"

He'd looked right at her when he answered. "Like you walking into the Cat's Paw. That was the best thing that had happened to me in a long time."

She was sorry now that she hadn't asked him to come to the meeting with her. The only person who was looking at her with any sort of friendliness at all was the barely twenty-something redhead who'd brought her into the room, and whom Tony hadn't even bothered to introduce.

Tony made a steeple of his fingers and gazed at AnnieLee. "I'm a straight talker, AnnieLee," he said. "And I'm going to be honest with you: right now, you're just a pretty little nobody."

He paused a moment to let the words sink in, and AnnieLee felt her heart give a lurch.

"You've got a couple of things going for you, though," he went on. "One, Ruthanna Ryder says you're hot shit, and when a deity like that speaks, people like us listen. And two, we've heard your single. It's pretty fantastic."

"Thank you," AnnieLee said. "I—"

"But it takes more than a good face and a great voice to sell records," Tony interrupted. "And we've got a lot of girl singers here already. You're familiar with Susannah Dell, of course. She just hit number ten on *Billboard* Country Airplay this week, and she's going nowhere but up."

AnnieLee put her hand on her guitar case. "You got a lot of girl singers?" she repeated. "Well, shoot, I sure hope you do, considering women make up fifty percent of the population and most of the country music audience."

The redhead's eyes widened a little, and she gave AnnieLee a barely perceptible shake of the head. AnnieLee knew she wasn't being properly deferential, but she didn't care.

Tony's hands unsteepled as he leaned forward. "You think

you can rise above the crowd, AnnieLee? Do you know how many songs get uploaded to DSPs every day? Try *forty thousand*—to Spotify alone. There's so much noise out there. There's more music than ever before in history. What makes little ol' you think you've got what it takes to be heard? And not just to be heard, but to be *loved*?"

AnnieLee looked around the room at the people who, she now understood, were only here because Ruthanna Ryder had called in a favor. Tony Graham had made up his mind about AnnieLee before she even walked in the door.

It was the kind of thing that really got under her skin. That— and being called little.

"I won't pretend to be a city sophisticate, Mr. Graham," she said, "but you can stop talking to me like I'm as dumb as a turnip. I'm a straight talker, too, and I'm here to tell you that you've got a damn gold mine right here sitting across from you."

Tony Graham laughed. "A girl singer with an outsized sense of confidence."

"I believe in myself, and if you heard me play, you'd believe in me, too," she said. Fearless, shameless: she was playing the part well. And it felt good.

But AnnieLee was angry, too, thinking about the times she'd been underestimated or kicked around by someone bigger and more powerful than she was, someone who thought he had a right to tell her how things were going to be.

So without waiting for Tony Graham's invitation, she got out her guitar and began to play. She sang with hope and she sang with fury, and the ACD people sat so still they could have been statues. She blazed through three songs without stopping for breath. She wasn't going to give them a chance to show her the door until she'd shown them her talent, in all its gorgeous rawness.

When the last notes of "Firecracker" faded, AnnieLee put her guitar back in its case and folded her hands in her lap. "Well?" she said calmly.

Tony Graham wiped imaginary sweat from his brow and turned to the pale, red-lipped woman sitting next to him. His entire demeanor had changed. "She's *fire*," he said. "We want her, don't we?"

Everyone in the room nodded, and the assistant standing in the corner met AnnieLee's eyes and gave her a tiny thumbs-up. "You did it," she mouthed.

Tony Graham was already talking about the deal they would sign, and AnnieLee heard a bunch of numbers and big promises and terms like *synergy* and *omnidirectional marketing*.

AnnieLee listened, nodding, and when Tony paused for a breath, she said, "I want to keep my publishing." She saw a shadow pass over his face, and she went on before she lost her nerve. She was asking for the kinds of things a star like Ruthanna would ask for. "I want approval on the producer, and I want to coproduce, because I know my songs better than anyone else."

The room went dead quiet. Then Tony Graham started laughing. "I'm afraid that's just not possible," he said.

AnnieLee picked up her guitar. "Then I thank you for your time, sir," she said. "It was real nice to meet you all." She stopped in front of the assistant as she headed out. "What's your name, hon?"

"Samantha," she said. "Sam."

"Sam," AnnieLee repeated. "Thanks for being here today. I'm rooting for you, too."

CHAPTER

43

AnnieLee spun through the revolving doors and stumbled forward into the noise and the crowds of a midtown sidewalk.

"Hey, watch it!" a man shouted as her guitar careened off his briefcase.

"Sorry," she gasped as the street blurred and wavered in front of her. She staggered up the block, crying not so much out of sorrow but out of frustration and fear. She'd stormed out of the ACD offices without thinking, and now the weight of what she'd done felt as though it would crush the breath out of her. In less than fifteen minutes, she'd managed to ruin the incredible opportunity that Ruthanna had put together for her. What if it was her only one?

And would Ruthanna be able to forgive her?

She'd asked for too much—that was obvious. She should have been nicer and more grateful. Why was she still thinking about the advice of an aging barfly whose name she'd never even asked? What did that woman know about being fearless?

She swiped angrily at her tearstained cheeks. She cared so

much about her words, her creative expression, when what mattered to everyone else was the bottom line. *Everything* was a business—even art. She'd written the songs, but she wouldn't be able to truly own them. Not if she wanted the rest of the world to hear them.

AnnieLee felt like kicking herself. She'd made so many sacrifices in her life—why hadn't she been prepared to make just a few more? Wasn't a bad deal better than no deal at all?

She was dimly aware of shouting behind her, but she didn't turn around. She wanted to lose herself in the sea of people. She wanted to walk until she was too exhausted to cry.

You idiot, she said to herself. *You're not hot shit. You're just—*

AnnieLee felt a hand on her arm, and she whirled around, ready to fight whatever purse snatcher had spotted her for the country rube she was.

But it was Sam, breathless and panting. AnnieLee saw now how the assistant's shirt was too big for her, and her shoes were cheap, and her heart went out to this girl who looked just as lost as she was.

"What are you doing here?" she asked. "Did you storm out, too?"

Sam gave a grim laugh. "No. I came because they want you back upstairs."

"What for?"

"They just told me to go get you," she said. "So here I am. Will you come back?"

AnnieLee pointed to her stricken face. "I can't go in looking like this."

Sam reached into her bag and handed AnnieLee a pack of tissues. "I always have some with me," she said. "But I haven't cried in the office for a week, so things are definitely looking up."

People streamed around them as they stood there, AnnieLee drying her cheeks and trying to get her emotions under control while Sam soothed her with small talk about the Pennsylvania town she'd come from and the railroad apartment in Queens she'd been subletting since she moved here nine months earlier.

"You don't ever think about going back home?" AnnieLee asked as the two of them walked back toward the building.

Sam gestured to the gleaming office buildings, the honking taxis, the whole loud rush of city life. "You know what they say. *'If I can make it there…'*" She laughed, not bothering to finish the lyric.

They walked back through the lobby and rocketed up to the conference room. Tony Graham was the only one left. He stood up when AnnieLee entered, and his smile was genuine this time.

"The thing is," he said, "whenever I hear someone play—whether it's in a crowded club or an inhospitable conference room—I close my eyes. And if I can imagine that person playing Madison Square Garden, then I know I've found something real."

AnnieLee held her breath. Madison Square Garden was a damn high bar.

Tony Graham took a gold pen from his pocket and began spinning it on the tips of his thumb and forefinger. "I had a feeling when you left the room, AnnieLee. And that feeling was that it was in my best interest to get you back inside, whatever it took."

"So you got me," she said.

"And we aim to keep you," he said. "By whatever means—or concessions—necessary."

CHAPTER
44

AnnieLee burst into the coffee shop shouting, "Ethan, Ethan!"

He knocked over his chair as he ran to her and caught her by the arms. Her hair was wild and her eyes were an electric blue. "Are you okay?" he demanded.

"I'm great. I'm so good! Why are you flinging furniture?"

"I thought something was wrong," Ethan said, dropping his hands and shoving them into his pockets. "I mean, considering your recent experiences…"

"No, no—everything's right!" Then she reached out and took his face between her palms and kissed him on the cheek. Immediately she stepped back, embarrassed. "Sorry. I couldn't help it."

Ethan bent down to pick up the chair so she wouldn't see the way he flushed. "It's okay," he said, thinking, *Do that again and again*. "I take it the meeting went well?"

"The second one did," she said. "I'll tell you all about it. Let's go!"

He laughed at the way she was nearly bouncing up and

down. "Go where?" he asked, following her outside, into the sunshine.

"Let's just *walk*," AnnieLee said. "Let's walk until we can't even feel our feet anymore. Let's look at everything in the city until our eyes start to cross."

Though he might've wished that he weren't wearing steel-toe boots, Ethan was hardly in the mood to argue. He'd never seen AnnieLee so happy, so alive. And why not celebrate her incredible news? Did she even comprehend how lucky she was?

He decided not to ask her. Instead he said, "North or south?"

"Like I know which is which!" she said, laughing. "Come on!"

Soon they found themselves on Ninth Avenue, walking through the neighborhood known as Hell's Kitchen. Passing walk-up apartment buildings, pizza joints, and laundromats, they bought bright-green apples from a fruit vendor. They wandered farther south and west, peering into the windows of the Chelsea art galleries, and then came upon Pier 25, with its playgrounds, fountains, and volleyball courts jutting into the Hudson River.

"Want to get whipped in a round of mini golf?" Ethan asked.

AnnieLee laughed. "Not by the likes of you, no thank you."

So they kept on going, down into the financial district, where the buildings were so tall and close together it seemed to Ethan as if they walked along the bottom of a canyon of steel. He kept thinking about reaching for AnnieLee's hand. But he didn't do it.

AnnieLee had explained her deal with ACD—or at least what she could remember of it, the point being that they'd given her almost everything she asked for, including the purchase and promotion of her self-released single, "Driven"—and now she was chattering on breathlessly, sometimes about what she and

Ethan were seeing and sometimes about the kinds of songs she imagined putting on her first album.

Ethan was quieter, and not just because he couldn't get a word in edgewise. He was wondering what sort of person would live in a place like this, surrounded by traffic and noise and lights at all hours of the day and night.

He'd been here once before, when he was very small. On a road trip north with his parents to see family in New Hampshire, they'd driven into the city. They'd planned to spend the day sightseeing, but his parents were so overwhelmed by the crowds and the giant buildings, not to mention the pedestrians who seemed to fling themselves into the streets without regard for DON'T WALK signals, that they'd headed straight back out again.

"Did you ever take family vacations?" he asked AnnieLee as she was perusing the menu outside an Italian café.

"Not hardly," AnnieLee said.

"We camped in the summers, if that counts," Ethan said. "Though once we stayed in a hotel in Kitty Hawk. It had a pool *and* a hot tub, and I thought I'd died and gone to heaven. I didn't set foot on an airplane until I went into the army."

"What flavor of gelato do you think *stracciatella* is?" AnnieLee asked. "Should we try some?"

She was trying to change the subject, however ungracefully, and Ethan felt what might've been a small flare of annoyance. But it was her day—so why not let her talk about whatever inanities she wanted to?

"Sure. One scoop of whatever that is, and another of chocolate," he said.

"I'll be right back."

When she came out again, she had a double-decker cone for each of them. "This represents twenty bucks' worth of gelato, so it'd better be amazing." She took a bite and her blue eyes got huge. "It is," she sighed.

Ethan laughed. The city thrilled her today, and even if she wouldn't open up to him, he loved watching her delight. Everything seemed brighter and fresher through her eyes. He wished he could tell her so.

But instead, he slung his arm around her as they walked. And when she leaned into him, he felt the world go a little brighter for him, too.

CHAPTER
45

AnnieLee rested her forehead against the window of her hotel room, gazing out at the jagged skyline, the glittering city lights, and the people rushing by far below. She felt giddy, exhausted, electrified. She couldn't have imagined a day like this, not ever.

After walking around for hours, she and Ethan had returned to the lavish Mark Hotel on the Upper East Side, collapsed onto the sofa in her suite, and ordered room service—burgers, salads, and Cokes—which they'd devoured while watching the end of *Die Hard*. Then Ethan had called Ruthanna to give her the report on the ACD deal. AnnieLee heard a gleeful shriek through the phone, and not ten minutes later, a hotel attendant had appeared in the doorway with a magnum of Dom Pérignon.

Which meant that AnnieLee, who'd never tasted champagne before, was now perhaps a little bit drunk on it.

She turned her back to the view and watched Ethan noodling with her guitar on the couch. He was leaning back against the cushions with his boots on the coffee table, and there appeared to be a large spot of ketchup on his white T-shirt.

He was probably half drunk, too.

"Almost heaven, East 77th Street," he sang, channeling John Denver.

"Velvet sofa, soft slippers for my feet," AnnieLee sang, pushing away from the window and sitting down on the couch, a careful distance away from Ethan.

Ethan poured them both more champagne, and then he held up his glass. "A toast," he said, "to today's great news. And to country music's future number one star."

AnnieLee clinked her flute against his. "Oh, Ethan, I don't know," she said, suddenly feeling overwhelmed. "It doesn't feel real."

"Well, it is," Ethan said. He lightly pinched her arm. "See?"

"*Ow,* unnecessary!" She laughed, swatting his hand away. "I mean, *the deal's* real. But success isn't guaranteed." She took a big gulp of champagne. She couldn't tell if the wine was making her feel better or worse, but it was delicious.

"Nothing's guaranteed, obviously," Ethan said. "But if you ask me, your chances of success are pretty damn good."

AnnieLee fell back against the pillows. "I'm so tired," she whispered.

"Maybe I should sing you a lullaby," Ethan said. *"Hush, little baby, don't you—"*

"No covers!" AnnieLee said. "Sing me one of your new ones, why don't you? I'll bet you're writing all the time."

She watched his profile as he pondered this request. From watching him at the Cat's Paw, she knew he didn't always like playing what he'd written; he preferred to hide behind other people's words. That might've seemed strange to some, but not to AnnieLee, who'd been hiding something bigger than lyrics since long before she got to Nashville.

She scooted a little closer to him. "Come on," she said. "You won't find a friendlier crowd than yours truly."

Ethan laughed. "I can think of a lot of words I'd use to describe you, but *friendly* isn't way up there."

AnnieLee crossed her arms. "Oh, really? What is?" *This is going to be interesting*, she thought.

"Fierce. Ornery. Stubborn—"

"I'm waiting for the compliments," she said.

"I'm getting there!" Ethan protested. *"Talented. Enthusiastic."* He hesitated. *"Enigmatic. Gorgeous."*

AnnieLee felt herself blushing. "Okay, you can stop there, Blake. Otherwise I might get a big head. Just sing, why don't you?"

"What, you're not going to list *my* top qualities?" he asked.

She bit her lip. What was she supposed to say? "Well, you're strong and you're loyal," she said haltingly. "And protective…"

"So's a golden retriever."

She threw a pillow at him. It was impossible to say more, impossible to tell him the truth—that he was handsome and kind, that he drew her to him like a magnet. That she thought his voice was one of the best sounds in the world. That when he put his arm around her, she felt his touch like an electric shock.

"Oh, just play," she commanded.

With obvious reluctance, Ethan began to pick an unfamiliar tune. When he started to sing, his voice was barely more than a whisper.

Don't know why I've been lost for so long
Why can't I write a new life like I can write a new song?

He stopped and looked over at her. "Forget it," he said. "It's terrible."

"Do you really feel lost?" AnnieLee asked. The question startled both of them. They'd never gone deeper than banter and small talk; AnnieLee had always turned the conversation away from anything serious.

Ethan picked a few more notes before he answered. "I used to. I don't know if I do anymore."

She didn't ask him what had changed. *What if he said it was her? Worse, what if he didn't?*

"Keep singing," she said, and he obeyed.

Sometimes the world seems to move too fast
You find something real but it's not gonna last

Then he stopped again. "It's not right somehow."

"Ethan," AnnieLee said, "it's great so far. But it's so… melancholic." She giggled. "I know, it's a big word for a hayseed like me, isn't it? Tony Graham thought I was dumb, too."

"I don't think you're *dumb*, you idiot," Ethan said. "But the best country songs are about heartbreak."

"Not all of them." AnnieLee reached over and grabbed the guitar from him. "What if you made it more up-tempo? What if your lost man realizes he was wrong to feel that way?" She began to play, tweaking the melody, making it brighter. "Maybe," she said, "you could give the song a happy ending."

Ethan got up and grabbed a beer from the minibar. When he turned around, his expression was almost haunted. "I don't know much about those," he said quietly.

AnnieLee's fingers found a D major open, one of the simplest and most optimistic chords there was. "Me, either," she said. "But I bet we can write one anyway."

CHAPTER
46

So she rented a bridal gown, he rented a tux
A bouquet of blue bonnets in his fancy new truck

Ruthanna was running through the song she and AnnieLee had been working on when her phone rang, and she jumped as if she'd been caught doing something wrong. Then she laughed. Who did she think was calling, the retirement police? Of course it was only Jack, checking in on her the way he did every Sunday.

"How are the roses?" he asked as soon as she picked up.

"The blooms are all gone now," she said, "but my damask roses should blossom again in the fall." She nudged the guitar away from her with a painted toe. "What's shaking, Mr. Holm?"

"I can't believe you let her go into that room alone," Jack said, and Ruthanna had barely figured out who he was talking about before he was barreling on. "The last time we talked about AnnieLee, you told me she wasn't ready for professional representation. And then you sent her all the way to New York—

not with a lawyer, either, but with that cowboy guitar player of yours. For all you knew, she might've signed an exploitive 360 and offered up her firstborn to those guys!"

"She's not *stupid,* Jack," Ruthanna said.

"But that's not how you do things," he said, exasperated. "You know that!"

"Do I?" she asked, affronted. She wasn't used to being challenged like this. "All I know is that if there were rules, I broke them—my whole damn life. You know who helped me for the first five years of my career? Me—that's who. I was *alone.*"

She remembered being sixteen and singing at one VFW hall dance after another, with hair so big and shoes so high she made a six-foot silhouette with a five-foot-two body. *God, those were long days,* she thought. *Correction: they were long* years.

She'd sung at county fairs, rodeos, weddings, showcases, and talent competitions; she'd lurked outside radio stations all over the South, accosting everyone who walked in to try to get them to play the songs she'd paid to record. She'd started at the bottom, and rung by rung she'd climbed her way to the top.

"I just meant—" Jack began.

"I worked my rear end off," she interrupted, "and I never stopped—not until I left the business."

"Honey," Jack said, his voice gentle now. "I *know* that. I know just about everything about you."

"Oh, do you, now?" Ruthanna was simultaneously offended and touched by Jack's claim. Of course he didn't know *everything.* But he knew more than almost anyone else. Way more.

And then suddenly she wasn't thinking about her past, or AnnieLee's career, or anything but Jack, good old familiar Jack, there on the other end of the line.

"I miss you," she heard herself say.

He didn't answer right away, and Ruthanna quickly wished

she could take the words back. It didn't matter that they were true.

"Well," Jack finally said, "if you *really* mean that, then today might be your lucky day."

"Oh, yeah? How come?" she asked.

"Because I'm right outside your gate."

"Oh, for Pete's sake!" Laughing, blushing, Ruthanna punched in the gate code, and five minutes later Jack was coming into the yard, where she sat in a white lacy dress and Balenciaga sunglasses, her hair and makeup perfect. Of course.

"Were you expecting someone?" he asked, glancing around the garden.

"I don't leave my own bedroom without looking red-carpet ready—you know that. And it's a good thing, too, the way some folks show up *unannounced*." She smiled up at him as he set a bottle of white wine on the table. "What's that for?"

"A gentleman never shows up empty-handed," Jack said. "Anyway, don't we have something to celebrate?"

"What?"

"My management agreement with AnnieLee."

"You old snake," Ruthanna said approvingly. "Calling me up to yell at me when you'd already got it all figured out."

"We'll bring in PR and a social media manager immediately," he said. "And she's got to get a lawyer. Do you think we should go with Nelson at Fox Klein Nelson?"

"Work all this out with *her*, why don't you? I'm retired."

Jack glanced over at the guitar that was leaning suspiciously close by, and then at the new lyrics he could see scribbled on the back of a receipt. But he didn't say anything; he just gave a little smile, which Ruthanna pretended not to notice.

"Are you going to open the wine, or what?" she asked.

Jack's smile got wider. "I'll be right back."

He returned with the bottle opener and her Riedel stemware. "I saw that AnnieLee's single is at number thirty-seven. She's a phenom."

"Once they took her on, ACD put serious money into promoting 'Driven.' Not bad at all for a kid nobody's heard of."

"It sure isn't." Jack poured the chardonnay into their glasses. "The spotlight's going to come back to *you*, you know."

"Why do you say that?"

"Because you've made AnnieLee your protégé," he said. "Maybe not even on purpose. But think about it: You hear a pretty kid singing in a bar one night, and your interest is piqued. Good Samaritan that you are, you pick her up and dust her off, and lo and behold, you find a star underneath the hillbilly dirt. Hell, not even a star: a potential *supernova*. People are going to eat that story up like ice cream. And mostly because *you're* in it."

"But it's not my story," Ruthanna protested. "It should be all about AnnieLee."

Jack laughed. "You just don't get it, do you? People will grab at even the tiniest scrap of information they can get about you, Ruthanna. You left the business when you had the whole world at your feet. You were the biggest star Nashville had, and you just *quit*. No one can understand it, though believe me, they've tried." He took a sip of wine and made a face; he was a whiskey man at heart. "The world still wants more from Ruthanna Ryder: more songs, more concerts, more everything. And the fact that they aren't getting any of it? Well, *that*, my dear, is just one of the reasons why everyone's still completely fascinated by you."

She laughed at his words, and at his tiny grimace. "You're cuckoo. What makes you think that's true, anyway?"

He waited a moment before he spoke, as if he wanted to make sure he had her full attention. "Because *I'm* still fascinated by you, Ruthanna," he said. "And I, of all people, should be damn well sick of you."

His voice was low and intimate, and Ruthanna felt the flush move from her cheeks all the way down to her chest. They'd known and loved each other for so long, hadn't they? They'd always been such good friends.

But feelings could change, and one kind of love could blossom into another when you least expected it. Was that what was happening now? Or had it already been happening, slowly but surely over all those years? What would it be like if she didn't send him home tonight?

Flustered, she took a big gulp of wine and nearly choked on it.

"You okay?" he asked, looking at her quizzically.

Instead of answering, Ruthanna reached out and grabbed her guitar. Holding it against her like a shield to guard her heart, she felt better instantly. Everything was under control.

"You want to hear a song?" she asked.

Jack gazed at her for a moment, and then he sort of shook himself and smiled. "Retired," he said. "Yeah, right."

"It's a yes or no question," Ruthanna said.

"Yes," he said. "Of course I do."

CHAPTER

47

"Okay, you sit down right here," Ruthanna said, gently pushing AnnieLee toward a poolside chair. "And don't be nervous: Poppy's a brilliant hairstylist."

AnnieLee, who'd played the last eight nights in clubs all around Nashville, was more than happy to follow any orders involving the word *sit*. She felt as though Poppy could shave her head bald and she'd be too tired to even care.

Poppy, whose wide face and high cheekbones made her look like a young Debbie Harry, ran her fingers through AnnieLee's long hair, which was still wet from the shower.

"Virgin?" Poppy asked.

AnnieLee stared at her in shock. "*Excuse* me?"

Ruthanna burst into laughter, but AnnieLee couldn't imagine what was so funny. "What? What does she mean?"

"She meant has your *hair* ever been colored," Ruthanna said. "Virgin hair is unprocessed."

AnnieLee could've died right then and there. "Oh," she said. "I thought—"

Poppy gently brushed one of AnnieLee's dark waves away

from her cheek. "It was pretty obvious what you thought, love," she said.

"I've used a box dye once or twice," AnnieLee said stiffly, trying to regain some of her dignity. She'd never had a professional haircut, though, and the mani-pedi Ruthanna had treated her to yesterday was her first.

"Well, the color is gorgeous," the stylist said. "I won't mess with it."

As Poppy began combing, misting, and snipping strands of her hair with the utmost care and tenderness, AnnieLee started to relax again. She was toying with a new melody in her head, feeling almost as if she could drift into a nap, when Ruthanna's phone dinged with a text.

"Okay. Eileen Jackson will be here any minute," Ruthanna said.

"Who's Eileen Jackson?" AnnieLee asked drowsily, and only to be polite.

"She's the publicist you're hiring," Ruthanna said. "She's flying in from Los Angeles."

"Wait. What?" AnnieLee said, sitting up straight and suddenly wide-awake. "What for?"

Ruthanna took a sip of the smoothie Maya had pressed into her hand. "Jack says that now you've got a label, it's time you got a publicist, and since he's your manager, you're supposed to listen to him."

Poppy's scissors clicked across AnnieLee's back, and the bright, metallic sound reminded her of brushes tapping on a snare drum. "I thought he said I needed a lawyer," AnnieLee said.

"And he was right. But the bigger you get, the more people you need," Ruthanna said. "You'll probably want to think about hiring an assistant at some point, too." She flashed a sly grin at Maya. "Though I'd recommend one who *doesn't* make you drink kale and bee pollen smoothies, or whatever the heck this is."

"Don't even pretend you don't love them," Maya said huffily.

"Is this a 'fake it till you make it' kind of thing?" AnnieLee asked. "Sure, I'm getting a name around Nashville, but I don't even have an album yet."

"If I had to bet, I'd say this was the calm before the storm. It's best to get your team in place."

AnnieLee's hair was just beginning to fall into long, elegant layers when Eileen Jackson appeared on the pool deck in a chic white dress and towering, leopard-spotted heels. Her cool, confident demeanor wavered ever so slightly when she saw Ruthanna, and AnnieLee thought she detected an expression of barely concealed awe.

AnnieLee smiled to herself. Ruthanna Ryder tended to have that effect on people.

But Ruthanna, ever the gracious Southern host, rose to greet her. "Welcome to Nashville," she said. "I hope your flight was all right."

"Turbulent, but the Bloody Mary helped." Eileen smiled. "It's such an honor to meet you." She looked over at AnnieLee as Poppy twisted a section of her hair and pinned it on top of her head. "An honor to meet you both," Eileen clarified.

AnnieLee offered up a tiny wave and said, "Hi, I like your shoes," because it seemed like a friendly thing to say. Certainly it was better than *Nice ankle breakers,* which had been her first thought.

Eileen said, "You're taking such good care of your little discovery, Ms. Ryder."

Ruthanna laughed. "I wouldn't call her *little* if I were you."

AnnieLee would rather not be called anyone's *discovery,* either—it wasn't as if Ruthanna had found her underneath the tree near the Cumberland River—but she kept her mouth shut.

"Are you enjoying the pampering?" Eileen asked her.

AnnieLee stretched out a leg to admire her pedicure. "I'm definitely not complaining," she said.

"Well, good, because it comes with the territory," Eileen said. "Celebrities should look like the glittering stars their fans think they are. Right, Ruthanna?"

"I try to look reasonably nice most days," Ruthanna allowed — an understatement if there ever was one.

"But I'm not actually a celebrity," AnnieLee pointed out.

"You will be," Eileen said firmly.

"You got a crystal ball in your purse?"

Eileen looked at her very seriously. "No, AnnieLee, I don't. I can't see into the future. But I've been in the business for a long time, and I'm excellent at seeing what's inside a person. Talent's not enough, I know that for sure. You've got to have something else. Something bigger and deeper. People call it star power, I guess, but the fact is, you've got to have it in spades *before* you're a star."

Poppy unclipped AnnieLee's hair and came around to inspect it from the front. "Almost done," she said.

Eileen perched on the edge of a glass-topped table and crossed her long legs at the ankles. "My job, AnnieLee, is to help the world *see* that you're that star. We'll start with social — Instagram, TikTok, and Twitter — and build you a following. ACD's very big on social, and you want to show them that you're a team player. Then we'll focus on interviews with magazines and late-night. Eventually we can get endorsement deals, too; those are great. I'll make good things happen, AnnieLee." She ran a hand through her glossy bob. "And if *bad* things happen — like if you trash a hotel room or shoplift a six-hundred-dollar scarf from Bergdorf's — I'll keep it out of the tabloids."

AnnieLee nodded slowly, taking this in. She'd spent a decade of her life dreaming of being up on a stage, but she'd never thought about anything beyond the music. She hadn't imagined that trying to make it as a singer would involve so many other people and so many new obligations.

She closed her eyes as Poppy began blow-drying her hair. Eileen's chatter sounded like a lot of promises to her. A lot of things that didn't have anything to do with song-writing.

"The question is," Eileen said, "what story are we going to tell the world about you?"

No one said anything for a while, and AnnieLee realized that they were waiting for her to speak. She opened her eyes to find Eileen gazing at her.

"Who are you, AnnieLee?" the publicist asked.

AnnieLee felt a sudden jolt of adrenaline. "I'm not sure what you mean," she said, as calmly as she could. This was a professional question, wasn't it? There was no way this woman could actually know any secrets about her past.

"Can you turn that dryer off for a minute?" Eileen asked Poppy. Poppy obediently clicked it off.

"Are you the girl next door, AnnieLee?" Eileen asked. "Are you country music's Cinderella story? Or Ruthanna's anointed successor? Or just a backwoods innocent, stumbling into super-stardom?"

AnnieLee swiveled around to look at Poppy. "Actually, could you please finish the blow-dry?" she asked quietly.

As the hot air rushed around her head, AnnieLee squeezed her eyes shut again. She'd only come to Ruthanna's for a haircut, and this line of questioning felt overwhelming. Eileen was tough and smart, but did she expect AnnieLee to pick out a persona the way she could pick out a dress? And what was wrong with who she was right now? Did she have to put a label on herself for the world to understand her?

She could hear Eileen talking about how important it was to take the image aspect of her career seriously—that social media was a necessity these days, and that building a brand identity was the best way to keep ACD happy.

AnnieLee remembered the night she'd sung "Two Doors Down" for Spider, and how she'd left the bar that night feeling like she'd been part of something new and bright and real. Would any of those people care if she posted selfies on Instagram? If she had an endorsement deal with Vitaminwater?

The dryer whined, blowing a D and a B flat simultaneously, as Eileen went on about maximizing followers and building synergistic partnerships.

"Is she even paying attention?" she heard Eileen ask eventually.

Ruthanna gave a low chuckle. "Oh, believe me," she said, "AnnieLee's tracking every word." She paused. "She's going to take it all in and turn it all over. And she'll do whatever she thinks is right."

The blow-dryer finally shut off, and Poppy appeared in front of AnnieLee with a handheld mirror. "Behold the glory that is you!" the stylist said, without even a trace of irony.

AnnieLee's dark hair fell in smooth, luxurious waves over her shoulders, while a sweep of a shorter layer slipped teasingly down in front of her right eye. She looked sultry, innocent, and defiant all at once.

"Prettier than a picture," Ruthanna said.

"Speaking of pictures," Eileen said, pulling out her phone and snapping one. "It's perfect for your Insta."

AnnieLee was about to protest, but then Eileen knelt down and looked her in the eye. "We can handle the social media. Just think hard about who you are," she said gently. "And who you want to be. The truth—whatever that may look like—doesn't really matter. There's only what you tell us, and what you'll have us believe."

AnnieLee rubbed her hip, where there was still the faintest ghost of a bruise, a visual marker of a past that didn't want to leave her alone.

The truth doesn't matter? she thought. *If only it were that simple.*

CHAPTER
48

"All this for *us*?" AnnieLee asked, glancing around the clean white cabin of Ruthanna's small private jet. "Shoot, I was impressed by Delta. They had those cute peanut packets."

"A Bombardier's a little nicer than Delta," Ethan agreed. "And it's a *lot* nicer than hitchhiking."

"No kidding." AnnieLee set down her duffel bag and sank into her seat. "I still can't believe any of this is happening." She shot a warning look at Ethan. "But you don't need to pinch me again, in case you were thinking about it."

He held up his hands in surrender. "Never."

It had been an exhausting, exhilarating few weeks. First she'd moved out of the Pepto-Bismol motel room and into a rented cottage in the neighborhood of Hope Gardens; it felt like the first real home she'd had in years. And then, after talks with her manager, her lawyer, and her label, AnnieLee had released two more singles on the same August day. Though ACD had initially been against the idea, AnnieLee had insisted that the songs go out into the world together, like the A and B sides of an old-fashioned 45.

Even more unusual than a double release, the tracks weren't fully produced, perfected, and mastered. Instead, they were the ones that she'd recorded in Ruthanna's home studio: the Cellar Sessions, AnnieLee called them. People loved them, even more than she'd dared to hope, and an influential music critic tweeted that AnnieLee would be the next Taylor Swift—"but fierier and fiercer, with a voice so raw and gorgeous it'll make your jaw drop or your eyeballs leak. Or both." ACD was thrilled, and now— rather than release an EP—they wanted AnnieLee to write more songs so she could put out a full-length album instead.

Ethan waved a hand in front of her face. "Hello? Buckle up," he said, and soon the jet had risen above the clouds, where it then seemed to float as smoothly as if gravity had suspended its rules just for them.

AnnieLee gazed out the window at the endless blue sky. "I'm scared," she whispered.

"Try riding in an Apache over a Taliban stronghold," Ethan said.

"That sounds terrifying," AnnieLee said. "But I didn't mean I was afraid of flying."

She'd been profiled in *Rolling Stone's* "Ten Women to Watch Out For" feature, and so she was heading to LA for a photo shoot and an interview, which was far more frightening than streaking along at thirty-five thousand feet above the earth. Far too soon, the plane made its graceful descent, landing at Van Nuys Airport, twenty miles from downtown Los Angeles, where a car was waiting to take them to the photographer's studio.

On the top floor of a refurbished warehouse in the Arts District, Eileen Jackson greeted them like old friends—even Ethan, whom she'd never met but took an instant liking to.

I'm sure it has nothing to do with his smoldering good looks, AnnieLee thought wryly.

Eileen directed Ethan to go wait in the studio, and then she took AnnieLee by the elbow and steered her into a stark room lined with three large clothing racks, all of them full.

"As you can see, we've sourced pieces from a number of designers," Eileen said. "This is Rachel, who'll be styling you today."

Rachel was tall, pretty, and probably deliberately underfed. "Who do you like to wear, AnnieLee?" she asked.

AnnieLee looked down at her outfit: jeans, Fryes, and a T-shirt she'd stolen from Ethan that said CASH NELSON JENNINGS on it. "Don't you mean *what?*"

Rachel laughed as if AnnieLee had made a joke. "I meant which designers. Rag & Bone? Burberry? Oscar de la Renta?"

The stylist clearly had no idea what a ridiculous question this was. "Honestly, I don't give much thought to clothing," AnnieLee said, "as long as it covers the bits it's supposed to."

Rachel gave another bright laugh, although it seemed a bit forced this time. "No worries," she said. "We'll just play around, then." She slid several dresses off the rack to her left and laid them out on a table. "A classic little black number, something with a little flounce—and how about this Monique Lhuillier? Oh, and try this one, too. The garnet works great with your coloring. It'll make your eyes pop." She spoke over her shoulder as she kept thumbing through the clothes. "You can just change right here. Try this one, too. And this." Then she turned around and blinked at AnnieLee and the pile of dresses on the table. "All right, that's good for now, don't you think? I'll go grab shoes."

Then she was gone, and AnnieLee was alone among a couple hundred thousand dollars' worth of clothing. After a moment's hesitation, she undressed. She grabbed the black sheath that Rachel had picked and stepped into it. The fabric felt cool and elegant against her skin. She zipped it up, gathered her hair into a topknot, and stepped barefoot in front of the mirror. She turned this way and that, squinting at this new version of herself.

"You look like Audrey Hepburn!" Rachel exclaimed, coming back in with an armful of heels.

"Really?" AnnieLee said. "I think I look like I should be going to a funeral."

"Try the garnet Burberry, then," Rachel suggested. "You want to love what you're wearing."

The Burberry was beautiful, but it showed too much cleavage. AnnieLee didn't like the flouncy Carolina Herrera at all, or the minidress with the eyelet trim. Finally she slithered into the floor-length yellow gown that Rachel had picked out for her, and when she looked in the mirror, she almost gasped. It fit perfectly, from the graceful neckline to the way it skimmed her slim hips. The dress was exquisite, delicate—"totally handsewn," Rachel said proudly.

"Wow," AnnieLee whispered. "I didn't know I could look like this."

Rachel beamed at her. "Just wait until you get out of hair and makeup."

In another room, sitting before a huge, illuminated mirror, AnnieLee watched as a makeup artist rubbed bronzer and then blush into her cheeks, brushed smoky gray eye shadow onto her lids, and outlined her eyes in black kohl. A neutral lipstick with a touch of gloss made her mouth look lush and pouty. Then a stylist curled and sprayed AnnieLee's dark locks, arranging them into cascading waves with even more care than Poppy had taken.

Once the makeover process was complete, AnnieLee went out to meet the photographer, Tyson Mitchell, in the studio. He was standing in front of a carefully constructed set that looked like the dark corner of a dive bar, complete with a nicked table, two crooked chairs, and a handful of empty beer cans placed artfully here and there. A guitar leaned against the painted backdrop.

Tyson Mitchell held out his arms in delight as she approached. "You look like an absolute queen," he said. "I'd fall down at your feet, but my knees don't allow that kind of thing anymore."

Eileen giggled girlishly. "Tyson is a relentless flatterer," she said. "It's one of the reasons I love working with him."

But AnnieLee couldn't help staring at the complicated background and all the equipment necessary to capture it—and *her*. There were lights, umbrellas, softboxes, cameras, and fans. It almost looked like a movie set. She could feel the adrenaline tingling through her limbs.

"Are you nervous?" Tyson asked. "Don't be, darling. We're going to have so much fun."

"The idea is one of contrast," Eileen explained. "The dusty honky-tonk with the sparkling new talent. Glamour versus grit."

"Two-dollar beer versus two-thousand-dollar dress," Annie-Lee said softly. She was thinking about the first time she walked into the dive that was the Cat's Paw, hungry and desperate and smelling like a Popeyes. What would that AnnieLee think of this one?

She heard a surprised "Whoa" from behind, and she whipped around to see Ethan walking in, holding takeout from the taqueria on the ground floor. He looked her up and down in wonder.

"What do you think?" she asked, smoothing the dress self-consciously.

"You look incredible," he said. "And…really different."

Even as he said it, she knew that it wasn't a good thing. And she realized that she'd known it even before she walked out of hair and makeup. This glittering, made-up princess wasn't

AnnieLee Keyes at all. She still wasn't exactly sure what story she wanted to tell—she only knew it wasn't this one.

She looked at Eileen and Tyson. "You'll have to excuse me for a minute," she said.

Then she turned and tottered into the dressing room, where she took off the dress and put on her jeans and T-shirt. In the bathroom, she scrubbed off most of her makeup and ran a brush through her shining hair.

When she reappeared in the studio, Eileen gasped in what might have been horror. AnnieLee walked onto the set, picked up the prop guitar, strummed a loud, wildly out-of-tune chord, and grinned. She felt a million times better already.

"You said I ought to love what I'm wearing," she said. "And now I do. So let's get this party started."

I truly can't believe you did that," Sarah Ortega said. The *Rolling Stone* writer was young, with a black pixie cut, a nose ring, and tattoos of cascading stars across her knuckles. "Maybe that's my lede: How up-and-comer AnnieLee Keyes blew up a famous photographer's perfect shoot. Talk about a woman to watch out for!"

"Please, no," AnnieLee begged. They were sitting at the back of a cozy tea shop on West 3rd Street, and she was still wondering if she'd screwed everything up. Tyson Mitchell had ended up shooting her for two hours, but Eileen was convinced that AnnieLee's defiance would come back to haunt her.

"I didn't mean to. I just..." She stopped and took a sip of hibiscus tea. It was as bright red as Kool-Aid, but it sure didn't taste like it. "I just wanted to feel like myself."

Sarah placed a recorder on the table between them. "Look, I get it," she said. "And in a way, it's not even that surprising. Your songs are kind of defiant, don't you think? Like when you sing '*A rough road, we'll walk it. Never give up, we'll talk it.*'"

"Yeah, there might be some truth to that," AnnieLee allowed.

"And 'Driven' is almost painfully catchy," Sarah went on. "I belt it out whenever I'm driving to work, which sucks because I can't sing."

AnnieLee laughed and then glanced over at Ethan, who was sitting at a nearby table, seemingly reading a newspaper but more likely eavesdropping on their conversation. Eileen was supposed to be here, too, but there'd been an emergency with one of her other clients and she'd been called back to the office to do damage control.

"You've had your fun today, AnnieLee," she'd said as she ducked into an Uber. "So it's time to be nice and cooperative. Stay on message. Remember, the truth is what you want it to be."

AnnieLee intended to try. Now the question was only whether or not she could convincingly deliver the autobiography she'd constructed for herself while smiling for Tyson Mitchell's camera. Lies were dangerous—she knew that. But the truth could be even more so.

Sarah checked her device to make sure it was recording. Then she scooted forward, as friendly and confidential as a girl at a slumber party. "Okay, the big questions. Where'd you come from, and where are you going?"

AnnieLee took a deep breath. She'd rehearsed the story the way she rehearsed her songs. There was a verse of truth, and then a chorus of deceit. Or was it vice versa?

"I'm from Tennessee," she said. "From a place so small it didn't even have a real name. Some people called it Little Moon Valley, and some called it Old Mud Creek. My mother used to say that what you called it depended on your outlook." AnnieLee gave a slightly abashed laugh that she hoped sounded genuine. "To me, it was Little Moon Valley. It's a nice name, isn't it? Anyway, we lived off the grid pretty deep in the woods. My dad was a mechanic, but his real talent was music. He could play the banjo as good as Earl Scruggs himself." She paused then, letting a faraway look creep into her eyes. "My mom sang and played the guitar."

"Did you guys have a family band?" Sarah asked. "Like the Carters?"

AnnieLee laughed. *Yeah, right.* "Well, my folks were too busy making ends meet to play music as much as they might've liked. It takes a lot of sweat and time to grow your own food." She paused, and then added, "Or to hunt and kill it."

"So were you survivalists?" Sarah asked in a fascinated whisper. She said *survivalists* the way AnnieLee might've said *aliens.* She was clearly a city kid.

"Well, we didn't exactly use the term, but sometimes it did feel like surviving was just about all we were doing."

As she went on, talking about the beauty and hardship of growing up in the woods, AnnieLee could see Ethan out of the corner of her eye, sitting with his arms crossed and his brow furrowed. She knew what he was thinking: that she'd never told him anything, even though he'd asked a dozen times, but suddenly here she was, blabbing on to this stranger, answering every question as though she'd been waiting her whole life to be asked it.

How could AnnieLee explain to him that this was just another performance? He wouldn't get why she had to do it. And she couldn't ever tell him.

"AnnieLee?" Sarah's voice called her back to the interview.

"Sorry," she said, trying to regain her focus. "Okay, well,

here's the depressing part of my story, if you want to hear it. My parents are dead. The fields are full of weeds. The house still stands, but no one's in it. Unless you count some possum, or maybe a family of raccoons." As AnnieLee spoke, she could imagine the cozy cabin and the green meadow around it, and for a moment she mourned her happy wilderness childhood as if it had actually existed.

She shook her head, clearing the image. "Anyway. It was a fine place to grow up. But a valley in the middle of nowhere starts to feel small after a while, and I guess I started hoping that music might be my ticket out of there."

"It seems like it was," Sarah said. "Can we talk about the inspirations for your songs?"

AnnieLee was prepared for this, too. "They come from my life," she said. "And so they're true, but only up to a point. I want to tell stories that everybody can relate to. And I want to wrestle with the big questions, too—you know, ones about love, or about being brave, or about learning how to trust yourself."

"Maybe you'll write a song about refusing to wear a gown when you're told to."

AnnieLee laughed. "Who knows? I just might."

They talked for another half an hour or so until Sarah said that she'd gotten great material. They stood up and shook hands, and Sarah thanked AnnieLee for her time, and left.

"Finally," AnnieLee said, walking over to Ethan's table. "I'm starving. Let's go get burgers and milkshakes."

But Ethan only looked at her searchingly for a moment before shaking his head. "No, but thanks," he said. "I think I'm going to head back to the hotel. Our flight leaves early in the morning."

He strode outside, and she gathered up her things and

hurried after him, figuring that she could convince him to find an In-N-Out as they rode together in the hired car.

But though the car and driver were waiting for her outside the tea shop, Ethan Blake was nowhere to be seen. And she didn't lay eyes on him again until they got on the plane to go home.

CHAPTER

50

When Ethan opened the door to his truck, which he'd left in the Nashville airport's economy lot, a blast of hot, stale air rolled out. He gritted his teeth and slid onto the scorching vinyl seat. AnnieLee clambered in the passenger side, and a few seconds later, the engine started up with a roar.

"Are you going to talk to me now?" AnnieLee asked as Ethan piloted Gladys out of the lot.

He didn't say anything until they got onto the freeway. It took a little while for the old truck to come up to speed. "I wasn't *not* talking to you," he said.

She snorted. "Oh, okay, sure. You were just asleep the whole flight home, I guess."

Of course he'd been faking, leaning back with his eyes closed and a Merle Haggard playlist on his iPhone. He hadn't expected AnnieLee to fall for it, but he'd needed to be alone with his muddled thoughts and Merle's hard-living anthems. And she'd played along and let him be.

Now, as the early fall air came rushing in through the window, he wasn't any closer to figuring out how he felt about the trip, or his role as chaperone, or AnnieLee Keyes herself.

No, scratch that last part. He knew how he felt about AnnieLee; he just wasn't at all sure that he wanted to feel it.

He thought about the guitar he'd built in his garage workshop, with its dark slender body and its neck polished so smooth it felt like satin. He'd made it for her; he could admit that now. But he didn't know if it'd ever feel right to give it to her. It would be like handing her his heart.

"Hello?" AnnieLee said. "You're definitely not asleep now, seeing as how you're *driving*, so I don't know why you still aren't talking to me."

He couldn't help smiling. She was as funny as she was infuriating. "Fine. Tell me what you want me to say."

"Now that would just defeat the purpose, wouldn't it? If I told you the words that I wanted to hear?" AnnieLee asked. "But you seem to need help, so here goes. You could tell me what you thought of LA or give me your opinion on the hotel breakfast. *Or* you could explain why you've been ghosting me since the tea shop."

Ethan flicked on his turn signal, glancing in the rearview mirror. As he moved into the right lane, suddenly there was a black pickup behind him, so close it was practically riding Ethan's bumper.

"Whoops. Sorry, buddy," he said reflexively. "Didn't see you there."

AnnieLee threw up her hands and stared in obvious annoyance out her window. "Won't say boo to me, but he'll talk to the dude behind us who can't even *hear* him," she muttered.

"He has good taste in trucks," Ethan said. "The new F-150s are slick." He accelerated a little and looked sideways at AnnieLee.

"All right, if you really want to know what I was thinking, I'd say I thought the hotel pancakes were undercooked."

"You're so annoying," AnnieLee said. But a smile flickered at the corner of her mouth.

"You're one to talk," he said.

But he didn't know what to say next, and so they rode in silence for a while.

"I think I know why you're so quiet," AnnieLee finally said. "When you saw me in that dress, you were so stunned by my magnificence that it rendered you speechless for eighteen hours."

"Bingo," he said.

She was joking, yet in a way she wasn't wrong. She'd taken his breath away when he saw her in the studio. But her beauty had been so burnished, so glittering and unfamiliar. It was as if, at that moment, he realized how little he really knew AnnieLee Keyes. And despite all the time they spent together, he wasn't sure she'd ever let him get to know her better.

He turned on the radio, and Tim McGraw's voice came faintly out of the truck's old speakers. "Okay," he finally said, "here's what I was thinking. We see each other almost every day. We play music together. We've written lyrics together. But if I hadn't been sitting in that café yesterday, I wouldn't know any of that stuff about your life until I could read about it in a magazine. Don't you think that's weird?"

AnnieLee hesitated. "I think a lot of things are weird," she said, glancing in her side-view mirror. "Like why this jerk in the truck won't just pass us."

At first Ethan was annoyed that she seemed to be changing the subject. But then he looked backward and saw the black truck still there, not exactly riding his bumper, but almost, and he knew it wasn't right. Quickly, acting on instinct, he took the next exit off the highway. The truck followed, keeping a steady distance behind them.

Though Ethan couldn't see any real reason to worry, the back of his neck began to tingle. Some deep, subconscious part of him sensed the presence of danger. In Afghanistan, where gunmen could be around any corner or roads could suddenly detonate, that part of him had helped keep him alive.

Ethan made a right past the 76 gas station and then took a left on the next road without even seeing what it was called. He slowed, and the black truck slowed, too. He made another left, and then a right. The truck stayed behind them, maybe a little closer now. He squinted into the rearview mirror. It wasn't one of his friends messing with him, was it?

Whenever Ethan varied his speed, the black truck did, too; the same went for the turns. Whoever was driving certainly wasn't trying to pretend that he wasn't following them.

It couldn't be one of his friends.

Ethan looked over at AnnieLee, pale and now silent. He thought of the night she was mugged, and the night that she was attacked outside the bar. And he understood, suddenly, that these events probably weren't random after all. They were connected.

AnnieLee kept her eyes straight ahead, as if she knew what was happening but didn't want to see it. She held tight to the door handle. Her knuckles were white.

"AnnieLee," he said.

"Hush," she said curtly. "Just drive."

They were driving along a narrow road of modest ranch houses, somewhere between the airport and the city. Ethan sped up again, and so did the truck. He cursed under his breath. There was no way Gladys could outrun that thing, and he couldn't lead whoever this was to AnnieLee's place.

Ethan's fingers tightened on the steering wheel. There was one thing he knew he could do, one thing the driver would not be expecting.

"Hold on," he said to AnnieLee. He was about to turn a retreat into an attack.

As they neared a four-way stop, Ethan slowed to give a quick glance in all directions, and then he ran the stop sign. In the middle of the intersection, he swung Gladys all the way around, tires squealing, so he was heading straight toward the black truck. Ethan could almost see the driver's face, but the man responded quickly, whipping a screeching, tight U-turn. He barely stayed on the road, but then he regained control of the big truck and raced back the way they'd come.

Ethan slammed the gas pedal to the floor. Gladys shuddered and her engine screamed.

"What are you doing?" AnnieLee cried.

"Tactical vehicle intervention," Ethan said through clenched teeth. They were closing in on the truck, which was now stuck behind a slow-moving combine that took up a lane and a half of road. "I don't know about you, but I'd rather fight than run."

He knew how to do it: get right behind the truck, line up his front bumper with its rear one, and give it a gentle tap. If he timed it right, the big black truck would spin out but then come to a safe stop.

AnnieLee was yelling something at him, but all his focus was on driving. He was six feet behind the black truck, now five. Then it started swerving, making it impossible for him to get in position. He dropped back, paused, and accelerated again. Five feet, four—and then AnnieLee was suddenly halfway into his lap, her hands reaching for the wheel. He tried to push her away, but she grabbed the steering wheel and yanked it hard.

They went careening off the road and tore into the flat gravel of a construction site.

Ethan slammed on the brakes, and Gladys came to a shuddering stop. He turned to AnnieLee. "What the hell?" he yelled. "Why did you do that?"

AnnieLee's blue eyes widened, and he watched in shock and confusion as tears welled in them, overflowed, and went spilling down her cheeks.

CHAPTER

51

AnnieLee threw open the door, flung herself out of the truck, and ran stumbling toward the field on the far side of the gravel. She could hear Ethan shouting behind her.

"What the hell is wrong with you?"

Halfway into the tall grass she stopped and turned around. He was fifty yards away, standing with his shoulders hunched and his hands shoved into the pockets of his jeans. He looked furious.

Well, she was furious, too. Why on God's green earth had he decided it was a good idea to spin around and try to clip the back bumper of that truck? What kind of crazy cowboy move was that?

"If you don't come back and talk to me," he called, "I will leave you here!"

She didn't doubt him, and in a way, she wouldn't blame him. She'd nearly gotten them killed.

But none of it would've happened if he'd simply kept on driving her home the way he was supposed to, instead of trying to take matters into his own hands.

This wasn't his fight—it was hers. And she didn't want him involved.

"AnnieLee?" He squinted at her. "Can you please come here?"

She wiped her eyes and started walking back toward Ethan Blake. The tall grass scratched at her legs, and katydids flung themselves out of her way in huge, flying arcs. When she reached him, he took her shoulders in his big hands. His touch was firm but gentle.

"What came over you, AnnieLee?" he asked. He didn't sound furious anymore—he sounded tired and sad.

She didn't know what to say to him. At first she'd panicked when she saw that they were being followed. She knew who those men were and what they were capable of. But then she'd realized that they weren't going to hurt her—not then, not with Ethan there to protect her. They were just sending her another message. Reminding her that they weren't going to leave her alone. That no matter where she ran, they'd find her. And that in one way or another, they'd make her pay.

Fine, she felt like screaming. *I get the damn message.*

Ethan's grip tightened on her shoulders. "You have to tell me what's going on."

"I can't," she said.

"Is that because you don't know? Or because you won't tell me?"

AnnieLee stared down at her feet. Now that the adrenaline was fading from her limbs, her legs began to tremble. She felt almost nauseous.

Ethan dropped his hands. "Maybe I should call that *Rolling Stone* writer," he said. "Maybe you'd be able to tell her what's going on."

"That's not fair—"

"Not fair?" Ethan interrupted. "I'll tell you what's not fair.

You expecting me to be your sidekick and bodyguard but never—"

"I didn't ask you to do that! Ruthanna did," AnnieLee said, interrupting him right back.

"And you hated every second, didn't you?" he said, glaring at her. "You resented all the free rides home after your shows. You couldn't stand how I showed you around Nashville and helped you find a house to rent and furniture to fill it up. You couldn't stand my company."

"That's not what I meant," she protested.

"Did you know that I used to sit outside that crappy motel room of yours until you fell asleep? You thought you were so brave to stay there. But the whole time I was out in the parking lot like a guard dog. *Protecting* you."

AnnieLee inhaled sharply, as if she'd been punched. Of course she hadn't known. But what made him think he had the right to make her feel bad about something she'd never asked him to do? Instead of gratitude, she felt only anger.

"Well, you were on the clock, weren't you?" she said. "I'm sure Ruthanna paid you for your time. So the more hours you were watching me the better, right?"

Ethan turned away from her then. "Wow," he said. "I really don't know what to say."

AnnieLee kicked a toe into the gravel. "Maybe you don't enjoy your babysitting job anymore. Maybe you want to quit." Even as the words came out of her mouth, she couldn't believe she was saying them. She didn't want him to quit. She didn't know what she'd do without him.

Ethan took a step backward. His dark eyes grew darker. "If I quit now, you'll have to find your own way home," he warned.

But she couldn't back down. "Great," she said, tossing her head back. "I've missed bumming rides from strangers."

He took another few steps away. "AnnieLee..." he began.

"Just go."

She could tell that he didn't want to go any more than she wanted him to. But they were each stuck inside their own anger, and neither of them was going to give in.

"Go on," she said. "You don't have to worry about me."

"I've done a lot of worrying about you," he said. "But I'll try to quit that, too."

Then he walked away, climbed into his truck, and peeled off, spraying gravel behind him. And AnnieLee trudged back out to the road, pasted a bright, fake grin on her face, and stuck out her thumb.

chapter 52

Give me a chance, girl, open your eyes now, I'm not the enemy here
I'm a soft heart to lean on
A shoulder to cry on
Two good lips to kiss away tears

Ethan carefully folded up the lyrics he'd written on the back of an envelope. The song was a good one. But could it ever be true? Would AnnieLee ever really give him a chance?

Today he highly doubted it. He hadn't wanted to drive away from her, but she'd challenged his pride and forced his hand.

He thought back to the night he'd watched AnnieLee charm her way onto the Cat's Paw stage. If he'd known the havoc she'd wreak on his heart, would he still have introduced himself?

He could practically hear his grandma tsk-tsking him from heaven. *Yes, you would have, because when it comes to love you don't have the sense God gave a goose.*

He picked up an old rag and began oiling the fretboard and bridge of the guitar he'd finished right before leaving for LA.

He was trying to keep his mind open and empty, but the lyrics he'd tucked away kept swirling around in his thoughts.

Demons, demons, we've both had enough of our own
Demons, demons, we don't have to fight them alone

"I like that a lot," said a voice. "It's catchy."

Ethan spun around, startled by two things at once: that he'd begun to sing out loud without realizing it, and that Ruthanna Ryder was standing in his driveway, dressed as if she was about to have Easter brunch with the queen.

She shifted her weight from foot to foot, gazing up at the little apartment above his workshop. "So this is home, huh?"

Ethan smoothed his hair back and put aside the guitar. "For now," he said.

"I thought I paid you better," she mused.

"Please," he said. "You pay me plenty. I don't want anything more than this."

She turned her cool green eyes back to him. "But *desire*, Ethan, is where it all begins. If you don't want more, you don't get more."

He looked away. He wanted plenty of things, when it came down to it. But a bigger apartment wasn't one of them.

Then Ruthanna's face softened. "It looks like a nice place," she said. "Anyway, I had to come over because I broke the peg on my mandolin." She pulled a vintage instrument with a Florentine cutaway out of her handbag. "I thought you could fix it."

Ethan took the mandolin from her and knew instantly that this wasn't at all why she'd come. The instrument was student quality. She had a dozen better ones. This meant that she'd come because she'd spoken to AnnieLee, and the repair was only the excuse.

"Can you fix it?"

"Sure," he said. "Of course." He set it gently on his worktable.

Ruthanna folded her arms across her chest and looked at him. "So," she said, "you quit, huh?"

Ethan didn't bother defending himself by pointing out that AnnieLee had basically dared him to quit. "I don't think I should be her...whatever I was...anymore. It turns out we don't get along."

"Sounds like a lovers' quarrel, if you ask me," Ruthanna said, looking at him sideways.

Ethan snorted. "Hardly."

"It was nice of you to drop her bags off after she had to Lyft home," Ruthanna said.

Lyft, Ethan thought. *Is that what she said she did?*

And though Ruthanna was being sarcastic, he wouldn't take the bait. "Well, I'm nice. Too nice," he said. "Girls don't like the nice ones."

Ruthanna gave a great, braying laugh, and then she pointed a long pink nail at him. "Number one, that's a load of BS about girls. Number two, you're not *that* nice. And number three, I've got a job for you that'll help you prove exactly how not nice you are." She stepped closer and jabbed the nail into his chest. "You're going to talk to Mikey Shumer and find out what he knows about that black truck."

Ethan exhaled slowly. So this visit wasn't really about his argument with AnnieLee after all.

He knew Mikey Shumer—or knew of him, anyway. Mikey took talented, unknown singers and shaped them into hitmakers, skimming as much as he could from every check along the way. He drove a Mercedes-Benz SL65 AMG that cost upwards of two hundred grand, and he owned a fleet of vintage Mustangs and a penthouse condo in the Gulch. Meanwhile, his newest artists struggled to make rent, and he'd run at least two other managers out of town with threats and harassment. Ethan had encountered Mikey only once, but he knew him instantly for the kind of man who'd buy you drinks at a bar and then have you beaten to a pulp in the parking lot if it suited him.

In other words, this wasn't going to be a job Ethan would enjoy.

Ruthanna waited with uncharacteristic patience for him to say something.

Ethan picked up the rag and the guitar and started polishing again. "Okay," he said. "I'll go see him tomorrow."

"Thank you," Ruthanna said. "I knew I could count on you. Just…be careful."

"If he's scaring AnnieLee, he's the one who's going to need to be careful." Angry as Ethan was at her, he didn't want anyone messing with her.

"See? I knew you were the protective type," she said.

"You know just about everything, don't you?" he said.

Ruthanna flashed him a brilliant smile. "I've been around the block once or twice." She turned to go. "And I meant what I said about that song you were singing. I think it's got real potential."

CHAPTER

53

S ir, you can't go back there," the secretary called, but Ethan
was already striding down the office hallway, looking for
Mikey Shumer. He was almost to his door when two of the biggest men he'd seen since the army materialized out of nowhere
to block his path.

He pulled up short, sighing. He should've known this
wouldn't be easy.

Ethan took a step backward, holding his hands up in a gesture
of peace. "I'm here to see Mikey Shumer."

"Mr. Shumer's busy right now," the mustached one said. His
face looked as if it'd been carved from granite.

The bald man, who was shorter, just as muscular, and
ugly as a box of armpits, said, "Gotta make an appointment,
pretty boy."

Ethan hated being called pretty boy even more than AnnieLee
hated being called little, but he pretended he hadn't heard.
There was still a chance that this interaction would end well. "I
need to speak with him now."

"That's not possible," said Baldy.

"Real sorry, bro," said Mustache.

Ethan felt his hands clench into fists. He was coming up on the point of no return, and though he'd wanted to keep things civil, he wasn't leaving without talking to Shumer. He said, "I don't think you're sorry, and you definitely ain't my bro."

"That's it." The bald man slapped his enormous hand around Ethan's biceps and tried to shove him back in the direction he'd come, but Ethan shook him off. Mustache made to grab his other arm, but Ethan was done being touched by these goons. He swung at Mustache. The blow glanced off his jaw, but the attack took him by surprise, and he stumbled backward. The bald one reacted quickly, shooting a straight jab at Ethan's face. Ethan ducked, coming up again and bringing an uppercut from way down low to connect with Baldy's chin. Ethan's knuckles exploded in pain as he heard the man's teeth snap together. His head went back, he wobbled for a moment, and then he was on the floor.

Again Ethan faced Mustache, who was wary now, dancing around like a boxer. Big guys like these weren't used to being hit. But Ethan didn't have the time or inclination for a boxing match. He lunged forward, grabbed the man by the back of the head, and yanked Mustache's head down as he brought up his knee. Blood from the man's nose soaked Ethan's jeans.

The fight was over after that, and Ethan burst into Mikey's office, watching as the manager's face twisted under a barrage of emotions: disbelief, fury, and a grudging admiration.

"What the hell?" Mikey said from his chair behind his desk.

"They came at me first," Ethan said. He rubbed his sore knuckles. "I hate fighting, so I got it over with as quick as I could."

Mikey gave a low whistle. "Do you know the kind of retaliation I'm capable of?"

Ethan said, "I do," and left it at that.

Mikey looked down at his fists as if he was wondering if he should give them a go. But instead he cracked the top of a Red Bull and took a long drink. Then he said, "You must be a fighter."

"I boxed in the army," Ethan said.

"Class?"

"Middleweight." Ethan marveled that they suddenly seemed to be having a normal conversation, as if there weren't two giants in the hallway that Ethan had personally KO'd because he wanted to speak with Mikey without an appointment.

"Maybe I should hire you as my muscle instead of those jokers," Mikey mused.

"I don't think you'd like me," Ethan said.

"I like everyone, as long as they do what I want them to."

Ethan decided that there'd been enough chatter. "Are you harassing AnnieLee?" he said. "Because if you're trying to scare her into switching management and signing with your crooked operation, it's not going to work."

"Did Joe hit you in the head before he went down?" Mikey got up from his chair and walked over to the window. "Of course I'm not. I wouldn't waste my time."

"You wanted to work with her."

"I did, and if she was as smart as she thinks she is she would've signed with me," Mikey said. "But I don't hold a grudge."

"Yeah, that's what everyone in town says about you, especially the guy you dangled out a third-story window because you thought he was trying to poach your talent. 'Mikey Shumer, he's a real forgiving guy.'"

Mikey laughed. "You know what I think?" he said. "I think Ruthanna Ryder's getting paranoid. She's got no more career to keep her busy, so she cooks up conspiracy theories and sends you out to investigate them. How do you feel about being her errand boy?" He pitched his empty can into the wastebasket. "I hear you're a good musician. You ever try to do something with yourself besides dive bar open mics?" he asked. "I started Will Rivers, you know. He can only play about five chords, but his voice is good, and now he's got girls running up to him and asking him to sign their tits. Who knows? Maybe that could be you someday."

"No, thanks," Ethan said. "I'm good."

Mikey gave a dismissive wave. "You probably don't have what it takes to make it, anyway," he said. "Your little friend does. It's her loss she went with that old fossil Jack Holm."

"Well," Ethan said, "thanks for your time."

"Whatever," Mikey said. "Just don't let me see you around here again."

As Ethan moved to the door, he braced himself for an ambush. He figured he could sustain a few hits to the chest or stomach; he just didn't want to get punched in the face.

But when he got outside Mikey's office, the hallway was empty. He breathed a sigh of relief.

"Have a nice day," the secretary said as Ethan left.

AnnieLee walked along the Cumberland River, which ran green-brown and slow as it wound through Nashville. She passed joggers and dog walkers, little kids toddling behind their parents, and an old married couple creeping along with the aid of walkers. She hadn't slept well the night before, and she was trying to wake herself up with a giant coffee and a scone from the café on Commerce Street. So far it wasn't exactly working.

After a while she turned off the path and ducked into the trees, where little spots of shade provided relief from the sun, already blazing at 10 a.m. She was humming the song she'd almost thrown away—the one about the girl who'd hated being ignored until she found out that being noticed was worse.

I was invisible, invisible
Like shade at midnight, a ghost in the sunlight

Some songs came to her so fast it was like being jumped in an alley; others took months of frustration and hard work.

Encouraged by Ruthanna, AnnieLee had been working on this one for weeks, and she'd even played it in public. The experience had been nerve-racking for reasons she didn't want to dwell on.

Not to be cliché, but you could have heard a pin drop when you sang it. That was what Ethan had said, back when he was still talking to her.

But AnnieLee was resolutely *not* thinking about Ethan Blake this morning, because she'd already spent all night doing so. Every time her thoughts drifted in his direction, she pulled them back to the song. Something about the bridge wasn't right yet, and maybe the third verse wasn't so hot, either. She sang it softly, feeling the words take shape in her mouth as she kept walking, not paying attention to where she was going.

But then I grew up pretty and I grew up wild
Didn't look no more like a hungry child

Her phone rang, startling her. It was Jack.

"Are you sitting down?" he asked.

She felt her breath catch in her throat. "What's wrong?"

Jack's laugh came booming into her ear. "Nothing's wrong, kid," he said. "Like I said, you sittin'?"

AnnieLee shook her head, though he couldn't see her. "No."

"Well," he said, "you ain't got far to fall, I guess. So listen up. I've got you a chance to open up for Kip Hart."

AnnieLee gasped. Kip Hart had over a dozen certified gold albums, twice that many top ten singles, and his catchy "Live Fast, Love Hard" was *Billboard*'s number one country song of the previous year. She leaned against the nearest tree and then slid down it. Now she *was* sitting.

"You're kidding," she breathed.

"No, not kidding. Congratulations," Jack said. "You've got a date in Knoxville, and if it goes well, which I know it will, there'll be more."

AnnieLee squeezed her eyes shut tight and squealed like a little girl on Christmas. "Sorry," she said. "Did that hurt your ears?"

"Honey, I blew out my eardrums long ago," Jack said. "A hazard of the music business. I'm glad you're happy—you should be. Anyway, kid, I have to run. We'll do the details later." And then he was gone.

Holding back another scream of delight, AnnieLee opened her eyes as a crow squawked from a branch above. She looked around her, and suddenly she realized where she was: right near that smooth patch of dirt underneath the big old elm tree, the spot where she'd spent her first cold and lonely nights in Nashville.

A few yards away was the little hollow where she'd hidden her backpack as she wandered the city, looking for a place to sing her songs and a place to wash her face.

I'm back where I started, she marveled. *But now everything's different.*

CHAPTER
55

"T urn the offer down," Ruthanna said.

AnnieLee's mouth fell open. "What? What are you talking about?"

"You're not an opening act, AnnieLee. You're a star," Ruthanna said.

AnnieLee, who'd been idly pinching the flowering tops off the basil in Ruthanna's kitchen garden, stood up and put her hands on her hips. "I appreciate your belief in me," she said, "but I'm *not* a star yet. I don't even have an album out. I've got to work my way up."

"And you want to do that by playing second fiddle to a man?" Ruthanna challenged. "By warming up the crowd for a guy who can't write a song half as good as yours?"

"But he's huge," AnnieLee said.

"He's overrated," Ruthanna replied.

AnnieLee had assumed Ruthanna would be thrilled for her, and now she hardly knew what to say. She knew Kip Hart was no Hank Williams. No Willie Nelson or Brad Paisley or Kenny Chesney, either. But he commanded a big audience, and he was willing to share it with her. She had the chance to play for a crowd of thousands! Shouldn't she be jumping for joy?

"Sweetie," Ruthanna said, "when you were little, just learning how to sing along with the radio, women musicians sang about a third of the songs played on country stations. Now they're barely above ten percent. Things haven't gotten better since Tomato-gate—they're getting worse."

"I don't see what that has to do with me and Kip Hart," AnnieLee said.

"Kip Hart thinks he's better than you," Ruthanna said. "If he doesn't talk down to you, he'll try to get into your pants. Or maybe both."

"I dare him to try," AnnieLee said. "And I don't have to think he's a great guy, Ruthanna. I just need to sing some songs on that stage before he does."

Ruthanna folded her arms across her chest. "I don't like it," she said.

"But ACD loves it," AnnieLee said. "Aren't they kind of my bosses now?"

Ruthanna took off her sunglasses so she could look AnnieLee in the eye. "Don't ever let anyone else be your boss."

"That's a heck of a lot easier said than done," AnnieLee said. "Especially when there's lawyers and money involved."

AnnieLee heard Maya calling from the kitchen, and Ruthanna turned to go inside. "I know it is," she said. "Look, hon. I just want what's best for you. Maybe this is it, but maybe it isn't. There's more than one way up the ladder. You go on home and think on it a little more, okay?"

AnnieLee said she would as she gathered up her keys and bag. But she knew the decision had already been made for her, by her management and label. Okay, it wasn't perfect—but what ever was? It was her next big shot. Even if she could hold out for the ideal opportunity, she very well might be waiting forever. She wanted the opportunity that was in front of her right now.

Opening for Kip is a good thing, she thought as she drove home. *A great thing. Ruthanna can't tell me otherwise.*

When AnnieLee got back to her little rental cottage, Ethan was sitting on her front steps. She felt her heart give a lurch. She wanted to fling herself into his arms and celebrate her news. Too bad she was still mad at him, and he was probably still furious with her.

She stopped a few feet away and looked at him warily. "Did Ruthanna send you? Because if you're here to try to talk me out of opening for Kip Hart, it's not going to work."

"Why would I do that?" Ethan asked. "I came to say congratulations. It's great, AnnieLee, and you deserve it." He stood up and brushed off his jeans. "And I brought you something."

He walked over to his truck, and when he came back he was carrying a guitar. It was small and dark, and its polished wood softly gleamed. Mother-of-pearl inlay circled the sound hole and decorated the fretboard. "For you," he said, holding it out.

"Really?" She took it from him. It felt warm and smooth— almost alive. "It's beautiful," she said. "Is this really for me? I've never seen one like it. Where'd you get it?"

"I made it."

She stared at him. "You're kidding."

"Nope."

"No one's made me anything since my mom sewed me dresses in elementary school." She ran her fingers along the inlay, marveling at its detail. "Not that I even appreciated those dang things. I wanted clothes from the store like everybody else. But this—this is incredible."

She sank to the steps and cradled the guitar in her lap,

strumming G, then C, then D. The instrument had a silky, golden sound.

"I can't believe it," she whispered. She felt like crying.

Ethan stood watching her, and his foot began to tap as she played the opening bars to "Lost and Found," the song they'd worked on together in New York.

"It's probably not a stage guitar, since you've got Ruthanna's Taylor," he said. "It's more for songwriting, alone, late at night, when only the moon knows what you're up to."

She blinked, pushing back grateful tears, and then beamed up at him. "I love it. Thank you, Ethan Blake. And…I'm sorry."

He hunched his shoulders. "Me, too."

And then he sat down next to her and started to sing along.

Lost and found, unchained, unbound
No more second guessing, I know who I am
Now I'm on solid ground

CHAPTER
56

They didn't speak of their fight again, and Ethan resumed his duties as if quitting had never even occurred to him. Early in the mornings, he drove to Ruthanna's, where he and the band played the songs she couldn't keep from writing, retirement be damned. Depending on when they finished their studio session, he'd bring AnnieLee lunch or dinner at her cottage, where she was working on her own music day and night. ACD kept sending her songs written by professional songwriters, ones with track records of charting hits, but AnnieLee was certain that her material was better. She was a songwriter first, she said, and a performer second. "I wouldn't be me if I sang someone else's songs."

Busy as she was, she got a kick out of pretending that it was ridiculous of Ethan to bring her takeout every day. "Oh, it's the meals-on-wheels guy again," she'd say, laughing.

But Ethan had seen AnnieLee in her kitchen, and as far as he could tell, she barely knew a colander from a cantaloupe. Left to her own devices, she'd probably survive on canned beans, Pringles, and the occasional multivitamin at best.

Her gig as an opening act was less than a month away, and Ethan knew she was feeling a tremendous amount of pressure. No matter what Ruthanna believed about the relative talents of AnnieLee Keyes and Kip Hart, the fact remained that he was a mega-selling country hotshot, and she was still the new kid on the block. She had a lot to prove, and she knew it.

Gladys coughed as Ethan pulled up and parked in front of AnnieLee's house. Tonight he was bringing fried chicken from Arnold's Country Kitchen as a treat for them both. He knocked on her bright-red door, waited, and then knocked again. It took a few more minutes before AnnieLee appeared and said, "God, that smells good. I knew I forgot something today."

"Not even breakfast?" Ethan asked, stepping into her living room, the entire floor of which was covered in notebooks, pencil stubs, paper scraps, and guitar picks.

"Nope," she said. "Totally slipped my mind. But I've got this killer lick, and now all I need is, like, the riff, the melody, three verses, a chorus, and the bridge. We can figure that out tonight, right? Plus a title? Something like 'You Never Saw Me Coming.' Or 'It's a Long Way to the Top.' No, never mind: those stink." She had a pencil tucked behind each ear and two holding her hair up in a messy bun. She was bouncing on her toes and talking a mile a minute. She probably had more coffee running through her veins than blood.

"I think AC/DC beat you to that second title anyway," Ethan said. He set the take-out bags on the pinewood table he'd helped her assemble. "How about you take a break and have some dinner, and then you can play me what you're working on?"

She nodded. "Okay, okay, I can do that."

Ethan went into the kitchen to fetch plates, napkins, and utensils. As he grabbed two beers from the refrigerator, he noticed that AnnieLee had taped a photo of Kip Hart to the door. He recognized her handwriting scrawled across the bottom in Sharpie: "Don't embarrass yourself—or me. Love, KP."

He was chuckling when he walked back to her. "I like your motivational poster," he said.

"What?" she said. "Oh. That. Yeah, I made it at three o'clock this morning."

"You should be *sleeping* at three o'clock in the morning," he chided.

"Couldn't," she said. "Too much coffee." AnnieLee took the pencils out of her bun, and her hair fell in a shining dark cloud around her shoulders. "You know, I've been reading about Kip Hart. He's got a couple of ex-wives and two dozen former writing partners, but no one seems to have anything bad to say about him."

"Maybe he's a nicer guy than Ruthanna thinks he is." Ethan had his doubts, but he'd be happy to be proven wrong.

"I hope so," AnnieLee said. "Lord knows I've known more than enough mean ones."

Ethan didn't press her for any more information. He wouldn't get it, and anyway, it wasn't as if AnnieLee was the only one who had secrets. He had to remind himself of that sometimes.

She dug through a take-out bag to pull out the coleslaw. "I wish you guys were coming with me."

Kip Hart's management had made it clear that the singer was playing a stripped-down tour, in smaller venues, and that he wanted a solo opening act. Donna, Melissa, and Stan had been disappointed, but neither Elrodd nor Ethan had much wanted to be up on that stage. Let Kip Hart take a vacation back to his humbler roots; they could stay in Nashville and play in Ruthanna's basement—and at the Cat's Paw, if and when they felt like it.

"How many songs you got now?" Ethan asked.

"Eight that are rock-solid," AnnieLee said. "Two more that are so-so. I'm getting there." And then, with a half-mad gleam in her eye: "Unless I scrap everything and start all over again."

"Don't you dare," Ethan said. "And no more caffeine for you tonight, okay?"

AnnieLee nodded, slathering butter on a biscuit and grumbling about bossy know-it-alls.

When they were done eating, she walked over to the battered spinet piano that the previous renters had left behind. "Check this out," she said, and played a handful of high, tinkling notes that reminded Ethan of the opening bars to Patsy Cline's "Crazy."

She stopped and turned around. "See? Isn't that nice? I don't know what to do with it yet, but one of these days we'll have to get back down to the studio. We can put Stan on keyboards."

Ethan wanted to sing with AnnieLee again almost as much as he wanted to pull her into his arms. But neither of those things seemed likely to happen any time soon.

"I like it," he said, "but seeing as how you won't have a piano with Kip Hart, let's work on that other lick you were talking about."

They parked themselves on her couch and worked through songs until 2 a.m., when Ethan stood up and announced that he was going to the bathroom and then straight home. When he came back into the living room less than five minutes later, he found AnnieLee asleep against the couch's armrest, surrounded by lyrics, crumpled papers, and crumbs from Arnold's Country Kitchen biscuits.

He stopped and looked at her for a while. He'd never seen her so still, so peaceful. The chorus of his song came to him in the silence.

Lost and found, I'm safe and sound
No more drifting aimlessly, I've settled down

Then he carefully picked her up and carried her into her bedroom, where he took off her boots and covered her with a blanket. Without opening her eyes, she burrowed into her pillow, breathing slowly and calmly, as if she didn't have a care in the world.

He wished that could be true for her. But he knew that it wasn't.

He bent down to kiss her smooth, untroubled forehead, and then he quietly let himself out, making sure the door was locked behind him.

On the day of the Kip Hart show, AnnieLee woke before dawn. A light, misty rain was falling. She poured herself a glass of orange juice and paced her cottage as she drank it, feeling nerved up and jangly, like an animal about to be freed from its cage. Though Ethan had come to visit every day for the past month, she'd been working so hard that she'd barely left her living room.

Even if everything else goes wrong tonight, she told herself, *at least you'll be out of the damn house.*

She was making her fiftieth circuit of the room when she heard the doorbell chime. She opened the door. Ethan Blake stood on her stoop, his car keys dangling from one hand and a tray with two giant take-out coffees in the other.

"The way Gladys runs, it's about three hours away without traffic," he said.

"Ruthanna loaned me a car, remember?" AnnieLee said. "I'm good."

Ethan scuffed his toe against the doormat that said WELCOME

Y'ALL. "You ever been to Knoxville before? The coliseum's in a weird part of town, and parking might be confusing."

"If you're suggesting that I'm liable to get lost, Ethan Blake, let me remind you that I've been on this earth for two and a half decades and I'm not an idiot."

"Believe me, I know you're not an idiot, AnnieLee," he said. "I guess I just thought you might like a little company."

She softened then, telling him that she appreciated the offer, but she needed to do everything herself today. What she didn't say was that it'd be impossible to call up all the fearlessness and shamelessness she needed if Ethan came with her. Having just herself to rely on was what she was used to. And it was the only way tonight would work.

He looked disappointed. "At least take the coffee," he said. "Don't drink it on an empty stomach, though. This is Maya-strength brew."

"Aye, aye, Captain," she said, grinning.

He didn't smile back. Instead he reached out and gently brushed her bangs from her eyes. "Good luck tonight," he said. "I'll be thinking about you."

Impulsively she leaned forward and kissed him on his freshly shaven cheek. "Thank you," she said. And then she ducked back inside, closing the door behind her and hoping she wasn't crazy to turn him away.

Five hours later, she was standing in the wings at the Knoxville Civic Coliseum, listening to Kip Hart and his band run through their sound check as roadies and technicians finished assembling the stage for the night's big show. Two videographers kept their cameras pointed at Kip as he played "Runaway River," and then his party number, "Chasin' Tailgate."

AnnieLee couldn't help tapping her feet to that one, and she sang the chorus as she hurried back to her dressing room to get ready for her performance.

You and me in a parking lot
Let me pull you close, let me show you what I got

She laughed as she ran a brush through her hair. What a stupid song! And yet…it was catchy; she couldn't deny it. It almost made her want to dance.

She was sitting in front of the mirror, putting on a touch of mascara, when the door opened. In the reflection she saw Kip Hart himself enter the room, without so much as a knock or an invitation.

"Hey there," he said. "Sorry, but I figured since the door was unlocked…"

"Oh, oh, sure," AnnieLee said, stammering just a bit, thinking, *Ain't you learned to lock doors by now, girl?* And *I can't believe it.* Kip Hart *is in my dressing room.*

In person, the singer was more handsome than she'd expected. He was tall and long-limbed, his clothes were carefully rugged, and he carried himself like a man used to being admired. As he strode over to the couch and straddled its cushioned arm, she couldn't help but notice his hand-stitched boots. They'd set him back a solid four figures—she was sure of it.

"Do you know what happened when the country singer sang his song backward?" Kip Hart asked her. He pulled a pack of cigarettes from his pocket and tapped one into his palm. "He got his dog back, his truck back, and his wife back."

AnnieLee laughed, though she'd heard Billy tell that joke about five hundred times. That, plus the one about how it takes two country singers to change a lightbulb: one to do the work, and one to sing a song about the good times he had with the old lightbulb.

"So you're the famous AnnieLee Keyes," Kip Hart said, gazing at her.

"Oh, I sure wouldn't say that," she said.

"Well, everyone seems to think you're hot shit."

AnnieLee turned back to the mirror and swiped mascara onto the lashes of her left eye. "Have you heard me before? What do you think?"

She knew it was bold to ask him such a thing. But it was also pretty audacious to barge into a girl's dressing room half an hour before she was supposed to go onstage.

"Tonight'll be the first time I have the privilege." He put the cigarette in his mouth and lit it, winking at her.

"There's a No Smoking sign," AnnieLee blurted.

Kip laughed. "That sign's not for me, pretty girl," he said. "It's for all the bastards who aren't famous."

"Oh," AnnieLee said. She put a slick of gloss on her lips and then wiped it off again. She didn't like being called pretty girl, but at least he hadn't called her little.

Kip leaned forward as if he was about to impart a great secret. "You're new to this game, so let me just say that the more successful you are, AnnieLee, the better life gets. I was once like you. Scrappy and hungry, begging for buy-ons like this one. Those were fun times." He gave a great guffaw. "Just kidding. They sucked bull's balls. But you know what? I miss 'em anyway." He stood up. "All right, I'll leave you to it. Good luck tonight."

When he was gone, she let out the breath she'd been holding.

A buy-on? How had it not occurred to her that that's what this was?

Of course Kip Hart hadn't called her label and invited her to play with him because he was a big fan of hers. ACD had called *him*—and they'd offered to pay good money for her to warm up his crowd. And somehow no one had seen fit to tell her this, and she'd been too dumb to guess.

Damn it, she thought. *You thought it was about your talent. But it was really about someone else's cash.*

CHAPTER
58

AnnieLee gave a final check to her outfit as she stepped out of her dressing room: Levi's, a new pair of Frye boots, and a black T-shirt with sequined sleeves that Ruthanna had given her the week before.

"I bought it for Sophia," Ruthanna had said, pressing it into AnnieLee's hands. "I thought she might wear it onstage someday. But now it'll be you to take it up there instead."

The shirt looked good on her, but she would've worn a paper bag if Ruthanna had asked her to.

"AnnieLee Keyes on in three," said a stagehand, brushing past her.

AnnieLee felt a jolt of nerves so sharp it was like she'd just touched something electrified. Closing her eyes, she took a few slow, deep breaths. Her heart was pounding so hard that it ached. But after a minute the pain lessened, and she slung the guitar strap over her neck.

She walked down the hallway, flanked by men with headsets and ID badges who were saying things to her that she didn't catch. All her attention was focused on the murmur of the crowd, which grew louder with every step.

Right before she stepped onto the stage, she paused and sent a whispered prayer to the sky. *Don't let me screw this up.*

The spotlights were still off as she came out of the wings. It seemed to take ten whole minutes to walk to center stage. She stopped behind the mic and stood trembling in the darkness. She couldn't see the audience, or how many of the seats were filled. She could only see hundreds of blue, glowing screens.

All right, she thought, *you're in a huge room full of people, but they're so busy playing Candy Crush they don't even know you're on yet.*

She touched the mic stand to steady herself.

Breathe in, breathe out. Stop holding the guitar neck like you're trying to strangle it.

Then the spotlights slammed on, and AnnieLee was blinded by their glare. She froze like a deer in the road, not even breathing anymore, utterly overwhelmed. She'd never even had tickets to a concert like this before—and here she was up onstage. How the hell did this happen?

AnnieLee could hear scattered, distracted clapping. She glanced behind her, as if looking for invisible reinforcements. It felt as though someone's hands were closing around her throat.

Then she reminded herself of the countless hours she'd spent preparing for this night—not over the past month, but for two whole decades of her life. The first rehearsals began back when she was six years old and got her first beat-up plastic-stringed guitar from a church rummage sale. And she'd been anticipating a night like this ever since she wrote her first song, a sweet little rhyming ditty about a bee who fell in love with a flower.

You belong here, she told herself. *It doesn't matter how you got*

here, and it doesn't matter that you're not the one they came to see.
You belong.

She loosened her death grip on the guitar neck and gazed out
at a crowd she couldn't see on the other side of the spotlights'
glare. And then she started to play.

Is it easy?
No it ain't
Can I fix it?
No I cain't
But I sure ain't gonna take it lyin' down

As the song went on, she could sense the crowd's attention
turning toward her. People's phones pivoted up to take pictures
and record. AnnieLee could feel everyone's new appreciation,
and she didn't want that energy to end. Hoping not to break the
spell, she went straight into the next song without a pause, pulling the audience along with her. She played "Driven," and then
"Dark Night, Bright Future," and as she moved into the first
verse, she could see three teenage girls in the front row, loudly
singing along. So she sang right to them, holding out the mic
once in a while so their voices rang through the coliseum, too.

Everyone knows happiness
Everybody grieves
We all cry, we all smile
Everybody bleeds
Everybody has a past, things they want to hide
There's give, take, love, hate in each and every life

Six thousand people were in the room that night, and her
music called out to each person. She sang joyfully, and then

fiercely, and she could feel the way her voice soared and keened. She was electrified in a whole new way, and she never wanted the show to end.

But obviously it had to, and for her final song, AnnieLee danced around the stage playing Ruthanna's hit "Big Dreams and Faded Jeans."

> *Put on my jeans, my favorite shirt*
> *Pull up my boots and hit the dirt*
> *Finally doin' somethin' I've dreamed of for years*

The song was older than AnnieLee, but it seemed as though everyone in that giant room knew the words.

Then it was time to hand over the mic to the star, Kip Hart. But the applause for AnnieLee was thunderous. She took three, then four bows, and then she ran from the stage, triumphant.

A roadie held out a bottled water. "How d'ya feel now?" he asked.

AnnieLee took a long, grateful drink and then said, "Shoot, if I felt any better, I'd drop my harp plumb through the cloud!"

He laughed. "Think you might like to do it again sometime?"

AnnieLee looked straight at him, totally serious now. "Honey," she said, "I'm only getting started."

CHAPTER
59

Too thrilled and wired to sleep in a hotel room, Annie-Lee drove back to Nashville that night. She fell into bed at 4 a.m. and didn't wake until the afternoon. Even then, she didn't get up, but stayed warm beneath her down comforter, still feeling the faint electric buzz of her performance.

She'd been good and she knew it. Hell, she'd been great. She wondered where Kip would ask her to play next. Virginia? North Carolina? She didn't want to go back to Texas, but she'd certainly consider it.

Eventually she sat up and checked her phone. There were voicemails from Ethan, Jack, and Ruthanna, which she decided to listen to after she'd had her coffee. Then she checked the Instagram account that ACD had insisted Eileen set up for her.

AnnieLee didn't do the posting, but she had agreed to regularly text her publicist pictures, and Eileen had already put the ones from last night into her feed. There were a handful of backstage photos, plus a few shots that the stagehands had taken from the wings. These were blurry and slightly under-exposed, but AnnieLee had told Eileen that she wanted her

Instagram pictures to have the feel of casual snapshots. She didn't want anything filtered or Photoshopped or Facetuned, or whatever it was people did to make everything look better than it really was.

"I want to post the truth," she'd said, "or as near as I can get to it."

And though Eileen had hoped for a more carefully curated and slick-looking feed, she'd clearly decided to take what she could get.

AnnieLee scanned through the comments to the one semi-selfie she'd taken right before going onstage. It was a shot of half of her face, taken in the mirror, with a streak of light falling across her shoulder.

Ur so pretty, said one commenter.

OMG I wanna be you when I grow up, said another.

There were star emojis and handclap emojis, and people begging her to tour through their tiny midwestern towns. AnnieLee hearted all the comments and then got up to make herself breakfast.

She was in such a good mood that she didn't understand what Jack was saying in his message when she finally listened to it. She had to play it over and over again, in disbelief.

He had been driving, and so his voice was cutting in and out. "Kip...disappointed in the performance...different direction...future concerts. Sorry, AnnieL—"

She stood by the stove, stunned, as the French toast blackened in the pan.

It took the ringing of the phone to bring her back to herself. It was Ruthanna, and AnnieLee was already crying by the time she said "Hello."

"There's a video of the performance on YouTube already," Ruthanna said. "You damn near sang the roof off."

AnnieLee took the pan from the stove top and dumped the contents into the trash. Her kitchen was full of smoke now, and so she banged outside and stood shivering in her bare feet and pajamas. "If I was so good, why doesn't he want me back?"

"You just answered your own question right there, AnnieLee," Ruthanna said. "You outshone him. Maybe it wouldn't have happened if he was up there with his regular giant band and his big ol' pyrotechnic show. But this tour was supposed to be a simpler, smaller affair. And then you got up there with your tiny self, all alone, and you just blew everyone away with your big voice and your powerhouse songs. What man wants to follow that? Not Kip Hart. Not anyone I can think of."

AnnieLee stepped farther into her little backyard and stood beneath its one tree. A fall breeze kicked up, and a shower of red-gold leaves swirled down and around her.

"I was so worried about screwing up. I didn't think playing a great show would be the problem."

"Everyone's got an ego," Ruthanna said, "and stars' egos are usually the biggest and the most easily wounded."

AnnieLee caught a spiraling leaf and ripped it into tiny pieces. "*You* were never threatened by me," she said.

Ruthanna laughed. "I'm retired, don't forget. But if I were still playing out, I like to think I'd welcome you with open arms. I happen to believe there's enough love—and enough ears—out there for all of us." She paused. "You done good, kid. Don't let Kip Hart take that away from you."

After they hung up, AnnieLee went back inside and flung herself down on the couch. Hurt and angry, she picked up her phone again and went to her Instagram account.

That ol' hat act should've opened for *you*, said bellacatlady.

Damn right he should have, AnnieLee thought.

I've got a good fiddle part for Driven, said honest2goodness mandy.

DM it to me, AnnieLee wrote.

I know who you really are, said ark_north.

AnnieLee's breath caught. She looked down at the next comment.

Some songs can get a girl's jaw broke, said bax990.

AnnieLee dropped the phone as if it had turned into a snake. Every time she managed to forget all that she'd left behind, the past reared its mean, ugly head.

She got up and started digging through her old backpack. She pulled out old notebooks and holey socks and the musty sleeping bag that had once been her bed. Near the bottom of the pack, she felt the cold metal of the Smith & Wesson, and her fingers closed around it.

AnnieLee had never liked guns. But maybe it was time to start keeping hers closer.

W ell, well, well. What brings you back to these parts, little songbird?" Billy asked as AnnieLee came into the Cat's Paw, practically blown through the door by the blustery October afternoon.

"Not *little*, Billy, remember? Sheesh," AnnieLee said. "I'm meeting Ethan. We had a hankering for your French fries." She looked around the familiar, welcoming room as she climbed onto a barstool. There were only a few other customers scattered around, and Willie was playing on the stereo. She'd missed the festive Christmas lights, the smell of Bar Keepers Friend, and gruff but warmhearted Billy himself. "He's late, so that means he's buying."

Billy put four maraschino cherries on a little plate, shoved them toward her, and then poured her her usual drink of club soda with lime. "I was starting to think you'd forgotten about us," he said.

"Never ever," AnnieLee said. "I'm eternally grateful to you, remember? You gave me my first break." She looked at him ruefully. "But my so-called big break? Well, it didn't quite work out the way I thought it would."

"I'm sorry to hear that, kid. But no cowboy ropes every steer, if you know what I mean. Or cowgirl—whatever. And I still hear you on the radio, so you can't be doing that bad."

Maybe not, AnnieLee thought, but she'd like to be doing a whole lot better. Thanks to new expenses like cottages and publicists, she was still just scraping by. And ACD was mad about Kip Hart, even though they'd seen the footage and they knew it was hardly her fault.

She popped one of the cherries into her mouth. It was so sweet it made her teeth hurt. She cocked her head toward the stage. "You got anyone playing tonight?"

"I'm giving my ears the night off," he said. "If *you* were going to offer, though, now that would be something else."

She laughed. "I'm taking the night off, too," she said.

There was a bang from the back of the bar. Startled, AnnieLee nearly leaped off her stool. Billy glanced up in alarm as the emergency exit door swung open. But it was only Ethan striding in, followed by Ruthanna, her face nearly invisible behind huge sunglasses and a headscarf.

"Well, I'll be damned," Billy said. "Ten years she didn't set a high heel in this place, and then you come to town and she's practically a regular."

AnnieLee took a casual sip of her drink as if they hadn't just scared her half to death.

Ethan waved. "Sorry, we had to sneak in the back," he said. "I didn't want a mob following us in." He glanced around at the other customers. "These guys in here gonna be cool?"

"Yeah, they've pretty much only got eyes for their beers."

While AnnieLee was thinking about how weird it would be

to have to disguise yourself in order to walk into your own bar, Jack came in the front with a huge bouquet of sunflowers.

"What the heck?" AnnieLee said to Ethan. "I thought it was just you and me and a bucket of fries." She was still processing the Kip Hart fiasco, and she'd been hoping Ethan would make her feel better about it.

"We figured you could use some cheering up," Ruthanna said, freeing her spectacular hair from its silk scarf. "Surprise!"

"Well, shoot, I left the party dress that I don't own at home," AnnieLee said.

They all sat down together at a table near the empty stage. Jack pulled out Ruthanna's chair for her, and Ethan pulled out AnnieLee's, and she bit her tongue so she wouldn't say something sarcastic about how she couldn't have *possibly* moved that big ol' chair with her tiny lady arms.

Sometimes chivalry is just nice, she reminded herself.

"We'll take a round of martinis, please, Billy," Ruthanna said.

"And six orders of fries," Ethan shouted. Then he turned to Ruthanna. "I'm telling you—'Flowers' by Billy Yates."

"Ethan and I are having a disagreement about which country song is the saddest," Ruthanna told Jack and AnnieLee. "He's wrong, of course, but he's mule-stubborn. Everyone knows the saddest song is 'He Stopped Loving Her Today.'"

"What about 'Chiseled in Stone' by Vern Gosdin?" Jack asked.

"How about 'Gypsy, Joe, and Me'?" AnnieLee said. "That one sneaks up on you."

"Oh, you're so right!" Ruthanna exclaimed, nodding. "The tempo's upbeat, and it's got those climbing key changes. If you weren't listening to the lyrics, you'd think it was a happy tune." Then she smiled slyly. "Ten bucks says I can make someone cry if I sing it."

"Deal," said Ethan.

"Done," said Ruthanna. She walked over to the bar and said, "Billy, you got that new guitar I had sent over?"

"Sure do, ma'am."

"Well, give it to me, why don't you? And don't call me ma'am."

Ruthanna came back to the table and sat down, holding the guitar gracefully in her lovely, manicured hands. She strummed the opening bars, and then she began to sing.

We might have slept in the mayor's yard or camped by the river bank
We fed ourselves from the fruit of the land and quenched our
*   thirst with rain*

The words lifted and curled over the notes of the guitar, and everyone in the bar held their breath. The customers who hadn't even noticed Ruthanna come in stood suddenly frozen, awed, as one of the greatest country singers in the history of the genre sang to them in her angelic voice, just to win a bet.

By the time the song was over, AnnieLee's eyes were stinging and Jack was clearing his throat as if something was stuck in it.

"You win," Ethan said.

Ruthanna looked triumphant. "Damn straight I do. Cough up the cash."

Ethan handed her two fives as Billy, who'd been standing as still and awestruck as everyone else, brought over the food and drinks. Everyone pounced on the French fries, including Ruthanna. Jack put barbecue sauce on his pile, which Ruthanna told him was disgusting, and then the two of them got into a good-natured and obviously old argument about who had weirder taste in food, considering that Ruthanna thought hot sauce was acceptable on virtually anything.

"I once saw her put it on a *salad*!" Jack exclaimed to the room.

AnnieLee, listening in amusement, took a sip of her martini and then spluttered a little.

"What do you think of it?" Jack asked.

She grimaced. "It's sort of like what I'd imagine nail polish remover would taste like."

"Take a few more sips and you'll start to like it," Jack said, raising his glass to her.

They talked, teased one another, and traded jokes as the food and drinks kept coming. And for the first time in weeks, AnnieLee felt happy, a deep-in-her-bones kind of contentment. It was wonderful not to think about anything besides being there in that dim, quiet bar with the people she'd grown to love.

Then Ruthanna raised her glass and said, "I'd like to make a toast to my favorite firecracker, AnnieLee Keyes. Congratulations, kid."

"Congratulations for what?" AnnieLee said with her mouth full of fries. "Getting fired by Kip Hart?"

"Hardly," Ruthanna said. "See, Jack and I have been keeping a little secret from you today. You want to know what it is?"

AnnieLee washed down the fries with a gulp of her martini. "Yes, please, and hell yes," she said.

"ACD and Jack have worked out a deal, and they're going to send you on a twelve-city tour of your own. Small venues, but really good ones. So congratulations, girl, and Godspeed."

Ethan gave a gleeful whoop before AnnieLee could even react, and then Jack said, "You're forgetting something, Ruthanna," as he put his hand affectionately on top of hers.

Ruthanna smiled and kept her hand where it was. "The other thing you might care to know, Ms. Keyes," she said, "is that I'll meet you at your final performance in Las Vegas. And you and me are going to sing a few songs together."

AnnieLee felt her stomach drop down to her knees. "You're kidding."

"I most certainly am not."

"So you're coming out of retirement?"

"No, I'm just taking a break from it." Ruthanna glanced over at Jack. "We thought it sounded like fun."

Jack nodded. "That we did."

Ethan said, "I can just imagine the two of you, harmonizing on 'Blue Bonnet Breeze.' There won't be a dry eye in the house." He grinned. "Maybe I ought to make a few bets on that in Vegas."

"Who says you're invited?" AnnieLee challenged him.

He put his arm around her and squeezed. "You better let me come with you this time."

AnnieLee let her head fall against his shoulder. "I'll think about it."

CHAPTER
61

Merle Haggard had once called his career a thirty-five-year bus ride, and after barely more than a week, Ethan could sympathize with the man. Towns flew by, faces blurred together, and he couldn't remember the last time he'd eaten something that didn't come out of a paper bag that was handed to him at a drive-through window. Why hadn't anyone told him that they should've asked for fresh fruit, or at least a few carrot sticks, in AnnieLee's hospitality rider?

ACD wouldn't spring for a driver—a small tour required small expenditures, after all—so piloting the Sprinter van had become yet another one of Ethan's jobs.

"At least it means you get to come along," AnnieLee had teased him.

He definitely didn't mind the duty. But, unused to sitting still for hours in a row, he'd taken to drinking one kind of caffeinated beverage or another from the moment he woke up until he switched to beer at five. He also kept a bag of sunflower seeds in the door pocket because getting those little bastards out of their shells with his teeth gave him something to do besides hold the steering wheel steady.

"Whoo-ee, turn that Cash up!" AnnieLee shouted from the passenger seat.

"Are your arms broken?" he teased. "You do it. I'm driving."

Grumbling theatrically, she turned up "Sunday Morning Coming Down," and then she sang along with it at the top of her lungs, in a thick hillbilly accent, as they drove west along I-40.

Even when she was goofing off, her voice was wonderful, Ethan thought. And despite the boredom of driving and the exhaustion of the late nights, being on tour with AnnieLee could be a hell of a lot of fun.

Two hours later they were pulling up in front of Cain's Ballroom in Tulsa, Oklahoma. Beneath a vintage neon sign advertising long-defunct ballroom dancing classes, they unloaded the guitars and guitar stands, amps, pedals, extension cords, DI box, cables, loopers, and tuners.

"Can you imagine how hard this'd be if we had the whole band?" AnnieLee asked as she lugged a speaker down the hall.

But Ethan knew that she missed them, and that she wished they could have come on the tour. As far as ACD was concerned, though, the musicians who had played on AnnieLee's singles were an avoidable expense.

Once their gear was loaded in, Ethan went to meet the sound guy. He made a point of treating these men (they were always men) with special respect, since they would control how AnnieLee's voice and guitar sounded during the show.

Cain's sound guy, Jerry, was burly and talkative, and after AnnieLee's sound check, he invited Ethan to the bar for a quick pint. Hank Williams and Willie Nelson had played at Cain's, Jerry told him proudly, and Johnny Paycheck had gotten in one of his many fights there, and Bob Wills and his Texas Playboys had broadcast a radio show from its stage for eight years.

"Folks called it the Carnegie Hall of western swing," Jerry said.

Ethan had seen the pictures of Bob Wills, Ernest Tubb, and other departed stars on the walls, and as he looked around the big room, with its high, arched rafters and polished maple floor, he imagined he could feel their benevolent spirits in the air. Those musicians would've liked AnnieLee—Ethan was sure of it.

When he and Jerry had finished their beers, Ethan went to find her. She was backstage eating the potato chips that her rider did stipulate (she'd admitted to him that they were her favorite food) and scrolling through emails on her phone.

"Eileen sent me a review from Memphis the other night," she said, looking up at him from underneath tousled bangs. "The writer said I had the eyes of a saint and the voice of an angel."

"Did they happen to mention your heart of a hellcat and tongue of a serpent?" Ethan asked as he grabbed another beer out of the mini fridge.

AnnieLee laughed and threw her sweatshirt at him. It hit the side of his face, and in that instant, he smelled her—the scent of lilacs, pine, and sunshine. He didn't throw the sweatshirt back.

"Can I play in my socks tonight?" she asked. "My boots are too tight."

"I think you know the answer to that question," Ethan said, opening the beer and taking a long, cold drink.

"How about barefoot? Hillbilly style?"

He just shook his head. AnnieLee had learned a lot from Ruthanna, but she couldn't be convinced to care about perfect stage makeup or glamorous costumes. "If it doesn't matter what I look like when you're listening to me on the radio," she'd say, "why should it matter when we're in the same room?"

Ethan could see her point, but he felt that shoes onstage were nonnegotiable.

So AnnieLee wore her too-tight boots for her performance that night, along with a pair of loose jeans and a low-necked T-shirt that showed her delicate collarbone. He watched her stride onto the stage, gaze out at the crowd and up to the rafters, and then give the room a smile as bright as any spotlight. The crowd cheered, and she began to play.

"A rough road, we'll walk it," she sang.

"Never give up, we'll talk it."

Her voice seemed even fuller and richer than usual, and in between songs, she joked and bantered with the audience as if they were old friends. She was a born performer, Ethan thought. She fed off the crowd, and she grew more energized the longer she was onstage.

He was leaning back, relaxing and letting the music flow over him, when he heard his name coming through the PA. The front legs of his chair banged hard on the floor as he sat up, suddenly alert.

He looked over and realized that AnnieLee was staring at him from center stage. "You gonna come give me a hand or what?" she said into the microphone. Then she turned to the crowd. "Don't you want to hear my friend help me out with a little harmony?"

The answering applause made it clear that Ethan had no choice in the matter.

Man, he thought, getting up and shaking himself out a little, the way he used to do before a boxing match. *She really should've warned me. I would've done a shot.*

But then he jogged out onto the stage and took the second guitar from its stand. For a second, the instrument felt as foreign to him as the first rifle he'd ever held—like something he had no idea how to use. But then AnnieLee smiled her beautiful, wild smile at him, and his nerves eased. He knew how to do this; he'd done it a hundred times before. Smaller crowds, sure, and local ones—but did that really matter? He stepped up beside her and put his mouth to the second mic. He'd even remember to introduce himself this time.

"Hello, Tulsa," he said. "I'm Ethan Blake, and usually I'm just the chauffeur these days. But tonight I guess AnnieLee and I are gonna play a song for you."

He looked over at her. Her eyes were shining.

"I don't know about you," she said to him, "but I'm feeling like we should honor the woman who brought us together." She turned back to the crowd. "That's Ruthanna Ryder, everybody— and I know you all love her as much as I do."

As the crowd cheered, AnnieLee strummed a chord progression that Ethan instantly recognized. Tapping his foot to the beat, he joined her in song.

Big dreams and faded jeans
Fit together like a team
Always bustin' at the seams
Big dreams and faded jeans

He leaned into the microphone, the spotlight bright in his eyes, the stage solid beneath his boots, and AnnieLee by his side.

I could get mighty used to this, Ethan thought.

CHAPTER
62

Ethan rode high on their duet until they were heading back to their hotel at midnight. He was gliding down Cincinnati Avenue when he felt a sudden prickle of alarm along the base of his scalp. He glanced in the rearview mirror at the lights of the car that had been following him for several blocks. They didn't belong to a black truck—he could see that much. But this didn't necessarily reassure him. Camouflage was easy; anyone could rent a different car.

He looked over at AnnieLee. Her eyes were closed, her feet were on the dashboard, and she was softly singing the song she'd helped him to write.

Lost and found, I'm safe and sound
No more drifting aimlessly, I've settled down

She had no idea that he was worried, and he decided to keep it that way. He looked behind him again. *Maybe I'm just being paranoid*, he thought.

Without signaling, Ethan made a few leisurely turns so that he was now heading in the opposite direction. He passed a Dollar Tree and a gas station, and then a car lot, its empty vehicles gleaming under the streetlights. Whoever was driving the car behind him kept close, and AnnieLee remained oblivious. Soon she wasn't singing anymore. But it wasn't because she'd noticed anything. It was because she'd fallen asleep, her head against the window, cushioned by the jacket he'd given her.

Ethan was glad that she could relax, even as he felt the chill of certainty crawling over his skin. It wasn't paranoia on his part. Someone was following AnnieLee, and this wasn't even the first time he'd sensed it on tour.

He knew it wasn't Mikey Shumer. Crooked as Mikey was, Ethan had believed him when he'd said he had nothing to do with it. Mikey Shumer wouldn't waste his time or his money, not when he could nab the next hungry up-and-comer, especially one who'd be less stubborn than AnnieLee.

So who could it be? A fan with stalker tendencies? A crazy ex-boyfriend?

Who is it, AnnieLee? he thought. *And why won't you tell me?*

Still he drove, turning here and there, as if he hadn't already driven six hours today and then played part of a show he hadn't been expecting to play. The yellow lines wavered in front of him. His eyeballs felt as dry as dust.

Finally he couldn't take the slow-speed car chase any longer. He pulled into the parking lot of a Pizza Hut and waited to see what would happen next.

The car behind him—a Chevy Impala—slowed, and then it stopped in the middle of the road. Ethan tensed, waiting for it to follow him into the lot. He started to reach under AnnieLee's legs for the knife he kept in the glove compartment. But then, with a squeal of tires, the car sped off, its brake lights disappearing into the darkness.

Ethan sat back with his hands gripping the steering wheel. *Maybe*, he told himself, *it was just a pair of teenagers having their dumb idea of fun.*

Maybe.

Beside him, AnnieLee stirred. "Are we at the hotel yet?" she asked.

Ethan put the van back into gear and pulled onto the road. What she didn't know wouldn't hurt her. And he was there to protect her.

"Almost, AnnieLee," he said. "Almost."

CHAPTER
63

"Take a picture of me, will you?" AnnieLee asked, whipping her knitted cap off her head and holding out her phone to Ethan. She'd stopped on the sidewalk in front of the State Room in Salt Lake City, Utah, beneath a sign proclaiming in big black letters TONIGHT ANNIELEE KEYES. "It's my first actual marquee," she called. "Come on, cowboy! *Cheese!*"

Ethan dutifully took a few photos with her phone and then looked down at the screen. "You're squinting in every single one of them," he said.

"That's okay," AnnieLee said, cramming her hat back onto her head. "When Eileen told me to send her pictures for my so-called tour diary, she forgot to say they had to be good."

"You might be the least vain person I've ever met," Ethan said. "Dudes included."

AnnieLee took this as a compliment and told him so. "I'm trying to sing the truth, aren't I? So it'd be weird if I didn't show it, too."

"But you could keep your *eyes* open in a picture," Ethan said, sounding ever so mildly exasperated. "No one would say that's not telling the truth."

AnnieLee laughed. He had a point, of course, but she didn't have any interest in looking good in the photos. Her voice alone mattered to her. As far as she was concerned, beauty was little more than a liability.

AnnieLee spun around on the sidewalk with her arms out. It was so good to be out of the van that she felt like bursting into song. Salt Lake was a nice town. Hell, every town was a nice town. It was the highways in between them that were driving her crazy.

That, and the deep, unwelcome feeling that she should always be looking over her shoulder.

She worked hard to ignore that feeling. Most days, she was successful. She'd played ten good shows, and Jack said ACD was very happy with their decision to send her out. *There's nothing to worry about*—that's what she kept telling herself.

"So what's in this tour diary?" Ethan asked, bringing her back to the present moment. "You written anything about me yet?"

She stopped spinning, and the world tilted around her. Was she crazy, or was Ethan looking at her as if he hoped the answer was yes?

"It's just photos," she said. If he'd asked her whether she'd written any *lyrics* about him—well, that was a different story. "Love or Lust" was straight up about that man, not that she'd cop to it. "But I've taken a lot of pictures of you. Take a look if you want."

Ethan held out her phone. "I'm not going to just scroll through your photos."

"Why not? I've got nothing to hide." But this was an outrageous thing to say, and they both knew it. "At least not on my photostream," she added.

"Right," Ethan said. "You're a regular open book."

AnnieLee flinched a little at the hurt she heard in his voice, but she didn't protest. She took the phone back and tucked it into her pocket. *What I'm not telling you?* she thought. *Believe me, you don't want to know.*

She hunched her shoulders against the cold wind blowing up State Street. There was new snow in the Wasatch Mountains.

Ethan saw her shiver. "Well, we should probably go on in and make nice," he said.

"I guess we should," AnnieLee agreed.

She followed him through the door, politely shaking hands with everyone as Ethan introduced them both, but her thoughts had already turned toward the upcoming show: how big was the room, how were the acoustics, and how many of the seats would be filled?

But Ethan was naturally gracious, and he never seemed curt or hurried. He easily ingratiated himself with all the promoters and managers, and he'd dealt with their road troubles—a flat tire outside Wichita, a mild bout of food poisoning somewhere in rural Colorado—with good humor and patience. He was the steadiest man AnnieLee had ever known.

She glanced down at her phone, wondering what Ethan would do if she showed him all the threatening Instagram comments. There were new ones every day now. Would he call the police? Try to cancel the tour? Find the nearest Cabela's and buy a gun? She'd brought her own Smith & Wesson, hidden inside the makeup kit she barely ever opened, but that was another secret she was keeping.

AnnieLee's publicist had tried to reassure her that the messages didn't really mean anything, and that lots of younger artists—women especially—attracted strange and sometimes menacing online attention. "I know it's not fair," Eileen had said.

"It's how the world is, unfortunately. But our team is on top of it. They'll delete and report all inappropriate comments from creepy random strangers."

And they were doing their best. But what Eileen didn't know, of course, was that the comments weren't random, and they weren't from strangers. And that by posting tour dates and pictures to Instagram, Eileen was making it easy for AnnieLee to be found.

Or maybe the better word was *stalked*.

Even though she knew it was a bad idea, AnnieLee opened Instagram and checked her DMs. There was a link to the fiddle recording she'd asked the young musician to send her, an offer from an aspiring designer to send her some outfits, and a hundred sweet little fan messages full of hearts and praising hands emojis.

And then, as she'd known she would, she saw a new anonymous message, sent from the world she'd left behind. It was a picture of an unmade bed, and lying on the rumpled sheets was a curved and gleaming knife. Rose watch out, the note said.

CHAPTER
64

S he didn't think the message would rattle her—not really. It wasn't like it had been a physical attack. But as AnnieLee was putting her hair into two long braids, she saw that her hands were shaking. How was she going to keep her old life from ruining her new one?

Too soon it was time for her to go onstage.

She stepped out in her uncomfortable boots, waving and smiling, as the audience clapped and some rose from their seats in welcome. Blue and violet shafts of light beamed down from the lighting rig as she put her hand on the microphone in its stand, her guitar dangling from its embroidered strap. She opened her mouth to greet the room, but no sound came out.

AnnieLee cleared her throat, trying to quell the rising fear. She felt like she was outside her body, floating off to the side, looking at her small frame all alone on that big stage.

Poor girl, she thought. *She's in way over her head.*

Letting go of the mic, AnnieLee put her hands on the cool, solid wood of her guitar. She played a loud, bright chord to make the noise her mouth couldn't. A few more: E, F sharp 5,

G5, G sharp 5, and then A. Then her throat opened again, and she could speak.

"Hello, Salt Lake City," she said. "Sorry about that little hiccup—I think I got a Pringle stuck in my throat." She smiled brightly. "One of the hazards of touring, I guess. Constant low-level dehydration and a real excess of potato chips." She could hear a little waver in her voice as she spoke. "Anyway, I guess I'll shut up and play for you now."

As she strummed the intro to "Driven," she wondered if the audience could see the way her legs were shaking. She started to sing, but she had trouble calling up the lyrics. She skipped the second verse, and was as surprised as everyone else seemed to be when the song ended after two minutes.

"Well," she said, feigning breezy nonchalance, "I wrote it, so I guess I'm allowed to change it up now and again, right?"

But her chest began to burn with dread. And she knew that the tenser she got, the more mistakes she would make. There were three hundred people in the room who had paid to see her, and she couldn't let them down. She had to find her flow.

They don't want to watch you fail, she thought, *so don't make them.* She picked the beginning to "Firecracker."

Firecracker, I heard you callin' me
Firecracker, that suits me to a T

The song was up-tempo, and she could feel herself gathering a bit of momentum.

I'm full of fire and passion, wound tight and aim to please
But if you want to play with fire, be mindful and take heed
Standin' up for who I am and all that I believe

By the time the song was over, her legs had stopped trembling and her voice was coming out clear and strong. But she still felt vulnerable. Exposed. The audience was on her side—she'd won them over, at least until she screwed up again—but she couldn't tap into their energy.

She turned toward stage left, where Ethan was waiting just beyond the curtain. She couldn't see him, but she knew he was there.

He was always there.

And right now she needed him closer.

She called him out onstage, just like she'd promised she wouldn't do again, at least not without warning him. She saw him come shuffling out, more than a shred of reluctance to his step, and she motioned for him to come right to her side.

"I'm sorry," she whispered. "I really need you."

He nodded, head bent, concentrating on what she was saying.

"We're going to sing 'Love or Lust,' and we're going to do it on the same mic, okay?" She looked pleadingly at him. "I don't want to be alone up here tonight."

Ethan touched her elbow gently, fleetingly. "I guess you won't be, then," he said.

And then he stood so close to her that she could feel the heat of him all along the left side of her body, and their voices were instruments that they played together.

Love or lust
Do we doubt, do we trust?
Whatever it is, it's stronger than us

As they sang, she could sense the way the air in the room changed. A hush settled over the crowd. They were seeing something almost unbearably intimate: two people singing with and to each other, alone in front of hundreds of strangers. Two people who looked for all the world like they were in a love so deep there weren't even words to describe it.

Though they had rehearsed the song a hundred times, in hotel rooms and on empty stages, they hadn't rehearsed it like this.

When the music ended, the applause was so loud and long-lasting that AnnieLee and Ethan stood there, blushing, unable to say anything over the noise.

Then AnnieLee turned to Ethan. "Thank you," she mouthed.

He picked up her hand and kissed it. And then he left the stage.

CHAPTER
65

By the time they arrived at their hotel, AnnieLee was a delirious mix of elated and exhausted. The show had been teetering on the brink of disaster, but she'd pulled it back from the edge. She hadn't let the threats from her past drag her down.

As she and Ethan rode up in the elevator together, though, she grew quiet, almost shy. The reason that the show had worked, of course, was that she'd called Ethan onto the stage. She didn't mind admitting that he'd saved her; she didn't have a Kip Hart–sized ego. But if she scratched below the surface of that fact, she'd be forced to acknowledge that it wasn't about the song they'd sung. It wasn't about the lyrics or the pleasing thirds of their harmonies. It was the *way* they had sung them. It was as if they were lost in their feelings for each other, and nothing else—not even the audience— mattered.

What exactly *were* her feelings for Ethan Blake? That was something she wasn't ready to think about, let alone discuss with him.

But as they unlocked the doors to their adjoining rooms, AnnieLee found herself turning to him. "Do you want to come in for a drink?"

He barely hesitated. "I kinda think you owe me one, don't you?" he asked.

"Yeah," she said, nodding. "I do."

They walked into her hotel room, which looked like every other hotel room they'd been in: dark wooden furniture, a king-sized bed, a sultan-sized TV. AnnieLee kicked off her boots and opened the minibar. "What's your poison tonight?"

Behind her, she heard Ethan taking off his jacket. "Is there any whiskey in there?"

"Of course there is," she said, scooping up all six bottles at once. "Want to get us some ice?"

While he was gone, she poured two mini Jack Daniel's into each of their glasses, and then she stood in front of the mirror and looked right into her own eyes.

Don't let this go too far, she told herself.

In the bathroom she washed her face, took out her earrings, and pulled her long hair up in a knot on the top of her head.

When she came back into the room, Ethan was sitting on her bed. He must have seen the surprise on her face, because he said, "Not to be forward or anything, but there's no couch." He held out her glass, full of ice and whiskey now. "Cheers," he said. "It ended up being a great show."

She clinked her glass against his. "Thanks mostly to you," she said. She took a sip and shuddered. She still wasn't used to hard alcohol.

"Don't be craz—"

"Don't be selling yourself short," AnnieLee interrupted. "You saved me up there."

Ethan put down his whiskey and shoved his hands between

his knees. He, too, seemed suddenly shy. Embarrassed, even. "I was just doing my job."

"You're doing the job of ten men," she corrected him. "And I don't know if you know how much it all means to me."

She'd never spoken so directly to him before. Ethan looked down at his hands. Then he jumped up and took her guitar out of its case.

"When was the last time you put on new strings?" he asked.

She fell back on the bed and stared up at the ugly light fixture. *Fine,* she thought, *let him change the subject.* They weren't really in the habit of deep honesty, were they? No wonder he was unsettled. She was, too.

"I've never changed them," she told the ceiling. "I found that guitar in one of Ruthanna's closets, and I just started playing it."

Out of the corner of her eye she could see that he was looking at her like she was nuts. "It's a great guitar, but who knows how old the strings are? You could've popped one onstage. You need a new set." He started pawing around in the giant messenger bag he always carried on tour. It was full of bottled water, snacks, picks, batteries—and, apparently, a new set of Martin guitar strings. "I'll take care of it."

AnnieLee sat up. "Are you ready for another drink?"

"I wouldn't say no."

She looked at her own glass, which was emptier than she'd thought it would be. She figured she might as well get herself another while she was at it.

She flicked through television stations while Ethan changed her strings, and then he paced her room like he was casting about for something else to fix.

AnnieLee turned off the TV. "There's a spiderweb up there in the corner," she said, teasing him.

He looked at her uncomprehendingly. "What?"

"You were looking like you needed another job."

He laughed. "Sorry. I don't sit still much—unless I'm driving, that is."

"Try," she said softly. She took another drink of whiskey. She still didn't like the taste, but she liked the way it softened the edges of things. Her limbs felt looser, and she'd suddenly stopped worrying quite so much about what might happen next.

She patted the edge of the bed next to her. After a moment, Ethan came over and sat. Not too close, but not very far away, either.

Something was about to shift—AnnieLee could feel it. Beside her, Ethan held himself very still. She inched toward him on the bed. Like a diver at the edge of a high board, she paused: did she dare?

She dared. She put her hand on his leg and her head on his shoulder. She felt him inhale sharply.

"I have to tell you something," he said.

———

E than let his breath out, slow and steady. "I had a wife," he said.

He allowed that sentence to hang in the air for a moment, those four small words filling the room. "We were young—too young—but that's not how we felt. We were so sure of ourselves. We thought we knew everything." He shook his glass so the ice swirled and clinked. "Her name was Jeanine Marie. She went by Jeanie."

He risked a glance at AnnieLee. Her eyes had a faraway look in them, as if she was trying to imagine who he was back then. It felt like a lifetime ago, but he could still see himself perfectly, nineteen years old and crazy in love, with Jeanie by his side, glowing in her mother's wedding gown as they were married on a North Carolina beach.

It was still easy for him to call up those good early days. He told AnnieLee how they lived in a little two-bedroom brick house on a quiet street in Fort Bragg. Life on an army base wasn't that different from life in a regular small town, he explained. He'd loved the community, the routine, and the sense of purpose. He even loved the predawn ruck marches. But most of all, he loved going home to Jeanie at night.

He thought he might have sensed AnnieLee flinch ever so slightly when he said that. But it was the truth, and he owed it to her.

"I got deployed, though," Ethan said, "and suddenly there were thousands of miles between us. A seven-hour time difference. And completely different lives. She was working out at the gym and playing poker with the other wives, and I was sweating in hundred-and-sixteen-degree heat and watching my back for snipers. Seeing my friends get wounded or killed or just go plain crazy."

Ethan paused. He could go down that combat hole if he wanted to; it was a deep one. But there wasn't enough whiskey in the state of Utah for him to talk about the war *and* his wife tonight. That was just too much pain to bear at once. So he circled back to Jeanie.

"She took up with another man while I was gone," Ethan said. "A man who outranked me. I was furious. And when I came back, all we did was fight." He felt his hands clenching in his lap. "Maybe I should've just let her go. But I really thought we could fix things. I believed what I'd said on our wedding day—you know, till death do you part."

He looked up at AnnieLee. There was no way to sugarcoat it. "And death is what it took," he said.

AnnieLee sucked in her breath. "Go on," she whispered.

"It was winter. Not too late at night—I remember hearing taps, which they always played at nine—but I was drunk already. Walking around the neighborhood, I was looking at all those windows lit up gold against the dark and thinking how there were happy couples inside all of them. And there I was, cold and lonely, wandering the streets like a stray dog. I thought

I'd made a life for us, but it had all fallen apart when I wasn't there to keep it together."

He took another slug of whiskey. "When I got home that night, the back door was open. Jeanie was lying on the bed, and I thought she was asleep. I tried to wake her up to tell her that I was sorry. That she could go be with that other guy if that's what she needed. That all I wanted was for her to be happy." His throat ached with the telling. But he knew he wouldn't cry. He'd done that enough already. "But she was dead."

"Oh, Ethan," AnnieLee said.

She reached for him, but he flinched away. The story was about to become a darker one, and he knew that her expression would change from pity to suspicion.

"Jeanie had been strangled," Ethan said flatly. "And two days later, they arrested me for her murder."

"Ethan, I—"

But he didn't want to hear whatever she had to say; he had to keep telling the story. "I spent six months in jail before my trial," he said. "I can't tell you how bad it was, thinking I'd be convicted of killing the woman I loved. It was worse than war, worse than my parents dying, worse than anything I could've imagined."

"But—but you were acquitted?" AnnieLee's voice was a whisper.

Ethan smiled grimly. "Yes, or else I wouldn't be here. But the case was never solved. And I carried that…stain. People didn't look at me the same after that. And it just felt like my whole life was gone." He took another drink. "I guess because it was. Like it was blown up by a bomb."

Ethan got up from the bed and went to the door. He was going to leave before she asked him to. "So that's what I had to tell you," he said. "I'm going to go now."

But AnnieLee said, "No," and she came over and stood beside

him. She reached out and took his hand. Hers was so small, hardly bigger than a child's. But her fingers were warm and strong, and they squeezed his tightly.

"I know," she said. "I mean—I knew all this before."

He turned to her in shock. "What? But how?"

"Ruthanna told me," AnnieLee said. Her eyes searched his face. "I'm sorry. I know it wasn't her story to tell. But I asked her. I asked her to tell me where you came from."

Ethan didn't know whether to feel relieved or furious. How could Ruthanna tell—and how could AnnieLee pretend she didn't know? "And it doesn't matter to you?" he asked.

"Of course it matters," she said. "It matters like crazy, because it was a terrible thing that happened to you. And it was an even more terrible thing that happened to her. I'm so sorry, Ethan. I know you can't ever get over something like that." She pressed her free hand against his heart. "But it was never going to scare me away."

CHAPTER

67

E than stepped back from the doorway. "Maybe it's time you told me your story," he said quietly.

AnnieLee pulled her hands away, as if he'd suddenly burned her. She turned and walked unsteadily into the bathroom, where she splashed more water on her face. Were revelations tit for tat? Was that how he thought things worked? Did he really want her to dredge up the stinking muck of her past?

She wouldn't do it. She couldn't.

Whoever said time heals all wounds is full of shit, she thought. Those wounds were still there, buried beneath scar tissue and denial. Ethan had his scars—sure. But hers were so much worse.

Where was her damn whiskey?

In your guts—that's where, she told herself. *That's why your glass is empty.*

AnnieLee didn't know how much she'd drunk, only that it was too much. There was no Jack left in the minibar. She reached in and got rum.

Just in case, she thought.

Then she straightened up and looked at Ethan Blake. "It's

funny," she said. "You might think there's no way things can get uglier, but somehow they always can."

Ethan frowned in confusion. "Are you talking about this? Now? Us?" He gently took the rum bottle from her hand and set it on the dresser. She didn't protest.

"No," she said. "I'm talking about me. Back then." She flopped down on the bed. She was exhausted, and all she wanted to do was sleep. But Ethan had been honest with her, and she knew she had to give him something in return. It wasn't ever going to get easier.

Her fingers picked nervously at the comforter. "I guess I should tell you that I'm not from Tennessee," she said. "I'd never set foot in the state until I showed up last spring. So in case it isn't obvious, Old Mud Creek doesn't exist. Little Moon Valley, either, though it sounded so nice I sort of wish it did. I lived on a hilltop, though—not in a valley. Nothing but trees all around, and a stream that ran down to the Little Buffalo River." She closed her eyes. "God, I need some water."

She heard Ethan leave the room, and then a moment later he nudged her arm. "Here," he said. "Drink it all."

She sat up, opened her eyes, and took the glass from him. "How bad's my head going to hurt tomorrow?" she asked.

"Depends," Ethan said. "Keep talking."

"Where was I?"

"You were telling me where you grew up," he said. "And you were about to tell me how."

She found a loose thread on the comforter and began to tug on it. "It's going to sound like a real familiar story," she said, "but there's nothing I can do about that. I can't make it into a clever song. Believe me, I've tried." Then she got up and began to walk back and forth beside the bed. "My dad left when I was seven. You would've thought aliens abducted him, the way he vanished.

He left everything: his tools, his guitar, the motorcycle he built from parts. Hell, they even found his car two hundred miles away in Texarkana, so I guess he left that, too." She eyed the rum on the dresser and then thought better of it. "I was almost too little to grieve, you know? Or maybe I just don't remember those nights I cried for him. Anyway, my mom remarried, and things were all right for a few years. But Clayton, my stepdad, started to get mean. By then I had two little half sisters running around barefoot and dirty, and it was my job to keep them from getting lost in the woods or drowning in the creek. I was sixteen when Clayton decided I had to teach them, too, because he said that school would corrupt us." She pulled her hair out of its bun and then twisted it up again. "He was pretty sure we were corrupted anyway, though, and he thought the best way to rid us of sin was to beat it out of us."

She didn't mention that Clayton was the only one guilty of anything in that family. Wasn't that always how it went?

"Where was this?" Ethan asked.

"Does it really matter? This kind of thing happens every-where." Then she fell back on the bed. "Arkansas. Caster County. Dear God in heaven, I'd rather eat sixteen buckets of weevils than go back there for a single day." She sighed. "But someday I might have to."

She stared up at the ceiling again. Would that bit of her past be enough to satisfy him? She was tired and drunk and she didn't want to talk anymore.

"I get it," Ethan said quietly. "But I still have a few questions, AnnieLee. Like how and when you got out, and whether or not somebody from there might be trying to get you back."

She squeezed her eyes shut again. "That part I can't tell you about," she said. "Not yet. Maybe not ever."

CHAPTER
68

That was all she would say, and she was relieved that Ethan didn't press her any further. Instead, he'd gotten up from the bed, kissed her on the cheek, and wished her a good night. She'd passed out immediately, still in her clothes and not even under the covers.

She woke up late and stumbled down to the lobby for the free continental breakfast. Her head ached horribly, and she kept her sunglasses on as she poured herself a bowl of Corn Flakes.

Ethan, who'd clearly been up for hours already, gave her a sympathetic look as she sat down across from him. "How're you feeling?"

She pressed her fingers against her temples. "Like I got hit by a semi," she said. "Then dragged behind it for a while, and then thrown off a cliff."

He pushed a mug of coffee toward her. "I had them brew it twice as strong," he said. "It'll help."

She took a grateful sip. It was hot and bitter and delicious. "I need some water, too," she said, "and a wheelbarrow of Advil."

He started to get up. "There's some in the van—I'll get it."

She tried to shake her head, but she had to stop because it hurt too much. "It's okay. I'll take it when we're on the road," she said.

"I've already checked us out," Ethan said. "Once we start driving, we'll be in Vegas in about seven hours."

Seven hours. The thought made her stomach lurch. Las Vegas—her final show, and by far her biggest. AnnieLee stared down at her cereal, and instead of soggy flakes floating in bluish skim milk, she saw crowds of people streaming into a huge arena. She saw an empty stage, and herself waiting in the wings, clumsy and self-conscious, palms so sweaty she could barely keep hold of her guitar as lyrics flew from her mind like birds loosed from a cage.

She dropped her spoon and looked up at Ethan. "I'm petrified," she said.

He reached across the table and took her hand. "I know the feeling well," he said as he twined his fingers through hers. "Me and that feeling go way back."

But Ethan didn't seem like the kind of man who'd ever be afraid. "How far back?"

"All the way to my jail cell, if not before."

"So what did you do?" AnnieLee asked urgently. "How'd you manage?"

"When I was heading into court, I'd say to myself, *Nothing can go wrong today, because everything has gone wrong already.*" Then he withdrew his hand from hers and offered up a small, sad smile. "But that kind of thinking's not for everyone, AnnieLee. It only helps someone who's been hurt beyond what they think they can stand."

AnnieLee sucked in her breath and let it out slowly. "I might be one of those someones," she whispered.

"I guess I figured that," he said.

CHAPTER

69

Both AnnieLee's mood and her hangover improved as they headed southwest under a vast and cloudless sky. They found a satellite radio station playing nothing but classic country, stopped to stretch their legs every few hours, and filled up at a gas station that sold old-fashioned candy by the pound. Ethan bought a bag of caramel creams, and AnnieLee ate so many licorice jelly beans that her tongue turned blackish green.

They arrived in Las Vegas at dusk. As Ethan drove the Sprinter slowly down the Strip, AnnieLee leaned halfway out the window, taking in the flashing neon lights, the towering hotels, and the masses of people streaming along the sidewalks. They passed an Eiffel Tower, a Statue of Liberty, and a four-story LED sign advertising a BUFFET OF BUFFETS, "whatever *that* means," AnnieLee crowed. She couldn't believe a place like this could exist at all, let alone in the middle of a huge, dusty desert.

"Careful," Ethan warned. "You're hanging out that window like a dang spaniel."

Indignant, she pulled her head back inside, but before she

could protest such a comparison, he started singing "Ooh Las Vegas."

Ethan sounded nothing like Gram Parsons, but AnnieLee joined in on Emmylou Harris's harmony, and they sang their way past the Luxor's enormous black pyramid, past a showgirl grinding on an embarrassed-looking grandpa outside Mandalay Bay, and bridesmaids in bright feather boas skipping down the sidewalk like a bunch of drunk Dorothys in Oz.

Finally they reached the south end of the Strip, and Ethan turned the Sprinter around so he could point out the iconic WELCOME TO FABULOUS LAS VEGAS sign, shining like a beacon against the dark-blue sky.

"The only cigarettes I ever smoked were in Vegas," Ethan mused as they headed back north to their hotel.

AnnieLee brushed her windblown hair out of her eyes. "You've been here before?"

"Only once," he said. "I lost a lot of money, ate myself sick at the Emperor's Buffet, and got harassed by a prostitute. Then I got drunk at a dive bar with a bunch of Elvis impersonators, and that's the last thing I remember."

"Sounds…fun?" AnnieLee offered.

Ethan laughed. "Not exactly. I have a good feeling about this trip, though," he said as he pulled up to the Aquitaine Hotel. "It won't be nearly as low-rent, for one thing."

He handed over the Sprinter's keys to the valet, and a bellhop dressed like a French footman unloaded their bags. AnnieLee people-watched outside while Ethan went inside and checked them in. When he came back outside, he bowed facetiously to her.

"M'lady?" he said, holding out his arm. *"Allons-y!"*

"Say what?" AnnieLee said.

Ethan laughed. "It means *Let's go*—or so I was told. The lady at the front desk said it would impress you."

"Oh, definitely," AnnieLee said. "I'm seeing you in an entirely new light now that you can speak two whole words of French."

"What if I tell you that I've also got us a dinner res?"

"Even more impressive," AnnieLee said. She tucked her hand into the crook of his elbow as they walked down the street.

At a bistro straight out of *Moulin Rouge*, they gorged themselves on steak, salad, and red wine served in goblets as big as goldfish bowls. They kept their conversation light, mentioning neither their unfinished talk nor the upcoming show. AnnieLee was tired, and her nerves were revving up again. She felt as though the best thing to do after the chocolate soufflé was simply to go to bed.

"We have to make one stop first," Ethan said. He paid the bill, and then he led her along the sidewalk until they were standing on the edge of a huge, placid lake in front of the Bellagio Hotel.

She wasn't sure why Ethan wanted to show her such a thing, but she supposed she could admire it if he wanted her to. "Pretty," she said mildly.

"About twelve thousand bucks' worth of coins get thrown in there a year," Ethan said.

"That's a lot of wishes," AnnieLee said. "What do you think all those people want?"

"Probably to win at blackjack," Ethan said.

"Shoot, I can think of way better wishes than that," AnnieLee said. "You got a penny?"

He dug into his pocket and held out a nickel. She squeezed it in her fist, felt the cool coin grow warm against her skin. She was thinking about what to wish for when she heard what sounded like church bells chiming. She turned to Ethan. "What's that?"

He said, "You'll see."

A moment later, a rush of sound came pouring out of speakers placed all around the lake's perimeter, and the air filled with the soaring, symphonic opening to "Luck Be a Lady." Seconds later, hundreds of sinuous streams of water shot into the sky, matching the rhythm of the song. They waved back and forth, twisting and gyrating.

"The dancing waters," Ethan said.

AnnieLee laughed, leaning forward to feel the cool mist on her face. Flashbulbs popped, traffic on the boulevard slowed, and not ten feet away, she saw a man get down on one knee and hold out a ring to a weeping woman in a Boston Red Sox T-shirt.

When the song was over, Ethan put his arm around AnnieLee's shoulders, and she let herself lean heavily against him. "That was just about the most beautiful waste of money and water I ever saw," she said. "Thank you."

"Ready to go back to the hotel?" he asked.

"Yes. Just one more second," she said.

She straightened up and moved toward the railing again, the nickel tight in her hand. She wasn't going to leave without a wish, and there were so many things she wanted. She closed her eyes. Did a nickel mean five wishes? She sure hoped so.

She squeezed the coin again. She wished that her show tomorrow would be incredible. That Ruthanna would be proud of her. That lyrics and melodies would keep coming to her for the rest of her life.

She took a deep breath. She had two more wishes.

She wished that somehow, there might be a future for her and Ethan Blake someday.

And she wished she could keep her secrets forever.

She gave the nickel one last squeeze, and then she flung it into the water.

CHAPTER
70

After performing a hundred reps each of push-ups, crunches, bench dips, squats, and burpees—a holdover from army PT—in his hotel room, Ethan walked into the lobby café to grab a coffee and check in with Ruthanna, who'd been due to arrive last night.

U get in okay? he texted.

Not even two seconds later, his phone rang. "Morning, boss," Ethan said, sandwiching the phone between his shoulder and ear as he stirred sugar into his cup.

"*Dolphin* yoga," Ruthanna said indignantly. "Can you believe it? The concierge suggested I take the 'once-in-a-lifetime opportunity' to do yoga next to a dolphin tank. I think he must've been drunk."

Ethan laughed. He'd missed Ruthanna's orneriness, though, come to think of it, he got a fair dose of something similar, thanks to AnnieLee Keyes. "You going to try it out?"

"You're plumb crazy if you think that sounds relaxing," she said. "Imagine! There you are, trying to do mountain pose, and ol' Flipper's pressed up against the glass, staring at you like, *Get me the hell out of here!*" She giggled. "I got to hand it to these Vegas folks, though," she said. "They sure do keep coming up with new ways to separate people from their money."

"No kidding," Ethan said, thinking back to the previous night's three-figure dinner check, which had set him back deeper than he cared to think about. He knew Ruthanna would cover it if he asked her to, but he didn't want to ask her to. "How was it getting into town?"

"I tried to sneak in under the cover of darkness, but I forgot there's no such thing as actual *dark* around here," Ruthanna said, still sounding disgruntled. "You wouldn't believe the commotion! You'd think I was the Beatles."

Ethan could imagine the crush of hollering fans, and tiny Ruthanna trying to make her way through them with Lucas, her bodyguard, and whatever security team they'd pulled together before leaving Tennessee. "Wasn't it just a *little* bit flattering?" he asked.

"Yes," Ruthanna said thoughtfully. "But also…a little scary. I'm not used to it anymore, Ethan." She paused. "I'm not sure that agreeing to play this show was the best idea I ever had."

Ethan detected a note of fear in her voice. "It's a great idea," he said firmly. "Why else've you been writing all those songs? Why else hire me and the rest of the band to play music in your basement every week? Don't even say it's because you like the company, because everyone knows Elrodd drives you up two walls at once."

"And *you*, Ethan Blake," Ruthanna agreed, laughing. "You've been trying my patience since the day I met you." But when she spoke again her voice was serious. "Watching AnnieLee come up the way she did, appearing out of nowhere and taking folks by storm…I don't know, it made me nostalgic.

I thought it looked like fun. But I don't think I'm having fun yet."

"You're going to love being up onstage," Ethan assured her. "And you're going to kill tonight."

"Oh, what do *you* know?" she exclaimed.

But he could tell that a part of her believed him. Like AnnieLee, Ruthanna was a natural. And after four decades of life in the spotlight, she was also a trained and professional performer. She might think she was rusty, but she'd take the crowd by storm.

"Oh, I know it, all right," he said. "I'd bet Gladys on it."

"So about three hundred bucks, in other words?"

"Gladys is priceless!" Ethan said in mock offense.

"Sure she is. Well, thanks, cowboy." Then Ruthanna took a deep breath. "Listen, I want you to go scope the scene for tonight, okay?"

Ruthanna didn't need to say anything more; Ethan knew she wanted him to check out the venue's event staff and security protocols. "Of course," he said. "I'll see you later. After dolphin yoga. Say hi to Flipp—"

She snorted and hung up on him.

Ethan downed the rest of his coffee and hurried to the Aquitaine Event Center. Ruthanna's personal team would be assisting the venue's regular staff, which included over a hundred uniformed and plainclothes guards responsible for bag checks, pat downs, and crowd control.

The manager of the event center, a no-nonsense blonde named Mary, assured Ethan that there were only a few ways to get in, and reentry would be forbidden. "The venue is extremely nonporous," she said. VIP badges would be limited, and no one would have access to Ruthanna's backstage area without passing through a gauntlet of armed guards. Ethan scanned the huge, empty space and pictured it thronged with people.

Lucas, Ruthanna's driver and personal bodyguard, walked over and slapped Ethan's shoulder in greeting. He was six foot four at least, with a head shaved smooth and shiny. "Ten thousand seats," he said, "and every one of them sold. Ruthanna's fans sure didn't forget her."

"Let's hope the creeps did, though," Ethan said. Ruthanna had had her share of stalkers over the years, including a deranged man who'd managed to scale the fence of her compound before being arrested. Police had found knives, zip ties, and a pair of handcuffs on him, and Ethan still shuddered to think what the man would've done if he'd gotten into her house.

He stood at the railing on the three hundred level and gazed down. Could a person manage to slip a weapon past the guards? Would someone come to the concert intending to do harm?

Ruthanna was the real star tonight, and Ruthanna was the one who needed professional protection. So why was it that Ethan was more worried about AnnieLee?

Mary walked over, adjusting the radio earpiece beneath her short blond curls. "We've had multiple security meetings, and we've gone over media credentialing, where our singers will enter and exit, which gates will be used, blocking re-entry points, et cetera," she said. "We've got everything under control."

Ethan nodded, knowing that he should trust in Mary and her staff. And Las Vegas was a safe city. Every hotel, casino, nightclub, and theater had its own security team, and there were police on foot, on mountain bikes, and in patrol cars. There was no need to be afraid—not for Ruthanna, and not for AnnieLee.

His eyes swept the stage, which was crawling with workers

setting up projections, risers, and equipment for the band. If this were a Hollywood movie, the bad guy would already be hiding up in the lighting rig, ready to swoop down and kidnap the heroine as she sang her final, triumphant notes.

But thinking like that was crazy. Life had its dramatic moments, Ethan thought, but it sure as shit wasn't a Hollywood movie.

CHAPTER
71

AnnieLee had just stepped out of the shower when she heard a gentle knock and a polite voice calling "Room service" from the hall.

Wrapping herself in a fluffy white robe, AnnieLee padded over, unlocked the double locks, and stepped back to let the maid wheel the folding table inside. "Thanks a million," she said. "You can put that over by the couch, I guess." She headed back into the bathroom.

As she stood in front of the mirror, combing through her wet hair, she could hear the wings of the table clicking into place and the sound of water being poured into a glass.

"*Bon appétit,*" the woman said. "*Au revoir!*"

"Thank you," AnnieLee called. "And um…*au revoir* to you, too."

They really like their French around here, she thought.

With her hair brushed and her skin slathered with one of the fancy complimentary lotions, AnnieLee came back out, re-bolted the door, and then walked over to inspect the breakfast spread. Beneath a gorgeous spray of lilies was a bowl of cut fresh fruit, a basket of buttery pastries, and a cappuccino with a fleur-de-lis design in its foam.

She was too nervous to be hungry, but she took a croissant and made herself eat it as she paced around the luxurious hotel room, going over her set list in her mind. She'd open with "Driven," and then go into "Dark Night, Bright Future"...

Knowing that Ruthanna was the true headliner of the show took a tiny bit of the pressure off. But AnnieLee and Ruthanna hadn't sung together in weeks, and their only rehearsal time before the performance was in less than two hours.

The story is old
Has often been told
Of a rich city boy and a poor country girl

She sang through their duet—she had the high harmony, and Ruthanna the lower melody—and then she walked out onto the balcony to feel the sun on her face. She could see a turquoise pool glimmering a block away, and beyond that, the tip of the fake Eiffel Tower and the High Roller observation wheel. Somewhere even farther out lay the wide, flat desert— and, nearly two thousand miles beyond that, her little cottage in Nashville, Tennessee.

As wonderful as her tour had been, she wouldn't be sorry to get back to normal life, where she could take walks and write new songs and make plans for what would come next. She had an entire album to make, after all. And what if ACD wanted her to do music videos? Or perform on *SNL*? Or tour with Luke Combs? It was too much to think about now.

She went into the suite's bedroom and turned on the TV. Half listening to a young couple trying to decide which McMansion to buy, she finally opened the box that Ruthanna had sent to her room earlier that morning.

Inside blush-colored tissue paper was a halter-neck Proenza Schouler dress in a black metallic knit, with a fitted bodice and a tiered, ruffled skirt. "Ohhh," she breathed, lifting the dress to her shoulders and looking in the gilded mirror. It was a far cry from her usual jeans and boots, but tonight was a special occasion, wasn't it? Certainly Ruthanna would be dressed to the elevens, and it wouldn't do for AnnieLee to swagger onstage looking as though she'd outfitted herself at the nearest Goodwill.

You know what I say about "too much"... Ruthanna had written on the front of a little card that had been affixed to the box.

"What?" AnnieLee said out loud to the empty room, and then she looked inside the card. Out fell five crisp one-hundred-dollar bills.

I say I never, ever heard of such a thing! Break a leg tonight, kid. And then buy us ten rounds of drinks. Love, Ruthanna

Grinning, AnnieLee tucked the money into her robe and then reached into the tissue paper again. She pulled out a pair of black six-inch stilettos with sparkling rhinestone heels.

"Shoot, I probably *will* break a leg if I wear these," she said. She dropped the shoes onto the bed and picked up the dress again. She was about to slip off her robe and try it on when she heard a noise that made her freeze.

A low thud. It had been faint, but close by. Had it come from the TV? From a neighboring room?

Slowly, she reached for the remote and hit Mute; now the young couple on-screen debated kitchen design in silence.

The thudding sound came again, and then one more time.

It was coming from the hallway, AnnieLee realized, sighing with relief. People were walking by and brushing against the wall outside her door.

She was way too jumpy today—that was for sure. She flopped onto the bed and stared up at the crystal chandelier. *You just need to calm down for a minute,* she told herself.

She was counting her slow exhales when out of the corner of her eye she caught sight of movement. A flash of dark clothing, a gleam of metal. She barely had time to form the thought *Someone's here* before he was on top of her.

His legs straddled her midsection, his weight pressed her breathless. And he was holding a gun.

Her gun.

CHAPTER

72

For an instant, fear blinded her. But then she recognized that cruel, hated face. She knew that heavy brow and those hard blue eyes. She could smell him, too, a familiar, bitter smell of sweat and cigarette smoke.

"You," he spat, stabbing her in the chest with the muzzle of the gun. "You dumb hick, you thought you could run."

"Get off me!" AnnieLee yelled.

He clapped his hand roughly over her mouth. "Rose," he said, shaking his head. "Rose."

"I don't know any Rose." She spoke into his fat, hot fingers.

"Is that what you say these days?" he hissed.

She could feel her panic rising, threatening to overwhelm her. "I was never," she said desperately. "I wasn't—" Her thoughts raced and her heart hammered against her ribs. She didn't know what she could say to stop him from hurting her. Her breath was coming in sharp pants.

"You wasn't *what*, you skinny piece of trailer trash?" He sneered at her. "I took care of you—and this is how you repay me."

AnnieLee's eyes were wide above his sweaty palm. She tried to shake her head, but his hand was pressing down hard. She wanted to bite him so he'd take his hand away. But then he'd hit her.

Or else he'll just shoot me, she thought.

As he glared at her, waiting for her answer, she moved her right arm slowly along the bed, her fingers searching blindly in the sheets. If she could only reach…

"I wasn't going to say anything," she pleaded. The press of his hand made her teeth cut into her lips. She could taste her blood and his sweat. "Please," she whispered. "I won't tell."

"What do you mean? You're singing about it," he said.

She closed her eyes. "It's just a song," she whispered.

He dug the muzzle of the gun into her breastbone. She'd reached her arm as far as it could go.

Nothing.

"You *belong* to me," he said. "Remember?"

She reached a millimeter farther, and she could feel…leather. Her finger hooked around a strap.

"But you can't be trusted," she heard him say.

She took a deep breath and opened her eyes. *"You're right,"* she hissed as she grabbed the shoe by the sole and drove the stiletto heel into his eye socket. He hollered in shock and pain, and she bucked her hips up as hard as she could, unbalancing him. Another buck and he was falling off the edge of the bed. AnnieLee scrambled up and flung herself away, landing on her hands and knees. Then she sprinted out of the bedroom.

Behind her, she heard him crash into something, half blind and raging. She'd hurt him, but it didn't matter. He was coming.

As she rounded the corner, she saw that he'd blocked the door with an armchair. She'd never get it out of the way in time, not before he reached her. She screamed in rage and turned toward the living room.

She ran, nearly colliding with the huge, stupidly luxurious sofa. As she cleared the coffee table, she heard another crash behind her. Up ahead was her only escape.

A balcony leading to nothing but air.

CHAPTER
73

The hot, bright sun flared in her eyes. She could hear music floating skyward from the pool, the bass thudding like a distant heartbeat.

AnnieLee stumbled and caught herself against the doorframe. There was a crash from behind her as she stepped onto the chaise longue. It tipped under her weight, nearly unbalancing her, but she grabbed the railing and flung her leg over it.

Her stomach twisted in nauseated fear, and her courage wavered.

I can't, she thought. *I can't do it.*

But then she heard him calling for her, and she knew that she had to.

If she had to die, she was going to do it on her own terms. No way in hell was she going to let that bastard kill her with her own damn gun.

She was on the railing now, perched like a bird. It was time to fly. Either she'd know all kinds of answers soon—like if there was a heaven, and if her mother was waiting for her—or else she might know nothing ever again.

She turned her head and saw him coming, the gun hidden behind a pillow, and suddenly she almost laughed out loud. *He'd called her a dumb hick, but he thought a pillow actually worked as a silencer?*

But these didn't seem like proper last thoughts, and last thoughts they probably were. He was only going to fire once, and he was going to make sure it hit.

There was only one way out. She flung herself into the air.

Dry wind whipped at her face. She heard people yelling, but her own scream strangled in her throat.

Regret consumed her, hot as fire. *I didn't mean to, I didn't want—*

She couldn't take anything back. But she pinwheeled her arms, as if she could slow herself down. Her white robe billowed around her legs.

Below her was the glass canopy of the hotel entrance, glittering in the sunlight, rushing up toward her. It would be over soon. The fall—and maybe everything. She relaxed every joint, every muscle. She closed her eyes.

Then she plunged through the awning, shattering it into a thousand sharp and shining pieces. A second later she crashed down onto one of the boxwoods that lined the Aquitaine entrance, and then she spilled onto the golden carpet.

CHAPTER
74

She couldn't feel or see anything. She seemed to exist outside her body, painless and floating. She wondered if she was dead and her brain didn't know it yet.

She struggled to open her eyes, and when she finally could, she gasped to see where she was. She was lying on a sagging mattress in a dim, humid room. There was no comforter or pillow, only thin sheets. The air smelled like stale and unwashed bodies. Her body was too heavy and she couldn't sit up. She turned her head toward the window, where a few rays from a streetlamp shone through the vertical blinds. A thin wisp of cigarette smoke curled toward the ceiling.

No, she thought. *No, no, no.*

She blinked, but the vision didn't change. Sick as it made her, she knew the truth. She had always been here. Nashville was nothing but a dream—a warm, bright place she had conjured from a hundred dark nights of despair.

"Maybelle," she cried, blindly reaching to the side of the bed. If she had her guitar, she wouldn't be totally alone.

Then there were strong hands on her shoulders, shaking her, and her eyes opened for real in a room full of light. AnnieLee blinked in wonder. She was not in a dingy motel. She was lying in a hospital room, and a man's stubbled, handsome face hovered inches from her own.

"AnnieLee," he said. "You're okay, AnnieLee. You were having a bad dream."

"Who?" she said. She put her hands up to touch her damp cheeks, but the man gently took them away and held them in his own. Then she knew who he was, and who she was, and everything came back to her in a flood of color and relief.

"I lived?" she whispered. She clutched at Ethan's fingers, proving to herself they were real. "Or is this some kind of messed-up heaven?"

Ethan gave a bark of a laugh—a sound of utter relief. "This is definitely not heaven, AnnieLee." He glanced over at a steaming Styrofoam cup. "If it was, there'd be a lot of angels and much better coffee." He grinned. "And you're so damn ornery, I don't know if Saint Peter'd let you in." Then his expression turned serious and his eyes searched her face. "Oh, God, AnnieLee, I thought we'd lost you."

"Excuse me, sir," said a voice. A large nurse in a bright-pink uniform had pushed her way into the room, waving a blood pressure cuff. "I'm going to need access to the patient. We have a little business to take care of."

Ethan retreated to the far wall while the woman—her name tag said PATIENCE—checked AnnieLee's blood pressure and pulse and then shone a flashlight into her eyes. "Looking good," she said. "You play the lotto?"

"Never," AnnieLee said. "Why?"

"Because I never heard of anyone surviving a four-story fall with barely more than a few scratches. If you got that kind of luck, dear, there's no reason not to test it out. See if you can get yourself a piece of that three hundred million."

"Oh," AnnieLee said. "Right." She shifted her legs under the covers, still marveling that she had lived. That this room and everyone in it—herself included—was real. "I'm really okay? I don't think I can feel my feet."

Patience smiled. "You're pumped pretty full of painkillers right now because you've got a sliced-up heel and a gash along your left leg. But if someone asked me what'd happened to you, I'd've bet twenty bucks you just fell off a bike."

"Luck be a lady tonight," AnnieLee sang softly. Five heartfelt wishes, and survival hadn't even been one of them. She was luckier than she'd ever thought possible.

"Hmm?" Patience said as she wrote something down on AnnieLee's chart.

"Nothing. Just a song," AnnieLee said. "So if I'm not really hurt, when do I get out of here? I've got a show I'm supposed to—"

"Not any time soon, you don't," Patience said. "You just lie back and relax. I'll be back to check on you in another hour."

When she left, AnnieLee turned to Ethan. "I can't stay here," she said.

He came back to her bedside. "You don't have a choice. The concert's been called off, and the police want to talk to you."

Her heart gave a painful kick in her chest. "What for?" she managed.

"Because you plunged down fifty feet, AnnieLee, and it's a miracle we didn't need a spatula to pick you up." He sighed and glanced out the window and then toward the hall. "Because they think that maybe someone pushed you. Or that maybe you might have done it on purpose."

AnnieLee pushed herself up to a sitting position. She could

feel her breath coming faster. *Suicide? That's what they thought this was?*

The easiest thing to do—*tell the truth*—was also the impossible one. Because the story wouldn't stop with the man in her hotel room, and it was a tale she never wanted told.

"I fell. I didn't try to kill myself," she said. "But even if I did, suicide's not a crime."

Ethan took her hand again. "What were you doing, messing around on the balcony like that?" he asked.

She turned away from him. "I need you to go to my hotel room," she said. "Get me my bag and my phone and some clothes."

"You can't go anywhere," he said.

"I'm not going to!" she yelled. "I just want my things!"

Her voice was sharp and cruel. She wanted to tell him that she was sorry, but he was already gone.

CHAPTER
75

E than stalked into the hallway, angry at AnnieLee and more grateful than he could even fathom that she was alive and unhurt. When he'd come back from the event center and seen her strapped to the gurney, being loaded into the ambulance, he'd almost—

"Excuse me, Blake!"

He'd run right into Ruthanna, almost unrecognizable in a brown wig, huge dark glasses, and tennis shoes. "Sorry, boss," he said reflexively, and then without even knowing he was going to do it, he grabbed her and hugged her hard against his chest. He felt her arms tighten around his waist after a second's hesitation. "AnnieLee's fine," he said, shaking his head at the wonder of it. "She's absolutely fine."

Ruthanna pulled away from him and fluffed her wig in agitation. "Thank God," she said. "I've run a nonstop prayer since I heard. Poor Jesus must be up there going, 'Will someone please shut that woman up?'" She laughed nervously, twisting her pink-nailed hands in front of her. "She's really going to be okay?"

"Yes. But she has to stay here for a little while."

Ruthanna's expression grew grim. "Jack called. He said it's all over the Internet already. 'Woman falling from Vegas luxury hotel looks suspiciously like rising country star AnnieLee Keyes.' Eileen is doing her best to calm the rumors, but these people are vultures, Ethan."

But Ethan was distracted by the policeman now entering AnnieLee's room. The man left the door open, and so Ethan could hear him introduce himself as Officer Gates. *He looks like he's been out of the academy for all of five minutes,* Ethan thought.

Officer Gates took out a notepad and asked AnnieLee to tell him what happened at the Aquitaine Hotel.

"Isn't it obvious?" AnnieLee said, the fire still in her voice. "I fell off the balcony. I should sue the hotel for it!"

Gates gave a tiny, noncommittal nod. "Can you talk about what exactly you were doing on the balcony? And how you...fell? The railing's nearly four feet high, Ms. Keyes, and you're not particularly tall."

AnnieLee crossed her thin arms. "I don't see why you need to bring my height into it, Officer Gates."

"Ma'am—"

"And I am sure as shit not a ma'am."

"I apologize," Gates said as Ethan rolled his eyes in the hallway. They must not really think AnnieLee was a danger to herself, he thought, or else they would've sent someone who knew what he was doing.

"I went out there to get fresh air. To take in the view. I don't know what I was thinking. I mean, I used to climb all over everything when I was a kid. I was never afraid of heights. I could balance like that guy—what's his name? The one who walked the high wire between the Twin Towers."

"Philippe Petit," Ruthanna whispered beside Ethan. "I met

him once in Paris." Her hand now squeezed his forearm tightly. "She's telling the truth, isn't she? That it was an accident?"

Ethan thought carefully before he answered, remembering the tragic story of Ruthanna's daughter, Sophia. Ruthanna would never know if Sophia had been so heartbroken over the breakup with Trace Jones that she'd killed herself in that hotel room— or if it had all been some kind of terrible, drunken mistake.

He covered Ruthanna's hand with his. "I don't think she wanted to die," he said gently.

Ruthanna's tense shoulders dropped. "That means a lot. You know her better than anyone," she said.

Which is not saying much, Ethan thought.

"But I can't stop thinking: What if she wasn't ready, and I pushed her too hard?" Ruthanna said. "Sometimes a thing you think is a favor ends up being the heaviest kind of burden. But by the time you realize it, it's too late, and you don't know how to take it back…" She stopped and looked up at him through her big dark glasses. "I don't want it to be my fault," she whispered.

"It's not your fault," he said. "All we've ever done is try to help her. But sometimes I get the feeling that she's not used to being helped."

Patience, the nurse from earlier, approached. "Are you the husband?" she asked Ethan.

"Friend," he said quickly.

"Have you noticed any changes in her sleeping or eating lately?" she asked as she shut the door to AnnieLee's room.

"No," he said. He patted Ruthanna's hand. "She was happy. Excited. She has a lot to look forward to. I don't think she was trying to hurt herself."

But what, then, was she trying to do? he thought. The word came to him, sudden and surprising as a slap in the face. *Escape.*

"Sir?" Patience said. "I asked you if you knew any of her next of kin that we could contact."

Ignoring her, Ethan turned to Ruthanna. "I'm sorry," he said. "AnnieLee wants me to get her things, and I should probably go do that."

When he was almost out the door, he heard the nurse say to Ruthanna, "Do I know you, ma'am? You look awful familiar to me."

Ruthanna demurred in her low, rich voice. "Oh, I'm not from around here, darlin'."

CHAPTER

76

B ack at the Aquitaine Hotel, the manager visibly trembled as he let Ethan into AnnieLee's room. "... just beside our-selves," he was saying from the hallway. "Never in a million years would I ever..." He looked up at Ethan. "If there's any-thing we can do—"

"Thank you," Ethan said, and firmly shut the door in the man's tanned, worried face. The poor man was probably expect-ing to be hit with a lawsuit any minute, and Ethan would have felt sorry for him if not for the fact that every ounce of his own concern and worry was being used up by the infuriating, intoxicating AnnieLee Keyes.

As Ethan turned around to face the hotel suite, he felt a jolt of adrenaline. Without even taking another step into the room, he knew that someone else had been in there with AnnieLee, and that the man had not been invited.

There was the faintest whiff of cigarette smoke in the air— AnnieLee never smoked—and, even fainter, what seemed to him like the metallic scent of fear.

Ethan leaned against the wall and closed his eyes as an old, sharp anguish shot through him. He was back in North Carolina, walking into a room where his wife lay strangled. She'd been wearing the nightgown he'd bought her for her birthday, the one made of silk as red as blood.

He took a deep, shuddering inhale—*One, two, three, four*— held it—*One, two, three, four*—and let it out: *One, two, three, four*. He waited four seconds and did the whole thing again. Box breathing, Jeanie had called it, and she had said it kept her calm in moments of great stress.

If only, he thought, *it could have kept her safe.*

Then Ethan pushed himself off the wall, shaking his head as if he could rattle loose the memories of his wife. He still missed Jeanie, despite her betrayal. But it was time to worry about a living woman.

He crept silently through the entryway, though he knew that whoever had come in had long since vanished. The bedroom lay ahead of him, and the living room was to the left. He went into the bedroom first. The bed was in disarray, its covers kicked to the floor. He glanced over at the muted TV, which was broadcasting drone footage of an enormous cliffside mansion. Closed-captioning suggested that it could be his for a mere sixteen million euros.

A black dress with a muted sparkle dangled halfway off the end of the bed. He felt the heavy, expensive fabric as he read the card from Ruthanna: *You know what I say about "too much"*... He tossed the card back onto the bed—he did indeed know.

And it certainly explained the shoe he saw lying in the middle of the bed. A thin, impossibly high stiletto with a jewel-encrusted heel, it looked more like a weapon than it did footwear. He couldn't imagine AnnieLee ever wearing such a thing, though clearly Ruthanna hoped her protégé might be convinced. He spotted the other shoe by the wall, as if AnnieLee had flung it there in a huff after trying it on. He bent down to pick it up and noticed a pale bit of something clinging to the heel. He peered closer. It looked like...a scrape of skin.

Ethan stood motionless, even as his heartbeat quickened. Someone *had* used the shoe as a weapon.

He set it carefully on the bed and moved into the living room. The balcony doors were open wide, their pale curtains fluttering lightly in the breeze. A vase of roses had been knocked over, and water pooled on the coffee table, dripping down onto the thick cream carpet.

He walked out onto the balcony, gripped the railing, and looked down. He felt an almost overwhelming vertigo as he thought about falling that far. Below he could see the broken glass awning, and ribbons of caution tape blocking the hotel's front entrance.

Ethan stepped away from the railing and breathed slowly again, trying to calm himself. But it seemed he could feel AnnieLee's desperate panic, and the feeling caused him nearly physical pain.

Someone had come into her room, and this someone was a person she feared so much that she chose to throw herself off a balcony rather than face him. The realization of what this meant felt like a punch to Ethan's gut. The person couldn't be a crazed fan, or an anonymous petty Vegas criminal, or a random psychopath. He was someone AnnieLee knew.

Was he one of the men from the black truck? The driver of the Impala? Or someone so frightening that he was only now making himself known?

Ethan knew that he should call the police. But he also knew that doing so would most likely backfire. AnnieLee would be furious, and she would push against everyone, dodge any questions, refuse to cooperate. And how could the police investigate a crime that its victim said never even happened?

He stepped back into the hotel room. He'd played enough amateur detective for the day. Anyway, the answers weren't to be found at the Aquitaine Hotel. They lay with AnnieLee.

He found her bag and began to gather up what little clothing there was. And as he did, he asked himself, *What sort of person packed a tiny duffel bag for a three-week road trip?*

A person used to privation and lack—that's who. Ruthanna joked that there was no such thing as having too much, but suddenly Ethan understood that AnnieLee didn't even believe in having *enough.* He'd always thought that she wore the same too-small boots and the same two pairs of jeans because she was superstitious: she thought they were lucky. But now it seemed to him that there were darker, sadder reasons.

Either she didn't think she deserved more or she knew she needed to travel light, so that at any moment she could grab everything and run.

CHAPTER
77

"S o she really seemed okay? Body, mind, all of it?" Jack asked, pouring himself a Scotch from Ruthanna's minibar, though five o'clock was still a ways off.

Ruthanna nodded, her mouth full of fancy French chocolate. Low-carb diet be damned—stress like this called for truffles, or whatever the hell those delicious little cocoa-covered balls were. "AnnieLee was as impatient and headstrong as ever," she said. "But then she was sleeping when I left. I think they still want to do some kind of psychiatric evaluation." She picked up another truffle and then set it back down again. Maybe Scotch was the thing for stress. Or both. "I somehow still can't believe it," she said. "I keep thinking someone's going to pinch my arm and tell me to wake up."

"If only," Jack said, grimacing and rubbing his forehead.

Ruthanna hadn't seen him so rattled in years, and she patted a spot on the couch next to her. "Take a load off for a minute, hon," she said.

He sat down heavily and put his feet up on the coffee table. "I should be on the phone with ACD, and the Aquitaine Event

Center people, and about a thousand other lawyers and bean counters. But right now I just need to drink a little of this Scotch and be grateful that our sweet girl is okay."

Ruthanna turned to look at his familiar, rugged profile. *Our sweet girl.* It was as if AnnieLee belonged to them the way a child would, and the phrase sent a sudden rush of emotion through her. She was so grateful for Jack, she cared about AnnieLee so much, and seeing her lying tiny and alone in that hospital bed had just about broken Ruthanna's heart.

Had she done wrong by dreaming up this concert? She knew how much pressure AnnieLee was under, and how it was all new to her—she hadn't been performing since she was knee-high to a grasshopper the way Ruthanna had. AnnieLee hadn't had time to grow the thick skin that was necessary to survive.

Ruthanna let out a long sigh. Sophia hadn't grown that thick skin, either, and though she'd never truly wanted to be a performer, she had always been in the public eye. She'd resented it, too, which was one of the things that had made her relationship with Trace Jones so ironic. She'd finally gotten out of her mother's shadow, only to turn around and walk right into his.

And what if that was the thing that had killed her?

On the morning of Sophia's funeral, Ruthanna had stepped outside her house to find a helicopter over her lawn, hovering so close she could feel the wind on her face. Her phone had been ringing day and night with reporters who wanted to hear about her grief, as if her pain was something she owed them.

She didn't owe them anything but her music, but after that day she couldn't give it to them anymore. Sophia's death—and the world's fanatical fascination with it—had broken Ruthanna. She'd quit the business.

And now, years later, she was back, and another girl she loved was hurting. She couldn't bear to lose this one, too.

Jack put his hand on her leg and squeezed affectionately. "What about you? Are *you* doing okay?" he asked.

She was trying to figure out how to answer the question when her phone rang. It was Ethan.

"Hey, cowboy—" she began, but Ethan's words tumbled right over hers.

"I'm at the hospital," he said. "But AnnieLee's not here. Ruthanna, she's gone."

78

Ruthanna let the phone fall from her fingers onto the carpet. Jack began to rub her back, as if he could smooth away her rising panic.

"That damn fool girl *ran*," she said.

Jack bent down, picked up her phone, and held it out to her. "Call the hospital," he urged.

"What for?" Ruthanna snapped, her numbness shifting quickly to anger. "Should I ask how the hell they let a banged-up girl in a hospital gown and no shoes sneak out the back door?"

"You could ask if anyone saw anything—"

"Ethan's on top of that already, Jack," she said. "And you know full well what'd happen if I called them up. I'd pitch a hissy fit so big it'd have a tail on it, and there's no way that would help."

"It might make *you* feel better," Jack said.

"Yes, it might," Ruthanna agreed. "All the same, I think I won't do it." She put her face in her hands. "Why didn't I just stay with her?"

"Because you thought she was safe there," Jack said gently.

"I did," she whispered. And knowing how wrong she'd been about that made her want to cry. "I thought they were taking care of her." She squeezed her stinging eyes shut. She never should have left; she should've sat by AnnieLee's bedside until she woke up.

Unless, of course, AnnieLee hadn't really been sleeping in the first place.

Then Ruthanna heard Jack say, "Damn it," and she looked up to see him scrolling down his phone.

Her heart gave a lurch. "Damn what?"

He held up the screen so she could read the headline.

AnnieLee Keyes Jumps from Luxe Vegas Hotel
[Click HERE for DRAMATIC Photos]
Speculation the rising star was suicidal

Ruthanna grabbed the phone and clicked through, but when she saw the photograph of a blurry, white-robed figure— AnnieLee, caught mid-plunge—she put the phone down. "Suicidal? That's horseshit!"

"Anything to get eyeballs," Jack said.

"Don't I know it," Ruthanna said bitterly. "The people behind these gossip sites will piss on your leg and tell you it's raining. But it's one thing to say I'm having an affair with my personal trainer and another thing entirely to say my protégé flung herself off a balcony on purpose!"

"I'm sure Eileen is doing everything she can," Jack said. "But once these guys smell blood…"

Ruthanna didn't plan to read the article. "Are they saying that she tried to kill herself or that she already did?"

"Depends on which site you're reading."

"Maybe they're the ones I should call," Ruthanna said angrily. "'FYI, AnnieLee didn't mean to jump out of a window, but she *did* mean to up and vanish, so maybe you can pull your heads out of your—'"

"Ruthanna," Jack said, putting a gentle hand on her shoulder. "You know how this goes. We release a statement. 'AnnieLee Keyes was injured in an accident, and is recuperating under a doctor's care in an undisclosed location. She requests privacy,' et cetera. It's a terrible reality, but there's a standard PR line."

Ruthanna knew Jack was right, but it hardly mattered, because she didn't truly care what people said—she only cared that AnnieLee was safe. She dialed AnnieLee's cell, and it rang six times before going to voicemail. Ruthanna didn't bother leaving a message.

"I'm going to call the police," she told Jack. "I'm going to talk to someone who actually knows what they're doing, and I'm going to make them *find her.*"

She paced the room as she dialed. A few minutes later, she was connected to a woman who introduced herself as Officer Tucker.

"I'd like to report a missing person," Ruthanna said.

"All right," the officer said. "May I have the person's name?"

"Her name is AnnieLee Keyes," Ruthanna said. "K-e-y-e-s."

"And tell me about the last time you had contact with Ms. Keyes."

"I saw her this morning." Ruthanna swore she could hear the woman exhaling on the other end of the line, as if she thought she was dealing with some kind of nut.

"Just a few hours ago, then. Okay. Did you see her in person?" Officer Tucker asked.

"Yes. She was in the hospital." Then Ruthanna recounted what she knew of the events leading up to AnnieLee's fall— which, she realized, was almost nothing. How *had* that child fallen off a balcony?

"Do you believe she is a risk to herself?" Officer Tucker asked.

"No," Ruthanna said quickly. She spoke out of stubbornness and loyalty. But as soon as Officer Tucker began to talk, Ruthanna realized her mistake.

"If an adult wishes to spend some time alone," the officer said, "without notifying friends or family of their whereabouts, they are entitled to do that, ma'am. It sounds like she was under a lot of pressure. She might just be trying to take a little break."

Ruthanna took a deep breath. "I misspoke. I do think she is in danger," she said.

"All right," the officer said. "I want you to tell me more about why you think that. But first I do want to reassure you that over fifteen hundred people go missing a day in this country, and the vast majority of them are found safe and unharmed."

"But she wouldn't just walk away from everything!" Ruthanna said.

"Have you reached out to her family? Her friends? Anyone who might have been in touch with her after you were?"

Ruthanna sucked in her breath. AnnieLee's family? Her friends? Ruthanna had no idea who any of those people might be. She was trying to figure out how to explain this to Officer Tucker when she heard a sharp knocking at the door. Jack walked over to see who it was, and a moment later he returned with Ethan Blake, whose face was shadowed with worry.

Ruthanna motioned for him to sit. He didn't. "No, I don't actually have their contact information," Ruthanna said to the officer. "But it's extremely important that we find AnnieLee as soon as possible."

"Who's she talking to?" Ethan asked Jack, and when Jack said, "The police," Ethan reached out and took the phone out of Ruthanna's hand.

"Thank you for your time," he said to the officer. "We'll call you back." Then he hung up.

Ruthanna's mouth fell open. "What the hell do you think you're doing?"

"Calling the police won't help anyone, Ruthanna. AnnieLee doesn't want to talk to them, and she doesn't trust them. If she sees a cop, wherever she is, she's going to run. I don't know why, but I know I'm right."

"So, what: we just sit here and do nothing?" Ruthanna said. "Wait for her to call us on the phone she left behind and tell us that she's perfectly fine?"

"No, Ruthanna," Ethan said. "I'm going to go find her."

CHAPTER
79

AnnieLee pulled her baseball cap a little lower over her face as she made her way east along Tropicana Avenue. It had been almost disappointingly easy to slip away from the hospital, and though she'd set off an emergency exit alarm on her way out, she was halfway across the parking lot and hiding behind a Toyota minivan by the time the security guard poked his head out to see what the fuss was about.

Bent low, she'd wended her way to the road, and then she'd walked only a few blocks before finding a tourist shop full of cheaply made Las Vegas theme wear. Grabbing things almost without looking at them, she quickly outfitted herself. Where else on earth could a barefoot woman buy a hat, sweatshirt, sweatpants, socks, and sneakers with two hundred-dollar bills she pulled out of a pocket without making anyone bat an eye? It felt like a minor miracle.

Or else, AnnieLee thought, *it's just Las Vegas.*

She didn't have to wait long for a ride, either. The three bachelorettes pulling out of the 7-Eleven with Monster Energy drinks and a box of doughnuts took pity on AnnieLee, standing there with her big smile and little thumb, and they let her climb into the back seat.

"You look familiar," the one who was driving said. "Did we party with you last night?"

AnnieLee offered up a false and sparkling laugh. "Maybe so," she said. "There's a lot I don't remember about my whereabouts."

"You and me both," the driver said, rolling her eyes. "My name's Bella."

"I'm Rose," AnnieLee said. Then she sucked in her breath. It wasn't what she'd meant to say.

But no one noticed the way she paled. The other two girls were Molly and Taylor, and they were desperately hungover from the night before, they said, though Molly seemed possibly drunk still. The three of them had caravanned from New Mexico with two other friends, both of whom were still asleep in their hotel rooms—"and not alone, either," Bella said archly.

While they were heading southeast along Route 93, Taylor, who was in the passenger seat, put her head between her knees and said, "You gotta pull over, girl. *Now.*"

Bella sighed, flicking on her turn signal and pulling onto the shoulder. Cars whizzed past as Molly giggled and Taylor staggered out of the car, bent over at the waist and clutching her stomach.

Five minutes later she returned, wiping her mouth and pink with embarrassment while her friends made sympathetic noises and tried not to giggle. Taylor shook Tic Tacs into her palm and then passed the container around the car. "If I try to order triple White Russians ever again," she said to Bella, "I want you to punch me in the face."

Soon they were on their way again, and AnnieLee gazed out the window, trying not to think about where she was headed.

The city was already invisible behind them, and ahead lay nothing but brown hills dotted with desert sage. She looked down at her hands and realized that they were shaking.

Just what do you think you're doing? Have you gone crazy? How is this going to solve anything?

The voice in her head asked all sorts of questions she didn't want to answer.

She knew she was betraying everyone who'd ever been kind to her by running away. Ruthanna Ryder, who'd taken her under her wing. Who'd *come out of retirement* to sing with her at a show that would never happen. Kind, wise Jack, who'd worked so hard to build her audience, and the people at ACD, who'd taken a chance on believing in her.

And of course there was Ethan. Unlike the rest of them, he had nothing to lose if she destroyed her career. But leaving him felt worst of all.

She thought back to the conversation they'd had in that Salt Lake City hotel room. When Ethan told her about the pain of his past, she'd seen how a weight suddenly lifted from his shoulders, how the restlessness that always seemed to animate him suddenly quieted. He'd wanted a confession from her, too, probably because he thought that it would mean relief for both of them.

But she couldn't give him that, and she couldn't even tell him why.

She'd tried to imagine the explanation. *Your secret was about a bad thing people thought you'd done. But mine's about a bad thing that was done to me. And those aren't the same kinds of secrets at all.*

He wouldn't understand. And if he knew the truth, he'd never look at her the same way again. It wasn't the kind of thing a man could forget.

AnnieLee reached down and rubbed her wounded leg.

Whatever painkillers they'd given her had worn off, but the cuts weren't painful so much as they were uncomfortable and itchy. Her skin felt tight and hot beneath the bandages, and the thick cotton-poly sweatpants that she'd grabbed off the rack— they were the first extra-smalls she'd come across—didn't help matters. The right pant leg read LAS VEGAS RAIDERS. Was that a football team? She didn't even know.

She leaned forward, trying to see how fast Bella was going. Was she speeding? AnnieLee hoped she was going ten miles over the limit at least.

"How far are you going?" Bella asked. Molly and Taylor seemed to be asleep.

"Farther than you," AnnieLee said brightly. "So I'll ride along as long as you'll have me. And I'll fill up the tank at the next pump." She met Bella's eyes in the rearview mirror. "I've got money," she said. "Just...not wheels."

"We're glad to help out," Bella said.

Molly raised her head, blinked sleepily, and said, "Hos before bros, right?"

AnnieLee laughed, for real this time. "Sounds good to me," she said.

CHAPTER

80

A hundred thousand miles, huh?" Ethan said, squinting at the truck that was parked in front of a dilapidated ranch just outside Paradise, Nevada. It was a 2004 Dodge Ram, a quad cab V-6 with a towing package and a few other needless bells and whistles.

"Yeah, that's right," the owner said. He was a skinny, nervous-looking dude in a faded Golden Nugget T-shirt, a leather vest, and a pair of jeans that hadn't been washed in so long they looked like they could walk off somewhere on their own. "It runs like a dream."

The truck was newer and nicer than Gladys was, but it had none of her charms; it was a truck without a soul. Not that this mattered in the slightest. Ethan wasn't interested in the Dodge because he liked it; he was interested because he needed a reliable set of wheels that wouldn't make him look like a tourist or a cop when he was driving down the back roads of Arkansas, looking for AnnieLee. "Why are you selling?" he asked. "Trading up?"

The man glanced nervously back toward the house. Its cheap

aluminum siding was coming off in places, and its roof was badly in need of repair. In the front yard were a few broken lawn chairs, an upside-down laundry basket, and a baseball bat leaning up against a rusting Weber grill. "I gotta pay down a few debts," he allowed.

"Slots?" Ethan asked, not a hint of judgment in his voice.

"Blackjack," the man said. "And horses."

Ethan nodded sympathetically, as if he knew what this kind of desperation felt like. He'd never gambled, but he knew what it was like to be poor. He looked up inside the wheel wells, though cars didn't rust in the desert the way they did in wet Tennessee winters, and then he touched a smattering of dents in the back rear panel. "Someone use this for target practice?"

"My wife," the man said glumly.

Ethan could imagine she had good reason to let off a little steam. A man didn't have any business gambling away the money he needed to survive, not to Ethan's way of thinking. He opened the hood and looked at the engine.

"New spark plugs," the man offered. "And I just changed the oil last month." He pronounced it *oll*.

"I don't want to buy this truck," Ethan said.

The man seemed to visibly shrink. He kicked his toe into the weeds at the edge of the driveway. "I suppose I could go a little lower on the price."

"I want to borrow it," Ethan said.

The man gave a low whistle. "Well, I don't see how that helps—"

"I'll pay what you're asking," Ethan said. But he didn't want to own the truck. Didn't want to take advantage of someone so down on his luck, or be the reason this man had to ride around town on the busted-looking bicycle that was parked on the porch. "I'll give you the money and drive off. And then I'll bring the truck back to you when I'm done using it. It's a win-win. You never get those kinds of odds around here, do you?"

The man looked extremely doubtful. "You ain't going to use it in no crime, right?"

"I can assure you I'm not. Take my picture."

"Why?"

Somewhat impatiently, Ethan motioned for him to do it, and the man pulled out a cracked Android and snapped a photo.

"There," Ethan said. "Now take a picture of my license— there you go. You've got proof of who I am and what I look like, just in case anything bad happens. But nothing's going to." *God willing,* he added silently.

The man seemed overwhelmed by this turn of events. "Shoot," he said. "You sure about this? You ain't gonna take it for a test-drive, even?"

"I'm in a hurry. I'm going to pay you, and I'm going to leave. But if I hear anything funny, I'll be back and I'll be pissed. Because you told me it runs like a dream, and I chose to believe you." Ethan held out the envelope with six thousand dollars in cash that Ruthanna had given him. "You're an honest guy, aren't you? The way I'm an honest guy? But maybe it's best to stick around your yard for a while, just in case."

"Sure, sure, I can do that." He glanced up at Ethan, his darting eyes uncertain. "This is for real?"

Ethan knew that the man *could* run, of course, but he was willing to bet more than six grand that he wouldn't. "It is for real," Ethan said. "But I'm going to ask you to throw in the bat over there."

The man laughed, but then he stopped when he saw that Ethan was serious. "Okay, okay, sure, no problem." He handed Ethan the keys and then jogged over to retrieve the bat.

Ethan got into the truck. The cab smelled a little sweet, like pipe tobacco. He stretched his arm out the window to take the bat. "It's been a pleasure doing business with you," he said.

"When do you think you'll come back?" the man asked.

Ethan started the engine with a roar. "A few days, I hope," he said.

"Well, good luck," the man called as Ethan backed out of the driveway.

Ethan put the truck in drive and gunned it down the street.

He could tell right off that the truck ran smoothly and that it would get him where he needed to go. Fifteen hundred miles was all he asked of it for now, with another fifteen hundred to get itself back home.

Ethan turned on the radio, and Maren Morris was singing "My Church." He tapped his fingers on the wheel.

Soon traffic thinned and he'd made it into the desert. Desolate and brown, under an empty blue sky, it made him think of Afghanistan—a place he tried hard not to remember. Ethan Blake set his jaw and practiced box breathing. It was twenty-odd hours to Arkansas. He watched the speedometer climb up to seventy-eight miles per hour, and then he put the Ram in cruise control.

CHAPTER
81

It was five o'clock in the morning when AnnieLee walked up to the bright-yellow Freightliner parked at a rest stop outside Albuquerque and knocked on the window. She'd spent the night at a Roadside Inn a few miles down the highway—it was a major step down from the Aquitaine—and now it was time to get moving. She waited for a little while, shivering, and then she knocked again. A minute or two later, a sleepy, angry face appeared.

The man it belonged to motioned her away. "I don't want no company," he said, his voice muffled through the glass. "I don't do that kind of thing." He held up a ring finger. "*Married*, okay?"

This was exactly the information that AnnieLee was looking for. "I'm not a lot lizard, or commercial company, or whatever the heck you want to call it," she said. "I'm just asking for a ride." She gestured to the horizon, where it was just beginning to go a paler gray. "You're supposed to be driving pretty soon, I bet. If you let me ride along, I'll buy you all the Egg McMuffins you can eat and the biggest coffee they got."

The man turned away and stared out his windshield. Out on

the highway, only a few sets of headlights stabbed through the predawn dark. AnnieLee couldn't hear the man sigh, but she could see him do it, the way his shoulders lifted up and then fell back down.

"Fine," he said, and she was already up on the step when the passenger door swung open.

"Thank you so much," AnnieLee said, climbing in. "My name's Katie."

He told her that his name was Foster Barnes, and he was headed to Oklahoma City. Gruff and quiet at first, he warmed up after she bought him the promised breakfast at a McDonald's thirty miles down the highway. And once Foster got a few ounces of coffee in his belly, AnnieLee barely had to say a word; she just listened to him talk about his job, about fishing with his wife, and about the boat they were building in his garage whenever he wasn't on the road. After a solid hour of monologue, Foster turned to AnnieLee. "Well, I've sure talked a lot," he said. "What's your story?"

"I don't have one, really," AnnieLee said lightly, shoving her hands into the pocket of her pink VEGAS, BABY sweatshirt. "I'm just a girl without a car."

"Huh," Foster said after a moment. "Well, I hope you're being real careful out there."

"Oh, I am," AnnieLee said. Her fingers found the can of pepper spray she'd bought back in the Vegas shop. Small and hot pink, it looked just like a tube of lipstick.

Foster looked over at her, his expression serious. "I mean it, Katie!" Then he said, "Sorry. I didn't mean to speak sharply like that. It's just that a lot of people aren't as nice as you want 'em to be."

No shit, AnnieLee thought. *You want a list?*

But she pulled her hands out of the pocket of her hoodie.

"You seem nice, though," she said, and she could see the blush that crept up Foster's neck to his cheeks. She'd been right—he was one of the good ones.

"You seem pretty nice, too," he managed.

AnnieLee thanked him, though she wasn't nice at all. She'd kept too many secrets and abandoned too many people, and that wasn't even the worst of it.

"You got someone waiting for you on the other end?" Foster asked.

"I sure do," AnnieLee said. "All I got to do is find him."

And when I do, she thought, *I'm going to kill him.*

She didn't think Foster would want to hear about that.

They parted ways in Oklahoma City, a few miles away from the electronics distribution center that was Foster's final destination. Right before she hopped out of the cab, he held out a fifty-dollar bill. AnnieLee said, "Oh, no, I couldn't," but Foster Barnes shook it at her.

"If it means you can take a cab instead of one ride from a stranger," he said, "then that's all I ask." When still she hesitated, he said, "Consider it a favor to Foster Barnes."

She took the money and then she reached for his hand. "Thank you," she said, squeezing it.

"Best of luck," he said. "Go with God."

I'd sure like to, thought AnnieLee. *But it's the devil's help I need.*

82

Ethan felt the Ram's right rear tire go flat on the far side of Flagstaff. After pulling in at the next gas station to change it, he discovered that the spare, which should've been stored underneath the truck bed, was missing. He kicked the flat in anger. He hadn't even made it four hours down the road.

The gas station didn't have a repair shop, so Ethan got back into the cab and drove slowly back toward the city, hazards flashing, to the nearest Pep Boys, where he paced the lobby while a guy named Bobby worked on the Ram. He bought a bag of Lay's from the vending machine, ate them, and then bought two more bags for the road. Potato chips—AnnieLee's favorite food and probably her primary source of caloric intake.

Doubt crept into his head during the delay. What if his hunch was utterly wrong? What if she was still somewhere in Las Vegas?

He reached into his pocket and pulled out her wallet and her cell. The phone was locked, and her wallet contained nothing but a handful of prepaid credit cards, seventy dollars in cash, and a few receipts from Nashville coffee shops. There was nothing with her signature on it. There wasn't a single photo. He couldn't even find a driver's license. It was like holding the wallet of a ghost.

Ethan walked over to the lobby window and watched the passing cars slow down at the stoplight. If there was one thing he knew about AnnieLee, it was that she didn't back down from a fight. So if she'd run from the man who surprised her in her hotel room, that didn't mean the fight was over. It was more likely that she was circling back for the knockout punch.

Ethan pressed his forehead against the cool glass. The man in the Aquitaine had come from the part of AnnieLee's life that she couldn't bear to talk about—he was sure of it— and whatever terrible secret she insisted on keeping was tied directly to him.

That was why she was hitchhiking back home, to the place she said she never wanted to go again. Ethan would bet anything that he was right. Caster County, Arkansas. All he had to do was follow and find her.

He really believed he could do it.

The light changed to green, and the line of cars surged forward. Ethan watched them, wondering what sort of drivers had stopped for AnnieLee. Where, exactly, was her final destination? And what did she plan to do when she got there? These were the questions that set his teeth on edge.

"Found the culprit, sir," said a voice.

Ethan turned around to see Bobby holding up a two-inch screw.

"Sucker went right through your tire," he said. "But she's all patched up now, and you're good to go."

It was after 6 p.m. by the time Ethan was back on the highway. He figured he could go for another seven or eight hours before he needed to stop. As he drove, he thought about everything else he knew of AnnieLee, and about how little it added up to. She was stubborn and funny and beautiful, and her singing voice could give him chills. But he still knew more about his damn *dentist's* life than he did about hers.

So how was it that he loved her the way he did? How had she become as necessary to his life as oxygen? He opened his second bag of potato chips. The world was full of mysteries, he supposed, and the human heart—*his* human heart—had turned out to be one of them.

As Ethan was pondering it all, a red Ford pulled alongside him in the left-hand lane. For a mile or two, the truck stayed there, matching its speed to the Ram's. Ethan, finally glancing over to ID the incompetent driver, saw a man pointing and gesturing at him in some kind of wild pantomime.

What the hell? Ethan thought.

The man finally made a comprehensible motion: *Roll down your window.*

Ethan did, and the man screamed across the dotted line at him, "Your tire!"

Startled, Ethan realized that the steering wheel was vibrating, and the Ram was pulling to the right.

Another flat. Furious, he took the next exit off the highway.

CHAPTER

83

After saying goodbye to Foster Barnes, AnnieLee had wasted no time catching a ride to Fort Smith, Arkansas. But that was where her hitching luck had run out—not that she would have expected anything different from a state that'd ground her up and spit her out the way it did.

No siree, there was no place like home.

She'd walked east along Grand Avenue toward the university, hoping to find a college kid heading out of town for the weekend. But she'd waited for three hours now, and it was getting dark.

"Driven to insanity," she sang softly, *"driven to the edge…"*

Paying for another motel room would nearly clean her out, and anyway, she was determined to keep going. She started walking again. She felt rattled, jumpy; she had felt this way ever since she crossed the state line. She couldn't tell if the tightness in her chest came from anticipation or dread. Probably it was both.

Hearing the low hum of traffic from I-540 up ahead, she broke into a light jog. It was never a good idea to hitch at night, but right now she didn't even care. Whatever she had to do—

beg, hitch, or crawl the whole way on her hands and knees—
she'd do it.

Vengeance was one hell of a motivator.

Twenty minutes later, AnnieLee was scrambling up the embankment to the interstate. Cars rushed past as she stood on the gravel shoulder, forcing a smile no one would be able to see in the darkness.

When a woman in an old white Pontiac finally pulled over, AnnieLee got in and let herself be scolded for hitchhiking, for being out alone at night, for not having a proper coat, and for every other wrong choice the woman seemed to think she'd made in her life. AnnieLee just nodded gratefully, promising she would start going to church and turn herself around, and two hours later she got dropped off on a rural road barely twenty miles from her final destination.

She fingered Foster's money in her pocket. He'd said *If it means you can take a cab…*

But there weren't any cabs in the boondocks, or at least not any that she knew how to call on a phone she didn't even have. And so she put out her thumb again. She hoped a kind and decent stranger would stop for her. In a place so small that everyone seemed to know everyone else, she just needed a person who wouldn't recognize her. Someone who'd believe her name was Katie—or even AnnieLee Keyes.

She walked along the side of the road, sticking out her thumb whenever she heard a car approaching. After an hour or so, a battered Chevy passed by and screeched to a halt twenty yards in front of her. She ran up to meet it.

When the man—he was around her age, and alone—pushed the passenger door open, AnnieLee felt a humid cloud of beery air spill out and surround her.

She'd never seen him before, and this was such a relief that she overlooked the fact that he'd been drinking, and that she'd just promised that nice old lady that she wouldn't ever take a ride from a random man again. She got in. She was so damn *close* to where she needed to be, and she didn't know when the next car would stop, and already it felt like she was in enemy territory. She needed to keep moving.

"I thought you were a deer at first," he said. Then he laughed. "Shoot, woulda hit ya and turned you into steaks."

"Not a deer," AnnieLee said. She looked down at the empty beer cans in the cup holders. "You're going to keep us between the ditches, right?" she asked, buckling in. She pulled the man's coat out from behind her back and tucked it down by her feet.

"Pretty sure I can do that," he said.

"I hope so," AnnieLee said. "I've had enough near-death experiences for the week," she added, but she said it so quietly that he didn't hear her.

"Where you aiming to get?" he asked.

One of his headlights was out, and the other was dim and yellow. "A bit outside Jasper," she said. "On the way to Rock Springs."

"You from the hills?" he asked.

Out of the corner of her eye she could see that he was looking closely at her. "I am."

"Do I know you?"

"I don't think so," she said. "I've been gone a long time."

"Welcome back, then," he said. "You party?"

"Not so much," she said.

"Too bad."

He was quiet after that; he seemed to be concentrating on driving. AnnieLee sat as close to the door as she could get, with the window cracked to bring in fresh air. She wasn't worried about him running off the road anymore. But she couldn't say the same about what the next few hours would hold. Could she get this half-drunk hillbilly to take her right up to the door? Would the house be dark? Would anyone be home? Could she find the rifle that used to be hidden underneath the front porch?

She was trying to imagine what might happen next when she felt the pressure of a hand on her leg.

You've got *to be kidding me,* she thought. *Not this shit again.*

"You feel tense," he said.

She pushed his hand away. "Don't," she said.

He laughed. "Oh, don't be such a prude," he said. "I'm just being friendly. Let's go have a drink. I know a spot a little ways up the road. I think you'll like me. My name's Wade. What's yours?"

AnnieLee felt her arms go cold. "I think you'd better just let me out."

"Are you crazy? It's the middle of nowhere." Wade sounded disappointed in her.

He drove with both hands on the wheel for a while. But eventually the right one found its way to her leg again. She watched it moving up toward her crotch, and for a minute she just sat there, frozen and horrified. Where was her gun when she needed it?

Suddenly she remembered her pepper spray, and she reached into her pocket. But somehow the little tube was gone.

"Shit," she whispered.

"What, babe?" Wade said.

He ran his finger along the inner seam of her sweatpants. It tickled. And it made AnnieLee feel like she was going to vomit.

"Get your hand off of me, or else," she said.

"Or else what?" he asked. When he looked at her, he didn't seem drunk anymore. He seemed focused and dangerous.

AnnieLee's mind had gone numb, but her body clicked into

gear without it. She reached down, grabbed Wade's coat, and clutched it to her chest. When the car slowed to make the next curve in the road, AnnieLee threw open the door. She didn't hesitate, not even for a second. She flung herself out, holding the coat to cushion her fall. She landed with a horrific thud on the pavement and then rolled down into a ditch.

She lay there, panting, as the sound of the car engine faded. Her head was an explosion of pain and her vision was going in and out. But she gritted her teeth and tried to get up on her hands and knees. She didn't think she'd broken anything, but every part of her hurt.

She crawled a little ways, unsure if she should try to make it back up to the road or drag herself into the woods like a wounded deer. Which was less dangerous? It felt impossible to think, and it was getting harder and harder to keep her eyes open. The world was spinning way too fast suddenly. She felt like she needed to lie down. She saw a flash of light and looked up toward the road.

She held her breath so she wouldn't cry out in pain. Was someone coming to help her? She squinted through the dark.

It was Wade, picking his way down the hill.

"No," she whispered. And then she blacked out.

CHAPTER
84

Ethan woke stiff and sore after five hours of fitful sleep in a convenience store parking lot thirty miles east of the Texas border. It was cold inside the cab and chilly outside, too, though he knew it'd get plenty warm once the sun got a little higher in the sky. He slipped on his boots and stumbled into the shop, where he bought himself a coffee, a bag of sunflower seeds, and a microwavable egg sandwich. After filling up the tank, he was back on the road.

Despite the flat tires, he was making good time. When Ruthanna called to check in, Ethan told her that he'd be in Arkansas before the day was out.

"And then what?" she asked. "Maya spent hours yesterday trying to find AnnieLee online—her hometown, her high school—and she didn't come up with anything. It's like she doesn't even exist."

Though this wasn't the news he'd hoped for, it wasn't exactly what he'd call surprising.

"So how're you going to find her?" Ruthanna demanded.

"Drive around the state calling her name out the window? Light a fire and send up smoke signals?"

"Eight hundred square miles," he said. "That's all I gotta cover."

"What?" Ruthanna said.

There was a cop up ahead, and Ethan slowed down a little. "The county she's from, Caster—that's how big it is. But that was a joke. I don't have to drive the whole thing. She grew up in the woods, right next to a creek that drains into the Little Buffalo River. I'll find her."

"Hang on," Ruthanna said.

He could hear her tapping something into her phone, and a minute or two later she came back on.

"Caster's nothing *but* woods and creeks!" she exclaimed. "Ethan, this is never going to work."

"Yes, it is," he said stubbornly. "Someone's going to know her, Ruthanna, and that someone's going to tell me where she is."

"Call me the instant you have news," she said.

"I will," he said.

By 4 p.m., he'd found a run-down-looking shack with a flickering Budweiser sign in the window that called itself the Reel 'em Inn. Though Caster County was dry, its neighbor, Boone, could serve liquor starting at breakfast time.

The bar was smoky and dimly lit, and over the sound of a TV football game, Ethan could hear Hank Williams singing about how lonesome he was. Ethan parked himself on an empty stool and ordered a pint of what the window advertised. Even though he could tell by the beer's wet dog smell that the tap hoses hadn't been cleaned recently, if ever, he still felt his shoulders relax as he took the first sip. He let himself get halfway down the pint before he asked the bartender if he'd ever heard of a girl named AnnieLee Keyes.

"Doesn't ring a bell," he said.

A bearded geezer down at the end of the bar snorted. "That's because we don't get no women in here," he said. "Used to, but it's too much of a dump now."

"You hate it so much, Bucky, go someplace else," the bartender said.

Bucky spun around on his stool. "Nowhere else to go, bro."

Ethan pulled up a picture of AnnieLee on his phone. "This is what she looks like. She grew up around here."

"You a cop?"

"No," Ethan said. "Definitely not."

The bartender looked down at the screen and then up at Ethan. "She run off on you?"

Ethan hesitated. "Yeah."

The bartender poured a shot of Jack Daniel's and set it in front of Ethan. "Women are more trouble than they're worth," he said. "That's why none of us are home with the ones we got."

"Damn straight," the geezer called.

"Shut up. Yours is dead," the bartender said.

Ethan knocked the shot back and set the glass down on the sticky bar. "Thanks, man," he said. He put the phone back in his pocket. "I guess you'd remember a girl like that, wouldn't you?"

"I would," the bartender said. "A girl as pretty as that, though? She's not here—I can tell you that much. She'd get the hell out as soon as she could, and she wouldn't never come back."

CHAPTER
85

Ethan spent the night lying on the bench seat of the truck, barely sleeping, and in the morning he began his search in earnest, driving from one tiny, run-down town to another in search of someone who could tell him what he needed to know. Trees and meadows were on every side; he rarely even passed another car.

The countryside was wild and beautiful, but the abandoned buildings crumbling at the corners of empty crossroads seemed almost haunted. A hundred years ago, these little places had been thriving; now, most of them seemed long since dead.

In a place called Bensonville, Ethan passed a shuttered butcher shop with a hand-painted sign advertising turtle and coon meat. Next to it might've once been a hair salon. Now it was nothing but an empty room with a dusty tiled floor.

There were no cars parked along the main street, but down at the end of the block, Ethan saw someone sitting on a bench. As he drove closer, he saw that it was an old man dressed in a pair of faded Carhartt overalls. For all Ethan knew, he was the only inhabitant of the whole town, and he looked like he was waiting for a bus that was never going to come.

Ethan pulled over and rolled down the window. "Morning," he said. "Are you familiar with the Keyes family?"

The old man looked at him for a long time before he spoke. "I know some Lockes," he said, and then gave a great guffawing laugh.

Ethan hated puns. "Thanks for your time," he said. He drove away without bothering to show the man the picture.

Half an hour later, he came upon a much bigger town. It was almost picturesque, with flowers planted in old whiskey barrels along the main drag, and the Little Buffalo—the river he was aiming for—was running along the north side of the road. Ethan saw an antiques shop, a Christian bookstore, a pawn-broker, two motels, and a café with a blue-and-white-striped awning.

Ethan figured he'd kill two birds with one stone by going into the café, where he could eat breakfast and ask a question or two.

The woman who waited on him was young and fine-featured, with lively green eyes. Ethan tried to be friendly, but other than taking his order, she barely acknowledged his existence. Twenty minutes later, she brought him a plate of undercooked pancakes and overcooked bacon and was refilling his coffee mug for the third time when he said, "I wonder if I could ask you something."

She wiped a drop of coffee off the table with the corner of her apron. "I've got a boyfriend," she said.

Ethan was taken aback. "Seeing as how we've said less than twenty words to each other, it'd be pretty presumptuous of me to ask you out," he said. "And honestly, I think it's pretty presumptuous of you to assume that I want to."

She cracked a smile at that, the first friendly one he'd seen on her face. "Sorry," she said. "It's kind of a reflex."

Ethan dropped a sugar cube into the bitter brew. He didn't suppose being a pretty girl in the only café for a hundred miles was the easiest job in the world. "I just wanted to ask you if you'd ever heard of AnnieLee Keyes," he said. "She's a singer."

"Sure, I've heard of her," the girl said. *Dark night, bright future,"* she sang. *"Like the phoenix from the ashes, I shall rise again…"*

"You've got a great voice," Ethan said. It was high and clear, with a faint vibrato. "And I'm not hitting on you, either."

"Sure, sure, I believe you," the girl said. It was unclear whether or not she meant it.

"Have you ever seen her?" Ethan asked. He brought out his phone and showed her a picture he'd taken of AnnieLee backstage. Her hair was messy, her cheeks pink and sweaty from the spotlight. She looked tired and gorgeous and radiant.

The waitress leaned in, and then she frowned a little.

"What is it?" Ethan asked.

"That's what she looks like? Do you have any more pictures of her?" the girl asked.

"Swipe left," he said.

Ethan watched as the girl thumbed through his photos of AnnieLee onstage, backstage, and in the passenger seat of the van. The girl was squinting at first, and then she began to lightly shake her head. After another moment a smile broke over her face. And pretty soon she started laughing. "No shit," she was saying. "No freaking *shit.*"

"Why are you laughing? What's so funny?" Ethan asked.

"That's not AnnieLee Keyes," she said. "That's Rose McCord." She swiped to see a few more pictures. "Yeah, she looks real good. I liked her better with her natural hair, though."

Ethan felt as though he'd been punched in the gut. He shoved his plate away and looked up at the waitress. "What color is her real hair?" he asked. Immediately he wished he could take the question back, because the answer didn't matter at all. What mattered was that AnnieLee—or Rose McCord, or whoever the hell she was—hadn't just been *unforthcoming* about her past. She'd been lying about everything.

"Caramel blond, I guess you'd call it," the waitress said. "It was real long, real pretty."

Ethan clenched his fists under the table. He was pissed and embarrassed that he hadn't known the actual name of the woman he loved, but he struggled to keep his emotions in check; he had to remember that she was in danger. "Do you know where Ann—where Rose used to live?" he asked.

"Outside of town somewhere," the waitress said. "I don't know, really. I just used to see her around. She was a few years older than me, but she wasn't stuck-up. She was nice. But then she got herself a boyfriend, and it seemed like she kinda disappeared. I assumed she married him and moved away. That's the dream, right? Get the hell out?" She tucked a stray curl behind her ear. "Easier said than done, though." She glanced down at Ethan's still-full plate. "You done already?"

"Yeah," Ethan said. "It was delicious." He took out two twenties and laid them on the table. "Do you know anyone who might know where she lived?"

The girl narrowed her eyes at him. "Does she want you to find her?"

"Maybe she didn't at first," he said. "But I think she does now."

"You her boyfriend?"

"No, I'm her…" Ethan paused. "Bodyguard."

The girl picked up the plate. "So Rose McCord really became AnnieLee Keyes?" she asked. "And she's writing songs now?"

"She sure is," Ethan said. "She's really good."

"That's incredible," the waitress said. "Damn, I'm happy for her."

Ethan stood up. "Any information you could give me—"

"Go ask Blaine over at the pawnshop," she said. "He knows just about everything about everybody, and sometimes he's in the mood to talk."

Ethan thanked her and left without taking his change, which amounted to a nearly 300 percent tip.

The waitress followed him outside and waved to him as he walked down the street. "I lied about having a boyfriend!" she called.

B laine wore a high and tight, but Ethan knew instantly that he wasn't military and never had been, though Ethan could imagine him spending a semester in JROTC before being kicked out for smoking a blunt in the school parking lot. He seemed vaguely high now, Ethan thought, or it could've been that he was just on the slow side.

He certainly wasn't interested in acknowledging Ethan's existence, at least not until Ethan picked out a fishing rod and a messed-up-looking ukulele and set them on the cracked glass of the counter. Ethan watched as Blaine did a quick calculus—shitty rod, busted instrument, out-of-towner—and said, "Hundred."

Ethan laughed and said, "Twenty-five."

Blaine grunted his assent.

As Blaine was putting the money in the cash register, Ethan casually asked him what he knew about Rose McCord and who her people were. "I think her stepdad's name was Clayton."

Blaine sucked his teeth and said, "Uh-huh, I know him.

Clayton Dunning's a mean sumbitch. Give him half a chance and he'll knock the pretty right off your face."

Ethan immediately thought about showing Blaine just who could knock what. But that went against his rule. *Don't start fights,* it went, *just finish them.* So he faked a smile and said, "How about you tell me where I can find him so he can do that for me? I'm sick of being so damn good-looking."

Blaine snorted. "Nearest hospital's an hour away."

Ethan gritted his teeth. The joke was getting old fast. "I need you to tell me where he lives."

"Yeah, yeah, okay," Blaine said, coming out from behind the counter. "Just don't tell him I did."

Two minutes later, Ethan tossed his purchases into the back seat of the cab and headed northeast out of town. He stayed on the main highway for twenty miles before turning onto a narrow road leading into the woods. As he drove, the road grew narrower and rougher—the kind of road that would've rattled Gladys to pieces. Pretty soon it was just a dirt track, and it seemed like the trees were closing in on him from all sides. Feeling claustrophobic, he rolled down the window and breathed in the scent of leaves, moss, and a nearby creek. A rabbit skittered in front of the truck, and Ethan touched his brakes as it disappeared into the woods.

"You're going to think that you've gone too far, and you're lost," Blaine had said. "But you won't be. You're just supposed to feel like it."

As he drove, Ethan tried to convince himself that he'd find AnnieLee just up ahead. There were girls she loved and a man she hated living off this road, so it wasn't so crazy to think she'd be there.

Finally he came to the tree Blaine had told him he'd find, the dead maple with the NO TRESPASSING notices nailed all over it. Two children's dolls hung from the broken branches, one upside down by her plastic legs and the other by her neck.

"That's the warning for any trespassers who can't read," Blaine had said, laughing. "You have yourself a nice visit."

87

A dog barked as Ethan drove up the dirt track toward the crooked jumble of tar paper and cheap siding that was Clayton Dunning's house. There were rusting machine parts scattered all over the yard and one incongruously shiny Chevy pickup with a gun rack and a brand-new deer hoist. Weeds grew around a pile of broken beer bottles and through the rigging of a wrecked trampoline.

Shit, Ethan thought. *No wonder AnnieLee left.*

As he walked toward the house, the front door opened and a man came onto the porch. "Who the hell are you?" he said as he lifted a rifle and pointed it at Ethan.

Ethan stopped in his tracks. He held up his hands a little—not a gesture of surrender, but an indication that he was unarmed. "The name's Ethan Blake. Clayton Dunning? I'm here because I'm looking for your stepdaughter. For Rose."

Clayton Dunning squinted at him. He was a bulldog of a man, round and ugly and unsmiling. Behind him, a teenage girl poked her head out of the house, and she looked Ethan up and down with a quick, almost animal curiosity.

"Get back inside," Clayton said.

"Hey," Ethan called to her. "You look a little like Rose."

Surprise flashed over the girl's face. "Rose? You know her?"

"I sure do," he said. "I'm trying to find her. Has she come around?"

"No," the girl said, and then she turned and yelled back into the house, "Shelly, he knows Rose!"

"I told you to get inside," Clayton said. He shoved the girl with the butt of his rifle and she vanished from view. Then he pointed the weapon back at Ethan. "You're trespassing."

"I was hoping a friend of the family wouldn't be considered a trespasser," Ethan said mildly. He gazed at the gun like it was a curiosity instead of a threat. "Is that a Winchester Model 70? I used to have one of those."

Clayton hocked a loogie into the yard. "You ain't no friend," he said. "And Rose ain't no family. Not my blood."

Then the teenager came around from the back of the house, holding the hand of a younger girl who looked even more like AnnieLee—rosebud lips and bright-blue eyes and everything.

"He knows Rose," the older girl said.

Ethan turned to them. "Have either of you seen your sister?" he asked. "Or heard from her lately?"

They shook their heads solemnly, and Ethan struggled to push back a growing sense of unease. He *knew* she was close. Why wouldn't she reach out to them?

"Listen," he said, "I know Rose came back this way, and I'm trying to find out where she is."

"She ain't here," Clayton said, stepping down off the porch. The dog started barking again. "Shut up!" he yelled, and it whined and lay down. "I don't know where she is, and I don't care. I just know that whatever they did to her, she deserved it."

"Deserved what?" There was a sharp edge to Ethan's voice. "Who's *they*?"

Clayton spat again and said nothing.

"We haven't seen her in a couple years," the teenager said quietly.

"Is she gonna come visit?" the younger girl asked. "I miss her."

Ethan looked at them with overwhelming pity. How hard it would be to live out here with only that angry man for family. "She'll visit," he said. "I'm sure she's on her way."

"That girl had the devil in her," Clayton said. "Couldn't beat it out."

Ethan stiffened, but he didn't want to start a fight with Clayton, not with his daughters standing right there.

He made a subtle beckoning motion, and the girls saw it and followed him toward his truck. "Are you okay?" he whispered as he opened the door.

The big one nodded. "Is Rose?"

"I hope so," Ethan said. "I have to find her. If you hear from her, you call me, okay? I'll be in town." He gave her his cell number, and he could hear her repeating it to herself as the girls walked back toward the house.

Then he felt something sharp stabbing him in the low part of his back.

"You better go on if you want to keep your guts inside you," Clayton said.

Ethan whirled around so fast the other man didn't have time to react. Ethan grabbed the barrel of the rifle and yanked it out of Clayton's hands, throwing it into the Ram's cab at the same time he brought a left hook to the side of Clayton's head. Clayton stumbled sideways, hollering, and Ethan jumped into the truck. Then he was spinning it around in the dirt yard and peeling away down that sorry excuse for a driveway, AnnieLee's stepfather roaring in rage behind him.

When he'd made it to the main road, Ethan glanced over at the rifle. He'd been right: it was a Winchester Model 70, just like he used to have.

CHAPTER
88

T hat evening, Ethan parked on the edge of town in front of a building whose sign proclaimed it the PROUD HOME OF POSSUM TOM'S LIVE BAIT. But Possum Tom, whoever he was, was long gone; the windows of his store were boarded up and trash littered the doorway.

Ethan watched as a fat raccoon slowly descended a nearby tree and proceeded to nose its way along the sidewalk, as casually as if it was out for a twilight stroll.

"Be careful, buddy," Ethan said as the creature ambled by. "Don't want to end up as someone's dinner."

Ethan's own dinner came out of the messenger bag he always carried: two protein bars, a bag of sunflower seeds, and a bottle of Gatorade left over from a greenroom back in Colorado. After he ate, he sat there with the stolen gun in his lap, absently running a thumb along its smooth stock. He was trying to keep his mind as empty as possible, because otherwise it was filled with awful visions: AnnieLee being picked up by someone dangerous. Being taken somewhere she didn't want to go. Being hurt or kidnapped or—

He shook his head. *Enough.*

And what about those girls he'd met today—her half sisters? Did Clayton hit them the way he'd hit AnnieLee? Ethan hoped Clayton was kinder to his own flesh and blood.

He couldn't imagine what it'd be like to grow up in the middle of nowhere like that, in a house that looked like a strong wind could blow it over. As beautiful as the land was, Clayton's mark on it was nothing but ugliness.

Ethan set the gun aside and reclined a little, listening to the deep quiet of an Arkansas night. Somehow he must have fallen asleep, because the next thing he knew there was a loud banging on his window. He sat straight up, his heart racing and the rifle already back in his hands.

But the face on the other side of the glass didn't belong to a threat. Peering in at him was a scared-looking girl. It was AnnieLee's teenage half sister, the one whose name he didn't even know.

He rolled down the window. "Hey," he said, his voice hoarse with sleep. "Come around, kiddo. Get in."

A moment later she was climbing into the passenger side. "I shouldn't be here," she said.

"Are you okay?" he asked.

"Considering I stole my daddy's truck and drove it without a license and made it all the way here without killing myself, I'd say I'm doing pretty good." She held out her hands and looked at them, flexing her fingers. "I was holding on to that damn steering wheel so tight I must've got blisters." She looked over at him, and her eyes were huge in the darkness. "Clayton's gonna kill me if he finds out, but I just...I needed to talk to you. And you didn't answer your phone."

Ethan reached into the pocket of his bag and pulled out his

phone. There were four missed calls. "Shit," he said. "I'm sorry. I sure don't want you to get in trouble."

"Too late for that, most likely," she said. She put her feet up on the dashboard and then took them down again. "But I don't care, anyhow."

"I didn't ever catch your name," he said gently.

"Alice," she said. "Alice Rae."

Ethan had to ask. "What happens when you get in trouble, Alice Rae?"

"Oh, my dad'll lock me in my room for a couple of days," she said nonchalantly. "Whatever."

"He won't hit you?" *If he does,* Ethan thought, *I'm not letting her go back.*

"No, not anymore," she said. "He used to, and Rose always got the worst of it. But a couple of years ago, after she left, he had a scare. He passed out down by the creek, and we didn't know where he was until the dog led us to him."

She gave a bleak laugh. "That was ironic, seeing as how Clayton's never said a nice word to Bandit in his whole damn life. But dogs are loyal and dumb, so whatever. After Clayton comes around, up he goes to the doctor, and he finds out he's got a bad heart. Doc says he shouldn't get agitated anymore. And I guess that mellowed him out a little."

Alice was braiding and unbraiding her hair as she spoke. "Anyway," she said, "you don't care about him and neither do I, or anyways not near as much as I should, considering he's half the reason I'm here on this earth."

"I can help you," Ethan said.

"No, you can't," she said bluntly. "But it doesn't matter. Me and Shelly'll be okay. It's Rose you came here for." She stared right at him again, and now she looked scared. "And I think she's in danger."

Alarm shot through Ethan's body like an electric shock. "What do you mean?"

"If she made it this far and she didn't come see us, it's because she wanted to see somebody else first. And it didn't go well." Alice looked down at the rifle, still in Ethan's hands. "She went to find Gus Hobbs—I'd bet anything," she said. "And now she needs your help."

"Who's Gus Hobbs?" Ethan asked.

Alice clutched her hands together in her lap, twisting them in agitation. "He's a really bad man," she said. "And he's Rose's husband."

CHAPTER

89

Three hours later, driving up yet another rutted road in the middle of thick forest, Ethan bitterly wondered if he'd ever come to the end of AnnieLee's secrets. *Husband?* He couldn't even fathom it.

Of course, maybe Alice Rae was a liar, just like her big sister.

Branches brushed along the side of the truck, and the Ram's headlights hardly seemed to penetrate the predawn darkness. Adrenaline coursed through him. So did a swirl of conflicting emotions. Never had anyone messed with his head and heart the way AnnieLee had.

"You'll see a fallen-down shack on your right, and then you'll know you're getting close," Alice had said.

Hopefully Alice is at least telling the truth about directions, Ethan thought darkly.

After another half hour of driving, he saw the shack, a crumbling shell of what might've once been a homesteader's cabin. There was an illegal dump just beyond it, full of old couches, mattresses, and car skeletons. Ethan's headlights picked out the eyes of some nocturnal creature scuttling among the refuse.

As instructed, he went five hundred yards past the dump. But then he pulled onto the shoulder and cut the engine. He paused for a second, gathering himself, and then he grabbed the rifle and got out of the truck. He picked his way along the side of the road until he spotted what he was looking for: the red reflector nailed to a post, which—if Alice Rae wasn't trying to get him lost forever in the Arkansas woods—marked the turnoff to Gus Hobbs's house.

The night was very still, with barely any wind, and a half-moon offered just enough light to see. Ethan walked softly and deliberately toward his target, every sense on high alert as he followed the dirt track up the hill.

Suddenly, sound and motion exploded on his right. He jumped back and simultaneously brought up his gun. A deer shot across the way in front of him and crashed into the brush on the other side.

Ethan listened to its footsteps fade as he stood there, panting. "Shit," he whispered. When his heartbeat had slowed, he continued on.

He'd walked nearly a mile before he saw the house up ahead, dimly illuminated in the moonlight. It was a hand-built cabin, standing in the middle of a swept-dirt yard that was as neat as Clayton's had been messy. Ethan was so focused on the silent house that he walked right into the barbed wire that had been strung across the road fifty yards in front of the place. He stifled a cry of pain as the rusted spikes sank into his flesh at his waist and thigh. Gritting his teeth, he stepped back, tugging his skin and clothes away from the wire.

Whoever Gus Hobbs was, he had a knack for simple deterrent technology, Ethan thought. After ducking under the wire, he walked more carefully, in case Hobbs had hidden a bear trap in one of the potholes. Hobbs didn't seem to have a guard dog, but

Ethan could think of any number of defenses that were cheaper, quieter, and more lethal.

He held the rifle loosely as he went. He wasn't going to walk in shooting. But feeling the weight of the weapon in his hands reassured him, the way it had when he was a soldier. The years in Afghanistan weren't ones Ethan could say he'd enjoyed, but they'd shaped him. They'd turned him from a scared, uncertain kid into a man who understood honor and duty, and who recognized the kinds of sacrifices those ideals often required.

As Ethan thought about Antoine and Jeanie and others he'd lost along the way, he told himself that he wasn't going to lose AnnieLee, too.

He crept past two cars and walked up to a dimly lit window. Inside he could see the kitchen, its counters full of cereal boxes, chip bags, and beer cans. On the left-hand side of the room was an interior door, closed. He put his fingertips under the sash and lifted. The window slid open with a sigh.

Damn. Was this how he was going to do it? Just *climb in*?

It was almost like a written invitation. If someone caught him halfway through the window, he'd be the easiest target imaginable—but it still felt like better odds than trying to get in through the front door.

Ethan guided the rifle through the window, balancing it on its stock against the inside wall. Then he took a deep breath and pulled himself up onto the sill.

His boots scraped noisily on the side of the house, but there was nothing he could do about that now. He got his torso through, and he was slithering the rest of the way inside when the door at the end of the kitchen swung open.

CHAPTER

90

E than didn't have time to move. Caught in the window frame, he was face-to-face with a pair of green eyes.

And whiskers.

And two black, triangular ears. Then a low, sinewy body slunk into the kitchen, making for a food bowl in the corner. The door swung shut behind it.

Ethan nearly choked with relief as he pulled himself the rest of the way into the room. A damn *cat*! The creature, oblivious to the fact that it had nearly given him a heart attack, sniffed disdainfully at its dish. Then it brushed past Ethan's legs and hopped outside the way he had come in.

Ethan bent down and picked up the rifle. He could hear the faint buzz of talk radio coming from the other side of the kitchen door. Taking a few noiseless steps forward, he reached out and turned off the light. Then he waited, letting his eyes adjust to the darkness while he listened for movement in the other room. Hearing nothing but the same low, staticky radio voices, he opened the door.

Though it was nearly pitch-black in the room, Ethan could

make out a couch along the back wall and an exterior door on the wall opposite. Another doorway opened to what he assumed was a hallway leading to the rest of the cabin.

"*So keep your dial tuned to 860 AM,*" the radio voice intoned, "*for all your sports and weather news…*"

The radio voice seemed to be coming from the far corner of the room. Edging closer, Ethan could see what looked like a large recliner—and the body of a sleeping man in it.

Gus Hobbs.

Ethan carefully leaned the rifle against the wall. Then he launched himself forward in the darkness. He didn't want to stand back and threaten this man; he wanted to beat him to a bloody pulp.

Hobbs woke with a start just as Ethan was on top of him, and the guy only had time to throw up his hands before Ethan was driving his fists into his head and arms. Hobbs started yelling and trying to block the blows, but Ethan was wide-awake and enraged, and there was nothing Hobbs could do but try to scramble backward out of the chair to avoid him.

"Stop! Shit!" he was yelling. "Man, stop! Shit!"

Ethan finally pulled back and stood above him, panting. "Where is she, Hobbs?" he yelled. "Where is she?"

Brilliant overhead light flared in his eyes, blinding him. Squinting, Ethan turned to see another man in the other doorway, calmly leveling a pistol at his chest.

"That fool ain't Gus Hobbs," he said. "I am."

CHAPTER
91

E than sucked in his breath. He wasn't afraid: he was furious. He'd let his emotions cloud his judgment, and he'd attacked without knowing the size, strength, or even the *identity* of the enemy. What a stupid, rookie mistake.

He stood up to his full height, as if he wasn't looking down the wrong end of a pistol at all. "Where's Rose?" he demanded.

Hobbs didn't answer, and the other man wiped angrily at his bloody, swollen face. "Shoot him," he said. "Shoot that bastard."

Gus Hobbs turned his cold gaze to his partner. "Maybe I should shoot *you*," he said.

"I just closed my eyes for a minute—"

"Exactly," Hobbs said viciously.

Hobbs was lean but muscular, with a hard, almost handsome face. If Clayton Dunning had been a bulldog, then Gus Hobbs was closer to a wolf. Had AnnieLee really married this man? Had she lived here in this very house? Ethan still couldn't believe it.

But whatever the truth was, it didn't matter. All that mattered was finding her safe.

And, he thought grimly, *not getting killed trying.*

"Step outside," Hobbs said to Ethan, gesturing with the gun.

The other man laughed as he wiped his bleeding nose on his sleeve. "He don't want to get the floor messy when he shoots you."

"Shut up," Hobbs told him. To Ethan he said, "Hands up. Go on." He motioned toward the front door, which was just to Ethan's left.

Ethan put his hands up and slowly turned. But he turned the long way around, to his right, so that he could see the kitchen door and the rifle he'd leaned against the wall next to it. Maybe it was because the Winchester was the same color as the wood paneling, or maybe it was impossible for Hobbs or his flunky to imagine someone having a weapon and not using it, but neither man had noticed the gun. Ethan figured it was eight feet away from him. *Doable,* he thought.

Finally Ethan rotated so that he was facing the front door. "I can't open this with my hands in the air," he told them.

"Jesus," Hobbs said. "Open it, Rick."

As Rick came toward him, Ethan's right hand dropped down and he yanked the knob as hard as he could. The door went smashing into Rick's face. At the same time, Ethan dove backward toward the rifle, landing hard on his side. He grabbed the gun and rolled onto his back in one smooth motion, and then pulled the trigger and shot Gus Hobbs.

Or…he shot where Gus Hobbs had been.

The bullet punched a hole in the wall as Hobbs disappeared around the corner. Ethan swung the gun toward Rick as he got to his feet. "Run or I'll shoot," he growled.

Rick hesitated. Ethan fired, and the bullet grazed Rick's biceps. The man needed no further encouragement to leave.

Then Ethan, alone in the living room, inched toward where

Hobbs had gone. Crouching low, he peered through the doorway. He saw a short, empty hall and a back door flung wide open.

Hugging the wall, Ethan walked forward until the yard came into view. In the moonlight he could see patchy grass, a utility trailer, a shed, and a clothesline with a few yellowing towels on it. A moment later, Gus Hobbs's face and gun peered around the corner of the shed.

"Want to count to three and shoot each other?" Hobbs drawled.

Ethan fired, aiming right above Hobbs's head. The bullet hit the shed's overhanging roof. "Where is she?" he yelled.

Hobbs, who'd disappeared behind the shed, didn't answer.

Ethan dropped the rifle and jumped down the steps into the yard. He raced around to the other side of the shed and grabbed Hobbs by the legs as he was trying to run into the woods. They both went down hard in the dirt. Hobbs's gun spun out of his hand and landed out of his reach.

Hobbs kicked at Ethan's chest but Ethan held on, hauling himself up along Hobbs's body until he was astride him. He pushed Hobbs's face into the dirt.

"That kid from the gas station found her—Wade," Hobbs gasped. "Said she hit her head, passed out cold, then woke up cross-eyed and saying my name." He gave a kick and then lay still. "The stupid little prick brought her here. She always caused more trouble than she was worth, so I did what I had to do. Shit, man, that hurts!"

"You have no idea what *hurts* means," Ethan said. "Where is Rose McCord?"

Hobbs started to laugh—a wild, unhinged laugh that sent chills down Ethan's spine. "I threw her damn body in the cellar," he said.

CHAPTER

92

A pit opened in Ethan's stomach. *Her body?* He got up and yanked Hobbs by the belt until he was standing.

The man reeled, coughing and cackling. "She deserved it," Hobbs said, rubbing the dirt from his face with his shirt.

If Ethan hadn't dropped the rifle back by the steps, he would've shot Hobbs for real. "Take me to her now."

Hobbs straightened up. "If you say so."

Dread and fear made Ethan detach; he felt like he was watching himself walk through the yard behind Hobbs, who was still laughing softly but maniacally. Ethan saw himself pick up the fallen gun as Hobbs went to the cellar doors and heaved them open.

"Have at it," Hobbs said.

"You go in first," Ethan heard himself say.

Hobbs cursed and descended the ladder. Ethan followed close behind him, keeping the tip of the rifle aimed between Hobbs's shoulder blades.

The ceiling was low, and Ethan couldn't see anything. "Light," he said.

He heard Hobbs fumbling around, and then a flashlight clicked on. The beam was weak and flickering. It swept the perimeter of the room, revealing dirt, piles of gravel, and debris.

Then finally the beam found a human form. AnnieLee was curled in a corner, her hands and feet tied. Her eyes were closed and there was tape over her mouth.

"AnnieLee," Ethan gasped.

Her eyes flew open, wide and terrified.

Ethan felt himself slam back into his body, back into reality. *Dear God,* he thought, *she's alive.* His knees almost buckled.

But they didn't. He turned toward Hobbs, who was heading for the ladder. Ethan grabbed him by the collar and spun him around. Hobbs went to swing at him with the heavy flashlight, but Ethan ducked. Low and at close range, Ethan threw a vicious uppercut, tightening his fist right on impact. His knuckles slammed into Hobbs's chin with a sickening crack. Hobbs's head snapped back and hit the ladder. Then Hobbs careened sideways and dropped, unconscious. The flashlight hit the ground and went out.

Ethan didn't bother to hunt for it in the dark. He just crawled to AnnieLee, calling her name over and over, even though she couldn't answer. When he got to her, his desperate hands found her face and then her shoulders, and he pulled her to a sitting position, pulled her against his wildly pounding heart. His eyes stung and he wiped at them—he was crying. "You're okay, you're okay. Tell me you're okay," he begged as he tugged the tape from her mouth.

"Ow," AnnieLee said as the tape came away. She leaned forward as he struggled to unbind her wrists. Her hair was damp; she smelled like sweat and fear. "I'm okay," she said, her voice cracked and raw. "But I've sure as shit been better."

Ethan nearly shouted in relief. Then the knots were undone and her hands were free. He helped her to stand, and she stumbled toward the ladder. He sent up a prayer of thanks as he followed her out of the cellar, just as the sun began to rise in the sky.

CHAPTER
93

Two hours later, AnnieLee Keyes—née Rose McCord— was sitting in a small-town police station, wrapped inside one of Ethan's flannel shirts and looking tired, pale, and angry. Ethan was standing and sipping from a Styrofoam cup full of weak Folgers and watching as the police chief, a paunchy, mustached good ol' boy by the name of Anderson, tried to coax out the story of what had happened to her.

It wasn't working.

"I don't care to talk to you," she told him for what must have been the tenth time. A sharp edge had crept into her voice, and she sounded older. Harder. Anderson had given her a cup of coffee, too, but she hadn't touched it.

The chief looked up at Ethan like he needed backup.

Ethan gently touched AnnieLee's shoulder and straightened the collar of his shirt underneath her tangled hair. He still couldn't really think of her as Rose. It was such a beautiful name, but it sounded so soft. "He's trying to help," Ethan said.

AnnieLee gave him a sharp look. "You don't know him," she said.

"No, but he's an officer of the law. He's sworn to protect and—"

"This *officer,*" AnnieLee interrupted, "has never protected me. In fact, he did the opposite."

Ethan dropped into the metal folding chair beside her. This wasn't what he'd expected to hear. "What do you mean?"

"I mean," AnnieLee said, "when I used to call the cops on Clayton for hitting me, they said I was a troubled teen. They said that I was a liar and I just wanted attention. You'd think the bruises on my arms would be proof, wouldn't you? Well, they weren't." She folded her arms over her chest. "The chief grew up here, just like Clayton did. They rode their damn Schwinns around town when they were little, and they got drunk in the same Boone County bars when they grew up. They were friendly. Which meant that when I called on Anderson, he took Clayton's side."

Ethan turned to look at the police chief. As a soldier, Ethan respected rank, and he wanted this man to tell him that this wasn't true, that it had all been some kind of terrible misunderstanding. But Anderson wouldn't meet his eye.

The police chief cleared his throat. "Domestic disputes can often be exaggerated by—"

"See what I mean?" AnnieLee practically hissed. "Three times I ran away, and three times they sent me right back to the man who was hurting me. That doesn't sound like protecting and serving to me. Does it to you?"

Ethan crushed his empty coffee cup in his hands. Though AnnieLee had never been as open and honest with him as he wanted her to be, he knew she was telling the truth right now. "AnnieLee, would you be able to talk to someone else?"

Slumped in her chair, she seemed to nod.

"We need to speak to another officer," Ethan said to Chief Anderson.

Anderson hesitated for a moment, but then he got up. When he returned a few minutes later, it was with a young, round-faced woman with coppery hair. "This is Officer Danvers," he said. "She can take your statement." He didn't meet AnnieLee's glaring eyes, but he gave Ethan a curt nod of farewell and walked out.

With Anderson gone, AnnieLee visibly relaxed.

Officer Danvers sat down behind the chief's desk. "I'm so glad you're safe," she said. "And I'm sorry you had to go through what you did. Do you want a warm-up on the coffee? No. Well, then, let's dive in, okay? I wonder if you can tell me what happened with Gus Hobbs."

"I came here to kill him. I still might," AnnieLee said fiercely.

Officer Danvers looked taken aback. "Let's focus on the crime that was committed against you, Ms. Keyes. What concerns me now is how and why you came to be tied up in Hobbs's root cellar. How did that happen?"

"I don't know. I just woke up down there," she said.

Ethan turned to Officer Danvers. "She was hurt. Some kid found her and took her to Hobbs."

"I was going there anyway," AnnieLee said.

"Well, I doubt you were aiming for the cellar," Ethan said.

"No, sir, I was not," AnnieLee said. "I was aiming to blow his head off, but it didn't work out that way."

"I'm not sure you should—" Officer Danvers began.

"Please, AnnieLee, start at the beginning," Ethan interrupted. He knew the story began a long time ago, and he wanted to hear it all.

AnnieLee drew a long, deep breath. "I've known Gus Hobbs since I was twenty years old and still getting beat on by my stepdad, Clayton Dunning. I thought Gus was going to rescue me from all that," she said. "And I guess he did for a little while."

She stopped and stared down at her hands. Neither Ethan nor the police officer said anything. They just waited. Ethan watched as AnnieLee rubbed at a raw place on her wrist.

Then she looked up again. When she spoke, her voice was calm and flat. "But then something changed in him. And pretty soon he'd dragged me so deep into hell I thought I'd be down there forever."

Ethan sat there, barely breathing, as finally the truth began to come out.

———

"Tell me what you mean by *hell*," Officer Danvers said.

AnnieLee gripped the cold metal seat of her chair. She didn't know if she could do it. Ever since she'd left Houston, her survival had depended on denying everything she'd been through.

She stared at the cup of coffee she hadn't even tasted. Her throat felt tight, as if the words she needed to summon wouldn't have room to come out. It was so hard to admit the truth.

"Take your time," said Officer Danvers.

AnnieLee's gaze shifted to the clock above Danvers's head, and she watched as the seconds ticked by: *One thousand one, one thousand two…*

"Gus was so charming at first," she said finally. "He told me that I was the most beautiful girl west of the Mississippi River. 'Probably east of it, too,' he used to say, 'but I ain't ever bothered to cross it.'" She gave a derisive snort. "Can you believe that BS? Well, I could, because he was just about the first person to be nice to me since my mother died. I thought we were in love."

"Did you…marry him?" Ethan asked in a low voice.

"Sir," Officer Danvers said, "please let her continue without interruption."

AnnieLee turned to Ethan, whose handsome face was full of pain. "No, I didn't," she said. "I told Clayton that we'd eloped so he'd let me move in with him. And things were good for a handful of months. Gus was really protective. Controlling, too, but I thought that was just his way of taking care of me."

AnnieLee stopped and looked at Officer Danvers. "Has a man ever held your hand just a little too tightly, officer? And suddenly you realize that you're not strong enough to get it free, and you just have to wait until he decides to let you go?"

"No," Officer Danvers said quietly.

"Well, Gus liked to do that. He wanted to remind me who was stronger. And he said that there were people out there who wanted to hurt me, and so it was important that I didn't go anywhere by myself." She grabbed a ballpoint pen from a mug on the desk and began clicking its point in and out nervously. "He never left me alone."

Officer Danvers pushed a box of tissues toward her, and that's when AnnieLee realized that tears were sliding down her face. She pulled the box into her lap and went on.

"I wanted to get away," she said, "but he told me I couldn't leave. He said I owed him." She dabbed a tissue onto her cheeks. "And that I needed to earn back what he'd spent on me." She got up, walked over to the door, and rested her head against its cool metal.

"You're safe now," Officer Danvers said.

A sob forced its way up through AnnieLee's throat. "I haven't even gotten to the worst part!" she cried. "Gus said I wasn't obedient enough or grateful enough. So he…*sold* me." She was crying so hard now that she could hardly speak. "He sold me like a goddamn used car."

CHAPTER
95

I f Ethan had known any of this when he was at Gus Hobbs's house, the police would've had to arrest him for murder. But he sat very still now, listening intently, as AnnieLee told the rest of her story.

A man from out of town — "Everyone called him D," AnnieLee said, "but I never knew his real name or where he was from" — had taken her away in the middle of the night. He informed her that she belonged to him now, and that if she didn't do exactly what he said, he would go back and get her sisters. The younger they were, he said, the more they were worth.

He set her up in a house with three other women on the outskirts of Little Rock. Later he took her to a motel in Houston. Then they moved on to Tulsa, Oklahoma City, and then back to Houston again.

"I never saw daylight," AnnieLee said. "Just the insides of one shitty motel room after another and my own dead eyes in the bathroom mirror."

Silence fell over the room. AnnieLee was crying, and the pain in Ethan's chest made it feel like he was being slowly stabbed with a thick, dull knife.

After a while, Officer Danvers cleared her throat. "How did you escape?" she asked.

AnnieLee wiped her eyes. "One night D got really drunk and fell asleep in front of the TV. He'd done that before, but he was a light sleeper—he'd wake up if I so much as cracked a knuckle. But this time it was different—I could tell. So I sat there and watched him for a long time, thinking about what to do. I was so *broken*. I knew that if I ran and he caught me, he'd kill me. But what was death compared to where I was? Death was a damn picnic. So I ran, and now…well, here I am."

"AnnieLee," Ethan said, rising. He tried to reach for her, but she backed away as if she were afraid of him. He dropped his hands. "Please," he said.

AnnieLee looked at the floor for a long time. And then, ever so slowly, she moved toward him. He waited until she was an inch away, and then he wrapped his arms around her. "I'm so sorry," he breathed.

She sank into his embrace with a sigh. "They came after me," she said. "Me and my big mouth. I was always saying how someday I was going to make it to Nashville. I guess it wasn't too hard to find me there."

"Who's *they*?"

"I don't even know who they were, or if they got sent by Gus or D. Does it matter which man thought he owned me? That what started as some kind of common-law marriage was more like a common-law kidnapping? All I know is that in Vegas, D came for me himself. As far as he was concerned, I'd betrayed him, and he was going to take me back or kill me. But I didn't want to die anymore. I wanted to fight. I wanted to *live*."

Ethan rested his cheek against the top of her head.

"But you see why I didn't want to tell you anything, Ethan," she said, her voice muffled against his chest. "I didn't want to remember it, and I didn't want you to know. Because you won't be able to forget—not the way I made myself forget."

Any of the words of comfort that Ethan could think to say seemed so small and empty. So he just stood there, rocking her gently in his arms. Her tears dampened his shirt and her thin shoulders shook.

He hated those men. When he thought about what they'd done, his teeth clenched so hard that pain shot deep into his skull. He wished he would've done worse than break Hobbs's jaw, and he wondered how hard it would be to find D—

"You're squeezing me really hard," AnnieLee whispered.

"I'm sorry," he gasped. "I was thinking about…" He didn't finish the sentence; he didn't have to.

"I know," she said. "I could tell."

Ethan let his arms drop and then reached out and took her small, cool hands in his. He bent his knees so that his head was level with hers and he was looking right into her blue eyes as he spoke. "Listen to me, AnnieLee, please, because this is important. I told you that when you walked into the Cat's Paw that first night it was the best thing that had happened to me in a long time. But I lied." He paused. His throat ached with emotion. "It was the best thing that had happened to me ever in my whole damn life. I love you, AnnieLee. And I promise, I won't let anyone hurt you ever, ever again."

NINE MONTHS LATER

A nnieLee Keyes and Ruthanna Ryder in four," came the
voice through AnnieLee's earpiece.

Her heart did a somersault and she reached out to squeeze
Ruthanna's hand.

The country star squeezed back. "Take a big ol' deep breath,
firecracker," she said. "Release all those butterflies."

"Butterflies, hell," AnnieLee said. "I feel like I've got an entire
flock of pigeons in my stomach." She gave a nervous bounce on
her toes and then nearly toppled over, thanks to the crazy-high
heels she'd let Ruthanna talk her into wearing.

"It's the CMAs," Ruthanna had said, "and you can't show
up in jeans and cowboy boots when Nicole Kidman's going to
be swanning around in head-to-toe Versace, and yours truly's
going to be sporting more sequins than all the contestants on
RuPaul's Drag Race combined."

AnnieLee had laughed and agreed, not even reluctantly,
to have a dress made for the occasion: a form-fitting, floor-
length sheath so golden and shimmery that she felt like an
Oscar statuette come to life. Her hair had been pulled into an

elegant chignon at the base of her slender neck, and diamond drop earrings—on loan from Harry Winston—brushed lightly against her shoulders.

Really, the only problem was the damn shoes. She bent down and fidgeted with the thin leather straps.

"You look great," Ruthanna assured her now, "but more importantly, you're going to *be* great."

Ruthanna was wearing an ombre gown whose scarlet neckline sequins faded into the palest pink by the bottom hem, and her hair floated like a red-gold cloud around her beautiful face. She looked, AnnieLee thought, like a star-spangled angel.

"Are *you* nervous?" she asked. "You haven't performed live in years."

"Haven't you heard what they say?" Ruthanna asked. "It's just like riding a bike." She smiled. "Or maybe a Harley-Davidson."

She leaned in close and whispered, though there was no one nearby to overhear her, "Did you know that Jack bought us matching motorcycles? I told him I'd sooner ride naked down Lower Broadway on a horse than get on one of those. And what does he do? The fool buys me three months of motorcycle lessons." She rolled her eyes theatrically. "And I'd always thought he was so sensible!"

Ruthanna might pretend she was scandalized, but AnnieLee could tell that she was thrilled—maybe not about the Harley itself, but about her relationship with Jack. It was a match made in country music heaven.

AnnieLee was thrilled, too. Back in Caster County, Officer Danver had built a strong case against D and put him in jail. As D awaited trial, AnnieLee gained the confidence she needed to recall her darkest days. Ethan listened to every word with patience, love, and understanding.

At that moment, the black curtain in front of them began rising into the air.

"Here goes nothing," Ruthanna said.

Still holding hands, the women stepped forward into the blazing spotlight. On the other side of it, the entire Bridgestone Arena was packed, the front rows occupied by nearly every big name in the music industry.

"Ladies and gentlemen," intoned the emcee, "Ruthanna Ryder and AnnieLee Keyes!"

The applause that greeted them was thunderous. When it died down, AnnieLee and Ruthanna looked at each other, smiled, and let go of each other's hand. The drummer gave the count, and the band began to play. AnnieLee closed her eyes as the music filled her. The sound was so big and loud she could feel every note ringing in her body.

Ruthanna sang, *"Put on my jeans, my favorite shirt..."*

"Pull up my boots and hit the dirt," sang AnnieLee.

Then their voices rang in harmony: *"Finally doin' somethin' I've dreamed of for years..."*

Even before the first chorus, the crowd was on its feet, singing so loudly AnnieLee could hardly hear the band in her earpiece. But it didn't matter; the song pulled them along, weaving their voices together the way it had when they'd practiced it beside Ruthanna's pool, in her studio, and even at the Cat's Paw, late at night after everyone but Billy had gone home. It had become the song of their friendship, a symbol of the indomitable spirit they shared.

When the last notes ended, Ruthanna stepped forward and bowed gracefully. "It's been so good to be with you tonight," she said to the cheering crowd. "So good, in fact, that I might just have to do it again soon. But right now I'm going to let my little friend here take over." Then she giggled. "Whoops. I'm *really* not supposed to call her *little.*"

Ruthanna blew her a kiss as she exited the stage. And AnnieLee, alone beneath those hot, bright lights, felt a sudden and exhilarating sense of gratitude—and determination.

She hadn't planned on speaking, but the words came almost unbidden, and they came from her heart. "My name isn't actually AnnieLee Keyes," she said. "Even though that's the name on my album, and it's what you've all gotten used to calling me. My real name is Rose McCord. And I want you to know that it's taken more than a handful of miracles for me to be here—and to even be alive. As long as I live, I will never, ever stop being grateful for this moment, and for every sweet, free breath I take."

She glanced to the side of the stage, where Ethan, Ruthanna, and Jack were waiting for her to join them when she was finished. "I owe a lot of my success to my manager, Jack Holm. And I owe much more than that to Ruthanna Ryder—you all know her! But I also owe my life—and my happiness—to someone you don't know. His name is Ethan Blake." Then she held up her left hand, where a small, bright diamond sparkled on her third finger. "I figure you might get to know him, though, because unlike my fancy earrings, this isn't a loaner." She laughed in giddy amazement. "You guys, this has been a wild, wild ride. Anyway, enough of me talking. Let's play some music."

A stagehand ran out and handed her her guitar, and she looped the strap over her neck, relishing the instrument's cool, familiar weight. She strummed the opening chords, and then Rose McCord did what she was born to do.

She sang.

Dark night, bright future
I'm on my way, I start today
I'm gonna be all right

Dark night, bright future
It's darkest just before the light
And though it's been a long dark night
Blue sky on the other side

SONGBOOK

SONGS BY ROSE McCORD

Run

Intro:

Run-run-run, a-run-run
Run-run-run, a-run-run
Run-run, run-run, run

Verse one:

When you find yourself in a mess of trouble
Trapped amongst the trash and rubble
Prayin' for relief but gettin' none
You wanna start your life anew
You just don't know exactly how to
Find your opportunity and run

First chorus:

Run, run, and run some more

Clear the premises before

The same old problems pull you back again

Run, run, and just keep goin'

'Til you get to where you're knowin'

You can rest, catch your breath

Know how it feels to win

Oh, run-run-run, a-run-run

Run-run-run, a-run-run

Run-run, run-run, run

Verse two:

You want to keep the hounds at bay

Don't give up, you'll find a way

Refuse to be controlled by anyone

And the walls that you run into

Break 'em down, you know you have two

Choices, you can stay or run

Second chorus:

Run, run and just keep movin'

Heal the past, keep improvin'

You can face your troubles one by one

You're gonna have to face your problems

You need time and space to solve 'em

Then you'll bloom just like a rose kissed by the sun

So run-run-run, a-run-run

Run-run-run, a-run-run

Run-run, run Rose run

Bridge:

Take your chances, you can do it
Make a plan and then stick to it
Make a choice to really be someone
Break away, run to freedom
Break old habits, you don't need 'em
Break the cycle, those ol' days are done
You have two choices, you can stay or run

Third chorus:

Run, run, and run some more
Clear the premises before
The same old problems pull you back again
Run, run, and just keep goin'
'Til you get to where you're knowin'
You can rest and catch your breath
I know that you can win
So run-run-run, a-run-run
Run-run-run, a-run-run
Run-run, run-run, run

Tag:

Come on, run-run-run, a-run-run
Run-run-run, a-run-run
Run-run, run-run, run
Run, you can run
Run-run-run, run-run
Run, you can run
Run-run-run, run-run

Firecracker

First chorus:

Firecracker, I heard you callin' me
Firecracker, that suits me to a T
A tiny stick of dynamite laced with TNT
I'm a firecracker, hot as I can be

Verse one:

Now I'll explode if you insist on lightin' up my fuse
If you ignore the danger of breakin' all my rules
A ragin' fire can be ignited from a tiny spark
If you don't pay attention all hell can blow apart

Verse two:

I'm full of fire and passion, wound tight and aim to please
But if you want to play with fire, be mindful and take heed
Standin' up for who I am and all that I believe
Is makin' me a firecracker, that's just what I'll be

Second chorus:

Firecracker, if you can't take the heat
Firecracker, just stay away from me
That pretty much sums it up, so handle cautiously
I'm a hunk-a, hunk-a burnin' stuff, you'll feel the burn
    from me
(Thank you very much)

Bridge:

Boom-boom, bang-bang, pow-pow-pow
I will blow up in your face right here and right now
Handle with care, with respectability
You can lose a finger if you're pointing it at me
Firecracker, yeah you can call me that
Firecracker, 'cause I will fight you back
Now I'm not out for trouble, but if it comes around
I'll go at you tooth and nail; there'll be no backin' down

Verse three:

Firecracker, more than proud to be
Firecracker, that suits me to a T
A little stick of dynamite laced with TNT
Firecracker, as hot as I can be

(Turnaround:)

Yodel-lady, yodel-lady, yodel-laaaady
Hee-hee hee-hee hee-hee

Half bridge:

Boom-boom, bang-bang, pow-pow-pow
I will blow up in your face right here and right now
Firecracker, handle cautiously
Firecracker, now don't you mess with me
Firecracker, full of TNT
Firecracker, just as hot as I can be

Tag:

Firecracker, hey don't you mess with me
'Cause I'm full of P and V

Firecracker, yodel-lady, yodel-lady
Firecracker, a little stick of dynamite full of TNT
Firecracker, hey don't you mess, don't you mess
Don't you mess with me

Woman Up (and Take It Like a Man)

Verse one:

Is it easy?

No it ain't

Can I fix it?

No I cain't

But I sure ain't gonna take it lyin' down

Will I make it?

Maybe so

Will I give up?

Oh no

I'll be fightin' 'til I'm six feet underground

First chorus:

I'm gonna woman up and take it like a man

I'm gonna buckle up, be tough enough

To take control and make demands

Look like a woman

Think like a man

Be as good as or better than

Gotta woman up and take it like a man

Verse two:

Do I want to?

No I don't

Will I surrender?

No I won't

It's a long hard life for a gal

But I gotta live it

And it's a dang shame if you ask me
Workin' so hard
Just to be free
Whatever it takes then I'm more than glad to give it

Second chorus:
So I'm gonna woman up and take it like a man
Gotta buckle up be tough enough
To give 'em hell and take command
Soft like a woman, strong like a man
Stick to my guns and have a plan
Gotta woman up and take it like a man

Bridge: (gang sing)
A rough road, we'll walk it
Never give up, we'll talk it
Soon enough we can chalk it
Up to experience and payin' dues
And I'll speak my truth

Third chorus:
(Sing it girls)
Woman up and take it like a man
And I'm gonna buckle up be tough enough
To take control and make demands
Look like a woman
Think like a man
Be as good as or better than

Gonna woman up and take it like a man
I am, I am
I'm gonna woman up and take it like a man
I am, I am
I'm gonna woman up and take it like a man

Driven

Verse one:

Driven to insanity, driven to the edge

Driven to the point of almost no return

Driven to think awful thoughts, do awful things

But at least I'd like to think I've learned

I'm driven, driven to be smarter

Driven to work harder

Driven to be better every day

Driven to keep on and on

To achieve the things I want

I'll be sorry if I don't

Make the most of livin'

I, I-I-I-I, I, I-I-I-I, I, I-I-I I'm driven

Bridge:

I've got drive

I try to do more than survive

Reachin' out to take what life has given

One thing you can say for me is

I, I-I-I-I, I, I-I-I-I, I, I-I-I I'm driven

(Turnaround:)

I-I-I I'm driven

Second chorus:

Driven, driven to be smarter

Driven to work harder

Driven to be better every day

Driven, yes you gotta be
Nothing you cannot achieve
Take the wheel and just believe
That you can change your life
Just say I, I-I-I-I, I, I-I-I-I, I, I-I-I I'm willin'
I, I-I-I-I, I, I-I-I-I, I, I-I-I I'm driven

Tag:
I'm driven, I'm driven
Driven...willin'
I, I-I-I I'm driven
I, I-I-I I'm driven
Driven, driven

Dark Night, Bright Future

First chorus:

Dark night, bright future

Like the phoenix from the ashes, I shall rise again

Dark night, bright future

I've been hurt and broken but I am on the mend

Got so much ahead of me

The past is gonna set me free

Learn from it and just believe

That I can touch the sky

Verse one:

Everyone knows happiness

Everybody grieves

We all cry, we all smile

Everybody bleeds

Everybody has a past, things they want to hide

There's give, take, love, hate in each and every life

Second chorus:

Dark night, bright future

Like the phoenix from the ashes, I shall rise again

Dark night, bright future

I've been hurt and broken, but I am on the mend

Got so much ahead of me

What's in the past, I'll leave it be

Learn from it and just believe

That I can touch the sky

Bridge:

Forgiveness is a magic wand, makes things disappear
Kindness wipes away regret, hope can conquer fear
Tenderness, a soothing balm, healing wounds and scars
Love says we can start anew right from where we are

Third chorus:

Dark night, bright future
I'm on my way, I start today
I'm gonna be all right
Dark night, bright future
It's darkest just before the light
And though it's been a long dark night
Blue sky on the other side

Half chorus:

Dark night, bright future
Like the phoenix from the ashes, I shall rise again
Dark night, bright future I've been hurt and broken
But I am on the mend

SONGS BY RUTHANNA RYDER

Big Dreams and Faded Jeans

Verse one:

Put on my jeans, my favorite shirt
Pull up my boots and hit the dirt
Finally doin' somethin' I've dreamed of for years
Don't know quite what to expect
A little scared, but what the heck
My desire is always greater than my fear

Chorus:

Big dreams and faded jeans
Fit together like a team
Always busting at the seams
Big dreams and faded jeans
Just my ole guitar and me
Out to find my destiny
Nashville is the place to be
For big dreams and faded jeans

Verse two:

Put out my thumb and wish for luck
To hitch a car, a semi-truck
Sooner or later one will catch me
    in their beams
Then I'll be on my way at last

Find a future, lose a past
Waiting silent as the passion in me screams

Half chorus:
Big dreams and faded jeans
Fit together like a team
Always busting at the seams
Big dreams and faded jeans

Bridge:
May the stars that fill my eyes
Guide my path and be my light
And may God provide the means
To accomplish my big dreams, my big dreams

Third chorus:
Big dreams and faded jeans
Fit together like a team
Always busting at the seams
Big dreams and faded jeans
Like the song "Bobby McGee"
I'm just longin' to be free
Take me where I want to be
Big dreams and faded jeans

Tag:
And there are many just like me
With big dreams and faded jeans
Mm-mm-mm-mm, mm-mm-mm-mm
Mm-mm-mm-mm, mm-mm-mm
Big dreams, big dreams and faded jeans
Oh-oh-oh-oh, oh-oh-oh-oh

I'm just longing to be free
Take me where I want to be
Big dreams and faded jeans
Mm-mm-mm, mm-mm-mm-mm-mm
Mm-mm, mm-mm-mm-mm
Mm-mm-mm, mm-mm-mm-mm...

Snakes in the Grass

Verse one:

Snakes in the grass
You'd better move fast
You'll be poisoned or be strangled to death
Their fangs, they bite deep
And their venom will creep
Inside you 'til you're gasping for breath

Verse two:

And you can't get away
From these Godawful snakes
They will bite and suck 'til they bleed you dry
And when they're done with you
They'll be stalking someone new
Aw, trust me, you'll be lucky to survive

Chorus:

And they won't let you go
They're creepy, they're cold
So beware of the snakes in the grass
They strike in a flash
So you better watch your ass
Or fall victim to those snakes in the grass

Verse three:

Snakes in the grass
It's hard to move past
When they're waitin' coiled and ready to strike

So you best be alert
Or you're gonna get hurt
Be mindful of their poisonous bite

Chorus:
And they won't let you go
No, they're creepy, they're cold
So beware of the snakes in the grass
They strike in a flash
So you'd better watch your ass
Or fall victim to the snakes in the grass

Tag:
Be careful where you step
'Cause I've been there myself
Beware of the snakes in the grass
Ssssnakes in the grass
Ssssnakes in the grass

SONG BY RUTHANNA RYDER AND ROSE McCORD

Blue Bonnet Breeze

Chorus:

Blue bonnet breezes bring precious moments
    to mind
Blue bonnet breezes
Stirring up memories
Of romance and passion, making a sweet place
    in time
A girl and a boy
With high hopes enjoyed
Doing whatever they please
With love in their eyes
'Neath the wide open sky
Making love in the blue bonnet breeze

Verse one:

The story is old
Has often been told
Of a rich city boy and a poor country girl
Their families tried hard
To keep them apart
But they became each other's world
He'd ask her to marry
Of course she said yes

When he knelt there on his bended knee
They promised forever
No matter whatever
As they kissed in the blue bonnet breeze

Chorus:

Blue bonnet breezes bring precious moments to mind
Blue bonnet breezes
Stirring up memories
Of romance and passion, making a sweet place
    in time
A girl and a boy
With high hopes enjoyed
Doing whatever they please
With love in their eyes
'Neath the wide open sky
Making love in the blue bonnet breeze

Verse two:

The father said no
In a voice loud and cold
Oh, what's of your future and school?
This won't be allowed
His mother said proud
We won't let you be such a fool
I'm your Juliet, I'm your Romeo
They said as they walked hand in hand
They knew in their hearts
They could not live apart
So they started making their plans

Recitation:

So she rented a bridal gown, he rented a tux
A bouquet of blue bonnets in his fancy new truck
They drove faster and faster, as fast as could go
'Til they crashed in a field of blue bonnets below
They placed a marker saying "May You Rest in Peace"
Now their souls soar together in the blue bonnet breeze

Chorus:

Mm-mm, mm-mm-mm, bringing sweet memories
   to mind
Mm-mm, mm-mm-mm, marking a sweet place
   in time
Oh, oh, mm-mm-mm-mm, doing whatever they please
Mm-mm, mm-mm-mm, mm-mm, mm-mm-mm, making
   love in the blue bonnet breeze
Ah-ah-ah, mm-mm-mm, mm-mm-mm, mm-mm-mm-
   mm-mm, mm-mm, mm-mm

SONGS BY ETHAN BLAKE

Secrets

Verse one:

Secrets, you're good at keeping secrets
Especially your own
Aw, come on, open up and let me in
Everybody needs a friend
Want you to know you can depend on me
(Mmm-mmm)

Verse two:

Secrets, all those things you hold too
 close
That you're afraid to share
But I care
Don't be afraid to open up
I'm someone that you can trust
And I will keep it between us
I swear

Chorus:

No matter what's gone on before
Don't hold it in a moment more
I'm here to lend a sympathetic ear
Don't fear
You don't have to hold inside

Things that need to see the light
I won't judge or criticize
Just know you're safe with me
(Mm-mm, mm-mm, mm-mm)

Verse three:
Secrets, you're good at keeping secrets
Especially your own
You're not alone
You'll feel much better if you try
To put some faith in you and I
I don't gossip, I don't lie
Try me

Tag:
Secrets, I'm good at keeping secrets
Especially my own
(Mm-mm-mm)…secrets

Lost and Found

Verse one:

Lost count of all the countless things
I've lost throughout the years
Lost friends and time and interest in
The things I should hold dear
Lost sleep just pondering the things
That have been lost to me
Especially the loss of love
I've needed desperately

Verse two:

I find it doesn't help at all
To sit around and brood
I find nobody gives a damn
About your petty moods
At least that's what I thought
Until the day you came along
Now I find my restless soul
Has finally found a home

First chorus:

Lost and found, I'm safe and sound
No more drifting aimlessly, I've settled
   down
I finally came around
No more to roam, those days are gone
I was alone, now I know I don't have to be
Since your amazing love has found me

Second chorus:

Lost and found, unchained, unbound
No more second guessing, I know who I am
Now I'm on solid ground
'Cause this love you've shown, like none
   I've known
All hope was gone, now I can see eternity
Since your amazing love has found me

Tag:

So much has changed, you've healed my pain
It's not the same, I know it never will be
I once was lost but now I'm found
Since your amazing love has found me
You found me

Demons

Verse one:

Give me a chance girl, open your eyes now, I'm not the
  enemy here
I'm a soft heart to lean on
A shoulder to cry on
Two good lips to kiss away the tears
So if you're looking to fight
You have come to the wrong guy
With you, I refuse to throw darts
I've had enough fighting
I'm more into righting
What's wrong when it's broken apart

Chorus:

Demons, demons, we've both had enough of our own
Demons, demons, we don't have to fight them alone

Verse two:

I've been fighting demons most of my life
So fighting with you makes no sense
I need some heaven and I've had enough hell
I'm an expert in pain and torment
So if you can't be with me
Then please just dismiss me
I guess when it's all said and done
We've all had our demons
I guess I was dreamin'
To think we could fight them as one

Chorus:

Demons, demons, we've both had enough of our own
Demons, demons, we don't have to fight them alone
Somewhere inside me I truly do believe together we could
    win the fight
The demons we've both known
Let's slay them and move on
I will if you're willing to try

Tag:

Demons, demons, we've both had enough of our own
Demons, demons, we don't have to fight them alone
The demons we both know, let's slay them and move on
We don't have to fight them alone
Hmm, mm-mm-mm

SONG BY ETHAN BLAKE
AND ROSE McCORD

Love or Lust
(Duet)

Verse one:

I blush at the thoughts I have when I'm with you
Can't hardly express how I feel
I want to hit you, I want to kiss you
A mixed bag of feelings so real
I've never felt it, how can I accept it?
Are we lovers, something other than friends?
All I know for certain, it's a good kind
    of hurtin'
Is it love, is it lust that we're in?

Chorus:

Love or lust
Do we doubt, do we trust?
Whatever it is, it's stronger than us
It's both, I suppose
Where it ends heaven knows
But we feel it with each look and touch
What is it, which is it?
I truly don't know
I suppose, though, that with any luck
The glow won't diminish

And we'll go 'til we finish
Whether it's love or lust

(Turnaround)
Chorus:
Love or lust
Do we doubt, do we trust?
Whatever it is, it's stronger than us
It's both, I suppose
Where it ends heaven knows
But we feel it with each look and touch
What is it, which is it?
I truly don't know
I suppose, though, that with any luck
The glow won't diminish
And we'll go 'til we finish
Whether it's love or it's lust

Tag:
Whether it's love or it's lust
Time will tell if it's love or it's lust
I'd like to believe it's love (let's believe)
Is it lust?
I'd like to believe (I believe) it's love

ABOUT THE AUTHORS

Dolly Parton is a singer, songwriter, actress, producer, businesswoman, and philanthropist. The composer of over 3,000 songs, she has sold over 100 million records worldwide and given away millions of books to children through her nonprofit, Dolly Parton's Imagination Library.

James Patterson is the world's bestselling author. Among his creations are Alex Cross, the Women's Murder Club, Michael Bennett, and Maximum Ride. His #1 bestselling nonfiction includes *Walk in My Combat Boots*, *Filthy Rich*, and his autobiography, *James Patterson by James Patterson*. He has collaborated on novels with Bill Clinton and Dolly Parton and has won an Edgar Award, nine Emmy Awards, and the National Humanities Medal.